SHE SHOOTS
TO CONQUER

**Center Point
Large Print**

Ellie Haskell Mysteries by Dorothy Cannell
available from Center Point Large Print:

Withering Heights
Goodbye, Ms. Chips

**This Large Print Book carries the
Seal of Approval of N.A.V.H.**

SHE SHOOTS
TO CONQUER

Dorothy Cannell

CENTER POINT PUBLISHING
THORNDIKE, MAINE

This Center Point Large Print edition
is published in the year 2009 by arrangement with
St. Martin's Press.

Copyright © 2009 by Dorothy Cannell.

The text of this Large Print edition is unabridged.
In other aspects, this book may vary
from the original edition.
Printed in the United States of America.
Set in 16-point Times New Roman type.

ISBN: 978-1-60285-448-2

Library of Congress Cataloging-in-Publication Data

Cannell, Dorothy.
  She shoots to conquer : an Ellie Haskell mystery / Dorothy Cannell.
    p. cm.
  ISBN 978-1-60285-448-2 (library binding : alk. paper)
  1. Women private investigators--Fiction. 2. Country homes--England--Fiction.
   3. Yorkshire (England)--Fiction. 4. Large type books. I. Title.

PS3553.A499S54 2009b
813'.54--dc22

2009003875

For Andrew and Cosette Cannell, wishing you a world filled with the magic of books. With love always from Granna.

1

Sometimes I am compelled to give Mother Nature a stern piece of my mind. That mid-September evening, I pointed out to her with all the authority I could muster (given my bulging eyes and closing throat) that dense fog was all well and good in the appropriate setting. I wouldn't have said a word had I been snugly at home with Tobias the cat on my lap, a book and cup of cocoa to hand while Ben and the three children—nine-year-old twins Tam and Abbey and seven-year-old Rose—were cheerfully occupied nearby.

What I didn't go for was sitting in a state of unbridled terror next to my equally terrified husband as he drove at an uncertain creep down an unfamiliar country road with visibility reduced to a couple of inches at best. We had exited the motorway about forty-five minutes earlier, planning to stop for an early dinner at a restaurant recommended to Ben by a fellow chef who had described the food as superb and well worth a detour.

Not only had we not found the Duck Pond Inn, we had gone twenty miles past the village of Little Woppstone before seeing a signpost with its name on it; by which time it seemed wisest to press on into the wooly gray yonder. What road we were now on was a mystery. I prayed for a ditch into which we might slither and wait lopsidedly until things cleared. It had been ten minutes since we had experienced the small comfort of seeing red pinpricks of taillights ahead of us.

"You're doing wonderfully," I told Ben in a voice that wobbled, "so calm and steady." An image I couldn't hope to present with my long brown hair untidily escaping its coil and hands gripping my jacket collar.

His reply was a grunt which I deemed heroic and befitting his dark good looks. The poor darling was claustrophobic. He had to be desperately fighting down feelings of suffocation along with fear of an accident, but he still maintained that arresting tilt to his chin. Mrs. Malloy spoke from the backseat, causing me to jump. In my state of nerves, I'd forgotten all about her.

"Bugger of a night," she said with unnecessary relish.

I was unable to pry my lips open to respond, but Ben nobly managed another grunt.

"Puts me in mind," Mrs. Malloy went on, "of that ill-fated day when Semolina Gibbons got caught in the mist after saddling the master's wild-eyed stallion and riding out onto the moor to seek life-saving information from the curate's bedridden great-grandmother."

In general, I am very fond of Roxie Malloy. She has been my household helper at Merlin's Court

8

since shortly after my marriage. The children count on her as one of the beloved certainties of life, and she and I have from time to time worked as a duo in amateur sleuthing. When Ben and I went to Yorkshire to stay with our relatives Tom and Betty Hopkins, we had been happy to take Mrs. Malloy to visit her sister and brother-in-law in the same village. We had deposited her with them a week ago and picked her back up that morning for our return home, where the children were being looked after by Ben's parents, with help from my cousin Freddy who lives in a cottage on our grounds.

I knew immediately whom Mrs. Malloy meant when speaking of Semolina Gibbons. In addition to other common interests, she and I share an enthusiasm for novels written during what we grandly refer to as the Gothic Revival period of the 1970s. Doing so makes us both feel studious and intelligent. Indeed, we consider ourselves serious collectors of yellow-paged, dingy-covered paperbacks invariably displaying a spooky mansion as the background to a young woman with wind-lashed black hair standing on a rock. Whether it is always the same rock remains open to question—a topic we consider worthy of a doctoral thesis should either of us ever find the time to go up to Oxford and wander the halls of learning, brushing shoulders with tutors and dons and the fearfully clever young. Semolina was the beleaguered but valiant heroine of a recent acquisition titled *The Landcroft Legacy*, by Doris McCrackle. Okay, maybe such isn't Literature in its purest form. But to the scoffers I make no apologies for what they may view as escapism. Not all of us can be swept away upon burying our noses in *The Subverted Subconscious* or *Principles of Parallel Pragmatism.*

Allowances have to be made for the way the twig is bent, and my parents could never have been accused of overdoing reality. Had I (an only child) not arrived in the conventional manner, they would cheerfully have gone through life believing that storks brought babies to couples leaning out windows hoping to catch a glimpse of a pink or blue ribbon. Once they got over the shock, they were (so they told me) relieved that no assembly seemed to be required and got down to the business of remembering where they had put me and how long ago. Occasionally there were meetings at the dining-room table where they sat looking dubiously adult while seeking my advice on how to bring me up. Otherwise, I got to eat my dinner in the bath or wear my party dress to bed if I felt like it. If I developed a practical streak which caused me to decide against becoming a starving artist in favor of a career as an interior designer, it was because someone had to occasionally remember that the gas bill needed to be paid or the windows closed against sheeting rain.

Had Mother and Father been in the car with us now, they would have been delighted to hear Mrs. Malloy's recounting of Semolina Gibbons's visit to the curate's great-grandmother. As it was, she had to focus on Ben as a captive audience.

"Gone ninety was old Mrs. Weathervane and her the only person left alive, Mr. H, likely to know whether it was the archdeacon's first or second wife that disappeared after doing a series of brass rubbings in the village church sixty-three years previous. Your heart would have gone out to Semolina! Getting lost in the fog was terrifying in itself, but the worst was when she heard the muffled footsteps behind her and felt a hand close round her lily white throat, it's no wonder she went to pieces. Have to give it to her that between one scream and the next she tucked away the memory of her assailant whistling an evil little tune; same as she heard the butler doing a week later when she dined at the Deanery on Christmas night."

Momentarily distracted from our own tremulous situation, I gently corrected Mrs. Malloy. "It was New Year."

"Oh, well," she said dismissively, "the fact that the butler had been lost in the fog himself, and blindly grabbed hold of her to save himself from falling, don't alter the case that Semolina would have done better not to have accepted the man's offer to give her a tour of the pantries. She couldn't be sure, for all his apologies, that it weren't him as moments later had took a shot at her with an arrow. But of course, to be fair to the girl, she wasn't herself at the Deanery, what with thinking of how Lord Hawtry's good eye had darkened when she refused his hand in marriage."

"Perhaps if he hadn't produced it in a bloody paper bag she might have been more receptive," said Ben with an admirably steady chortle.

Mrs. Malloy did not appreciate the witticism. "Nothing of the sort; the reason she had to turn him down was because rumor had it he already had a wife floating around."

"In the goldfish pond or the trout stream perhaps?" This second quip and accompanying relaxation of Ben's clenched jaw confirmed my hope that the fog was thinning sufficiently for us now to be able to see a couple of feet ahead.

"Alive and well two villages away, serving up drinks at the Smugglers Arms, Mr. H; but, as I said to meself when reading along, Semolina shouldn't have been so ready to see obstacles. Then again perhaps I'm being too hard on the girl. I've always fancied meself married to a lordship and swanning up and down the stairs as lady of the manor."

We had nearly swanned into a tree that loomed up like an unraveling mummy before being sucked back into the void. Mrs. Malloy was still going on about how Semolina had shown great pluck when pierced in the shoulder by an arrow while sitting in the copse contemplating whether to make her escape that night, or remain until the following Sunday so as to honor her promise to assist with the altar flowers. But enough was occasionally enough. What I needed at that moment was a strong cup of tea accompanied by a Marmite sandwich. There is nothing like Marmite for convincing one there is light at the end of the tunnel. But . . . hold on a moment . . . perhaps such sustenance wasn't necessary in this instance. I heard Ben suck in a breath as I saw a faint ruby glow ahead of us.

"Taillights!" I cried. "We are not the only ones left alive on the planet!"

"It could be a mirage, Ellie, but I think a vehicle is beginning to take shape."

"Don't get too close," I urged.

"Of course the fly in the ointment, was I to get an offer of marriage from a lord of the realm," continued Mrs. Malloy, who would have got on with my parents a treat when in this sort of mood, "is I'd be leaving you to find someone else to drudge on alone at Merlin's Court, Mrs. H. But like I've always said, housework was never me true vocation, not a holy calling, so to speak, but a woman has to put bread on the table after being left in the lurch by four husbands. Or was it five, Mrs. H?"

These men all having come and gone before Mrs. Malloy and I crossed paths, I was ill-equipped to do a body count. Eyes riveted on the taillights ahead, I suggested that she round off the number to six.

"Oh, very nice," she breathed huffily on my neck, "make me out to be Henry VIII. And me the forgiving sort. Even in me worst moments, struggling to bring up young George on me own, I never wished none of them blighters on the chopping block. Except perhaps for number three," she conceded. Mrs. Malloy prides herself on her honesty. "It was him as ditched me for a bleached-blond barmaid that couldn't make change counting on her fingers, she had to take off her shoes and use her toes as well. Come to think of it, she's the one I should have done in. A blow to the back of the head would have taken the smirk off her face."

I saw Ben's face lift in a smile.

"To have been arrested for murder would not have been amusing," I said, having one of my priggish moments, at which he removed his hand from the steering wheel and jabbed a finger at the windscreen.

"That vehicle's left indicator just went on."

"Thank goodness," I craned forward, "we must be coming to some sort of decent road."

"I don't see a signpost." Mrs. Malloy is inclined to put a damper on things when she's feeling cooped up and in need of a reviving beverage, not necessarily tea.

"We still aren't seeing much of anything," Ben replied mildly, "although I can make out that it's a van."

So it was—a fuzzy object of no discernable color,

but one with a bread-boxy utility about it that suggested to my eager mind a return to its place of business in a street bristling with lampposts and petrol stations where we could refuel and seek directions. Mrs. Malloy was mentioning a long overdue sit-down in a proper chair as we took the turn, playing follow-the-leader rather too closely for my comfort. To be fair to Mother Nature, the wooly gray blanket must have thinned during the past few minutes, because I was able to make out the shift and shape of a pair of oblongs as we passed between them, and then the dusky darkness of some further encroachment as Ben crept us forward with his nose on the windscreen. I decided we must have entered an alleyway, which belief became a certainty when I perceived ahead of us a solid rectangle that was undoubtedly—even though viewed through the diaphanous veiling—a sizable building of some sort.

"Oh, goodie!" quoth Mrs. Malloy sardonically from the rear. "Looks like a hospital. We can all go in and have heart attacks. They let you sit down when you're in that condition and force liquids down your throats."

"I don't care if it's one of those Victorian-era insane asylums and we're met by a toothless hag with hoary locks whose instructions are to drag us to the lichen-coated ward," I agreed heartily. "I'll bet that van's parked itself outside the emergency entrance. Come on," I patted Ben's arm, "let's get out and talk to the driver."

"I'm ashamed of you, Mrs. H!" A thump on the back of my seat signaled Mrs. Malloy's search for her handbag and the hat without which she wouldn't have been seen dead stepping out of the car. Not when she was on holiday and hoping to be taken for the sort of person who never stayed anywhere less déclassé than Claridges or the Dorchester. "Fancy you making jokes about lunatic asylums after living page by page the hell Wisteria Whitworth endured when her husband, as hadn't been able to get her to sign over her inheritance to him, had her spirited away at dead of night to that dreadful place deep in the heart of the forest."

The aforementioned excerpt was from *Perdition Hall*, another gem by the prolific Doris McCrackle, but I refused to be drawn. "Sorry, I forget at this moment where the wicked hubby incarcerated her. I tend to be heartless after driving nowhere for hours."

"Persimmon Hall. Known to the locals as . . ."

"Perdition Hall."

"And shrouded that night, if you care to remember, Mrs. H, in a fog as bad as this one!"

"Intensifying the sinister aspect of bleak turrets and barred windows to a bone-chilling degree," I agreed, while thinking that what could be seen of the building in front of us looked extremely dull in comparison. No veiled glimpse of pursued flight across the rooftops or ghostly slither down a drainpipe into the waiting arms of the constabulary. And to make for the further mundane, there were lights from within several of the windows.

"Oliver Twist lived it up at the workhouse in comparison." I was looking at Ben, who hadn't budged in his seat.

"More than the lichen-covered walls and rotting floorboards, it were the description of the communal chamberpots that fair broke me heart. And Wisteria, a young lady used to her privacy if you didn't count the maid standing ready to hand her the warmed towel when she got out of the bath." Mrs. Malloy exhaled an anguished breath down my neck. "But for me the worst moment came when the poor dear tried to flee the ward and a hand shot out from under one of the beds to grab her ankle. No wonder her lovely black tresses turned white within the hour. Still," sentimental breath this time, "the happy ending made up for a lot is how we have to look at it. That thrilling moment when Carson Grant, the handsome lawyer, philanthropist, and social reformer, broke into the secret room and rescued her just as the evil Dr. Megliani was strapping that dreadful device to her head that would have destroyed her brain . . ."

A sweetly anguishing moment . . . Wisteria's wondrous topaz eyes opening to light and love . . . Carson Grant's steely sensitivity in determining to allow her time to adjust to the news that her husband was dead, the valet having tied his master's cravat rather too tightly that morning. It was these memories that caused me to ask Ben if he would continue to love me if I were subjected to a mind-altering procedure and had white hair to boot.

"Of course not." He had never sounded more distant. But before my heart could break, I realized from his blank stare that he hadn't heard what I'd just said and very likely not a word of the conversation regarding Wisteria Whitworth's sufferings on the road to true love.

"What's wrong, darling?" I placed my hand over his.

"That isn't a hospital out there, Ellie."

"I said it looked like one, not that it was for sure," said Mrs. Malloy at her mostly bristling.

"Nor is it a post office, or a department store."

"So what is it, Mr. H?" Her tone suggested that had she been close enough she would have elbowed him in the ribs. "The Houses of Parliament?"

That I knew was ridiculous. There was no way we could have gone so far off course as to be in the center of London. Although . . . the various thickening and thinning of the mist did create an uncertainty to all things, including the van that had been our beacon. With its lights off, it dissolved and reappeared from moment to moment. Several people-sized shadows had emerged and likewise drifted in and out of vague view.

"It's a residence. This isn't a road we've turned onto. We're on someone's private drive."

"Well, what's so bad about that?" I actually laughed, before taking in his anguished expression and instantly regretting my blatant insensitivity. Men feel these situations far more deeply than women, believing that a sufficient supply of testosterone should have provided them with an inner compass. Maps were invented for sissies, the asking of directions entirely a woman's province. Before I could flounder a meaningless palliative, Mrs. Malloy broke the hollow silence.

"Carson Grant described Wisteria's new hair as moonlight spilling into the dark places of his soul. Some men just have the knack of making a woman feel good about herself. You need to think about that, Mr. H, instead of fretting that you've made a fool of yourself. And," she had to go and add, "your wife and me."

"Now we're here," I said quickly—for fear Ben would shoot the car into reverse taking us back onto the road to nowhere, "I'll get out and ask for directions to the nearest town."

"Coming with you." Sounds of Mrs. Malloy opening her car door. "You'll need my arm to hold on to, Mrs. H, or if I know tuppence you'll get yourself lost before putting one foot in front of the other. Stay put when you're out and I'll come and get you." She is a woman who can't bear to be left out of anything, however small, which is not to minimize her genuine, if often disgruntled, concern for my welfare. What I didn't put much faith in were the four-inch heels she invariably wore except (possibly) to bed.

"No, you stay by your door," I responded firmly, and on the wave of Ben's dejected sigh exited the car, to be met as I rounded the bonnet by his fog-bulked presence. Given the feeling of standing in damp fur, it was a relief to feel his hand cover mine. Mother Nature, having eased up on us, was back to demonstrating how quickly and thickly she could knit up a gray angora blanket. The van had been absorbed into the mix of plain and pearl, and it was with relief that I felt someone speaking with Mrs. Malloy's voice bump into my side.

"A good thing my vision has always been so good, Mrs. H!"

This was a surprise to me; she had always claimed the opposite when I would casually mention the cobwebs dangling from the ceiling. But there are times when it doesn't do to nitpick.

"I can see the outline of steps going up the building. And those blobs moving up them have to be the people that was in the van. There!" If she pointed, I couldn't see her hand. "We just need to move straight ahead. Do you have hold of Mr. H?"

"His hand, I don't know if the rest of him is tagging along. Are you there, darling?"

A response came in the form of a grunt.

We shuffled forward . . . or it was to be hoped

that was the direction we were taking. I felt myself becoming increasingly disorientated until my foot touched an impediment that suggested we had reached the bottom step. Galvanized by presumably reaching this same conclusion, Ben reclaimed full use of his voice.

"Ellie," he said with irritable vigor, "do not make excuses for the situation by complaining that the drive should have been better posted. And for God's sake don't agree to a cup of tea if they offer. Let's just get the hell out of here."

"Not getting good vibes from the place?" Mrs. Malloy snorted dismissively as she tugged us onward and upward. "Some of us is too suggestible, is what I say. Seen in a good light it'll be just another stately home . . . with a history of course, that I suppose could include murder and mayhem given its age."

"We don't know anything about its age," Ben rebutted.

Not true, I thought with a lack of wifely loyalty. My impression during that thinning of the fog had been of eighteenth-century construction. Another sobering thought emerged. Were we shuffling up the steps of one of England's stately homes? Would we be required to purchase tickets before requesting information of the admittance person in braided uniform? Excitement stirred. My work as in interior designer was often sparked by seeing how the upper crust lived. If as Mrs. Malloy had suggested we'd been preceded up the steps—which were certainly of a length to suggest awaiting grandeur—by the person (or people) from the van, it seemed likely they were already inside by now.

An eerie silence enveloped us along with the fog, broken only by the intermittent wheeze of our collective breathing and the tentative tap-tapping of Mrs. Malloy's high heels. The damp chill had worked its way within my light jacket and it was a relief when my extended hand touched a flat wooden surface. Surely a door! Sir Edmund Hillary could not have felt greater triumph when stumbling to the top of Everest. Not to belittle his achievement in accomplishing his scenic hike, in the pleasant month of June 1953 all that was then required of him was to bask in the moment with his fellow ascender and plant the triumphal flag before nipping back down for a cup of cocoa. Far more taxing to my mind was the need to locate either a knocker or a bell.

"You know what I think," gasped Mrs. Malloy over my shoulder, "it'll turn out this isn't an imposing house like I could feel properly at home in, but a bloody great block of flats. Talk about disappointing, Mr. H!"

I stood immobile—not only because I had been counting on touring a gallery of ancestral portraits after sipping tea from priceless Sèvres cups in the formal salon, but also due to the daunting prospect of pressing any number of bells before making contact with a static voice inquiring after our bona fides in palpable fear that we were either bill collectors or the police. Whether Ben would have suggested turning tail must forever remain questionable because a sound reminiscent of Big Ben shredded the gauzy mantle of gray tranquility.

"Must have hit the buzzer with me knee," came Mrs. Malloy's voice. "It's this reckless leg syndrome I've been plagued with ever since I heard about it on the telly."

"Restless," I corrected.

"Does it matter?" Ben snapped.

We might have gone on to discuss other medical ailments if the door had not opened inward with a grotesque creak to reveal a rectangle of yellowish light surrounding a figure, rather in the manner of a card depicting the image of a saint proffering hope of succor to all who wander parched and weary upon life's barren plain.

"I'd a feeling there was more of you outside," said a male voice that sounded more cockney than saintly, as the three of us scuffled an entrance accompanied by some elbowing in the ribs and trampling on each other's feet. "Didn't seem likely to me and Mrs. Foot that there'd only be them two that just arrived."

Did a fog routinely bring in a stream of lost souls? I should of course have focused on what the man continued to say, but there was the distraction of Ben's rigid discomfort and Mrs. Malloy's jabbing me in the side as she adjusted her hat, which would have been a bit overdone even for Ascot. Added to which I am one of those shallow types as much drawn to the environments into which I find myself catapulted as to those who provide admittance. Rather than wondering if the man was the home owner and who were Mrs. Foot and *them two* mentioned, I let my gaze pass through him to roam the vastness of a baronial hall shrouded in shadow so thick in places it was as though we had brought some of the fog inside with us. The yellowish light issued from a barely visible fixture suspended from some forty feet up, along with wall lamps that resembled the sort of torches held aloft by wild-eyed wretches screaming for the heads of their oppressors.

A snatch of a maudlin song warbled years ago by a great-aunt infiltrated my head, something along the lyrics of: *In the gloaming . . . oh my darling . . . when the lights are dim and low . . .* And lo, all these years later, I stood in the gloaming ignoring my own darling in the process. My eyes found the staircase. It stood a quarter of a mile down to my left, and despite the poor visibility there was no mistaking its baronial splendor. Straight ahead in the distance was a fireplace vast enough to roast more than one proverbial ox . . . or equally possibly a couple of recalcitrant peasants to be removed when necessary from the correspondingly large log bin to the left of the hearth. On my more immediate right was the outline of a carved screen that might well have been pinched from a cathedral. A trestle table that could have seated an army stood loaded with murky miscellany, and adding to the confusion were numerous squares and rectangles that could feasibly be packing chests brought in on moving day several centuries distant.

One thing was clear. Either I had mistaken the exterior of the building as eighteenth century or this hall dated back to an earlier part of a revamped structure. Tudor? No, I thought, undoubtedly doing some wishful thinking . . . Lancastrian or even further back to Plantagenet times. The name Geoffrey of Anjou filtered back to me from childhood history lessons, but I chose to indulge myself with the image of Henry II sporting a sprig of yellow broom tucked into his crown. By the time Mrs. Malloy pointed out that I was standing there gawking, the number of living persons in hall had dwindled by one.

"I expect you hurt his feelings by not listening to a word he said." She stood majestically, smoothing down the front of the emerald green taffeta jacket to which were pinned enough sparkling brooches to ransom half the nobility of Europe. Clearly she wasn't speaking about Ben, who was pacing on the spot, but in recognition of my stupid look she clarified for me. "Him as let us in, and I'd have thought you'd have thrilled to every syllable, Mrs. H!"

"Who is he and what did I miss?"

"Mr. Plunket."

"That's his name?" Call me persnickety, but as a sobriquet for a member of the landed gentry this one left something to be desired.

"So he said, and I don't see why he'd say so if it weren't true. Not one of your more romantic names, is it? 'Course, maybe it was pronounced French at one time. 'Ploonkay' has a certain air to it . . ."

"Possibly if he wanted to be a fashion designer, but maybe he's happy as he is."

"Happy is what he didn't look, Mrs. H, when he took an eyeful of you."

"Me?"

"Could we continue this rather banal conversation outside?" Ben paced further into the gloaming, allowing Mrs. Malloy to ignore him without seeming to be downright rude.

"Never mind that, Mrs. H, before you get all upset, Mr. Plunket is not the owner of this lovely big house."

"No? Then what is he? A policeman directing traffic?"

"The butler." Mrs. Malloy shook her head at my dimwittedness, then, perhaps feeling she had been unnecessarily crushing, added: "Not that he looked the part. More like he'd dressed out of the ragbag."

"I didn't notice."

"What difference does it make what he was

wearing?" Ben made an irritable turn and collided with a suit of armor, which made a metallic protest but mercifully did not draw its sword.

"And a face like a gourd," continued Mrs. M remorselessly. "Still, as I remember thinking on being introduced to my second . . . no, third husband, ugly is as ugly does. Like my American friend says, Abraham Lincoln never won any beauty pageants."

"And where is Mr. Plunket now?" I asked.

"Gone for a word with his nibs, is how he put it." Mrs. Malloy pointed at a door which I estimated could be reached without getting winded by anyone in reasonably good shape.

"About giving us directions? Why couldn't he have done that on his own?"

"Some people can't point the way to the end of their own noses. But never mind that, Mrs. H." Her eyes flashed like a cat's in the dark, and it was finally borne in on me that she was sizzling with excitement. "Get this! Them two people he mentioned as getting here ahead of us—the ones from the van, that is—they're part of a television crew, cameramen, audio, and such. Seems they've come to film a documentary! The director's French, if you can believe it!"

"God! What a ghastly stroke of luck!" Ben paced back into view, his footfall echoing up from the flagstones like the march of thousands. "We can't intrude at such a time! What if we get caught on camera explaining we couldn't find our way from point A to point B because of a little mist that wouldn't have stalled a kid on a tricycle. Ellie"—there was a note of pleading in his voice that would have undoubtedly touched my very core had I not been considering the likelihood of the director's name being François and whether he would wear a beret and sit in a canvas chair with his name on the back.

It shames me to report that I turned away from Ben to ask Mrs. Malloy a vital question. "Did Mr. Plunket say what sort of documentary?"

"So now you're interested." She struck a pose indicative of pondering her best side if presented to the camera. "He didn't get round to that. He ran off, it seemed to me"—she paused to give me the gimlet eyes from under penciled brows—"when he took a good look at you, Mrs. H!"

"Keep rubbing it in. I'm sorry I missed his reeling back in horror."

"You don't say. Anyway, from the look on his face it was like he'd seen a ghost."

"What rubbish!" If my laugh sounded hollow, it was due to the acoustics produced by the mile-high ceiling that vanished to a glimpse of the dependent light fixture and a railing girding what was presumably a gallery. I preferred the thought of lepers to minstrels. Was that a grotesquely dehumanized face peering down at us? Ridiculous! My overactive imagination had conjured a bedraggling of

28

hoary locks out of a trick of light. And yet, in my defense, a place like this, reeking with antiquity and seemingly serious neglect, might cause even the normally unsusceptible to overreact.

"It was right after eyeballing you that Mr. Plunket said he'd ask his nibs about the directions. Scuttled off he did like the hounds of hell was at his heels." Mrs. Malloy stood savoring the memory, while Ben took a detour around the trestle table before fumbling his way toward the fireplace. I inhaled a thought.

"Maybe that's the reason for crew and the documentary."

"What you mean, Mrs. H?"

"Ghosts. I wonder if this place is to be part of a series on haunted houses. I can't imagine it having been chosen for the glimpse it provides into the golden glory of aristocratic living."

"I'll bet you've hit the nail on the noggin." My trusty cohort is not one to hand out praise on a shovel and she did not now beam approval, but her nod conveyed agreement of sufficient fervor that her hat shifted a couple of degrees.

"What can be keeping the butler fellow this long?" Ben again passed the suit of armor without so much as a nod of acknowledgment. Did the sensation of being preyed upon by unseen eyes and ears emanate from that chunk of metal? Or was there some other hovering presence counting the seconds until Ben dragged Mrs. Malloy and me out the door that would thud heavily and inexorably against us as we went fleeing back into the night? Aware that this was a chapter I had read more often than was good for me, I banished the chills and thrills and concentrated on the logical.

"Very likely Mr. Plunket has interrupted a session between his nibs and the director of the television show and is having difficulty stirring up interest in our trivial situation." I felt regretfully compelled to add: "Under the circumstances, I think you're right, darling, we are making nuisances of ourselves, and from what Mrs. Malloy said of Mr. Plunket's reaction to me, I don't suppose he'll mind one bit returning to find us gone."

Being . . . or thinking . . . myself good at picking up atmospheres, I imbibed waves of gratitude flowing my way from Ben, coupled with even stronger vibes that boded well should he and I ever be blessed in entering our own bedroom once again. But before he could utter more than a reprieved sounding half-syllable, Mrs. Malloy responded vehemently. "That's right, Mrs. H, go blaming me for forcing us to do a bunk. Well, I for one don't hold with bad manners—them being precluded in Article Forty-nine, paragraph fourteen of the CFCWA [Chitterton Fells Charwomen's Association] Charter. Besides, it could be the reason Mr. Plunket's not back yet is that his nibs and the director are talking about inviting us to be extras"—her face became a beacon far outshining the inadequate wattage of the hall—"or even give us speaking parts."

To be on television? My shallow nature thrilled to the prospect. And, I reminded myself, on the practical side the exposure would be good for my career and Ben's. He could casually mention his cookery books and the bistro. I could display a charming knowledge of furniture styles, fabrics, and ambience before the camera panned to my logo and business e-mail address. A couple with three children and a cat to support must sensibly seize opportunities offered. Besides . . . my incredibly beautiful fashion model cousin Vanessa would be sick with jealousy, as would that woman at church who always looked down her nose at me because I don't know one opera from another . . . and there was that friend of hers who talked all the time about going to Paris for lunch . . .

Upon catching Ben's eye, I reined in my delusions of approaching fame while being sufficiently resentful of his wet blanket attitude to move away from him and Mrs. Malloy and prowl over to the suit of armor. We have a pair at Merlin's Court positioned against the staircase wall, and I was interested in discovering if there was any familial resemblance. If so, I could give this one an update on how often ours, according to the children, came alive when they thought no one was watching.

"Well," said Mrs. Malloy in a defeatist voice, "could be I'm getting ahead of meself about us being included in the show. Not that it matters to me; it was you I was thinking about, like always, Mrs. H. I expect the truth is his nibs is ninety years old and Mr. Plunket is having trouble waking him from his nap."

"Or deciding if he's dead," muttered Ben nastily. "In this lighting, his viability could be questionable for days."

"No need for jokes, Mr. H, I don't think it's nice considering—now I come to remember—that Mr. Plunket said this had been a difficult evening already." Either Mrs. Malloy or Ben sighed gustily; there followed the irritable tap-tap of her high heels. Without turning my head, I was aware of her standing with her back squarely to me a yard or so from the staircase.

"Good evening," I addressed the suit of armor with the courtesy I had instilled into my children during the process of introductions. "What, my fine fellow, can you tell us of this place?"

Its visored face showed only slightly more expression than a guard at Buckingham Palace.

"Ever get an urge to scratch an itch?"

Oh, the folly of thinking oneself witty at the expense of the immobile. Foolish . . . infantile assumption! Before the smirk fully adhered to my face, I experienced a sharp pain above my right foot, and just as I started to hop, I saw the metal arms begin to rise through the grainy gloom and draw together . . . the metal paws curled inward . . . closing around the general vicinity of my throat.

Did I imagine the macabre chortle and the gleeful murmur of "Who's immobile now?" Would I have stood there trembling on the edge of reason until those salad spoon hands closed around my throat, choking out every last spluttering gasp as my eyes stood out like Ping-Pong balls and . . . with a final expiring breath my nose blew off? It is not a question I allow myself to ponder in the dead of night when the ghastly memory returns. I was saved by a scream of unholy terror from behind me. Had I been capable of coherent thought, I would have assumed Ben or Mrs. Malloy had paused in thinking about themselves to notice my imminent danger. As it was, I turned in automated slow motion to witness Mrs. Malloy with her mouth opened in size to the entrance to a cave. For teeth she had stalactites and stalagmites. But what did it for her appearance was her wearing a hat on top of a hat—one with a circle of corded fringe cutting her face in half.

"I can't see! I'm blind! Blind!" Her screech was one of reverberating panic. Immediately, Ben was at her side making the necessary adjustment to what I realized, on the verge of hysterical laughter, was a lamp shade. His attempts to pull it off completely were unsuccessful. Apparently the hat underneath, having first dibs, refused to give an inch.

"Why are you wearing that?" I asked her in a voice as deadened as the rest of me.

"It dropped from above."

"Better a lamp shade than the roof of the temple. Poor old Samson had it worse!" Ben laughed comfortingly while placing an arm around her, drawing her into a hug, a gesture I would have found endearing had I been capable of the least flicker of emotion. "I expect someone took it off to dust and set it down on a piece of furniture or even the banister railing, forgot about it, and some vibration sent it toppling off balance." His words may have helped soothe Mrs. Malloy but did nothing for me.

"Unfortunately, it's not becoming," I pronounced tonelessly. "Suit yourself, but I wouldn't make it the basis of any future outfits." Somewhere deep inside I recognized the cruelty. I should have told her that the lamp shade elongated her figure . . . provided an Audrey Hepburn elegance . . . but when one has come close to being murdered by a suit of armor something within the soul dies.

"Ellie!" Ben protested. Could this be the wife he revered except for those times when she failed to pass on telephone messages or interrupted when he was watching football?

"Oh, that's all right!" responded Mrs. Malloy with a pathetically resigned look on her face. "Some people can never bear others being the center of attention, even when it's the nasty sort."

At that I started to shake. "A lamp shade fell on your head! Go ahead and sue his nibs! Insist that he tear down this horrible mausoleum. You won't get any complaints from me. That thing . . . that evil thing kicked me, and that . . . that was before it attempted to choke me."

"What thing, sweetheart?" Ben was at my side in an instant.

"That!" With an immense effort I twisted around to face the suit of armor, my pointing finger gyrating out of control.

"It looks harmless now." The laughter that had been in Ben's voice was back. And, adding insult to injury, Mrs. Malloy relented toward me, saying magnanimously that after all we'd been through it wasn't any surprise that I was overwrought.

"Probably you bumped into it and it tilted forward. Them legs and arms have to move some or the person inside wouldn't have been able to stagger into battle holding his crossbow, or sword, or whatever."

Of course what she said had to be true. It must have happened that way. But it hadn't! It hadn't! I stared at that metal, triangular-fronted face with hatred. If I'd had a tin opener at the ready, I would have gone whirring into action as if it were a tin of Heinz Tomato Soup. "Take that, you metal cretin!" I railed silently. In my defense, it had been a tense evening from the moment the fog descended through to our entrapment, or so it seemed, in this oppressive hall. It is almost certain I would have rallied to laugh with Ben and Mrs. Malloy at my overly vivid imagination, but recoiling from the disbelief in their eyes I looked up to see a face above the banisters.

Its features were blurred, but even without the distortions of distance and shadow it was grotesquely, terrifyingly recognizable by its straggling locks and toothless gape as the face of the wardress of the insane asylum in which Wisteria Whitworth was incarcerated by her brutal husband. Could there be any doubt that I was on the verge of a similar fate? Under such melodramatic circumstances, there was only thing to do. Regrettably, I did not have a history of fainting, but it's amazing how quickly one can develop the knack. The room spun, the floor went out from under me, and I went down into blessed oblivion.

2

I was vaguely surprised that the flagstones onto which I'd swooned weren't as hard as might have been expected. Indeed, they felt reasonably comfy. I explored them gingerly with my hand . . . the word *horsehair* seeping into mind . . . before opening my eyes to see someone standing over me. This person resolved into Ben, and behind him stood someone who closely resembled Mrs. Malloy, except that she was considerably taller than I remembered.

"It's the lamp shade," I whispered, and saw a

relief flood Ben's face. "How are you feeling, sweetheart?"

He knelt down to take my hand and I forced my eyes to blink my surroundings into clearer focus. We were no longer in the hall, although this huge room, whatever it was, bore a decided resemblance in overcrowding, and there was the same sense of decaying antiquity. The lighting, however, was somewhat better, although not sufficiently strong to hurt my eyes. It was the back of my head that ached. Not terribly, but with a dull throb.

"I'm on a sofa." I stretched out my feet tentatively and saw, as if looking through a telescope, that they appeared properly attached. It was my shoes that had been removed. "Did you carry me in here?"

"That was our host; he came out into the hall, saw you on the floor, and insisted." Did I detect resentment in Ben's voice? Surely not. What husband achingly concerned for his beloved would resent another man doing what he could to help by swooping her up into his manly arms? I remembered driftingly that I had pictured his nibs as being almost as ancient as his abode and the thought of him tottering precariously across the flagstone under my weight became so sad that I blinked back tears. I peered around, searching for a figure huddled in a chair shakily trying to find his face with an inhaler.

"Where is he now?"

"Gone to tell his housekeeper to bring you a cup of tea and a blanket."

"Thank God, you've come round, Mrs. H!" Mrs. Malloy pressed a heavily ringed hand to her bosom. "I could have sworn you was a gonner."

"Now don't say that!" a male voice exclaimed rather too loudly for my head. "One death this evening is more than enough! Very difficult these last few hours for his nibs! And him so looking forward to the filming. Not fair to him is what Mrs. Foot, Boris, and me—that works taking care of the house—has been feeling."

A face swam into view. Even to my numbed thinking, this could be no other than Mr. Plunket. My glimpse of him through the front doorway had called to mind the image of a medieval saint, but that had to be due to a blurred halo of saffron light surrounding poorly delineated features. It was Mrs. Malloy's description of his having a face like a gourd that told the tale. A flesh-colored gourd sprouting pale nodules, not an attractive sight for someone coming out of a faint. His nose was flat, his eyes lacked color, and his mouth was no more than a horizontal crease among the vertical ones. Not that he could help any of that. Not all men are born to be as darkly, dashingly handsome as Ben. Indeed, as she had demonstrated when unloading the fog, Mother Nature had her moments of being difficult just for the malevolent joy of it. Mr. Plunket was also not helped by his attire. He was wearing a threadbare navy suit, several sizes too skimpy for a man of his rotund build, a dishwater-gray shirt, and a badly creased tie, all of which looked as though they had previously been used as polishing cloths.

"Who died?" Interest stirred . . . coupled with the insensitivity of hope. If the deceased had been strangled by the suit of armor, it would be proved beyond argument that I had not imagined his attempt to attack me. As for the face above the banisters, I would think about her later . . . much later.

"Ellie, try to relax, you gave yourself a real crack on the head." Ben placed a soothing hand on my brow before getting to his feet and staring around the room as if in search of reinforcements. Had a doctor been sent for? Surely not? To disprove the need, I attempted to sit up. Unfortunately, my head went into orbit and an accompanying ringing in my ears forced me to lie back down.

"Who died?" I repeated fretfully.

"One of the"—Mr. Plunket paused, and despite my still swimming head I sensed he was making a verbal adjustment—"people . . . expected to descend on his nibs for the coming week. The others aren't due till tomorrow morning. But this one asked if she could show up this evening. Had been invited to spend the day with someone in the area, she said. Why she couldn't have spent the night with whoever it was is what Mrs. Foot,

Boris, and me wondered, but his nibs said he'd no objection."

"So what happened?" Mrs. Malloy is not one to suffer the long-winded gladly, with the exception of herself, of course.

"It was the fog . . ."

"An accident on the road?" Ben's gaze met mine. He had to be thinking this could have been our fate if we had gone on, and feeling better about having followed the van onto the private drive. How puny was embarrassment to the male psyche when compared to the hovering visage of the Grim Reaper.

"No, right outside." Mr. Plunket pointed to the window behind my sofa. "Happened three hours or so ago, when the visibility was even worse than when you got here. His nibs had said for us to keep our ears open for the sound of her car approaching the drive. And it was Boris that went out, but not quick enough. If he hadn't lost time looking for a torch and not finding one, things could have been different."

"So, cutting the story short," urged Mrs. Malloy with all the authority provided by the lamp shade still on her head.

"I blame myself for not getting outside ahead of him with the hurricane lamp that's kept in the grandfather clock, to guide that poor woman in safe." The nodules on Mr. Plunket's face were the more evident as he moved closer to the standing lamp at the foot of the sofa. "Gone off the drive she must have done onto the side lawn and through a broken section of a garden wall, down into the ravine that's thick with trees. Like I said, Boris got out of the house too late. When we heard the crash, his nibs, Mrs. Foot, and me followed as quick as we could with the help of the lamp. But there wasn't nothing could be done. It was a job getting the car door open but we managed between us. Luckily the interior lights worked. His nibs felt for the pulse in her neck. Nothing. She'd snuffed it all right and we come back inside so he could phone the authorities."

"Did they have trouble getting here?" Ben began pacing, his eyes shifting from me to the door and back. I knew what he was thinking and he was right. I desperately needed a cup of tea or if possible something stronger to keep me from starting to cry. Unfortunately, if there were a bottle of brandy in the room, a team of detectives would be needed to find it. An automobile accident amply explained by the fog would not have caused investigators to linger on the premises. Routine for them, while to us the deceased was a nameless, faceless stranger, but surely she was someone's loved one . . . wife . . . mother . . . daughter . . . friend. What an agonizing shock for the bereaved to receive by phone or a knock at the door!

"It's what they're used to, isn't it? The police and medical people, I mean, getting to places in the worst possible conditions, and of course Lord Belfrey turned on all the exterior lights for them."

Hadn't they been on when the woman arrived? This thought blocked out any other.

"Not that they was likely to do much good, that fog being thicker than a sheepskin coat."

"Lord Belfrey," echoed Mrs. Malloy, as if prayerfully reeling off the names of a dozen holy martyrs.

"That's his nibs," replied Mr. Plunket with a prosaic scratch of a nodule below his lower lip.

"A proper lordship?" Mrs. M pursued hopefully, while sinking into an armchair that looked as if it had been rescued after being set out next to a dustbin a hundred years ago.

"What other kind is there?" muttered Ben, his eyes fixed anxiously on my recumbent form.

"Oh, you know," an airy wave of a ringed hand, "the sort as is given for your lifetime only—that doesn't get passed on through the family. Or don't you get made a lord for being a famous jockey or actor?" Her rouge brightened at this possibility. "Maybe that's just for *sirs* and *dames* and all that lot."

"The title's been in the Belfrey family all of six hundred years." Pride was evident in every throb of Mr. Plunket's voice. And despite my increasing headache it struck that he had evinced no emotion of approaching scale when describing the appallingly recent death just beyond the doorstep.

"Have they lived here the whole time?" Mrs. Malloy inquired in a breathless rush.

"Give or take the times it was taken away on account of them being on the wrong side politically. Tudor times was the worst, from what Mrs. Foot, Boris, and me understand it. And for what? is what we ask ourselves. Roman Catholic . . . Protestant! Who gives a flaming candle?"

My mother-in-law for one, I thought dizzily. There is a woman who has never voluntarily missed mass a day in her life and can discuss the impenetrables of transubstantiation with the best of them, including St. Augustine had he paid her a vision. My Jewish father-in-law might not have made him quite so welcome; he's a crotchety man, not at all welcoming to drop-in guests at the flat above the greengrocer's shop in Tottenham.

"But there's an end to everything, even bloodthirsty kings and queens," said Mr. Plunket as if reading from a pamphlet on sale for twenty pence at the entrance booth. "The Belfreys always came back home to Mucklesfeld Manor, and some of them—the ones that wasn't given over to living it up wild—went about setting it back to rights, just like his nibs has made up his mind to do. Although who can say as to what will happen now that woman's been taken away in a body bag. Mrs. Foot and Boris both talk like it won't make no difference but . . . ."

Mrs. Malloy cut into his ruminations. "Mucklesfeld?" Her voice was sharp-edged with disappointment. "Not Belfrey?"

I heard what sounded like a hiccupping cough, but looking to where Mr. Plunket still stood at the foot of the sofa, I realized he was chortling. In the sallow light cast by the lamp nearest him and others scattered stingily around the vast room, his heightened color did not look good. A decidedly unbecoming greenish-orange that confirmed the pimply-gourd effect.

"Belfrey? Now that would set the place up as a joke, wouldn't it? Bats in the belfry, there'd be no stopping the schoolboy silliness. No, the place got its name from the old muck fields hereabouts. Famous they was; some said the best in all England. Wonderful it was for growing celery. But then they went and dried up, just like the family money did. As his nibs can't be blamed for." He stared down at Mrs. Malloy in her chair. "He only came into the title and property last year after his cousin that was then Lord Belfrey died. Spent much of the last thirty years in America, he did—Alaska mostly, although I always thought that was Russia."

"Whatever, it's abroad, isn't it?" Mrs. Malloy responded ingratiatingly. "I'm sure his lordship was glad to get back to the UK; a title in America has to be as much use as a fur coat in the tropics." If she expected an appreciative chuckle from Mr. Plunket, she was disappointed. He stood smoothing down the too-short sleeves of his jacket.

"From all we've heard, the cousin was a miserable old blighter that let Mucklesfeld go to rack and ruin while he shut himself away from the world."

This topic would have been fascinating if I'd been sufficiently unwoozy to be my usual nosy self. Even though I seriously doubted I'd slipped gracefully to the floor during my faint, I thought it more likely my headache was due to emotional stress than physical injury. For whole minutes at a time my mind successfully warded off the memory of the Metal Knight clawing at my throat, but the nightmarish face peering down at me through the upper banisters refused to be banished. Stupid of me. Once I could think clearly I would hit upon a logical explanation for both incidents, but the aura of malevolence that had accompanied the latter . . . would I be able to convince myself that it had arisen entirely out of my penchant for the Gothic novel?

"And like I said, his nibs has been hoping to refill the coffers at Mucklesfeld. He's had to make a decision that many a proud man wouldn't have the guts for. This television show . . ."

Ben cut him off. "I realize this isn't a cottage. But how long should it take for your employer to come back and inquire after my wife or at least send one of the other members of the staff with a reviving beverage?"

"Now then, Mr. H." Mrs. Malloy sent him the

admonishing glance of a nanny who doesn't appreciate being shown up when bringing a little person down from the nursery into the drawing room. "Mr. Plunket has explained why things are bound to be a bit topsy-turvy this evening. To top it off his lordship has them television people here and we all know how temperamental people in show business can be, even without that poor woman being killed." No doubt she would have added that it never rained but it poured or something equally platitudinous, but Mr. Plunket was off down his own road.

"Very inconvenient, that was." His lugubrious tone did not quite make up for his word choice.

"Inconvenient?" Ben raised an eyebrow at him.

"As well as sad," Mr. Plunket amended, "tragic more like. That goes without saying, of course."

"Was she . . . the deceased woman . . . a relative or close friend of his lordship?" I roused myself to ask.

"Never met or spoken with her. She was one of the contestants, you see."

"The what?" Ben added his echo to that of Mrs. Malloy, while bending over the sofa to smoothe back my hair and search my face with anxious eyes.

"Contestants." Mr. Plunket shuffled on his feet, which like his clothes appeared too small for him. "She would have made the sixth. The other five will be getting here tomorrow if it's not decided to put them off."

46

"What are they contesting for?" That was Ben asking, while looking toward the obdurately closed door.

"The position of Lady Belfrey."

I actually heard Mrs. Malloy's chin drop.

"One of the lucky ladies will . . . if the filming goes forward . . . be awarded his hand in marriage during the final segment. That's as Mrs. Foot, Boris, and me understand things. The director, Monsieur Georges LeBois—French like you might guess—hasn't had much to say to us since he arrived this morning. All he's been going on about is how bad the food has been."

If Mrs. Malloy hadn't already been seated, she would have sunk into the nearest chair or wastepaper basket.

"We can only hope the rest of the crew that just got here won't turn their noses up at what's on the table because it isn't snails and frog legs." Mr. Plunket wasn't looking at anyone in particular; indeed, his eyes had disappeared into his gourd face.

Clearly in desperate need of something to hold on to, Mrs. Malloy finally removed the lamp shade and her hat along with it. "You told us earlier out in the hall that they're doing a TV reality show. Are you saying it's one of them bachelor ones?"

"I think he's spelled it out," Ben snapped at her, something he almost never does.

"What's the show to be called?" she inquired

dreamily while crushing the shape out of the lamp shade.

"*Here Comes the Bride.*"

"My, don't that sound lovely! And I expect the contestants are all lovely young things with perfect figures and faces that have never been used." She was all eager wistfulness as she continued to pulverize the hapless lamp shade.

"Not chosen for their looks they haven't been," replied Mr. Plunket. "The idea, as presented to his lordship by Monsieur LeBois, was for something different from other programs of the type. That's the attraction what they're banking on to garner—I think that's the word—a big audience. The contestants have been picked because of other qualities: their willingness to muck in at Mucklesfeld is how his nibs puts it. Deal with all that's wrong with the place, pitch in with the cleanup, show they are up to the job of being Lady Belfrey while the ceilings come down about their ears."

"Hardly romantic." Ben paced over to the door, opened it, and closed it again.

"Oh, I don't know." I found myself sitting up on the sofa. Had I thought about it, I would have realized that neither the horrible face peering through the banisters nor the aggressive Metal Knight had terrorized my thoughts for the past few moments. "A woman with a strong practical streak can have her appeal, especially if she makes the most of her looks, something the beauties of this world don't have to bother about, hopefully, until it is too late. Did Lord Belfrey make the selections, Mr. Plunket?"

"That was done by Monsieur LeBois from the hundreds of written applications and photos sent in. He and his nibs met some six months ago in London, introduced by a mutual acquaintance. The idea for the show came out of their conversation. They got together again. You can see the mutual benefit to the winning contestant and his nibs. She'd get to become a titled lady and he'd be able to use his share of the financial proceeds from the show to set Mucklesfeld back on its feet."

"But now things are up in the air," I mused.

"They always was in a way." Mr. Plunket oozed despondency. "Monsieur LeBois hasn't managed as yet to get a firm commitment from any of the stations, he's filming on spec—is how I think it's called—but as Mrs. Foot, Boris, and me understand it, there's been considerable interest."

"Is Lord Belfrey content to marry for what it can bring him?" I felt, rather than saw, Ben's lip curl.

"It's how things has been done in the great families for centuries and it's not as how his nibs is young and wild to trot. Fifty-six is what he'll be come his next birthday. Can't say he's not of an age to know his own mind and stick to it down the years. Besides, his heart's already taken by one he can't have. That said, he'll choose the one that's right for him and Mucklesfeld and do right by her through the years."

But would it be a case of separate bedrooms, as had at first been the case when Wisteria Whitworth married the estimable Carson Grant after the timely death of the husband who in order to gain control over her fortune had contrived her removal to the hellish confines of Perdition Hall? A woman subjected to the suspect ministrations of Dr. Megliani, whose medical degree had been bought from a cloaked figure with a glass eye and a missing forefinger in the backroom of an opium den in a back street of Soho. An acknowledged beauty, once the toast of London, now reduced to being force-fed lumpy gruel by the slatternly female warden (I winced away from this image) could not be expected to cast care behind her like a silk stole and respond instantly to the overtures of a man who had been a notable rake before gaining fierce self-control over his baser self.

That he was regarded as the handsomest man in England, was fluent in all modern and dead languages, rode to hounds as if born in the saddle, and fenced like the Count of Monte Cristo, added not a whit to his conceit. Though his love for Wisteria invaded every aspect of his being, Carson Grant—whom I had naturally pictured as a young Cary of the same last name—had held his seering passion in check with an iron will and a clenched jaw.

Tormented beyond his limits, he had removed

himself to his study; and when inclement weather prevented his stripping off his intricately tied cravat and French cambric shirt and diving into the deep stillness of the lake behind the formal rose garden, he strode off on a twenty-mile walk across the moors, returning only when he knew himself too weary to accost her with anguished beseechings to permit him his rights as a husband. Of course, one hundred and thirty some pages later, all had ended as it should, with her wistful acknowledgment that a marriage in name only left something lacking, including the possibility of an heir.

Back to life at Mucklesfeld Manor. At fifty-six, Lord Belfrey might have no interest in siring children, making youth, or lack thereof, insignificant in the selection of a bride. My eyes met Mrs. Malloy's and a tremor seized me on perceiving their dreamy glow. I knew with appalling certainty that she was inwardly humming "Here Comes the Bride." Mr. Plunket had stated that his lordship was not seeking a dainty delight of a woman to take to wife but a sturdy helpmeet, one willing to roll up her shirtsleeves and trouser legs and begin setting his house to rights. And who better to do that than a woman who had spent her working life cleaning other people's homes? Tragically, one of the contestants was dead and a vacancy yawned.

I could understand from whence hope sprang. But even if his lordship and the director did by some remote chance add her to the list of hopefuls, the odds were five to one against her being the one chosen to become Lady Belfrey. And Mrs. Malloy was the worst of bad losers. She had snarled for a week after not winning Pin the Tail on the Donkey at Rose's last birthday party. No, no! I could not risk her being mortally wounded on the path to a loveless marriage. She must be wrested from Mucklesfeld Manor without delay.

"Sweetheart, your eyes are glazed. Did you doze off?" Ben was all tender solicitude.

"Just drifting." I gave him a staunch smile. Shuffling my legs off the sofa from a semi-reclining position produced an involuntary wince. My headache had gone from minor to full-blown. I was sure I looked like death. Which in this house was perhaps not a novelty. Mr. Plunket appeared not to notice.

"There's no denying that the lady's death puts his lordship in a difficult position." He looked more than ever like a talking gourd. "Will he think it right to go ahead with filming *Here Comes the Bride*? Would it seem right to the sponsors of the show? Would it be a turnoff for the viewing audience?"

"But that's what them shows is all about—high drama and cutthroat angling for the main chance," responded Mrs. Malloy stoutly from her chair. " 'Course, I don't want to sound callous, but there it is. Talk about grabbing the audience by the throat—revealing the tragedy up front and going on from there. Especially if his lordship could find himself a replacement candidate in the nick of time . . . right out of the blue, so to speak." The dreamy glow had returned. Clearly no time was to be lost in rescuing her from her giddy aspirations. At any moment Lord Belfrey might swan into the room to find himself a marked man. "His nibs is a sensitive bloke." Mr. Plunket's voice quivered. "He'll not want to show what could look like disrespect to the deceased, may she rest in peace. Trouble is, he's up against Monsieur LeBois. With him it's all about the finances, what he's already put into the project, along with whatever he's agreed on paying his crew, including the cameraman and the staging fellow that showed up minutes ahead of you three. Can't just send them off with a flea in their ear is what Mrs. Foot, Boris, and me heard him saying."

Ben stood seething, lips compressed; eyes blazing the color of the emerald (a genuine fake) mounted in one of Mrs. Malloy's rings, waiting to break in the instant Mr. Plunket paused on a shaky breath.

"No disrespect to your boss," he enunciated bitingly, "but his sensitivity appears to be lacking where my wife is concerned. It's been a good twenty minutes since he absented himself and has neither returned to inquire how she is feeling or seen to be providing her with any refreshment."

"Now then, Mr. H," Mrs. Malloy shoved in her

oar, "there's no need to get rattled. Like Mr. Plunket's been saying, his lordship's got a lot on his plate. Could be he's on the phone with the dead lady's family or the funeral home. It don't do to be selfish. Besides," she looked at me and added with what I considered extreme callousness, "Mrs. H quite often gets a headache when she gets herself worked up. Tension ones, they're called. My next-door neighbor is a martyr to them. And it's not like Mrs. H fell hard back there in the hall, just slumped down, bottom first, as I saw it."

Forgive her, I thought nobly; she had to be jealous that it was me, not her, whom Lord Belfrey had swept up in his aristocratic arms and deposited on the sofa. Also she very likely had a point. My nerves had been stretched to the limit during the drive through the fog. In addition to which we had failed to find the restaurant we had been seeking and I'm a person inclined to go all hollow and wobbly without food. Perhaps with a good helping of fish and chips inside me I wouldn't have succumbed to foolish terror and fainted. I started to say this to Ben, but he was still glowering at poor Mr. Plunket, who was making apologetic noises to the effect that his nibs had intended for Mrs. Foot and or Boris to bring in a tea tray.

"But as you can imagine, sir, they're discombobulated themselves."

"In that case, let's not inconvenience them or yourself." Ben attempted to contain his irritation.

"If you'll direct me toward the kitchen, I'll put on a kettle and . . ."

"Now, I don't know as that's such a good idea," Mr. Plunket passed a hand over his pimpled brow, "the stove's that old and unreliable, none of the knobs turn unless you've got the trick of it, and if you manage, which I never can, the gas flames shoot up to take off your eyebrows. No, no, begging your pardon, better to wait on Mrs. Foot or Boris. Can't risk an accident, so hard on this other. His nibs would never get over it if worse come to worst and you was to blow yourself up."

"I really am feeling loads better," I announced valiantly, "so much so that I think we should leave right away. I am sure Mrs. Malloy agrees with me. We are all eager to get home at the end of our holiday. The fog's bound to have lifted sufficiently by now."

"I wouldn't think so," Mrs. Malloy demurred.

"I'm a chef," Ben informed Mr. Plunket. "I'm entirely capable of dealing with the most resistant kitchen equipment and making my wife a cup of tea."

"A chef!" Mr. Plunket sounded taken aback.

"That's correct. I've even written some cookery books that have been reasonably well received, so if you would kindly direct me toward the kitchen . . ."

"What kind of meals? English . . . or the Frenchified sort?"

But for my increasing headache, I might have pondered the intensity of Mr. Plunket's response. Before Ben could demand either a compass or a map, the door opened to admit a tall, gangly man with very black hair and eyes in contrast to his chalk white face. Even though not at my sharpest, I was struck by his resemblance to Lurch of the Addams family. He stood gaping, awkwardly dangling a hand on the knob, presumably in hope of preventing the door from closing on the woman endeavoring to enter behind him.

"Ah!" Ben sucked in a relieved breath and shot toward her to remove the tray she was carrying. Not surprisingly, she appeared startled at finding herself standing hands spread, holding up thin air by the handles. But her surprise was nothing to mine. Hers was the face I had glimpsed through horror-glazed eyes peering down at me through the banisters. In the dimly lit room there was the grainy quality of a bad photo to her form and features, but she did not now send a chill through my bones.

Truth be told, it was impossible not to experience a woman-to-woman pang of sympathy for her unfortunate appearance. She was tall, so often a good thing, but in her case not an enhancement. She loomed in the manner of a man playing the part of a woman in a farce. Her smile, uncertain . . . experimental, was cruelly ridiculed by the absence of her front teeth. The shapeless dress and plodding shoes seemed as false as the clumpily curled shoulder-length gray locks that elongated her nose and chin to an extreme degree. Sadly it probably wasn't a wig which could be taken off and tossed in the wastepaper basket. Remembering how often I had condemned my own form in the mirror, I internalized a prayer of gratitude for mercies received. I dared not look in Mrs. Malloy's direction, but counted on her being a churchgoing woman, when she remembered it was a Sunday, not to exude an air of smug complacency.

"This here's Mrs. Foot," Mr. Plunket waved a hand in my direction, "her as is his nibs's housekeeper."

It could have been Mrs. Danvers, I reminded myself, as I added my murmur to Ben and Mrs. Malloy's chorus of "A pleasure to meet you, Mrs. Foot." Ben had placed the tray on an already crowded table and now poured and passed me a cup of dishwater-colored tea, accompanied by a biscuit of the same shade of gray as Mrs. Foot's hair. Her smile broadened, losing the uncertainty but gaining in the display of missing teeth.

"And that there behind her," continued Mr. Plunket, "is Boris, his nibs's odd job man."

Lurch flopped a flaccid white hand, intoning in an expressionless voice: "Can always count on Boris."

"One in a million." Mrs. Foot was now positively beaming as she clumped further into the room. "Always the one to get the job done when needed." She even sounded like a man pretending to be a woman and I mentally dared Mrs. Malloy to titter. "Feeling better, are you, dearie?" She stood staring down at me, and I have to admit to feeling a quiver of—not exactly revulsion . . . more awkwardness—on spotting the curiosity verging on thirsty fascination in her pale, globular eyes.

"Much better." I took a resolute sip of tea. "Thank you so much for bringing this."

"You do have more color." Ben sounded as relieved as if he'd just noticed I was coming out of a ninety-day coma. A few more minutes and surely we could politely leave. Mrs. Malloy accepted her cup and saucer while settling even deeper into her chair. We might need a forklift to move her, but we'd get her out of here, too.

Mrs. Foot shifted her gaze from my face to fix it upon Mr. Plunket. "There is a strange resemblance, isn't there? No wonder his nibs got his self in a tizz. Spooky, you could call it."

"Now then, I wouldn't say that." Mr. Plunket nudged his way cautiously around the words, as if one too many might trip him up. "It's ever easy to imagine things in this house."

"What sort of resemblance?" Mrs. Malloy, who does not enjoy sitting on the sidelines, made a valiant effort to sound pleasantly interested.

"To a lady in one of the family portraits."

"Really?" I completely forgot my woozy state and the desire to escape back into the fog. "I'd be interested in taking a look at the painting if it wouldn't be an imposition."

"It's no longer in the house." Boris must have spent hours in a dank cellar perfecting his sepulcher intonation. He was now standing directly behind Mrs. Foot, hunching first one shoulder, then the next, in an automated fashion that brought to mind the terror that had assailed me in the hall.

Turning on the sofa to face the assembled more fully, I said with determined lightness: "You said just now, Mr. Plunket, that it's easy to imagine things in this house, but I don't think it was imagination that caused me to faint." I came to a halt, aware that it wouldn't do to mention that I had mistaken Mrs. Foot for a ghoulish visitant. "I'm quite sure," I plunged on, "that the suit of armor tried to attack me."

"Oh, sweetheart," Ben bent over me, almost oversetting the teacup, "that has to have been a nightmare."

"It was, but not one produced by the faint," I responded firmly. "I was scared stiff. Its hands would have closed around my throat if I hadn't nipped back in time."

"That's our Boris!" Mrs. Foot reached back a hand to pat his arm. "Always tinkering about for the fun of it. Last year he got the dining-room chandelier to spin. Oh, his nibs did have a good laugh! We all did. Couldn't stop chortling for ages, could we, Mr. Plunket?"

"Always good to see his nibs enjoying himself."

"My, what fun you all have at Mucklesfeld Manor." Mrs. Malloy oozed rapt admiration, drawing Mrs. Foot's attention not so much to her as to what lay at her feet.

"Now how did that get in here? It's the one from the gallery table lamp."

"It dropped from the banisters onto my friend's head," I said.

"And if I'm not complaining who should," fired back said friend, "a very handsome shade and no damage done to me hat, as isn't my best by a long shot. I've a much smarter one at home that me friends," her voice took on a most unbecoming simpering quality, "call me lady of the manor hat."

I was watching Mrs. Foot as closely as possible, given the weak lighting. She was shaking her head, batting the gray locks against her neck. Her look of amused wonderment was perfect, but I again felt the prickle down my spine that spread to a subzero chill. She was smiling her jovial gap-toothed smile, but I saw the face peering malevolently through the banisters. Did she believe I hadn't seen her?

"Well, isn't that something!" She looked from Boris—who had shifted further to her side—to Mr. Plunket, and back again. "I was up there at the time crawling around the floor doing a last-minute bit of dusting, and when I got to my feet you'd," turning those globs of eyes on me, "you'd gone down in a faint and I can't say I noticed the lamp shade on the other lady's head, let alone saw it go over the railing. Like I've said, odd things do happen at Mucklesfeld that have us all scratching our heads."

I hoped she wouldn't put action to words. That hair of hers looked as though it had been around far longer than she had been on this earth and I was afraid of what might fly out.

"How's the tea?" she asked.

The truthful answer would have been dreadful, but I said it had put life back in me. To prove the point, I attempted to get off the sofa, but was compelled by an upsurge of ridiculous dizziness to sink back down. The nibble of gray biscuit had clearly not sat well with me. And the headache was back in sickening force. I wondered if I had a migraine. I'd never had one, but as the cheerful cliché goes, there is a first time for everything. Given the stresses of the day, coupled with an atmosphere that seemed ripe for a lifetime of languishing as an invalid waiting for the doctor to arrive with his medical bag stuffed full of leeches and the recommendation to keep the hartshorn always at hand, I wouldn't be surprised if I'd come down with something worse. Ben eyed me worriedly, but Mrs. Malloy appeared cheerfully oblivious. The thought even crossed my mind that she was looking on the bright side of things.

"Mrs. Foot makes a very good cuppa." Mr. Plunket's face creased into admiration.

"Best tea maker in the world." Boris cracked a smile that was ghastly to behold. Mrs. Foot's smile was pleased but modest.

"That's going a bit far. But wouldn't say much for me if I hadn't got the hang of it after brewing up more pots of tea than was ever seen in China during all the years I was a ward maid, trundling the trolley around to the patients. Poor dears, it was what they lived for—a cup of char and a biscuit."

Unbidden, I pictured her handing Wisteria Whitworth a cup of pale slop and ordering her to drink it down or could be her next treatment wouldn't go as nice and smooth as would be hoped. I was being unfair. Blame that on the fact that even Florence Nightingale's cool hand upon my brow wouldn't have brought me bounding back to life.

"Yes, poor dears is right. Sad, it was, how few visitors most of them got. I used to say to the doctors it wasn't right them lying there without a loved one's hand to hold when they got weepy. 'Course there was exceptions . . ."

"I must get my wife to a doctor." Ben was out of patience. He is always at his most handsome when agitated on my behalf. A pity I wasn't up to appreciating the flaring of his nostrils, the muscle twitching in his left cheek, the arrogant set of his dark head. "Is there one nearby that I could phone and ask to see her?"

"There's Dr. Rowley, him that's his nibs's cousin

and has his surgery in his house this side of Grimkirk village," replied Mr. Plunket, looking all at once like an important pumpkin. "But there's no need for you to get on the blower. Right after bringing the lady in here, his nibs went off to fetch him. Said, given the fog, he'd walk rather than take the car. Sensible after what happened earlier. Could be he got there to find Dr. Rowley was out or just couldn't go at a quick pace . . ."

He was interrupted by the door opening to reveal a man who was the living image of an older, silver-haired Cary Grant . . . or equally believably Carson Grant. He who had loved with invincible tenderness Wisteria Whitworth. Behind him came a lesser member of the male species holding a doctor's black bag. My headache and queasy state notwithstanding, the centuries-old, murkily lighted room came suddenly and vibrantly to life. Amazingly, it was obvious as he crossed the room that this impossibly handsome . . . virile . . . author-itive (need I add urbane?) man had eyes only for me.

3

※🙂🙃※

How are you feeling?" He stood looking down at me, and it was a moment before I realized that Ben had stepped aside to make room for him or that Mr. Plunket, Mrs. Foot, and Boris had ebbed out the door. The doctor, a rotund five foot six to his lordship's magnificent six foot three, also might not have been there. The same could be said of Mrs. Malloy, who had stood up in acknowledgment of Lord Belfrey's general greeting. Preen though she might, she was a shadow on the wall. I was in shock: Cary Grant . . . Carson Grant! Down to that entrancing cleft in the chin. Was I in a movie or a book? "Forgive me if Mrs. Foot forced one of her abominable cups of tea on you. She considers brewing up her main mission in life."

His voice enhanced his every other charm; it was deep-timbred, with a slight blurring around the edges. I shifted to a more upright position on the sofa, the better to bask in his smile, which so engagingly crinkled the skin around his eyes. He had a wonderful mouth . . . perfect teeth, particularly remarkable for a man in his fifties. Poor Mrs. Foot, with that sizable gap. I regretted every unkind thought about her.

"Really," I insisted, "there's nothing wrong with me but a tension headache. It was nerve-wracking driving in the fog, and I haven't eaten in ages because we couldn't find a restaurant. That must have been what caused me to faint."

"A sandwich and a glass of brandy would have been helpful." Ben sounded none too friendly, especially it seemed to me when adding, "Your lordship."

"Of course. Although I'm not sure anything prepared by Mrs. Foot would have made you feel any better." A wry and utterly beguiling smile. "Georges LeBois, who is here for the filming, is refusing to eat. And regrettably I don't keep alcohol in the house on account of Plunket having a weakness for anything that isn't orange juice"— again the kindness came through—"but if my cousin Tommy, here"—placing a hand on the doctor's shoulder—"prescribes a medicinal dose of brandy, or better yet cognac, for Mrs. Haskell, it will be fetched. A relation of ours lives within walking distance and she keeps an excellent cellar."

"Quite right." The doctor nodded his head vigorously. He had the round, guileless face of a schoolboy, his brown eyes shining with goodwill and his white hair fringing his forehead. His upper teeth (I was really noticing teeth or the lack thereof at Mucklesfeld) gave him endearingly goofy looks and a slight lisp. "I'm a teetotaler myself, for no reason other than I prefer lemonade, but it will be no trouble for me to walk over to Witch Haven, Celia's house."

"She's the daughter of our cousin Giles, who was at Mucklesfeld before me," explained his lordship.

"Interesting," said Ben.

"I'm also a Belfrey, or should be," the doctor chimed in cheerfully, "but my father chose to adopt my mother's maiden name. He was estranged from the family, believing he'd never been fairly treated as the third son. Silly, these family feuds. Now, if you do not object, Mrs. Haskell, I will take a quick look at you." He was opening his bag with great importance, encouraged by his wearing his big-boy suit instead of his play clothes. I pictured his mother agreeing on the condition that he didn't play in the dirt.

"What sort of a look?" I asked uneasily.

"Nothing that will require any undressing. Just an examination of your head and eyes. It's entirely possible," he continued cheerfully, "that you fractured your skull or suffered a concussion in that fall."

"It wasn't a fall," I protested. "It was a . . . slide. And please," feeling a ridiculous desire to be made one of the family, "do call me Ellie."

"Short for Eleanor?" Did Lord Belfrey frequently display that knack of indicating a vital interest in something of minor importance?

"Giselle." Mrs. Malloy assumed the role of speaking for me, given that the balance of my mind was disturbed. "Her husband is Ben," no appreciative smile from that quarter, "and my name's Roxie."

Lord Belfrey acknowledged this information with a smile that puffed up Mrs. Malloy's bosom under her taffeta ensemble and doubtless turned her knees to water. Could I begrudge her the thrill? Yes! She would get him alone at the speediest opportunity and propose herself as a contestant on

Here Comes the Bride. No sooner thought than done. She made her move. The hussy coyly suggested to his lordship that it might be proper for the two of them to leave the room while his cousin examined me. His consummate gallantry would have demanded this of him, but I watched him go with more regret than was appropriate in a woman with a husband of ten magical years standing devotedly at her sickbed . . . sofa.

Dr. Rowley—Tommy, as he urged me to call him—produced one of those eye-inspecting gadgets with all the enthusiasm of a schoolboy pretending to be a grown-up.

"A bright light!"

"Yes." I wanted to ask him what he thought of Lord Belfrey's plan to find a wife.

"Wear glasses?"

"No. Your cousin . . ."

"Aubrey?"

"An aristocratic name."

"And I got stuck with plain old Thomas." He chuckled while setting aside the instrument and beginning to probe the back of my head with enthusiastic fingers. "That hurt?"

"Some. Mr. Plunket mentioned that his lordship inherited the title from another cousin."

"Lie still, sweetheart," Ben urged.

"That was Giles." Tommy was now probing my neck. "Our paternal grandfather had three sons. Each of whom fathered only one child. The eldest produced Giles, the second Aubrey, and the youngest got stuck with me."

I murmured a protest before saying: "Didn't Giles have children?"

"Another *only* and this time a girl." Tommy continued to beam encouragement while laying my head back on the cushion. "Celia, who lives at Witch Haven and is likely to have brandy in the house. What does that make her to Aubrey and me? Daughter of a first cousin! I always have trouble working these relationships out. Always seem like something out of Genesis to me, this begetting or is it begatting? Too much to work out for a simple country doctor. That's the trouble with being the son of the third son, means a job. Not that Aubrey didn't have to work." Tommy blushed, embarrassment written all over his cherub face, as if in anticipation of a rebuke from his form master. "He went out to America as a very young man and stayed there, working for an insurance firm, until coming back last year when Giles died."

America! So that explained his sounding, as well as looking, like Cary Grant—another transplanted Englishman.

"It seems he didn't return with the proverbial fortune." Ben's tone was hard to read.

"No." Tommy was standing, repacking his bag in readiness for another game of let's pretend to be a big, grown-up doctor. "The firm went under. Unethical behavior on the part of several of the high-ups. Hard on Aubrey. Clean as a whistle in his own dealings." His voice deflated like a ball bounced too often. "Anyone can tell that, even after only a year of getting back to knowing him. And now when he'd come up with this plan, which couldn't have been made lightly, to restore Mucklesfeld, we have this evening's tragedy."

"My wife is going to be all right?" Ben demanded sharply.

"Oh, yes. I don't see any reason for alarm." Did Tommy sound ever so faintly disappointed? Was he aching for the chance to do a bit of delicate suturing or better yet wield a laser gun? "I was speaking of the car accident that took the life of one of the contestants."

"You were brought in on the scene?" Ben did not sound abashed by his error, which was understandable, given the husband he is. I hoped Tommy would see it that way. He was very likely a married man himself.

"Oh, yes! Aubrey, after discovering that the phone was out, as happens not infrequently here when the weather is bad—he drove to my house knowing I have a cellular, which he doesn't. After getting in touch with the police, I came back with him in his car. It was that drive that made him think it would be better—quicker—for him to walk, as I had done on returning home, when he needed me again. Don't remember such a fog! Not at all surprising what happened to the poor woman—Aubrey told me her name was Suzanne Varney." Tommy's round brown eyes shone more brightly than ever with what had to be the gloss of tears. My heart warmed to his childlike sensitivity. "Only forty-five, so Aubrey said. Severe blunt chest trauma. The autopsy will get to the nub of it. Only minor damage to the face. It was obvious she had been a pretty woman." A tear trickled down a rounded cheek. "She won't need much fixing up by the mortician to have her looking her very best for the funeral if the family chooses an open coffin. That'll be a consolation."

"Let's hope," said Ben.

Tommy wiped away the tear with his jacket sleeve and drew a shaky breath. "You'll have to excuse me; I'm a sentimental old bachelor. My daily helper, Mrs. Spuds, keeps going on at me about getting a cat. It is a temptation. But I'm not sure I'm ready after losing Blackie. It still hurts too much after forty years. He was my birthday present when I was ten, and twelve and a half when he got out onto the road and was hit by a . . ."

I wondered sadly—with thoughts of my own Tobias—if there had been any fixing Blackie up for the funeral.

"But enough of myself." Tommy blinked bravely.

"My wife?" Ben prodded, not looking quite as moved as I was.

"Indeed, yes. I think you have it right—although

I could be wrong, we doctors so often are. A bad tension headache, possibly—or perhaps a migraine."

"She fainted." Ben sounded determined on a bleak diagnosis.

"Explained most likely by the stress she mentioned."

"She fell."

"Yes, well . . . uhmm." Tommy appeared rattled. Maybe he wouldn't be a doctor when he grew up. Clearly patients could be awkward, expecting a fellow to be sure of his facts. Better perhaps to go back to wanting to be a fireman or a bus driver. But hadn't his mum and dad always told him not to be a wussy puss? Suddenly he straightened to his full five six, squared his shoulders, and stuck out his rounded chin. Time to assert himself. "People usually . . . generally . . . almost invariably, although this is arguable, don't fall hard when they faint. They . . . crumple."

"The latest medical term?"

"Oh, Ben, please! Dr. Rowley has to know what he's talking about. He must see hundreds of patients."

"I can't say that," demurred the truthful boy. "Grimkirk is a very small village, just a couple of shops and a strip of cottages. But I do see the occasional farmer and person on holiday. Let's say," chuckling convincingly, "I keep my hand in."

"I'm sure you do." My maternal instinct was

aroused, and I was further touched on seeing when he bent to unlatch and re-latch his bag that there was bald spot on the back of his head. What he needed more than a cat was a grown-up wife to tell him he was wonderfully clever. I wondered about his daily—Mrs. Spuds (who could forget such a name?). A woman who liked cats had to be nice, but like as not she already had a husband who wouldn't take kindly to her marrying someone else, bigamy not having the cachet it once did.

"Ellie," Ben sat down beside me on the sofa, "what sort of husband would I be if I didn't worry about you?"

"But I'm feeling better," I said, and realized it was true. Mrs. Foot's gray biscuit and dreadful tea had settled. I felt less queasy and my headache was barely noticeable if I lay still.

"My prescribed treatment," Tommy puffed out his chest, "is for you to go immediately to bed and once there be given a light meal and a drink, after which you will take the tablets I will leave for you. Two to be repeated every four hours if you should wake and feel the need."

Lovely as this sounded, I had to explain the obvious. "But I can't go straight to bed. We have to drive home or at least find a place to spend the night."

"Out of the question." Tommy was back to his beaming schoolboy self. "Aubrey will insist you stay here. If I know him, he will already be seeing that a room is prepared for you—preferably one that isn't layered in dust; although I could prescribe a mask." Radiating cheerful self-approval at this clever solution to what might or might not be a problem, he gathered up the bag and, saying that he would inform Aubrey and my friend of the situation, trotted from the room.

"Sweetheart," Ben got off the sofa to pace, "I don't put much faith in our Dr. Rowley."

"That was blatantly apparent. You must have hurt his feelings horribly."

"How do we know he's even a doctor? Mad as hatters, everyone in this house! Not a normal person among them!"

"Lord Belfrey . . . !" I protested.

"Him!" My adored spouse presented a nasty sneer. "The worst of the lot. Stalking around doing his impersonation of Cary Grant!"

"He can't help it if he's the spitting image. Besides," sidling my legs off the sofa the better to face him, "normal is highly overrated. My parents certainly thought so. To their way of thinking, normal was the real weird!"

"Sweetheart," Ben just missed colliding with a marble Aphrodite on a pedestal and a six-foot urn containing a dead shrub, "don't get worked up. You'll make your headache worse."

"And you shouldn't be ungrateful. You should be down on your knees in gratitude to Lord Belfrey for providing a port in a storm." This was nonsense. We rarely quarreled. But for some reason I couldn't put a lid on it. "I hope you enjoy the satisfaction of saying I told you so if Dr. Rowley's diagnosis proves wrong and I wake up in the middle of the night to find myself in a coma!"

"Is she always this much of a histrionic nutcase?" demanded a querulous male voice.

Ben and I froze in place, but Aphrodite jumped or . . . did a wobble on her pedestal. Gliding his circuitous way from the opposite end of the mile-long room was a man in a wheelchair. He was cloaked in shadow, as the cliché goes, which to my bewildered mind made him appear the more ominously substantial. He cleared the edges of the table bearing the tea tray and rolled to a silkily soft halt a few yards from the sofa. An enormously stout man, with a bloated bloodhound face, and sparse, greasy black hair combed over a high, bald dome. His eyes bored into mine, conveying a distaste that flattened my back to the sofa. Only by biting down on my lip did I prevent myself from quiveringly inquiring what right he had to call me histrionic. Then he smiled, a jovial smile that seemed instantly part and parcel of his brown and yellow checked waistcoat and voluminous cravat.

"I was teasing, my dear. Only teasing! I adore a spirited woman. You are a lucky man, sir," he swiveled around to look up at Ben, "what zest she must put into your life and so captivating in her looks. I have always been an admirer of the subtle

74

beauty of the woodland nymph fleshed out to full womanly glory."

"Ellie and Ben Haskell," I said hastily. "Wherever did you spring from?"

He performed a half-swivel this time, waving a vastly plump hand as he did so. "Through an archway beyond the dark reaches of all these hellish medieval furnishings. What possesses people to accumulate the hideous? The British nobility and their excesses! Take the Empire, for one small example. Ah, but as someone, possibly myself, so pertinently phrased it—vulgarity on a vast enough scale achieves a certain grandeur. For myself, I prefer the Spartan elegance of midcentury modernism in my London and Paris pieds à terre. But each to his own, and Aubrey Belfrey is a decent enough chap, perhaps not to be blamed for the sins of his forebears. One has to be broadminded."

"My wife is an interior designer." Ben offered this tidbit warily.

"We don't have your name," I pointed out.

"Apologies! Apologies! Did I not say? It is Georges LeBois. Forgive the lack of a French accent." He performed another of those hand flourishes. "My formidable English nanny, may she rest in peace," eyes raised heavenward, "drilled it out of me. She was less successful in inuring me to milky puddings and toad-in-the-hole." His vast stomach quivered noticeably at the horror of memory. "Is it any wonder that I escaped into the world of make-believe and at the conclusion of my incarceration within the vilely conceived British public school system studied film and became a director? I am here, at the aptly named Mucklesfeld Manor, for the making of *Here Comes the Bride*."

"So we have been told." It really was too bad of Ben not to make an effort to sound impressed. Monsieur LeBois might look and sound like a self-satisfied, overfed bloodhound, but he might also be a very nice man. Although perhaps not fanatically truthful. I doubted that he was French. The only trace of an accent he possessed sounded as if it had been born within sound of Bow bells. Probably started out as George Woods and had the imagination to reinvent himself. I doubted the nanny and the posh schooling, too.

"And I have been told that you are a chef." A stark hunger came into his eyes as he looked at Ben. "Have you any idea what a godsend that makes you in this house, where that gruesome female in need of wooden teeth to go with her Georgian male wig serves up food that a starving rat wouldn't eat! My dear, noble sir! In one day I have become the shadow of the man I once was. I endure torturous rumblings"—he placed his fat hands tenderly upon the enormous waistcoated stomach—"soon, I fear, there will be an outcry from within equal to that of the mob that stormed the Bastille! Believe me, I have not suffered such outrage to my constitution since the horse-riding accident that placed me in this wheelchair. An egg, one superlatively cooked simple egg, is all I ask of you. Even that foul creature cannot get inside the shell of an egg to pervert its intrinsic goodness. And your wife!" The purplish bloodhound jowls shook with emotion. "Surely you will not subject her to being poisoned before your eyes, when all that is required of you is to follow me down a warren of damp corridors to the kitchen."

"What state is it in?" All Ben's professional instincts were aroused, as evidenced by the tilt of his dark head, the flash of blue-green in his eyes, the fact that he proceeded to turn his back on me. For the moment, my headache and I were nothing to the intriguing challenges to be met behind a green baize door.

"A dungeon. All the well-rusted implements for drawing and quartering. Livestock in the pantry, I wouldn't doubt, and typhoid in the drains!" Georges LeBois eyed Ben narrowly through puffy lids, a professional sizing up how far to push his actor, shifting and leveling the camera to get the reaction he wanted. "A challenge surely no chef of any spirit with an ounce of stuffing inside him could resist." I was wondering where his assistants were lurking when Ben asked Georges how he had discovered he was a chef.

"From Plunket. And I do, despite my aversion to

men with pimples, have to give the mealy-mouthed fellow some points for trying to cheer me up upon seeing how low I was feeling following the accident. You know we lost one of our contestants? Most unfortunate—particularly for the woman herself, of course—but five is an awkward number to be left with. Still, I knew if I pressed that point too hard, Belfrey was liable to back out and we wouldn't want that. I'm convinced this one could be a winner."

Something flickered behind his eyes. Did I glimpse a cold-blooded ruthlessness that would let nothing stand between him and what he saw as his big chance to become a household name? I'd certainly never heard of him before today, not that that meant much. Or was he a man driven to the edge of reason by a frenzied desire to rend a pork roast limb from limb?

"Ben makes superb omelets," I said.

My beloved had eyes for me once more. "Would you like one, sweetheart?" he asked tenderly.

"Well, yes—I would rather. If you can find a mixing bowl and utensils to sanitize and a pan could be radiated." I broke off when the door opened to reveal Lord Belfrey and Mrs. Malloy, and all thought fled at the sight of her smug smile. His lordship's expression was that of the concerned host. He said he was pleased to see that we had met Georges LeBois and explained that Dr. Rowley had spoken with him, expressed relief that

I hadn't seriously injured myself, and hoped I would pass a comfortable night in the bedroom that was ready for me.

"Is it the room that was to have been Suzanne Varney's?" I asked. Somehow I hated the idea. I pictured her setting out on her journey to Mucklesfeld, a pretty woman, so Tommy had said, not all that much older at forty-five than myself. Had she been excited? Nervous?

"Not that one," Lord Belfrey assured me, "but I'm afraid there weren't many to choose from. What were the family apartments and the nursery wings are in a bad state of disrepair, which leaves the servants' quarters. Small rooms with space only for single beds." He looked questioningly from me to Ben, who said it wouldn't bother him to sleep on the floor. Of course I wouldn't let him do that; we could squeeze cozily in together. Even as I thought it, I knew he wouldn't agree to that. He'd insist that I get an undisturbed night's sleep.

His lordship provided an alternative. "The room I picked has a cubbyhole attached that has a small window. I had Plunket set up a bed in there, and I think you may be quite comfortable despite the rather tight squeeze, Mr. Haskell."

"Ben. This is very good of your lordship."

"My pleasure. Shall I show you both the way?"

"Who'd have thought when we set off in the car, Mr. and Mrs. H, that we was in for such an adventure?" Mrs. Malloy fluttered her false lashes, attempting to look soulful, but merely looking as though she had something in her eye.

"I'd like my next adventure to be that omelet we were talking about." Georges LeBois spun his wheelchair in a circle and brought it back to face Lord Belfrey. "You do know this man's a chef, Aubrey?"

"Plunket told me."

"Manna from heaven, my dear fellow. Do what it takes to keep him here. Choose him as your bride! Now that would be a reality show!"

His lordship smiled and Ben did not. What had happened to my beloved's sense of humor? My headache was coming back full force. I barely restrained myself from snapping at Mrs. Malloy when she suggested accompanying us.

Lord Belfrey eased the moment by encouraging her to stay and get acquainted with Georges. After a momentary pout, she set her face back to rights and waved me off as if watching a liner shift away from the quay to carry me to parts unknown. Which was the truth of the matter in the small scheme of things. Icebergs and squalls might not await, but as we followed Lord Belfrey down a corridor and up a flight of angular stone steps, I did have the feeling we were entering alien and possibly hostile territory.

Ben's muttering "Damn!" (for want of a worse word) upon stumbling in the ubiquitous half-light didn't help my increasing feeling that Mucklesfeld

Manor did not embrace a visitor with promises of warm and fuzzy delights to come. His lordship flipped light switches with efficient speed, but a candle would probably have worked better. Several more passageways and series of steps loomed. I felt rather like a piece being shuffled forward on the board of Snakes and Ladders—always in danger of shooting precipitously back down to the bottom and having to start the whole business over again. His lordship turned every dozen paces to make sure that we were comfortably keeping up with him.

"Where are we at this minute?" Ben asked with, I was pleased to hear, just the right amount of interest as we stood in a small room off a landing. It was lined with shelves containing nothing but dust and the occasional mildewed cardboard box.

"Used to be one of the linen closets in the days when there were mattresses on the beds and working taps on the baths." His lordship spread expressive hands.

"It must be next to impossible to keep places like Mucklesfeld up these days," said Ben conversationally as we passed into yet another passageway. I knew he was thinking that the time had come to throw in the towel . . . if there were any to be had.

"But we owe the past something, at least that's my assessment," his lordship replied, and it seemed to me that his eyes sought mine in hope of understanding. Or was he worrying that what seemed to have been a twenty-mile trek had exhausted my weakened constitution?

"I can appreciate the sense of responsibility," I said.

We plunged on, up another flight of steps to another landing, down again, and along what proved to be the last stretch. His lordship opened a door, flipped the switch to his right, and surprisingly the round globe in the center of the ceiling produced a sufficiently decent light to reveal a box of a room provided with a narrow bed covered with a faded paisley eiderdown. There wasn't much else to observe: a couple of clothes hooks protruding from the discolored plastered walls, a bentwood chair, a door in addition to the one we had entered, presumably giving entry to the cubbyhole in which Ben was to sleep, and a narrow window sliced into the sloping ceiling.

Lord Belfrey followed my gaze upward. "We are directly under the roof of the east wing. For centuries the female servants slept in one vast open space up here, but sometime in the early part of the twentieth century it was divided up into a warren of single or double rooms to provide them some privacy when they came off duty for the night."

"That must have been a treat," I said, adding with what I hoped was a cheery smile, "Is it much of a bus ride to the bathroom?"

"Right next door on your left. It is why I selected this room for you." His dark eyes seemed to take in my every movement as I sat gingerly down on the chair that didn't look as if it could support a Teddy bear. "I wish I had better to offer you." He did not embellish, there was no need. His voice said it all. "As for a meal, I'll take your husband to the kitchen and hopefully between the two of us we can concoct something that he can bring up on a tray." He turned to Ben, who was still standing in the doorway to the passage, and now asked him about the tablets Tommy had said he would let me have.

"We'll get them from him."

"Then best to get going." Ben cast me an anxious look that was not alleviated by my bright statement that there was no rush because I was feeling almost back to normal. "Lie down, sweetheart, and try to rest."

"What about my night things?"

"I'll get our cases from the car."

"Plunket can bring them up and put them outside the door," Lord Belfrey assured me in a voice equally soothing to that of my husband, adding that he'd had Mrs. Foot put a hot-water bottle in the bed. Perhaps I should have kissed them both before they left me. Ben was so incredibly dear, and his lordship emanated a secret sorrow that it was surely the duty of any compassionate woman to assuage. Let it be hoped, I thought rather woozily as I got off the chair, that in one of the contestants he would find a love that went beyond gratitude for helping him save Mucklesfeld. Perhaps an all-consuming passion was too much to be hoped for under the circumstances, especially as at the age of almost fifty-six he must have known and had his pick of countless women. Very likely he had been married in the past. At any other time I would have imagined a scenario to match his fascinating good looks, but I discovered that I was so desperate to lie down that I crawled under the eiderdown without worrying that it was filled with moths or that the pillow on which I laid my head had been around since the plague.

My feet searched out the hot-water bottle and discovered that it was lukewarm, which didn't surprise me given my opinion of Mrs. Foot's incompetence or malevolence . . . no, there I was being unkind. I turned on my side in hope I would find the lumpy mattress more comfortable that way. My original impression of her had been fueled by pure silliness. She was not the hag who had rejoiced in Wisteria Whitworth's subjugation at Perdition Hall. And if, as seemed credible, she had dropped the lamp shade on Mrs. Malloy's head, anyone doomed to live in this house might be excused for occasionally giving way to giddy attempts at humor. I lay thinking about the odd trio of Mrs. Foot, Mr. Plunket, and Boris, who presumably had a last name. Had his lordship hired them because they were affordable or because he was kind and doubted anyone else would?

If I lay completely still and kept my eyes squeezed shut against the light, which I should have turned off, but hadn't because the idea of complete darkness was even more unappealing, my headache receded. Except when the window rattled irritably. Checking the latch would have required standing on the flimsy chair and I did not want to risk a pair of broken legs that might keep me at Mucklesfeld beyond the morning. I was wondering what Mrs. Malloy was up to when a jolt jerked me up, and my eyes flew wide open, to find her there, arms akimbo, staring down at me.

"Did you have to bump into the bed?" I grumbled.

"I didn't." She was smiling dreamily.

"With the force of the *Titanic* hitting the iceberg."

"Not feeling better, Mrs. H?"

"I was. More to the point—why are you looking as if you just swallowed a dozen canaries?"

"Sure you're up to hearing?" She sat down at the foot of the bed, her ringed hands folded demurely, and I knew instantly what was coming. Even so, my heart gave a thump when she said the words. "I'm to replace the dead lady as the sixth contestant. Now, don't go looking at me like that, Mrs. H, it's not a case of me dancing on her grave, just being practical like, and after all we do owe his lordship for taking us in out of the fog."

"So you proposed marriage to him out of a sense of obligation?"

"What makes you think I asked him?"

"Well, didn't you?"

"And why shouldn't I?" she demanded haughtily. "Really, I don't know what's got into you, Mrs. H. I'd have thought you'd be thrilled for me, getting the chance to live out me romantic dreams. All them books we've both read with the blissfully happy endings."

I could have pointed out that these invariably occurred after a couple of bodies had turned up along the way, either in the millpond or the suspiciously locked turret additionally guarded by the yellow-eyed black dog, but I restrained myself out of concern for my head, which had been good to me over the years. "This isn't a situation that invites the grand passion, Mrs. Malloy, it's a reality show. Which some people might consider vulgar."

Understandably, she bridled. "You're saying that his lordship—my intended—lacks refinement?"

"No, no!" I protested hastily. "I'm sure only dire necessity drove him to this course . . ."

"Coarse?" Her voice rose, along with the rest of her, but fortunately she sank back down without grabbing my throat.

"Course of action. I suppose it could even be said that there is something noble in his desire to save his ancestral home. What really worries me is the thought of your being hurt when . . . if, he doesn't select . . . choose you as his bride."

86

"Well, that's the chance I'll be taking. Tomorrow we'll get to size up the other candidates, won't we?"

"We? But Ben and I will be going home first thing."

"What? Rush off before you've had breakfast?" She eyed me as if I had just produced a stake to thrust through her heart. "Or lunch. Well, I must say, that wouldn't be treating his lordship very nice after all he's done for you."

"He didn't say anything to me or Ben about his arrangement with you."

"And why should he?"

Why indeed? It was unreasonable of me to feel left out in the cold. Perhaps, despite Tommy's assurances to the contrary, I had injured my brain when I fell.

"It's not like I'm under age, needing a guardian's approval," Mrs. Malloy pointed out.

"I'm sorry. This house must be getting to me."

"What's wrong with it? I think it'll be lovely and comfy with a little tweaking."

Make that demolition, I thought.

"Although," Mrs. Malloy addressed the wall behind the bed, "being the gentleman he is, his lordship said as he wouldn't make the agreement final until he had a word with you and Mr. H. I suppose, despite me mature charms, he saw the vulnerable girl inside." Her purple-lipsticked mouth flickered like a butterfly landing on a dewy rose. Then her eyes hardened, giving off an iridescent sparkle to match her shadow. "But that doesn't go giving you license to stand in me way. Of course, I understand how you'll miss my slaving away for you at Merlin's Court, but it's not like I won't come over to visit you and Mr. H and the kiddies when I can find time away from opening the summer fête or hosting a ball."

"What about our partnership as amateur detectives?"

"Well, we still could—no, I suppose it wouldn't do." Faint sigh. "A proper husband wouldn't want his wife risking her life getting mixed up in the sordid."

So much for Ben!

"I didn't mention that aspect of me life to his lordship and I'd rather you didn't neither, Mrs. H; I wouldn't want him thinking I'd be the snooping sort. And then there's that requirement of his that the contestants all come from ordinary lives, not the glamorous pampered-puss sort. I've even wondered about keeping dark having been three times chairperson of the Chitterton Fells Charwomen's Association. That sort of office could come across as being snooty."

Before I could answer this one, Ben came though the doorway carrying a tray. While he was settling it in front of me and asking me to taste the tomato soup, which regrettably came from a tin, and sample the Marmite toast and fruit salad, also tinned, she teetered out of the room on her high heels, brazenly humming "Here Comes the Bride."

"How are you feeling, sweetheart?"

"Better."

"The tablets the doctor ordered are on that saucer. He said to take them as soon as you've eaten. That beverage in the glass is evaporated milk thinned with water. My poor darling, it seemed safer than what was in the bottle."

"Everything looks delicious." I smiled up at my husband while striving to keep my legs rigid in order not to create a tsunami.

"Georges wasn't so appreciative. There weren't any eggs. It looks as though the contestants are expected to prove their survival skills by going out and foraging in the woods." He shrugged expressively. "I suppose they think they know what they're getting themselves into."

"At least Mrs. Malloy has the advantage of having met Lord Belfrey and getting a glimpse of the reality involved." I studied his face as I went on to explain. When I concluded with the statement that I would hate to leave her behind when we set off in the morning, I was surprised that he merely said we would have to take tomorrow as it came.

4

I awoke in the night to the alarming sensation that I had wandered out of my life into someone else's disordered world. I had read enough books about time travel to make this seem perilously possible, if in this particular instance undesirable. Yes, it would be intriguing to discover oneself back in a past century, but what as? Certainly not someone compelled to sleep in a nasty chill on a lumpy bed the width of a plank in a room which in the shifting moonlight resembled a cell.

Fortunately, before clutching my throat in terror and watching my eyes roll down my cheeks, I spied the charcoal-edged shape of my suitcase, which Ben had brought into the room. Memory shifted its way out of the murky morass. Before his return to the lower regions to find himself something to eat, he had watched me dutifully swallow the tablets sent up by Tommy Rowley and instructed me tenderly to get off to sleep as quickly as possible. A likely prospect, I had thought, given his evasions when I tried to get him to talk further about Mrs. Malloy's determination to throw herself into the matrimonial fray. After a brief excursion to a bathroom that belonged in the Dark Ages, I returned to the room, inspected Ben's cubbyhole where he had deposited his own case, took grateful note that it was blessed with a window, albeit one not much bigger than a table napkin, got out my nightdress, and decided on also wearing my flannel dressing gown into bed. The water bottle was by then cold, but I was suddenly too sleepy to toss it onto the floor. What exactly were those tablets Tommy had given me?

My dreams thrust me into an episodic chaos fraught with impending doom. Up one flight of turret steps and down the next, through mazes and tunnels stripped of color I fled, hampered by feet that wanted to go the other way, knowing that beyond every locked door waited something even more unspeakable than that which padded silently behind me. At the moment of waking, I realized that the fog had liquefied and was spreading in puddles with hideously distorted human faces around my ankles.

Now, having somewhat regained my bearings, I discovered what had prompted that specific. My feet and legs were chillily damp. The cause didn't take prolonged pondering. The hot-water bottle had leaked. The cause? Either it was so ancient the rubber had perished or (more likely in my opinion) Mrs. Foot had failed to tighten the stopper. Shivering as much from aggravation as cold, I wiggled my way to the top of the bed to sit with my knees drawn up to my chin and try to find a bright spot.

Begrudgingly, I admitted there was one. My

headache was gone. Tommy's tablets had done their work. If Mother Nature had made her contribution, I wasn't about to thank her. But for her fun and games I wouldn't be currently incarcerated at Mucklesfeld. That Wisteria Whitworth had endured far worse did nothing to mellow my feelings. I was done with Gothic novels. The former wife who wasn't quite as dead as the master had hoped—having reinvented herself as the vicar's repressed spinster sister. The portrait of the cavalier in the ancestral gallery that came to life on the anniversary of Charles I's beheading. The . . . the—my insides buckled—the evil black dog that came hurtling through the window to land on the bed of a woman who was already suffering all the emotional and physical trauma of a leaked hot-water bottle! The mattress bounced, once, twice, thrice, before flopping back like a dead flounder.

I must be imagining the animal's thunderous leap onto a bed that had only been designed for half a person, not one full one and a dog. This appalling visitation was a delayed reaction to Tommy's tablets. The black dog with the yellow eyes and stalactite teeth was standard in the Gothic genre. I remembered how the ambience of Mucklesfeld had summoned up the image of one earlier. If any of this were real, Ben would have heard the commotion along with my scream . . . I was almost sure I had screamed, although in my panic I might have forgotten to do so. I wrapped my arms tighter around my drawn-up knees in a pathetic attempt to squeeze myself into invisibility.

"You do not exist," I informed the beast sternly. "You are a medicinal complication, for which I intend to sue Dr. Tommy Rowley if he hasn't fled the country. I am going to close my eyes and when I open them on the count of three you will be gone. One . . . two . . . ready for the magic number?"

My children would have been horribly embarrassed by this pathetic performance. Either the moonlight had grown stronger or we were closing on morning, but I could see with painful clarity that he still was there, eyeing me as if for him it was a case of love at first sight. Well, I was far from charmed.

"You did not," I chanted, "thrust that window free of its faulty latch. What would any real live dog be doing prowling around on a rooftop? I would summon my husband to get rid of you if there were any possible chance that he could see you."

The look on his face was nothing short of soppy. Head to one side, ears lolling, he began a cheerful pant as though eager to inhale every sweet inflection of my voice. His tail stirred into a wag that increased in enthususiastic speed to that of an orchestra conductor's baton. I had to blink to keep from becoming dizzy. His eyes, I realized, were not yellow but a melting brown, and I was forced to acknowledge that he actually looked more like a

Labrador who lived to fetch slippers and newspapers than the hound from hell. He was wearing a collar, but there were no tags. Reaching out a hand as he inched forward, I stroked his velvet head.

"Okay," I said, "you are real, but that makes it worse because obviously you're a housebreaker, probably one with a record a mile long, and if I had any public spirit I would notify the police at once. But let's pretend the phone isn't back on, which it may not be."

He continued to regard me with unstinting devotion. I told him he was shallow and I much preferred cats, they being creatures who preferred to be wooed than woo. What on earth was I to do with him? Should I let him stay as a replacement hot-water bottle until Ben woke and we could escort him downstairs and inquire if he was a member of the household? Surely that had to be the case. Out one window, in through another. And Mucklesfeld, like many ancient houses, must have a good-sized walkway around its roofline. I could have laughed at my silliness had my teeth not begun to chatter. With the window hanging open, I was chilled through despite my dressing gown. But closing the wretched thing, I remembered, would require standing on something and I had earlier decided that the chair was too risky. The only alternative was to drag the bed across the room.

I didn't see any problem there, but it proved unbudgeable even with the dog off it. Had it been nailed to the floor to prevent the kitchen maid from taking it with her when she ran off with the bootboy? Much as I disliked the idea of waking Ben prematurely—and my watch showed that it was only a little after five—I wasn't noble enough to climb back and freeze. I was on the point of going to rouse him when I looked again at the wide-open face of the window and came fully back to my senses (such as they are) and faced the truth. No dog that wasn't foaming at the mouth, mad from being bitten by a rabid wolf, and inclined to leap through fire if it stood in his way, would have hurtled itself off a roof ledge at a pane of glass with sufficient force to release the faulty latch. Besides which, the window opened outward.

There was only one reasonable possibility. The wind. There wasn't any now, but that didn't mean there hadn't been a raging gale earlier. Those tablets would have kept me from waking until . . . as must have happened . . . the chill was too much even for my subconscious.

"I maligned you," I informed the dog. "You are not guilty of breaking and entering. The window was open when you came trotting along the roof as any reasonably sane dog might do in the middle of the night. Your reasons are your own." He accepted my apology with a besottedly rapturous expression and a vast thumping of the tail. Sensing he was about to hurl himself into my arms and lick my face off, I raised a warning finger. "Kindly stay seated. This in no way excuses your leap onto my bed. And don't go trying to turn the tables and suggest I opened it in a half-sleeping state, because even your fur brain must recognize that I don't have the reach. Neither does my husband, a man of medium height. Even a six-footer like Lord Belfrey would need a pole hook to open the window."

The dog cocked his black head, intent on lapping up every nuance. Clearly I could have read off the instructions on a box of scouring pads and he would have been enthralled.

"Even if he could have done so, Ben would not have opened the window without asking me if I wanted to freeze to death. Someone's wacky idea of a practical joke? Now there's a merry thought. I'm inclined to think that no one in this house, other than his lordship, is entirely right in the head, which explains you if you live here, but this isn't quite the same as Mrs. Foot dropping that lamp shade on Mrs. Malloy's head. There would be maliciousness to anyone creeping in here while I slept . . ." I was brought to a halt by the memory of the Metal Knight reaching its glinting hands toward my throat. "But let me not dismiss Mrs. Foot's prosaic explanation for that.

"There is Boris, who looks as though he was apprenticed to Dracula," I conceded to my devoted listener. "Seemingly he takes pleasure in bringing inanimate objects to life. We all have our little hobbies, don't we? And bear in mind the suit of armor is in the hall, where the full effects of its gyrations can be appreciated by anyone unlucky enough to pass through. Not tucked away in a bedroom not normally in use. Okay! So here I am tonight. But why would Boris make me the specific target of his tricks? It's Mrs. Malloy, not I, who's intent on marrying Lord Belfrey and might decide with good reason—should she get the ring on her finger—to sack the staff of three in one fell swoop. As could be the decision of any of the other contestants, given the chance."

I paused to wonder in all seriousness if this possibility was a cause of hand-wringing concern to Mr. Plunket, Mrs. Foot, and Boris. If I were they, I wouldn't be counting my chickens, unless Lord Belfrey had made them a sworn promise to stand firm on their remaining at Mucklesfeld. Shame, not the dog, leaped up at me. Glibly I had dismissed them as an odd trio, but suddenly I was thinking of them as people trudging through life, hanging on to survival by a thumbhold, with no place to go if cast out of Mucklesfeld. If Mrs. Foot had got the idea that Mrs. Malloy and I were early arriving contestants, I could understand the irresistible urge to drop a lamp shade—for want of something heavier—on one of our heads.

"Let us be sensible and agree it was the wind that rattled the half-caught latch and blew open the window," I told the dog. "Mrs. Foot did say that spooky things happened at Mucklesfeld, but much as I'd like to I don't believe in poltergeists or other wayward spirits."

No disagreement from him. His melting expression and thumping tail assured me that every word I said was fact. I was as infallible as the Pope and he worshipped every inch of me.

"Let me remind you that I am a happily married woman and as such I am now going to take a peek into the cubbyhole," I pointed at the door, "and see if Ben's awake, so he can move that bed under the window. I'm rather surprised that being an early riser, especially when traveling, he hasn't already emerged to find me talking to you. Knowing me as he does, he normally wouldn't find that odd, but he's worried about me at the moment. Did I tell you that I slid into a faint on the hall floor?"

He raised a gentle paw and pressed it against my knee.

"Oh, cheese crackers!" I said. "I'm going to fall in love with you, which is wrong in every way. You're someone else's dog, and my cat would threaten to throw himself under a bus if he got wind that something was going on. And you know how cats have a sixth sense about these things."

He blinked as though squeezing back impending tears, before getting to his paws and following me to the cubbyhole door. It was now quite light, albeit with gray overtones, and I saw immediately that the narrow bed compressed against the right wall was unoccupied. Indeed, it didn't look as though it had been slept in. The eiderdown, as flat and faded as the one I'd slept under, was unrumpled, no impression that would suggest Ben had even sat down on it while removing his shoes for the night. His suitcase stood upright against the opposite wall. No sign of pajamas or dressing gown. Certain that he had not taken them out, I fought back a ridiculous feeling of abandonment. But mustn't let the dog see I was upset. He looked young and was bound to be impressionable.

As was I. It didn't have to be something as drastic as a dog leaping through the window in the middle of the night to startle me witless. An unknown face contorted by emotion suddenly peering at me through the glass was generally enough for my undoing. Which (violent start!) was now the case. I forgot the dog and the possibility of creating a neurosis that would keep him in canine therapy for years. I let out a yelp. The cubbyhole window was very small, making the face appear abnormally large.

The dog emitted a rumble deep in its throat before giving vent to a nice-sized bark. Not vicious—that would be overstating it—but certainly manfully assertive. The face vanished from the window, which was beside the bed across from the door.

"Good boy!"

He sat down with an attitude of pleased accomplishment, tail thumping wildly. But whoever was out there hadn't vanished in alarm. A hand appeared at the window and a tentative tapping followed.

Another deep-throated rumble. But this one struck me as of the inquiring sort. Was my furry companion wondering if we should let the person in? Had he perhaps realized that both face and hand belonged to someone of his acquaintance? His owner, in fact, out on the roof eager to rescue him after searching fruitlessly for a half hour?

"If you're wrong about this and you're forcing me into an acquaintance with a violent intruder, you'd better bare those fangs of yours and if necessary eat him or her." The dirty glass had made it impossible to tell whether the face was that of a man or a woman, let alone recognize it. Having at least made myself clear to the dog, I stared impotently at the window. A cardboard silhouette of a person couldn't get through it without being folded to the size of an envelope. I would have to return to the other room and pray like Samson for the blessing of brute strength in hope of shoving the bed under the window. Of course there was no saying that the person outside wouldn't have given up by that time and gone in search of another entry, such as a strategically placed door. Speaking of which, I suddenly spotted one halfway behind the bed, its dirty whitewash merging it almost imperceptibly into the wall. Even in my relief, the thought crossed my mind that there might also be an outside staircase that served as a fire escape. Also, as I raised the iron latch, why hadn't our visitor knocked on the door?

The dog stood close as I inched the door open as far as it would go, given the protrusion of the bed. It was a relief to behold a flat ledge of at least six feet that was barricaded by a waist-high railing. The only opening in sight provided access to a fire escape in direct line with the cubbyhole window. Pressed tightly against this, hands squeezing the wall, was a woman with dark hair in a suit the color of last night's fog. She was also wearing court shoes, which despite their sensibly sturdy heels did not look best suited to climbing to dizzy heights. Judging from her compressed profile, I had never seen her before. It was still misty and she was shivering badly from cold, fright, or both.

"Hello," I said ineptly as the dog inched his nose forward.

"Oh, thank God!" came the whispered reply.

"Would you like to come in?"

The dog added an encouraging woof to this idiotic question but did not rush forward to offer a helpful paw. If she were his owner, he had an inadequate way of showing it.

"I haven't been able to move, not even to turn my head since reaching the top of the fire escape."

This explained her not noticing the door no more than three feet away.

"It took everything I had to force my fingers to tap at the glass when I thought I saw movement in the room."

"I understand; I'm not particularly fond of heights myself," I said, stepping cautiously toward her after ordering the dog back inside; it would be dreadful if she backed up in panic and went tumbling down the metal staircase. Tommy Rowley might then find himself confronted with a severe head injury and multiple broken limbs if, I shivered, she weren't killed outright. Two fatal accidents at Mucklesfeld in the space of hours would lead to stories for years—centuries—to come of the ghosts of two women being glimpsed, one emerging behind the other to drift toward the house on nights when it seemed likely the hovering mist would turn into a full-fledged fog.

I felt clammy thinking about it. But anything was better than looking down. Murmuring encouragement, I reached her, succeeded in unclamping her from the wall, and got her into the cubbyhole one inching step at a time, whereupon I speedily closed the door and sat her down on the bed. The dog then proceeded to greet me with ecstatic wagging, but mercifully did not leap up at me. Someone must have trained him not to bowl people over, I thought. And he had been obedient about going inside when told.

The woman looked in need of a stiff drink, but Lord Belfrey had said that he didn't keep liquor in the house. Anyway, her prim seating—feet together, hands folded in her lap—caused me to sense that she wouldn't have accepted one if offered. I'm not much of a drinker, but after standing on a roof I would have swigged an entire bottle of brandy. Why on earth had she come up that fire escape?

"I'm Ellie Haskell." I smiled encouragingly.

"Livonia Mayberry."

"Feeling any better?" I asked her.

"It'll take a minute. I just need to breathe."

"Of course. I'll go along to the bathroom and bring you a beaker of water."

"Oh, no! Don't leave me! I'll fall apart if left alone." She had a small, fluting voice that reminded me poignantly of my nine-year-old Abbey.

"Then I won't budge an inch." This statement caused the dog to eye me as if witnessing a halo forming around my head. His interest in our visitor appeared only politely social. After a few moments of silence, I was relieved to see that her color looked better. She was rather pretty in the manner of a woman from the 1950s—the perm that was intended to last. No eye shadow or mascara, min-imal lipstick, and a powdered nose. Her light wool gray suit, the cream blouse with the Peter Pan collar, and the navy court shoes all spoke of that era.

"Is he yours?" She looked startled at the sound of her own voice.

"The dog? He came in through the window of the room next door where I was sleeping. I thought when I saw you peering in here that you'd come to claim him."

"I never saw him before tonight . . . this morning. But I did follow him up the fire escape. It was madness, but I had to—there was no choice. He'd made off with my . . ."

"My goodness!" Horror prevented my allowing her to continue. "How long were you out on that ledge?"

"I don't know." She twisted her hands together. "It seemed forever. Hours, days . . . weeks."

"Why didn't you go back down?" I knew it was a heartless question even as it left my mouth.

"I froze . . . shut down completely; I even blanked out about my reason for being up there"—she unknotted her hands to point a finger that looked as if it had been permanently bent in the process at the dog. "I don't think I would have seen him or my gloves if they'd both been right next to me."

"Your gloves?"

"He didn't bring them in with him, I suppose?" Despair mingled with pitiful hope showed in her blue eyes. "He made off with them when I got out of the car."

The dog put his head down on his paws.

I nipped back to my bedroom and checked. "No sign of them," I said on returning.

A pathetic, whispering sigh. "Mrs. Knox—she's

my next-door neighbor—was right when she said I would be punished for getting mixed up in such a mad scheme. She said only a fool would consider entering in a marriage contest, especially when there was dear Harold waiting so patiently in the wings. He gave me those gloves, and despite everything I can't bear the thought of losing them. Without them, I'm not sure I exist." A sharp intake of breath. "I'm so sorry . . . I'm still not thinking straight. You'll be one of them . . . of us, I mean. A contestant."

"Oh, no!" Not wanting Livonia Mayberry to think I disapproved of her involvement, as the neighbor had done, I explained—hopefully in not too bragging a voice—that I was married. I was about to add that a friend of mine had just been added to the list, but this would have required me to break the news that death had put one of the other contestants out of the running. "My husband and I and our traveling companion ended up here by accident during the fog and Lord Belfrey kindly allowed us to spend the night."

"Is he . . . did he seem nice?"

"Very."

"That's a relief."

"And very handsome. The reincarnation of Cary Grant."

"Really?" She reacted as if she had just heard that the date of her execution had been moved up to this morning and she had been denied the right to choose hanging versus beheading. "I'd hoped he would be quite ordinary. Good-looking men scare me, I always feel so intimidated around them. Harold is short and going bald and he wears glasses with very thick lenses. But don't get me wrong. I like his looks. He's my type; my mother said he was and so does Mrs. Knox. Do you think he will be annoyed that I arrived hours ahead of time and have created such a silly disturbance?"

"Harold?"

"No . . . well, he's already upset. He told me not to count on his overlooking my wanton behavior when I came crawling back, but I meant Lord Belfrey."

"Look," I said, "your showing up on the roof hasn't upset me. And if you would like to talk your situation through, I'll be glad to listen."

"Are you sure," she was knitting her fingers back together, "that you aren't dying to get rid me? I won't stay long, I promise. You will think me a coward, because that's what I am. All the sense of adventure has been shaken out of me. As soon as I feel steadier, I'm going to get in my car and drive home to Hillsbury."

I sat down beside her on the bed, and the dog, catching my warning look, lay down next to it. "How did you decide to be a contestant in *Here Comes the Bride* over Harold's objections?" It wasn't hard to picture him and the interfering Mrs. Knox.

"From meeting a woman who had already been

accepted. On a day trip to London I ran into an acquaintance from a few years back. She and I had got to know each other a little when my father and hers were in the same nursing home. Mine died first. Hers must have had a difficult time of it at the end because she said she couldn't bring herself to talk about it when we recognized each other coming out Selfridges. She remembered my speaking about Harold and I told her we were still together after courting for ten years."

"Most married people don't stay together anywhere near that long."

"That's awfully nice of you to say."

Ben and I had been lucky, I thought gratefully.

"But lately it had begun to seem as though there'd always be a reason why Harold didn't think it was the right time for us to get married. All very sensible, but I was forty-one on my last birthday and the other women at the bank where I'm a teller have stopped asking me when we're going to set a date." The blue eyes searched mine in appeal. "At the beginning—for the first seven years or so—I was in agreement that we shouldn't rush into things. It wasn't as though children would be an option. Harold had made it clear he wouldn't agree to them. A needless expense is how he put it."

"Really!"

"He feels the same way about pets. And I have always wanted a cat. But Mummy was allergic to them."

"Oh dear!"

"But I don't want to give you the wrong idea about Harold. He's practical, which is a good thing, and I suppose I'm a dreamer."

"Nothing wrong with that," I said, to which the dog responded with a look of rapt approval.

Livonia Mayberry stared wistfully into space. "Mrs. Knox says that in this day and age I should be glad of a steady man. And I did truly appreciate Harold accepting that with my being an only child I had a responsibility to stay at home and take care of my parents. But they've both been gone for over five years." Her voice cracked. "And after Mummy passed away, Daddy insisted on going into a residential facility. He said it was never his idea to keep me corraled—that was his word—with a couple of fogies, but he'd never been able to go against Mummy."

"Oh!"

"I didn't press him on that; but he couldn't have meant he was afraid of her. She was so sweet. Everyone, including Mrs. Knox next door, thought her absolutely wonderful."

Don't we all look better from a distance?

"It was just that she wasn't strong, and if either Daddy or I were ever a little thoughtless with her she would get terribly worked up and talk about being a nuisance and how it would be better for everyone if she ended it all."

"How awful!"

"Nothing I said could dissuade Daddy from going into Shady Oaks."

"And that was where you first met the woman you met again outside Selfridges, who told you about *Here Comes the Bride*?"

Livonia Mayberry stopped twisting her hands and sat motionless, her expression blank, her lips moving stiffly. "Yes. She said she had heard about it from a friend of hers who had come across it. She said the friend was a lot more adventurous than she was, but she was lonely after the breakup of a long relationship and sufficiently intrigued that she looked up the site on her computer and decided there was nothing to lose. It was a surprise, she said, to be notified that she had been accepted."

"What made you decide to give *Here Comes the Bride* a try?"

"Harold and I had an upset that evening. I was late with his dinner due to missing the train I'd hoped to catch coming back from London. He's in the habit of coming to my house for his evening meals three times a week as well as Sunday lunch. And really—I know this sounds boastful—I'm quite a good cook and always try to provide something tasty and nutritious with plenty of roughage. Harold is adamant about roughage."

He would be! I mentally conveyed this snide thought to the dog.

"But that evening he complained that the runner

beans were undercooked—I'd had to hurry them because he gets upset if we don't eat promptly at six thirty, especially if he has to go back to the office afterwards. Which has happened more frequently over the years as he's gone up in his job."

A high-rise window cleaner or a crane operator? I'd concede their claim to the dizzy heights, but somehow I didn't picture Harold as the fearless outdoor type.

Livonia Mayberry returned my look of inquiry. "He works as an accounts supervisor for a firm that manufactures hardware for doors. Sometimes he accuses me of not understanding the pressure he's under . . . the responsibility, having to constantly check that those under him are doing what they are supposed to do."

"Being a bank teller must bring its headaches, too."

"Thank you. It does. But Harold is a worrier; he'll talk for hours about someone having moved a paperclip on his desk and what could have been behind it. Sometimes, disloyally, I've wanted to tell him he might be just a little bit neurotic. And that particular night when he went on and on about the undercooked green beans and that there wasn't a proper pudding—just some jam tarts from Sainsbury's—I felt ready to . . ."

"Throw a paperclip at him."

The dog grinned up at me, but Livonia Mayberry did not crack a smile ". . . tell him what I'd heard the girls at the bank saying."

"Which was?"

"That I must be blind as a bat not to realize that he was stringing me along because of the free meals and all the other things I did for him—taking his clothes to the cleaners, mending and altering, doing the shopping for when he ate at his flat, to which I was rarely invited. That all those evenings when he said he had to go back to the office he was really seeing someone else . . . possibly several different women. But I couldn't get any of it out. I knew I would go to pieces if I tried. After he had gone, I just sat wishing desperately that I had a dear little cat so I could hold on to it and cry all over its fur. And the next morning I went on the Internet at work, during my lunch break, of course, and found the site for *Here Comes the Bride*. I felt I had to do something . . . anything to force Harold into a decision about our relationship."

"How did he take the news when you were accepted?"

"At first he thought it was a joke—a very bad joke—and I was about to cave in and say that was all it was and that I was sorry, when he called me a tart . . . a repressed tart of the Victorian spinster variety, incapable of a normal sexual relationship, and he shouldn't be surprised that this was what he got for his patience in allowing me to keep him at arm's length all those years."

"Brutal."

"And unfair. He'd never given any indication

that he was . . . eager to get me into bed." She blushed at the three letter word. "Sometimes I did wonder at his restraint. Never more than a kiss goodnight. I know the girls at the bank think it all very peculiar, but I always assumed he had old-fashioned morals and . . . perhaps a low libido. Mummy always said that men set the pace. And I would never have dreamed of broaching the subject and making us both uncomfortable."

"Did he break things off?"

"Not exactly. He said he'd have to think long and hard about giving me a second chance when I wasn't the selected bride, which I wouldn't be because no lord of the realm—however desperate to find an unpaid housekeeper—would pick me."

Why commit himself to giving up all those free meals and other entitlements? I placed a hand on her arm. "Oh, Livonia! I wish I could have been there to punch him in the nose for you. But," thinking it best to wrench the subject away from that cruel scene, "back to those gloves that my doggy friend made off with; you said Harold gave them to you."

"A couple of years ago at Christmas." Her face unfroze and tears melted her blue eyes. "It was such a lovely surprise; usually he gave me a wall calendar. Mrs. Knox said she couldn't think of anything more thoughtful, but the gloves—navy blue leather—I just couldn't believe he'd got the fit so right. I've always been a little vain about my hands." She held them out—nicely shaped, with slim fingers and oval nails coated with clear varnish. "Mummy said once that they were the prettiest thing about me."

How flush with the compliments!

"I know it sounds silly," Livonia looked more directly into my eyes than she had yet done, "but sometimes on nights when I was feeling down about how things were going with Harold I would take the gloves to bed with me and sleep with them under my cheek. When I set off in the car at a little after two this morning, I wore them not just because my hands were cold but because they made me feel that I hadn't completely burned my boats. What perhaps I haven't made clear is that even if by the longest of chances Lord Belfrey chose me for his bride, I wouldn't agree to marry him. I'd thank him, then tell him he'd be much better off with the runner-up. I just had to—and call it spite, that's what Mrs. Knox did—show Harold that I'd been his doormat long enough."

"And quite right, too!" The dog added applause by thumping the floor with his tail.

"But as soon as I set off, all the courage I'd squeezed up by talking to myself for hours began to seep away. I couldn't believe I was doing something so completely out of character. Yet I kept on driving." She paused. "I expect you're wondering why I allowed myself so long to get here, arriving hours before the appointed time, but I was afraid of getting lost—my sense of direction isn't good and I'm a nervous driver."

"Did you run into last night's fog?"

"A few patches of mist, but not enough to terrify me, and there wasn't a horrible amount of traffic. For once in my life I didn't make one wrong turn, so there I was parked outside the gates with the sun not yet up. I knew I'd have to take off again before someone looked out a window and came down to investigate and I'd come across as a pitiful idiot. But my legs were shaking and I was afraid I was going to faint."

"I've been there," I said in heartfelt tones.

"So I got out of the car to breathe in the fresh air, and after a moment took off my gloves to feel if my face was perspiring. I had them in one hand when he," pointing at the dog, "was suddenly there . . . racing around me in circles. My head started spinning and I dropped the gloves and he grabbed them up. I tried to tell him to put them down, but nothing came out, and the next second he'd raced off down the drive with them. I suppose I flipped. I was never a runner—Mummy said nice little girls shouldn't run and even when I had to be in a race at school I walked."

"Same here," I said. "I'd have been last either way."

Livonia Mayberry inched her hand toward mine to touch my fingertips. "But this morning I did run, if you could call it that, and every few yards or so he'd turn back and look at me and I had this mad thought that he was laughing at me—the way I knew some of the girls at the bank did—and I actually screamed at him to stop. Which of course made him take off faster than ever."

"Bad boy!" I told the miscreant, who abjectly licked my foot, causing Livonia to back up on the bed. "You're sure he still had the gloves in his mouth at that point?"

She nodded. "We reached the end of the drive, which seemed a mile long, and came to a low wall; he went through an opening and started to go down the slope. It looked steep even in the early morning light, and I could see that there were a lot of stones and rocks among the undergrowth, but didn't think about wrenching my ankle. All I thought was that if he dropped the gloves down there, I might not be able to find them. The thicket at the bottom looked like a wilderness."

I was momentarily distracted by the sober realization that this was probably the place where Suzanne Varney's car had taken its fatal plunge.

"Fortunately, he turned back and bounded off across the lawn. There was no way I could have got near to catching up with him, even if the ground had been level; besides, it was like an obstacle course, with overgrown flowerbeds popping up in front of me. He stopped close to the building, and when I came panting up, I saw the fire escape. He gave a bark that sounded like"—

she winced at the memory—"a ghoulish chuckle, and up he went."

"But wait a minute," I said slowly. "If he barked, he must by then have dropped the gloves."

The blue eyes stared at me in stunned amazement. "I didn't think! I . . . you know the rest. Harold would say this proves that I shouldn't be let loose a mile from home."

"Rubbish!" I said, rising from the bed. "I'm getting dressed and we're going down that fire escape to find those gloves. I think you do need them for the time being, as a reminder of just how little you got out of your relationship with Harold and how much more is waiting for you now you've escaped his clutches."

"But I can't stay here. When Lord Belfrey finds out about my foolish antics, he wouldn't want me as one of the contestants. He's in search of a sensible woman, capable of keeping her head at all times."

"I don't believe he'd blame you an iota for going after your property." His lordship's charming . . . captivating image rose before me. "If this is his dog, he'd be the one making the apologies. Anyway, how's he to know anything about it if you don't want him to? I'm not going to tell him and neither, I'm sure, will our naughty friend."

The dog appeared to take this designation as a compliment.

"You've been so kind." Livonia's voice trembled. "But I'm still so shaken, I think I'll have to go back home."

"Is that what your father would think best? You've told me how important it was to him that you make a new life for yourself. Maybe he thought that would mean marriage to Harold, but are you sure of that? What if he hoped you would spread your wings in an entirely new direction?"

She stared at me, her face solemn. "Mrs. Knox says that both Mummy and Daddy would be aghast by my present behavior. But I have the feeling that Daddy always wished that he'd had it in him to take more chances in life. And I don't think he liked Harold all that much."

"Then stay for him."

"Perhaps if you were going to be here for the week."

The imploring look got to me. If ever anyone needed someone in her corner, it was this woman. Yet even if I were to think about staying on, I couldn't imagine Ben going for the idea. True, his parents would be more than willing to continue holding the fort at Merlin's Court and the children would delight in the additional time with their grandparents. My cousin Freddy would cope at Abigail's on his own. But Ben would not wish to impose any longer than necessary on his lordship's hospitality. And why would Lord Belfrey want two extra people hanging around during the filming of *Here Comes the Bride*?

"You won't be alone with strangers," I said gently. "Your friend will arrive in a few hours with the other contestants."

"But she isn't a friend," replied Livonia. "Suzanne Varney is no more than an acquaintance. Very pleasant but . . ." She stared at me, obviously seeing the shock in my eyes. "What is it? What have I said?"

There was no getting round it. I had to tell her.

"Dead!" she whispered. "I can't believe it!"

"But it's true." I put my arms around her and felt no resistance. "A terrible tragedy. You, on the other hand, are here with the promise of a future ready to unfold."

So glib in giving advice! Did the restless spirits of Mucklesfeld Manor already have me in their clutches?

5

We found one of Livonia Mayberry's gloves at the foot of the fire escape, or to be more exact the dog—which I had come to think of as Thumper—performed this feat, bringing it to me with a look of undeserved pride. Thanking him profusely, I told him without much optimism to fetch the other one. This command sent him rushing around in circles, and I was about to accept that Livonia and I would have to go in search ourselves when he dashed forward, veered first to the left and then to the right, before returning with the glove dangling from his mouth.

They were, as advertised, navy blue leather. Luckily, they did not appear to have been chewed, but neither did they look as though they had been purchased at Harrods or some exclusive boutique. More likely, I thought spitefully, Harold had bought them on sale in a bargain shop and congratulated himself that Livonia—as had proved true—would be in transports at his thoughtfulness.

She expressed gratitude for my help, then took the pair without looking them over for signs of doggy mauling and put them directly into the pocket of the Windbreaker I had lent her. I took this as a positive sign that, despite the news of Suzanne Varney's tragic death and the emotional distress that had preceded that news, she might be coming around to the idea of making a more conventional entrance into the lion's den that was Mucklesfeld Manor. To test the waters, I suggested that we walk down to the gates outside where she had left her car, with the keys still inside, along with her own jacket, handbag, and suitcase.

I was disappointed to see her waver. "You're right . . . I'm almost sure you are, that Daddy would tell me to stay, that I should think of this coming week as a holiday with the chance to meet some new and possibly interesting people. But," she looked up at the vast rear of the house with its multitude of windows, almost indistinguishable in their heavily grimed state from the gray stone, "it does look grim—the sort of place where you could imagine terrible things having happened over the centuries. Murders that went undetected because the victims got locked away in secret rooms or walled up behind the paneling."

A woman with more in common with me and Mrs. Malloy than I would have thought. I shivered even though I was wearing a thick sweater over a long-sleeved linen shirt and woolen slacks.

"Any place of antiquity might look this way after years of abysmal neglect," I said more stoutly than I felt. "It will be interesting to learn why the former Lord Belfrey failed in his stewardship. Was his inheritance already seriously reduced when he took over at Mucklesfeld or did he squander the resources that could have sustained the property?"

A glimmer of interest showed in Livonia's blue eyes, and a pale glow of sunlight breaking through the gauzy veil of early morning brought out the sheen in the firmly set waves of her dark hair. "I wonder how much Lord Belfrey will tell us about the history of Mucklesfeld?"

"Not me," I reminded her.

"I still wish you weren't leaving."

"Even if I were staying, you wouldn't see much of me. You'll be caught up in activities from which I'd be excluded, especially when Lord Belfrey spends time with you and the other five contestants."

"There'll be your friend." She brightened marginally. "Is she easy to get to know?"

"Her name's Roxie Malloy. I'll tell her to take you under her wing." If she didn't without huffing and puffing, I thought grimly, I'd hide her makeup bag. Actually, it was more of a suitcase.

"Do you think we'll be divided into teams?" Unease trembled on her lips.

"I haven't thought about the format." Staring around the wilderness with its suggestion of having once been formal gardens, I found myself wondering about Georges LeBois's vision for *Here Comes the Bride*. It occurred to me that I had never been anywhere near the glamorous world of film. Our stressful arrival at Mucklesfeld Manor had blunted any latent groupie instincts; but now the questions jostled around my mind: How much individual time would Lord Belfrey spend with the contestants? Would there be competitons . . . described as Challenges to make them sound more dramatic? Such as a morning spent in a cellar slowly filling with algae-covered water, with floating rats leaking in from the now underground moat? Or a race to see who could swing fastest from one chandelier to another—while being smothered in cobwebs—down the length of the ballroom? Or, even more daunting, striving to be the first to finish a meal prepared by Mrs. Foot?

I took another glance round the grounds—as much as I could see of them from that vantage point—and felt a pang for the lopsided statues, moss-covered birdbaths, and capsizing garden benches scattered around what must once have been geometrically precise grassy terraces leading down to a scythed lawn with a central fountain—now reduced to a broken crock. All that stood in visible testament to a patrician past were group-ings of lordly trees, their lofty branches spread in benediction over what might once have been an Eden. Sinful the number that likely would need removing due to lack of pruning and neglected root systems. What chance was there that the proceeds from *Here Comes the Bride* would produce more for Mucklesfeld than the superficially cosmetic?

The dog woofed as if suggesting a penny for my thoughts and Livonia asked if I knew a lot about old houses.

"I'm an interior decorator—part time now that I have a family—and I did take a few courses on the architectural periods during my training. I can tell that Mucklesfeld's stone facade postdates the inte-rior by a couple of hundred years. And I think the grounds were probably re-landscaped at around the same time." My imagination warmed to the images invoked. "An eighteenth-century Lord Belfrey must have decided the place needed a face-lift, or perhaps the family coffers were over-flowing at that time and he did the manly thing—went on an out-of-control spending spree to make him feel good about himself."

"Harold thinks going mad on shopping is buying two loaves of bread at once."

Silently, much as I detested the man unseen, I conceded that in general this was more in line with the male psyche than my version. "Shall we go down to your car?" I suggested.

She accompanied me meekly toward the drive, which ended with the gapped and crumbling wall, while the dog trotted soberly ahead as if demonstrating that he was not the sort to run away from home. I was now convinced that he did belong at Mucklesfeld or had accompanied Georges LeBois. Regrettably, if the latter were the case, he didn't take his duties of canine assistance to a man in a wheelchair with an excess of dedication—unless he belonged to a labor union that required his being given designated time off.

"Perhaps he married an heiress, Ellie."

Momentarily I couldn't think who Livonia was talking about, but I was pleased by her comfortable use of my name. She had seemed so self-deprecating that I had imagined it would take months or even years for her to drop the Miss, Ms., or Mrs. with a new acquaintance. However, before flattering myself unduly, I recognized she now found herself in unknown territory.

"Oh," I said, "my eighteenth-century Lord Belfrey! The pragmatic marriage would have been the order of his day, wouldn't it? And now here is his current lordship engaging in a highly modern interpretation of selecting a bride with the most to bring to Mucklesfeld."

"It sounds cold-blooded," replied Livonia, as we skirted a sundial lurking in a tangle of tall weeds. "Still, I suppose it's understandable he would feel morally obliged to honorably fulfill his stewardship. With his not having children, in particular a son, who will inherit the title and estate at his death?"

"He has a cousin," I said, pleased that she was showing an increasing trickle of interest in Mucklesfeld and Lord Belfrey. "His name's Tommy Rowley and he's the local doctor. I met him last night." No need to go into details, although I would have to warn her at some point about the maniacal suit of armor.

She eyed me in puzzlement. We were now walking down the badly rutted drive that sloped fairly precipitously on our left into scrub woodland. "I'd have thought that if he's in line, his name would also be Belfrey."

"Rowley was his mother's maiden name. His father made the switch because of some family feud. I got the impression that he hadn't taken kindly to being the third son. Probably got his nose out of joint from being stuck wearing hand-me-downs and told his share of the ancestral inheritance would be a predisposition to severe acne and early balding."

"Did Dr. Rowley display any hostility toward his lordship?"

"They seemed friendly."

"I suppose he was at Mucklesfeld because of the car accident that took Suzanne Varney's life," Livonia continued before I could reply. "I still can't take it in. Did anyone say if she died instantly, or was she able to talk . . . if only to give them some idea what happened?"

"Tommy's belief was that she was killed on impact."

"It's simply too awful." Livonia swayed against me, stepping in a pothole. "I've always had a fear of getting into a bad accident. Harold says it's because I know nothing about how cars work, so can never be in complete control of a vehicle. He's right. I'm not the least bit mechanical, but I suppose I could take a course and hope the instructor wouldn't lose patience with me if I got the battery and the engine mixed up. In this day and age, a woman on her own should know how to fend for herself in a crisis . . ." She choked up.

There hadn't been much fending that Suzanne Varney could have done in her moment of ultimate crisis, I was thinking when we reached the tall iron gates that heralded the end of the drive. Parked against the roadside curb was a pale blue Volkswagen Beetle. Livonia opened the driver's side door with a timidity that suggested she was expecting an arm to reach out from the backseat to grab her round the throat. I wasn't all that surprised, therefore, when she screamed: "There's someone crouched down on the other side of the car. I saw the top of a head."

Even incoherent thought, let alone a verbal response, became impossible with Thumper barking agreement. Our blinking eyes perceived a woman coming round the front of the car.

"Did I scare you? Sorry. I'd got some gravel in my shoe and bent down to shake it out."

"Oh!" Livonia forced a tremulous smile.

"It's so early," I said with what I hoped was a light lilt, "we thought we would be the only ones out and about."

"An acquaintance kindly dropped me off and it had to be at first light because she has to be back in time for work at nine and it's a good two-hour drive. I was about to go for a walk and get the lay of the land around Mucklesfeld."

"Oh!" Livonia repeated, but this time there was interest in her voice. "Are you another of the contestants for *Here Comes the Bride*?"

The woman nodded. She was a diminutive female with short fly-away beige hair and a narrow, thin-featured face. Indeed, her overall appearance was beige—complexion, hiker's jacket, and twill slacks. The only touch of color came from her brown eyes and matching loafers. "And the two of you?" she inquired.

I explained about the fog and my overnight status. Livonia admitted tentatively to being a fellow contestant, but added that she was having some second thoughts now that a meeting with Lord Belfrey was at hand.

"Don't go getting cold feet," the other woman said. She had a quietly brisk, sensible voice. "You must have had compelling reasons for taking this step. In my case, it's the grounds." She stood on tiptoe to look around her. "When I read that once-glorious gardens and woodlands had reduced to a sad wilderness, I had to answer the call. My family owned a landscaping business, you see. My brother took it over and ran it into bankruptcy. My attempts to help him out financially caused me to lose my home with its two acres, and for the past few years I've been in a small flat with only a window box to satisfy my green thumb." Thumper extended a sympathetic paw, which she bent down and shook. "Nice dog." She looked from Livonia to me as she straightened up, her voice briskly pleasant. "Belong to either of you, or to Mucklesfeld?"

"Not ours," I told her. "But whether he belongs here or from somewhere else in the neighborhood isn't clear. For the moment I'm calling him Thumper."

"Suits him. Preferable to Dog Doe certainly." The narrow face creased into a smile that was reflected in the brown eyes. She extended a hand that was surprisingly workmanlike given her size. "I'm Judy Nunn. And you?"

"Ellie Haskell."

"Livonia Mayberry. Judy Nunn, you said . . . the name sounds familiar."

"I'm thinking the same of yours. Perhaps it will come to one of us. Meanwhile, we are still several hours early. Care to join me on a good long walk?"

Livonia looked less than enthusiastic. I spoke up.

"I should go back inside and talk to my husband about getting ready to leave for home. His parents have been taking care of our children while we've been on holiday." A panicked thought surfaced. They had been expecting us last night . . . but of course, my breath steadied, Ben would have phoned and explained the delay. Even so, I could not continue to dally outdoors. He was bound to be wondering where I had got to, although to be fair to me—I reminded myself in true wifely fashion—he had been the first to do a disappearing act.

"I think I'll come inside with you," said Livonia in the tentative voice of one who was used to having the most ordinary statement dissected prior to rejection, "if you don't mind, that is. I . . . I'm scared I'll lose my nerve if I wait any longer to face the music."

Oh, woe to Lord Belfrey, I thought with tender sympathy. Here was one woman who saw him merely as a means to causing Harold a momentary pang and another who seemed to be only after his garden. I refused to dwell on Mrs. Malloy and her silly fantasies. All it would take to squash them was the discovery that there were no bingo halls within a three-hundred-mile range of Mucklesfeld Manor. I wondered about the other three contestants as Livonia retrieved her suitcase and handbag from her car. Would there be one among the remaining trio eager to discover true love with the lord of the manor?

Judy, perhaps in the spirit of camaraderie or because it was beginning to sprinkle with rain, said she would forgo her walk for the time being and come inside with us. After disappearing around the side of Livonia's car, she reemerged with a small overnight bag.

"No case?" Livonia inquired worriedly, as if fearing that bringing luggage was an infraction of the fine-print rules of the competition.

"Never travel with one even on extended trips," Judy responded cheerfully. "I go by the two pairs of knicks rule. One on, one rinsed out and hung up to dry overnight. I've never understood why people have to take their entire lives with them when they travel."

"That's what Harold always said."

Oh, dear! I thought. I could hear Mrs. Malloy saying as clearly as if she were standing next to me that Livonia Mayberry needed a backbone transplant and if I didn't watch myself I'd be donating mine. It occurred to me at that moment that I did owe Livonia something for not blabbing to Judy Nunn about last night's fatal accident. Further relating of Suzanne Varney's death should be left to Lord Belfrey.

"That dog's going to miss you like the dickens. Devotion written all over him," remarked Judy as she set the pace on the walk up the drive. Head and shoulders forward, her feet scattered gravel right and left. Had there been a bulldozer in her way, I had no doubt she would have walked nimbly over it without missing a beat. Livonia already looked winded, and I had to suck in oxygen while glancing down at Thumper, who had kindly returned to stay at my heels after a sideways dive to encircle a couple of trees that swayed dizzily as a result. There was no doubt from his upturned face and the besotted glow in his eyes that his passion for me had not abated. If he could have done so, I felt sure he would have taken Livonia's suitcase from me (it was the kind without wheels) and carried it on his back. From his vantage point, ours was not to be a one-night stand. Yes, he had broken into my boudoir and thrust himself unencouraged onto my bed, but he had chosen to adore me on sight and (to play fast and loose with Browning) with God be the rest. Still, there was no use in either of us pining. Clearly he wasn't starving, nor did he show other signs of mistreatment. We would each have to forget our infatuation and move on. Although perhaps not with the speed that Judy Nunn was heading down the drive. We had reached the stone wall when Mr. Plunket came through the gap.

Even the thickening veil of rain could not disguise his unfortunate facade. It was also obvious from his labored breathing and hunched posture that he was not the outdoorsy sort. Judy Nunn halted a foot from him and stuck out the hand not holding the overnight bag with the spare pair of knicks.

"Lord Belfrey, I presume!" It was said with the utmost good cheer, but Livonia's reaction was not so sanguine. She gripped my arm with such force that I nearly dropped her suitcase on poor Thumper.

"Not his lordship!" I murmured soothingly. "This is his butler, Mr. Plunket."

"Then a pleasure to meet you, sir." Judy eyed him without visible sign of either relief or revulsion.

"Oh, yes, indeed!" Livonia let me have my arm back. "Such a lovely morning to be out and about, isn't it? Unless you're the sort who prefers to be indoors when it rains. Everybody's different, aren't they?"

Mr. Plunket stared blankly from her to Judy.

"These ladies, Livonia Mayberry and Judy Nunn," I explained, "are two of the contestants for *Here Comes the Bride*."

"Is that right?" He sounded as though he was still stuck in last evening's fog. "I was down in the ravine checking on that tree that got hit."

"Lightning?" Judy asked with the keen interest of one who thrills to the elements, however devilish.

Mr. Plunket either did not hear her or chose to

ignore the interruption. His hunted expression suggested he would much have preferred not to have encountered us on his morning constitutional. "Mrs. Foot's been that worried that a puff of wind could bring it down."

And cause bodily harm to a squirrel? I wondered. The area was well away from the house, but of course for all I knew the ravine might be the favored place of those who relished getting snared by brambles and scratched by thornbushes. Mushroom-hunters, I thought vaguely, or bird-watchers of the particularly dotty sort. Give me the verdant meadow, the velvet hills, the shady lane.

"Mrs. Foot?" Livonia whispered.

"The housekeeper," I told her. "And there's another household helper named Boris." I made a mental note to warn her about the suit of armor that Boris, who enjoyed tinkering, had brought to maniacal life.

"Lord Belfrey should fetch in an arborist to take a look at the tree you're worried about." Judy surveyed Mr. Plunket kindly.

"A what?" He batted away the rain as if it were mosquito netting.

"A tree doctor," I said, setting down Livonia's suitcase.

"Wouldn't a GP do for a quick look?" She squeezed out the words. "It's so awful to think of anything suffering a moment longer than necessary. What sort is the poor stricken tree?"

"An oak," Mr. Plunket sounded as though he was coming somewhat back into focus, "or maybe an elm or . . . a beech. I was never much good at nature study. It was my worst subject after English, maths, geography, and history. Like I used to tell my old mum, lunch was my best subject and I never got top marks in that, neither. His nibs will know what sort it is; for a gentleman of his superior background, knowing one tree for another will be bred in the bone along with Latin verbs and what sort of olive to put in a martini. But we don't want to go bothering him about trees, now do we?"

Given my presumption that the tree under discussion had been hit not by lightning but by Suzanne Varney's car, I agreed with him. Judy, if not Livonia, probably assumed Mr. Plunket was referring to the stress his lordship must be under now that the hour approached for his meeting with his prospective brides.

"So, if you ladies don't mind," Mr. Plunket turned up his jacket against the rain, "I'd appreciate your not saying anything about this little conversation to his nibs. I'm not the sort for early morning rambles in a general way and he might get to worrying that I'm going a bit funny in the head after last night."

"Oh, yes, of course!" Livonia flinched when looking into his gourdlike face, but the sympathy was there in her voice.

"Last night?" Judy met his eyes squarely. Not a flicker of an eyelash. Perhaps she saw the unfortunate man as an interesting botanical specimen, or was simply a nice woman who didn't think spiteful thoughts about other people's appearance. But this was not the moment to put on my hair shirt. Mr. Plunket's revelation of Suzanne Varney's fatal accident was likely to keep us standing outdoors longer than was desirable. The rain had petered out, but if I felt unpleasantly damp so must the others, and Livonia was shivering.

"I'm afraid I set Mucklesfeld at sixes and sevens yesterday evening, by fainting upon arrival," I said quickly. "So silly, but . . ."

"Oh, my goodness!" Livonia swayed against me. "Did you see a ghost?" She glanced fearfully toward the house, which did loom forbodingly as if prepared to sprout an extra turret or two and unleash its ivied tentacles.

"Nothing like that." I dismissed the Metal Knight from my mind. "It was just the stress from driving in the fog."

"Don't seem to get so many pea soupers these days," Judy inserted comfortably. "Certainly not the smog, thank God and cleaner burning fuel. Although I must say I always enjoyed a coal fire as a girl when coming in after a day spent digging up a field of potatoes. Now I make do with one of those fake electric log ones in my flat and . . ."

"Mucklesfeld has its ghosts and don't let no one

tell you different." Mr. Plunket's face, nodules and all, glistened with pride. "Wouldn't be proper in an ancestral home not to have them, would it? Shortchanging, you could call it. Might as well live in a caravan at Southend is what Mrs. Foot says, and Boris agrees with her. They've both seen the Lady Annabel Belfrey that went on a holiday to see her auntie during the French Revolution. Can't blame a woman for wanting to see the Eye Full Tower, I suppose, but . . ."

"Oh, but wasn't that built . . ." Livonia petered out.

"Went to the guillotine instead, she did."

A holiday in Southend might have been a better choice, I thought. The famous long pier, bracing salt air, walks across the mudflats when the sea was out, and yummy fish and chips.

"I suppose poor Lady Annabel has become the headless specter," said Judy with kindly interest.

"Oh, never!" Mr. Plunket rebuked this notion. "You'd not catch a Belfrey going around making a spectacle of herself is Mrs. Foot's opinion. And very particular about her appearance was this ancestress, from what his nibs and Dr. Rowley have to say on the subject—strong into the family history is the doctor. No, indeed, Mrs. Foot and Boris have heard she's always been seen wearing a silk scarf thing around her neck, tied tight enough to keep her head on straight."

"Oh, good!" said Livonia faintly. "Does she often put in an appearance?"

"Not all that frequent. Seems she was one to prefer her own company. You'll see her portrait in the library gallery. Mrs. Foot tried putting out a plate of biscuits and a cup of tea, thinking that could tempt Lady Annabel to show her face more often, but it don't seem to have worked."

Remembering the refreshments offered to me by Mrs. Foot, I thought the Guillotined Ghost showed a lot of sense for a woman who did not have her head screwed on right.

"It's Sir Giles's second wife that's been seen most recent, by both Mrs. Foot and Boris, slipping in or out one of the outside doors. I try not to take it personal that she hasn't seen fit to let me get a glimpse of her."

Abandoning any feigned interest in the conversation, Thumper sat scratching his ear.

"But it's hard not to get our feelings hurt, isn't it?" Livonia murmured sympathetically while either by accident or decision looking him in the face.

"None of us likes being left out by any member of his nibs's family living or gone," Mr. Plunket admitted, "especially one that seems to have captured his imagination with a special fondness. If you was to see her portrait—only you won't because it's at his cousin Celia's house—you'd see there's a strong resemblance between said Eleanor Belfrey and this lady here." Mr. Plunket pointed a stubby finger at me, and I found myself blushing.

Thumper appeared to find the sight adorable.

"Perhaps a family connection," suggested Judy.

"More like a coincidence," I answered quickly, eager to get off the subject.

"Were there children from her marriage to Sir Giles?" Livonia wanted to know. And who could blame her for attempting to brush up on the family history, if she had begun to picture Lord Belfrey as a man who reverenced the female . . . in other words, the antithesis of the horrid Harold.

"No, Celia Belfrey is the daughter by the first wife." Mr. Plunket sounded as though he were reading from a guidebook. He had taken on an air of pleased importance that was rather touching. For a man who had not initially seemed all that glad to have met up with us, he now appeared, having landed on a favorite topic, willing to chat on forever. "Mrs. Foot and Boris agrees with me that when Sir Giles married Eleanor something, anyway it was one of those hyphen names—oh, now it's come back to me, Lambert-Onger, my mother had a friend Mrs. Lambert as lived in Ougar—he must have had high hopes of getting an heir second time around. Her being almost thirty years his junior. Younger than his daughter, I've heard Dr. Rowley say . . . not disapprovingly— never a word said against the family by him, just a statement of fact. But as it turned out, Sir Giles, sad to say, wasn't to reap the fruits of his labor. The marriage was over before the year was out. His young wife did a bunk—vanished overnight—and to make matters even more wicked took the family jewels with her." Mr. Plunket stood, every nodule protruding, awaiting the gasps of consternation that were his due.

"Oh, how dreadful," breathed Livonia. "Where did she go? Was there another man?"

"Never sight nor word of her from that day to this."

"And the jewels?" Judy sounded as though to her this was the pertinent point.

"Never surfaced. Leastways, that's what Dr. Rowley says. His nibs don't talk about them, but you can be sure that things would have been different at Mucklesfeld if they'd been available for selling. And his nibs wouldn't find himself reduced to . . ."

"Quite!" Judy said.

Mr. Plunket now stood removing his foot from his mouth . . . or perhaps he was chewing on it while mulling over the evils of Lord Belfrey's situation.

"Perhaps Sir Giles was the sort of man who would have turned any wife of his into a villainess," said Livonia with surprising spirit. "What if he was constantly critical and never kissed her as though he meant it?"

Mr. Plunket looked uncomfortable, suggesting that he might have heard rumors to this effect from persons not one hundred percent loyal to the

Belfrey family . . . unpaid tradesmen, dismissed employees, Jehovah's Witnesses who'd had the door slammed in their faces. He remarked that it was beginning to rain again. Thumper looked nervously around for his tail as if the talk of theft had him wondering if someone had pinched it, before joining the rest of us in heading toward the house.

"The villainy I see," said Judy, eyeing the lopsided, moss-coated fountain sunk deep in its tangled dell, "is the way these grounds have been neglected. Even with money short, something could have been accomplished with a spade and a lawn mower."

"The weeds look healthy enough," I consoled her, as Mr. Plunket led the way through a door that looked better suited to a dilapidated garden shed than an ancestral home. Thumper kept close to my heels, for which I was eminently grateful. Should a rodent scurry to meet us, I was reasonably confident Thumper would get it while I was screaming my last breath. If this were one of the doors the ghost of Eleanor Belfrey had been spied entering rather than exiting, I admired her (no pun intended) spirit. My foot caught on a flagstone in the hallway, which smelled dismally like a tomb. Not that I had ever been in a tomb . . . I stumbled again as a question reared up belatedly.

How could Eleanor be a ghost if she wasn't dead? According to Mr. Plunket's account, she had departed from Sir Giles's life, not from this earth.

Of course, anything could have happened in the meantime, but Mr. Plunket had said that nothing had been heard of her since her sneaky departure. Were the sightings a result of wishful thinking on the part of Mrs. Foot and Boris because of their resentment that the Vanishing Bride had robbed the family jewel box?

Livonia grabbed my arm, causing the thought to flee and the suitcase to drop from my hand onto my foot. A specter was drifting our way with a gait that suggested a rattling assortment of bones hastily thrown together—oversized in height, parchment white of face. I was fortunate in that this was not my first sighting of Boris. Judy had impressed me as a woman capable of dealing with a roomful of vampires with aplomb—possibly to the point of inquiring into what blood types were most nutritious—but Livonia understandably emitted a pitiful screech.

"Boris," I whispered to her.

"Oh." Relief flowed out of her and not only, I thought, because she had feared that here was Lord Belfrey. Poor Boris; I picked up the suitcase and gazed upon him with compassion. It was a cruelty of fate for a man to look more dead while he was walking around than he would do in his coffin.

"Looking for me?" Mr. Plunket asked with a sprightliness that had the effect of increasing the gloom of the passageway. "I've been out for a morning constitutional."

"A what?" Boris, arms dangling to his knees, intoned out the side of his mouth.

"Walk. I felt a weird urge."

"Agghh!" The blank stare would have bored a hole in the ozone.

"And on the way back in, I met this lady." Mr. Plunket nudged an elbow my way.

"Ellie Haskell." I retrieved the suitcase.

"You'll remember her from last night."

"Agghh!"

"And these two other ladies that are among the contestants for the marriage show. I've been filling them in about the family history."

"Most interesting." Judy, snippet of a woman though she was and faded of coloring as if having been through the wash too many times, exuded a warmth that should have countered the chill that oozed up from the flagstones and out of the stone walls. She introduced herself and Livonia bravely did likewise.

"Agghh!"

Suddenly I saw what seemed to be a struggle for intelligent thought working its tortuous way from Boris's brain down his forehead and into his eyeballs. His arms battled rigor mortis to allow him to scratch the side of his nose with a reasonably lifelike-looking finger. "It was, I hope," he painstakingly produced the words with robotically even spacing, "a good walk this morning, Mr. Plunket. I hope you saw other things of interest to you besides these . . ." I expected him to say *creatures,* but he left the sentence hanging.

Mr. Plunket gave him a quelling look before turning to Livonia, Judy, and me. "Boris and Mrs. Foot keep hoping I'll catch a glimpse of Eleanor Belfrey so I won't go on feeling left out. But much as I appreciate their feelings," he redirected his gaze to Boris, speaking slowly and distinctly, "talking about it makes it worse. No, I didn't see anything, but I wasn't keeping my mind and eyes properly open to a . . . a sighting."

"Agghh!" Boris receded into his corpse to ebb out of the passageway. Thumper heaved a sigh of what sounded like profound relief and Mr. Plunket said rather snappishly that he didn't know what Mrs. Foot would say, seeing that she wasn't at all keen on dogs, but we'd find out about that right now. He pushed open a door to reveal a large room with a brick wall facing us.

Set into it was an archaic cooker that looked as though it would require arduous blacking to combat rust. As old-fashioned kitchens went, this one was not invested with an excess of charm. True, the heavily timbered ceiling and the same flagstones that had been in the passageway had their appeal, as did the vast deal table surrounded by an assortment of elderly chairs, but the sink looked like a pig's trough and the wall cupboards were lopsided and needed a fresh coat of paint. Back to a positive note, the place was appreciably more orderly and somewhat cleaner than I would have expected of a domain ruled by Mrs. Foot.

She came through one of several doors scattered around the room, with a jug in hand, the housewifely flowered bib apron contrasting quite horribly with her insane asylum wardress appearance. The hulking form and mangled gray locks fared even less well in daylight than they had done in the murky gloom of the past evening. Mr. Plunket hastened to take the jug from her before making the introductions. I set Livonia's suitcase down in a corner while she sank blindly into a chair. Judy also deposited her overnight bag, but I didn't get the feeling that at any point since setting foot in Mucklesfeld she had felt burdened either physically or emotionally. It was Mrs. Foot who looked as though she had been clobbered from all sides.

Mr. Plunket helped her to a bench by the side of the cooker and continued to anxiously hover over her to the accompaniment of ominous creaking. It wasn't a stone bench and clearly she wasn't made of that substance, either. Her features shifted as if formed out of Plasticine by a nasty-minded child. She waved a hand, almost taking out a cupboard that looked equally unhinged with its door hanging open.

"I came down to find the place looking like this, everything put away where I'll never be able to find anything. All my favorite slop cloths and the soup tins for keeping vegetable scrapings in—

gone. Everything off the floor where I could find what I needed at a glance or by stepping on it. We all have our own ways, like I used to explain when I was a ward maid and preferred taking my tea cart up the stairs to using the lift." She made this pitiful statement with a fixed smile that compressed her cheeks upward, forcing her eyes to pop.

I gave no thought to Livonia's sensitivity or Judy's imperturbability. I was picturing with painful clarity the deflated look on the face of the wardress when discovering that Wisteria Whitworth had escaped her clutches by fleeing Perdition Hall with Carson Grant. Back into a world of sunlight and hope—where far from being sneered at by the arbiters of fashion for the hair that had turned white from all she had endured, Wisteria set a trend that would one day be called platinum blond.

"Who was it that did this?" Mr. Plunket asked Mrs. Foot while patting her shoulder. "Who turned your nice cozy kitchen into an empty warehouse, the sort we used to hole up in when you, Boris, and me was homeless?"

Before I could absorb this information, the cry "Them!" broke from Mrs. Foot's lips. It carried with it a fearsome weight suggestive of mutant life-forms intent on reducing Earth to a series of crop circles, or an annual convention of euthanasia enthusiasts, or . . . Thumper, who had been standing discreetly behind me, gave a whine that indicated his guess was a truckload of dogcatchers.

"Them?" Livonia whispered.

"Georges LeBois was the steamroller."

"Who?" Judy asked in the voice of one not wishing to be overly nosy.

"The director of *Here Comes the Bride*," I told her.

"And the other one. Only too eager he was to shove in his oar." Mrs. Foot reached up to pat the hand with which Mr. Plunket was still patting her shoulder.

"Dr. Rowley?" I assumed she wouldn't have used that barbed inflection if she meant Lord Belfrey.

"Not him, sensible hardworking man that he is, he went home to get his rest. No, your husband—it was him that stole my kitchen."

"Stole" was an odd way of putting the matter. But then, Mrs. Foot had struck me as being on the far side of odd from our first encounter. It was Thumper who took umbrage. Coming out from behind me, he sat at my side and stared down the offender, to no effect because she gave no sign of being aware of his presence. Well, I thought, so that was why Ben hadn't been to bed or turned up after I was awake. I pictured him preparing my supper and putting together a meal of sorts for Georges LeBois under conditions that must have revolted his professional chef's soul. After which he would have felt morally obliged to work at restoring the kitchen to some degree of hygienic acceptability without going so far as to burn it down and start from scratch.

The look Mrs. Foot directed my way was not a pleasant one; gone was all affability and eager servitude as befitted a representative of Lord Belfrey's household. The eyes that I had thought colorless burned with a greenish-yellow fire. I felt certain that had there been a straitjacket to hand she would have bundled me into it and yanked the cords tight enough to give me the eighteen-inch waist Carson Grant had so admired in Wisteria Whitworth. Except in my case that elusive measurement would also become my bust and hip size.

"I'm sure my husband didn't mean to offend . . ." I began.

"Offend!" She spat the word across the room, causing Judy to duck her head and Livonia to cower in her chair. Thumper so far forgot his status as an unwanted guest to issue a growl, which brought a glower to Mr. Plunket's face but did nothing to put a dent in Mrs. Foot's rage. "Offend! That doesn't say nothing to how I felt. Heartbroken is what I was, and still am that your husband that his lordship took in along with you, Mrs., made off with Whitey right under my nose without so much as a *How do you feel about having your beloved pet marched away like he's vermin?*"

"And Whitey is?" said Judy.

"Her rat," responded Mr. Plunket mournfully.

"Cat?" Hope that I had misheard kept my knees from buckling.

"Yes, yes," Livonia pleaded, "do let it be a dear little kitty."

"Rat!" Mr. Plunket speeded up his patting of Mrs. Foot's shoulder. "Bought for her three Christmases back by Boris and me. Part Abyssinian, part Polish, with a little Italian on his father's side, the pet shop owner told us, and he'd have given us the pedigree papers to prove it if he could have laid his hand on them right there and then. A dear little fellow is Whitey, always cheerful and chirpy in his cage when he'd go in it."

"Where'd he hang out the rest of the time?" In my opinion, Judy didn't exude the requisite amount of horror, even in the face of Mrs. Foot's lugubrious response.

"Up among the saucepans that till last night hung from them hooks above the stove—when he wasn't in my apron pocket, that is. Loved to swing his self dizzy from the frying pan, did the little darling. You should have seen how Boris's face would melt watching him. Said Whitey's antics was better than any trapeze artist in any circus!"

Livonia made up for Judy's lack of finer feeling by uttering the awful mumble: "I think I'll have to go back to Harold."

The enormity of this pronouncement brought me sharply back to my senses—diminished though they might be after an evening's incarceration at

Mucklesfeld. And when Livonia cupped a hand over her mouth and fled the kitchen, leaving the door wide open, I said firmly: "I'm sure my husband and Georges LeBois have found a safe haven for Whitey. Somewhere he won't feel trapped in a stampede when the rest of the contestants arrive at ten o'clock, which," looking at my watch, "should be in a little over an hour."

"Wherever they've taken him, he'll be missing his mummy something cruel." Mr. Plunket looked on the point of tears, but Mrs. Foot appeared to be rallying. The greenish-yellow fire seeped from her eyes, leaving them as colorless as the rest of her face, but she was getting to her feet.

"I'll have to carry on in the face of nastiness just as I had to at Shady Oaks when some of the bed-pans came up missing and Sister Johnson gave me the eye like she suspected me of taking them to sell on the side . . . or that time old Mr. Codger's daughter looked at me funny when I was plumping up his pillows and he was getting awkward about it. His lordship's feelings are what count, not mine or Whitey's even, and I hope you'll tell Boris so, Mr. Plunket—you know how worked up he gets if he thinks I'm being upset."

Picturing Boris getting worked up was beyond me, but Judy was made of more compassionate stuff. Looking like a wood elf sitting in a people chair, she asked Mrs. Foot kindly if Boris regarded her as a mother.

"Too right he does." Mrs. Foot wiped the grubby sleeve of her grease-colored dress across her eyes and nose. "Him, Mr. Plunket, and me is family, along with dear little Whitey. Heaven help him," tears squeezed stickily out of her eyes, "if they put him down in the dungeon with the wild rats. They'll eat him alive—him having no street smarts, the poor little bugger."

"She's speaking of the cellars," Mr. Plunket explained; "there is no proper dungeon at Mucklesfeld." Being dwarfed by Mrs. Foot's hulking frame, he now had to make do with tapping her shoulder with the tips of his fingers.

"To think of Whitey put out of sight and a dog coming to my kitchen as bold as brass." Finally her gooseberry gaze fastened on Thumper before he skirted back behind me. "Well, he can't stay, that's for certain. Can't have a black dog bringing bad luck down on Mucklesfeld, just when it looks like Lord Belfrey may be able to save the place."

"Oh, come now," Judy rose from her chair to say reasonably, "just look at the nice old fellow . . ."

"I'm not suggesting he stay," I said. "He got in through my bedroom window in the middle of the night and I thought it likely he belonged here, but can't we at least give him something to eat and drink before trying to find out where he belongs?"

"Well, it'll have to be outside," Mrs. Foot answered, returning more or less to human form. "It's not that I'm hardhearted. Dogs aren't my cup of tea; still, I'd be hard put to be unkind to a living creature whatever's been done to my poor Whitey. But whatever you and this other lady," pointing a giant finger at Judy, "go calling superstition, a black dog at Mucklesfeld can't be tolerated, plain and simple as that. Not after what poor Lord Giles Belfrey went through after discovering that his bride of less than a year had made off in the night with the family jewels and Hamish the Scottie. And not a woof of protest out of the nasty little bugger, let alone sounding the alarm."

6

Alack, poor Thumper! Cast in the role of pariah because he was born a dog! Unfair, my heart cried out on his behalf! Nothing in his bark had suggested a trace of a Scottish accent that would lead one to believe he knew the entire works of Robbie Burns by heart and longed to wear the tartan.

"Whitey would have squeaked his dear little head off before being ripped away from Mucklesfeld, wouldn't he, Mr. Plunket?" Mrs. Foot was saying when Livonia came creeping back into the kitchen like one of the ghosts said to haunt the house along with the memory of a treacherous Scottie.

"Sorry for disappearing like that. I just needed a

moment alone," she whispered while returning to her chair next to Judy.

"And quite unstandable," began Mr. Plunket, to be interrupted by Georges LeBois rolling his wheelchair through the doorway and performing a nifty swivel in the center of the room in silent acknowledgment of his audience. I was surprised that Thumper didn't greet him as a relative of sorts with a friendly woof. But perhaps he took exception to hugely stout men wearing yellow and brown checked waistcoats coupled with crimson silk cravats tucked into aqua blue shirts. A prejudice I could not approve, considering I had once been plus-sized myself, which should have made me less critical of appearances in general, as in the cases of Mr. Plunket, Mrs. Foot, and Boris, instead of thinking wickedly unkind thoughts about them. It was Livonia, getting to her feet along with Judy, who broke the silence.

"Lord Belfrey?" The question combined hesitancy with an overly bright lift of the lips. She had a very readable face. Written all over it now was the awful dilemma of not wanting to find herself affianced to a stranger (she had made clear to me that being a contestant on *Here Comes the Bride* was only a charade intended to bring Harold either metaphorically or in actuality to his knees) while wondering how she could reject a man in a wheelchair if his choice fell upon her. Everything about Georges LeBois roared out that he was not a man to be pitied, that he did not view himself as handicapped, that he towered in his mind over his fellows with portable legs. They must plod through life while he spun circles around them, vast in size and knowledge of what was going on behind a timidly pretty face.

"'Course this isn't his nibs." Mr. Plunket sounded mortally offended by the suggestion. "It's Mr. Georges LeBois as is in charge of doing the filming of *Here Comes the Bride*."

"Oh!" Livonia released a quivery breath and tentatively followed suit when Judy moved to shake his hand.

He inclined his head, making three reasonably sized chins out of one humongous one. "Yes, yes!" A royal wave from a hand the size of a bowl of bread dough. "It will be interesting to see how you each comes through on film. You—the little washed-out beige thing—may be more alive to the camera than Ms. Teacup Face here. That's what makes for a good take, stripping away the flesh and bone to reveal what's hiding underneath, if anything."

"It's all very interesting, isn't it, Mrs. Foot?" said Mr. Plunket.

"Oh, indeed, Mr. Plunket," replied Mrs. Foot, with a return to the normalcy that I continued to find more scary than her greenish-yellow-eyed rampages. "I'd make you one of my nice cups of tea . . . and the ladies too, if I knew where the kettle had gone."

"On the rubbish heap, I devoutly hope!" Georges LeBois spun his wheelchair so that its back was toward her and Mr. Plunket. "As for you two," he notched his bellow down to a rumble in addressing Livonia and Judy, "don't stand there wasting your simpers on me. Go and announce your presence to Lord Belfrey, he's the one who may get stuck marrying one of you."

"And where will we find his lordship?" asked an undaunted Judy briskly.

"In his study."

Livonia tried but failed to unhinge her jaw.

"And where is that?" Again Judy posed the question.

Georges favored her with the bloodhound smile that could have gobbled up persons far larger than her less than five feet. Thumper might have been impressed had he not decided that the better part of valor was going to sleep at my feet. "My good woman, if you and your husband-seeking companion are incapable of locating a room without being led to it by the nose or by means of a map marked with a cross, you are patently not up to the gamesmanship of the contest ahead. And should forthwith make your absence felt. As you were informed on your application forms," Georges gestured mightily, "and in subsequent acceptance letters, Lord Belfrey is not looking for a bride of startling beauty or even above-average intelligence, merely one with the modicum of practicality that will prevent her going raving mad before the decorators are brought in to take the cobwebs down."

"Thank you for your assistance, Mr. LeBois," said Judy, and with Livonia in tow she serenely departed the kitchen.

"*Monsieur* LeBois," he swiveled to call after them as the door closed. "Hmm! That half rasher of bacon may be the one to watch in this race. The other's pretty and may have more to her than we're seeing now. But if looks mattered, the winner would have been the one that died . . . unless her photograph had been doctored, which I don't think it was. Ah well," the yellow and brown checked waistcoat swelled and the crimson cravat flamed to his grandiloquence, "that's life!"

"Not for Suzanne Varney, it isn't," I retorted roundly, "and you were horridly rude to Judy Nunn and Livonia Mayberry."

"It's his artistic temperament." Mrs. Foot eyed Georges ingratiatingly. "Isn't that right, Mr. Plunket?"

" 'Course it is, and Boris would agree if he was here. I expect he's looking for Whitey to give him a nice piece of cheese and tell him he'll be back among the saucepans, swinging his little heart out on the frying pan in next to no time."

"Over my fat carcass!" Georges roared with flabby-lipped relish. "As for the artistic temperament, you should know something about that, being married to a chef, Ellie Haskell, if that is your real name."

"And why shouldn't it be?"

"Because not everything in this house is entirely what it seems."

If his intent was to make me quiver and quake, he was to be disappointed. My temper was up. "Very likely," I said, "you're certainly no more a Monsieur than Whitey the Rat. My guess is you originated in Tottenham where my husband was raised."

"We never claimed the little dear was French." It was Mr. Plunket's turn to take umbrage. "Abyssinian and Polish is what we said, with a splash of Italian. Isn't that right, Mrs. Foot?"

Georges turned the wheelchair squarely on them. "I was referring, Mrs. Wife of the Chef, to the suit of armor that comes alive when one stands too close to it, inducing susceptible women to faint dead away."

"Nothing supernatural about that," I said, remembering that I had meant to warn Livonia about the Metal Knight. "Mr. Plunket explained that the extending arms and clawing mitts were the result of Boris's penchant for tinkering with inanimate objects."

"I did say that, though not with the Latin-sounding words," agreed Mr. Plunket.

"And no reason why you shouldn't have." Mrs. Foot loomed enormous behind the wheelchair.

"Very proud of Boris we both are. He's a genius in his quiet . . ."

"Unassuming," supplied Mr. Plunket, displaying his mastery of the English language.

"That's the word." Mrs. Foot nodded her head, causing the gray locks to shift like wooly clouds blown along by a fierce wind. "Unassuming, that's always been Boris. And unappreciated, only think what he's been put through in the past by them that had to be jealous of his looks and charm and cleverness."

"For God's sake, you two," Georges roared, "get out of my presence and indulge your delusions elsewhere."

"I still say what you need is one of my lovely cups of tea." Mrs. Foot spoke in the manner I imagined her perfecting when trundling her trolley through the wards of Lofty Poplars, Leafy Elms, or whatever the name was. That she sounded menacing in a slippery soft way rather than soothing was the fault of her hulking form, witch mane, and hag's grin, but instead of castigating Mother Nature for cruelty above and beyond, my sympathy went to the patients I pictured using every last ounce of feeble strength to hide under their sheets.

"Out! Out!" The purple mounting in Georges's face suggested a readiness to mow her down with the wheelchair if she didn't leap out of range and take Mr. Plunket with her. They took the hint and disappeared through one of several interior doors in the kitchen. Thumper, having staggered sleepily to his paws, sank down to continue snoring contentedly, perhaps happily reliving the moment he had leaped through the window onto my bed.

"You were saying," I prompted Georges coldly.

"Ah, yes!" He settled back into his wheelchair, spreading himself out to near overflow, with the blatant implication of taking the universe back on his terms. "I lay cheerful claim not only to being the brains behind Boris's tinkering with the suit of armor, but to instructing him in the setup of several other little surprises which will test the fortitude of the contestants."

"How interesting."

"For the bigger, more complicated work, including some whimsical visual effects, along with what I immodestly regard as the pièce de résistance, I sent in professionals earlier in the week. But what satisfies me most fully right now, Mrs. Wife of the Chef, is the hope springing in my . . ."

"Heart?" I stared at him in disbelief. "You're hiding one under that waistcoat?"

"I was referring to my self-serving stomach."

"Silly of me," I said, as he patted his designated organ of sensitivity complacently. "But do you seriously believe, after speaking to Mr. Plunket and Mrs. Foot as you did just now, that one of them will come out of the pantry—or wherever they went to cower—and toss you a crust of toast?"

"Those two cretins may seal themselves up and join the skeletons already stuffed behind the walls." The leer that accompanied this inappropriate remark was shocking to behold and I could only be grateful that Thumper did not crack open an eye to witness it. "Let it be hoped," Georges's eyes narrowed gleamingly above his Roman nose, "that their vile pet joins his fellows in gnawing at their bones. Meanwhile, I look forward to the epicurean delights your husband will provide for me during the coming week."

I stared at him blankly.

"I knew him to be a man after my own heart—were I to possess one—when he ignored the Foot woman's screams for mercy and banished the albino rat, after insisting it be first returned to its cage. My enthusiasm increased when he set about bringing this kitchen out of the Stone Age into something approaching the nineteen fifties by a great deal of scrubbing surfaces and throwing out of disgusting pots, pans, cutlery, and crockery. He agreed with me as I reclined in my chariot proffering the occasional word of advice as to which supplier would most speedily dispatch the caviar exquisite . . . the pistachio mushroom pâté delectable . . . the swordfish sublime . . . the loganberries lip-smacking that my stomach was announcing in impeccable French that it desired." Georges's oratory swelled into the operatic and I awaited the sound of wineglasses cracking. After studying my reaction, he abandoned his impersonation of Enrico Caruso and shook his head, puffing out the bloodhound cheeks as he did so. "The point I am making, Mrs. Wife of the Chef, is that before I retired for the night it was agreed between us that my gourmand interests were his."

"Yours and Ben's?" A woman who has been awake since the middle of the night and has not yet had a cup of coffee, let alone breakfast, should not be expected to be quick on the uptake.

"Who else?" He blew out a breath, deflating the cheeks, and grabbed the arms of his chair. "Very well, in words that sleeping dog could comprehend! Your husband has agreed to stay on as my personal chef at Mucklesfeld for the duration of the filming, which should take six days should there be no further complications—such as other contestants getting themselves killed."

"The person who is going to get killed," I fumed, "is your insufferable self. Of all the insensitive things to say! Poor Suzanne Varney! I hope her ghost appears to you in the middle of the night and wheels you out onto the roof and tips you over the edge. As for my husband promising to stay on and cook for you . . ." I choked on my fury.

"I would be willing to let others partake . . . Lord Belfrey and his doctor cousin, should he be called in to medicate a patient who is reduced to hysteria by one of the surprises in store. You yourself may join us at table if you care to do so. My good woman," he completed a circle in the wheelchair, "I do not see why you are making difficulties. Your husband said he suspected you already wished to stay on for the sake of your friend Mrs. Malloy, who is to take Suzanne Varney's place as a contestant, and because of your interest in old houses. He mentioned that you are an interior designer. As such," Georges tried but failed to look cajoling, "I would have thought you could happily wander around Mucklesfeld for a week, mentally redoing the place. It is even possible that when *Here Comes the Bride* achieves the success I anticipate and the money starts rolling in, his lordship might hire you to put your ideas into action."

"The opportunity to take down the cobwebs and possibly re-hand them elsewhere is certainly hard to resist," I said nastily, "but I think I can hold out. Coming, Thumper?" I looked down, flicked my fingers gently, and with my furry—possibly only loyal—friend at my heels, stormed out of the kitchen.

"Given the choice," Georges bellowed after me, "I prefer rats to dogs."

"Ignore him," I told Thumper. My attempt to slam the door behind us failed because it creaked and groaned, making clear that it was old and hated to be hurried. The hall appeared even more crowded than on the previous evening, with over-sized furniture from bygone eras that had reverenced excess, especially when it came to the hideous. Elbowing past a dresser with a bloated front that reminded me of a certain stomach, I continued to seethe! That I had been thinking it might be interesting to stay and watch how things turned out—not only for Mrs. Malloy but also for Livonia, who so desperately needed moral support, and for Judy, whom I had instantly liked—did not come into things. That Ben had made a commitment to Georges LeBois without consulting me wasn't how our marriage worked.

I was about to storm back to the bedroom when I realized that I didn't remember how to get there. I cast an irritable glance at the staircase, with its massively carved, age-blackened banisters and its look of having seen more than its fair share of coffins going up empty and coming down filled. Mounting those broad steps wouldn't get me anywhere fast because Lord Belfrey had taken me up by the back way last night. I made a rude gesture at the Metal Knight (who was definitely smirking), while balking at the idea of returning to the kitchen, stalking past Georges, opening the door through which Mr. Plunket and Mrs. Foot had disappeared, and asking one or both of them to guide me back to the attics.

I was stalled in making even a tentative move when the hall was invaded by two youngish men burgeoning with cameras, tripods, and assorted equipment suggestive of filming. My knowledge of such items was nil, but I admit to a small thrill coursing through my being. Who would have thought I would find myself this close to the production of a television show, whether or not it ever showed up on screen? Both men looked their part—wearing ragged jeans and sweatshirts and having longish, purposefully untidy hair, pierced ears, and artistic expressions. I took them to be the two who had preceded us into Mucklesfeld the previous evening. Both gave me a casual glance and one of them grinned at Thumper, who had moved in for a closer inspection but neither barked nor leaped up at them, for which I was relieved. That stuff they were carrying had to be expensive and Georges would undoubtedly make someone pay if it were dropped. That someone mustn't be Thumper.

They said something to each other, but whether or not they would have spoken to me remains open to question because the hall grew by two more people lugging technologically advanced-looking . . . things. One was a young woman with dingy blond hair and dragon tattoos on both bare arms, and the other an older man with gray in his hair but the same air of grungy glamour. The four converged without accident, conversing with an amicable intensity that made evident Thumper and I had faded off their mental screens. It was glaringly obvious that Georges's crew was on the move while he sat in the kitchen waiting presumably for Ben to come and feed him. Which might be a long time coming if provisions were yet to arrive. I knew nothing of the work ethics of directors, but it struck me that his did not set a particularly fine example.

The hall emptied itself save for Thumper and me. I was considering following the four in the hope that they would lead me to a back staircase that I would recognize, when Livonia came out into what passed for light at Mucklesfeld.

"Oh, how glad I am to see you!" Her face was flushed, her dark hair rumpled, and her voice trembled on the verge of hysteria. "I lost Judy within a couple of moments of going down that little corridor." Pointing into the morass. "She said it would speed things up if I went left looking for the study and she turned right, but when I had no luck and went after her, I couldn't find her, let alone any room that looked right. Just a couple with nothing in them. You don't think, Ellie, that she lost me on purpose?"

"I'm sure she didn't." I edged over to put an arm around Livonia while Thumper sat looking on with the soft light of sympathy in his eyes.

"No, of course not, that was awful of me to say. She does seem nice, doesn't she? Oh, I do hope this competition isn't making me paranoid already. You don't think that's the object, do you—to turn each of the contestants against one another?"

"Well," I hesitated, "it would make for more interesting television."

Livonia stared at me bleakly. "I've never watched a reality show, but I've heard the girls at the bank say the contestants can turn hostile . . . even bloodthirsty."

"That'll be Georges LeBois's aim," I conceded. "By the way, why did you and Judy go looking for the study down that hallway?"

"We decided it would be the best place to start after checking out here without any luck. The only door we didn't knock on and open was the one down there to our left," she pointed, "behind that huge jardinière with the dead plant. There was a sign taped to it with ENTER AT YOUR PERIL printed on it in great big black letters."

"That will be the study. Trust Georges LeBois to set you and Judy running in circles looking for the room that he'd designated off-limits. Beastly man! Perhaps," looking down at my faithful hound, "I can train Thumper to take a bite out of him that will cut him down to size. But Livonia, being fore-warned is your weapon against the man and his tricks. I think you should march over to that room this minute and see if Lord Belfrey is in there and have a talk with him as instructed. Point one scored against Georges. If Judy comes along within the next few minutes, I'll send her in after you. Livonia, you can do this!"

She shook her head. "I was right earlier about wanting to leave. I'm not cut out for this sort of thing; I've no stamina for conflict . . . Harold was correct and so was Mrs. Knox about letting wiser heads than mine prevail. He may not be perfect but . . ."

"Listen," I said, "I'll be here the whole week. Georges LeBois has persuaded my husband to stay on as his chef."

She brushed at her teary blue eyes. Hope faded from them as soon as it appeared. "But you can't be with me all the time, and you'll have your friend who'll expect you to be on her side exclusively . . . and rightly so."

"Roxie Malloy can fend for herself." This wasn't entirely true, of course. Mrs. M proclaimed herself capable of living her life without any help from me, especially when she was on her high horse, but over the years we had each come to depend on the other, though never before in matters of the heart. She might well resent my support of a rival . . . unless I could persuade her that Livonia merely wished to stay in the game as a boost to her self-confidence. I came out of my mulling to note the change of expression on Livonia's face. It was one of sharp surprise as if a penny had finally dropped with a clang.

"I've just remembered why Judy's name sounded familiar when she told us what it was and she said, didn't she?, that mine sounded familiar to her, too."

"Go on!" I urged, while Thumper showed interest by cocking his head.

"It was thinking about your friend that jogged my memory. Judy Nunn was the name of Suzanne Varney's friend—the one who told her about *Here Comes the Bride*."

"Which means," I said thoughtfully, "that were Suzanne here, it would make for three people with connections to each other in the competition. What are the odds of that happening by chance, if we suppose there were dozens, possibly hundreds of applicants?"

Livonia shivered. "Not strangers then . . . but people who are in some way woven together being set against each other. It sounds diabolical, doesn't it?"

"Or a shrewd move in grabbing the viewers' interest. In the case of *Here Comes the Bride*, Judy knew Suzanne and Suzanne knew you, so—if we are to follow a pattern of progression—you will know one of the other three contestants."

"Oh, I see! I see!" Her eyes now widened in horror. "Who could it be? But wait!" She held up a trembling hand. "Unlike Judy and Suzanne, I never told anyone except for Harold what I was planning . . . certainly not any of the girls at the bank. And Harold wouldn't have spread it around, would he?"

"Mrs. Knox," I reminded her.

"Yes, of course! I'd forgotten! I did tell her, but she's not looking for a husband. She's got one already. Oh, she wouldn't have said anything to anyone. It would have been so unkind! But if she did . . . and we call the person she told Contestant Number Four . . . then Four would have told Five and Five would have told Six."

"That's my assumption, Livonia," I was saying, and getting a look from Thumper that declared whatever I thought was bound to be right, when the front door creaked mightily before groaning inward, bringing the not unwelcome sight of Dr. Rowley. The tablets he had given me had certainly put paid to my headache and allowed me to get a few hours of sleep.

"Hello." I smiled while heading toward him with Thumper displaying a welcome in his springing steps and Livonia half hiding behind me. "I hoped I would have the chance to tell you that I am completely recovered."

"What great news!" He beamed his schoolboy smile on me. "Nothing could be nicer to hear after last night's tragedy." The radiant cheer vanished and his voice sank in sorrow. "I have just been down in the ravine laying a bunch of flowers from my garden at the place where it happened. So young a life cut short. I was in shock afterwards and it wasn't until I woke this morning that the full awfulness hit me! For the first time in years, I felt an overwhelming need for my old cat Blackie. Nothing like sitting with a cat on one's lap to make the world seem a better, kinder place." He reached into the pocket of the tweed jacket that fitted snuggly around his tummy and drew out a handkerchief, which he scrunched into a ball and rolled around in his hands. I pictured him doing the same as a stout, round-faced schoolboy endeavoring to appear manly when battling the urge to tear up.

I was wondering what I could say to him when I felt Livonia shift around me and heard her say with markedly less alarm than when she had made the assumption with Mr. Plunket, Boris, and Georges: "Lord Belfrey?"

"His cousin, Dr. Rowley," I explained.

"Oh, I see!" She continued moving forward until well out in front of me.

Tommy stepped sideways, stumbling to a halt when fully face-to-face with her.

"I'm Livonia Mayberry."

Why hadn't I noticed what a sweet voice she had? I waited for her to add that she was one of the contestants, but naturally she would assume he had already guessed.

"Tommy Rowley. I live in the village."

"Do you really?"

"Just a walk away."

"So close!"

"Mine isn't a large house, but it suits my needs. Or would do completely," Tommy returned the handkerchief with much fumbling to his jacket pocket, "if I could come home to someone . . . a cat . . . yes, a sweet-faced cat, waiting for me curled up in the armchair by the fireplace, with the lamplight shining on her glossy dark hair . . . I mean fur."

"You mentioned Blackie." Livonia cut down the distance between them by a couple of footsteps. "That sounds like a male sort of name to my ears, but then," she was blushing rosily, "it's so easy for me to be wrong about . . . everything really."

"Not in this case, Miss Mayberry." Tommy's voice took on a deeper timbre, "Blackie was a boy until his little operation—which we both regretted but I thought necessary."

"Perhaps next time a female would make a nice change."

"Indeed it would!" The round eyed, round cheeked schoolboy face under the thinning hair shone with enthusiasm.

There followed one of those silences that tend to become a little overwhelming. To break it—because Thumper looked a little anxious—I blurted out: "Dr. Rowley, Livonia knew Suzanne Varney." I knew at once that I had cruelly broken the spell cast by two people having what passed for a normal conversation at Mucklesfeld. Oh, to have stepped on my merciless tongue!

The roses faded from Livonia's cheeks. "And I haven't been thinking about her near enough." She twisted her hands together in the familiar way. "It's been all about me since I got here, hasn't it? Harold was right in saying I'm completely selfish." Tommy reached out a hand to her, but she backed away. I saw out of the corner of my eye a silvery glint, and heard, if they did not, a soft whirring . . . followed by the ominous creaking of metal arms rising stiffly to extend forward in preparation for closing around an unwary throat. Somehow I managed a warning yelp, which was echoed by Thumper; Livonia turned, perceived her peril, and stood frozen for the half second that it took Tommy to swoop her to safety. The metal arms lowered with a disappointed grinding sound as his closed around her.

"I meant to warn you, Livonia," I apologized.

"How did it come alive?" Her voice was muffled, due to her face being pressed against Tommy's.

"Georges LeBois's dictates! Boris's handiwork! A test of nerves for the contestants. According to the great man, there will be other fun and games." I expected Livonia to return to the theme of leaving Mucklesfeld without delay, but she was silent while remaining within the circle of Tommy's arms. It was an agitated squeaking (not her voice) that rent the air. My initial thought was that the Metal Knight was still readjusting its parts. But then came the scurrying . . . the flash of white bringing Thumper vehemently to life. What had been a mild-mannered gentleman of a dog became a bristling, springing, madly yipping and hollering wild animal. Across the hall he dashed in hot pursuit of . . . the ultimate fast food.

"Whitey!" I yelled in Livonia and Tommy's direction, before making my dash toward the staircase where the excitement was headed.

"It was Blackie, remember?" His voice floated my way.

No point in pausing to explain. I doubted Tommy would have heard me; he was fully occupied in shielding Livonia from the cruel world outside his arms. Stupid me, far better for her not to know that Mrs. Foot's beloved rat had escaped incarceration. Speeding up the stairs in Thumper's wake, I ordered him pantingly to stop. For once my word was not law and I reached the banister-railed gallery to see him spin in a circle—much as Georges did in his wheelchair—before diving left through an archway.

Why did I not leave him to do his worst when I have an absolute horror, bordering on pathological terror, of mice, let alone rats? The immediate answer was that it would be reprehensible for me to allow a dog for which I now felt responsible to go hounding through the house. Lord Belfrey deserved better from me, as did his staff. A second truth was that much as I loathed the very idea of Whitey, I would have considered myself wicked beyond belief if I had not made the attempt to save him from imminent death. This would have been the case whether or not he was Mrs. Foot's beloved pet and, therefore, also important to Mr. Plunket and Boris. It was a matter of unwished-for principle and I was stuck with it.

"Thumper!" I bawled, on catching sight of his tail disappearing around yet another corner. "Stop this minute! Weren't you ever told to pick on animals your own size! Bad boy! Okay, good boy!" Plowing up a skinny, twisting staircase that had appeared to my right, I continued to rant between puffs, but to no avail, as he was now racing down another, particularly dusky passageway. Perhaps a change of tone would work better. "Thumper—or whatever your real name is—come! Come to Ellie, there's a dear! We'll go and look for some nice bones without life attached to them!" He turned so abruptly that I collided with a door left standing open. I could not have seen well enough to read his expression even had I not been grabbing my shin, but I sensed his hesitation . . . a dog torn between duty born of affection and the call of the wild according to Jack London. A vile squeak settled the matter. Thumper plunged through the doorway, with me staggering behind.

This passageway was wider and better lit due to a couple of windows. Ahead of us, Whitey was groveling at desperate speed along the skirting board, until the revolting tip of his hairless tail disappeared after the rest of him into a hole in the wall.

Thumper belly-flopped back to earth, to lie with his limbs at geometrically impossible angles. His pathetically defeated whine tugged at my susceptible heartstrings, but, eyeing my scraped shin, which would undoubtedly develop a bruise, I did not allow my voice to soften when telling him that he was a disgrace to whoever had brought him up. Ignoring his melting eyes, I added that I would be glad to see the back of him. This was not true, and to my instant regret he seemed to take me at my word, getting to his paws and trailing on down the passageway, head low, tail drooping. I was about to tell him that I hadn't meant it—that I would miss him and would have liked him for my dog, but for the fact I had a cat at home who would be strenuously against the idea—when he halted and in his immobility radiated a renewed vigor, alert and cheerfully alive. He turned to look back at me, stepped forward, and turned again; clearly he was urging me to follow him. A closed door faced us, which I opened, instantly recognizing (as he had already done) that we were back on familiar territory.

"Okay," I said. "All is forgiven. We'll pretend this was your objective all along and say no more of the matter." His palpable gratitude followed me into the bedroom that seemed likely to be mine for the week ahead. Today was Saturday; I stopped counting forward when Ben emerged from the cubbyhole where he should have slept in the previous night. Perhaps it was the distempered bareness of the small space that brought into such stark relief his dark, curly-haired, olive-skinned, blue-green-eyed good looks. Or was it that it seemed an age since I had last seen him?

His first words should have been that he had

missed me terribly, prior to launching into an apology for agreeing to stay on as Georges LeBois's chef without waiting to talk to me about it. But after the briefest of glances he turned his attention to Thumper, standing like a very short sentinel at my side.

"What's that?" Ben raised an elegantly shaped eyebrow, but for once I was not one hundred percent charmed. A *Hello, darling, I feared you were dead and my life forever blighted* would have been nice.

"It's a dog."

"I can see that." He moved farther into the room, returning Thumper's equally intent look of appraisal.

"He," I stressed the pronoun, "is a black Lab."

"That too is apparent. I meant why is he with you?"

"A woman alone in the world needs companionship." I sat down on the bed, peeling my shoes off suddenly tired feet. So far I'd had more exercise in the first hours of the morning than I often got in a week, and after only a couple of hours' sleep at that. "As you may observe, Thumper here is my devoted slave."

The dear dog gave an authoritative woof of agreement.

"Looks like it."

Had I been a character in a book—Wisteria Whitworth for instance—I would have gazed up at

Ben through a sweep of long, curling eyelashes. But unfortunately I am not overly blessed in the lash department. His are the kind to make any woman's heart beat in envy. "Thumper," I continued piteously, "has filled a void in my life since I awoke to find you gone. You might at least pretend to have been worried about me."

"I was worried . . . I was panicked." Demonstrating the truth of this, Ben sat down on the bed and drew me into his arms.

"Panic sounds good." I admitted. "But I need to feel it."

"Like this?" He kissed me deeply. Even knowing Thumper was watching could not spoil the moment.

"Very nice," I said.

"I was panicked all right." Ben smiled wryly. "I thought Lord Belfrey had abducted you."

"If you were seriously afraid of that, why did you leave me alone all night?" I waited for him to tell me about his cleanup of the muck-filled Mucklesfeld kitchen and his talk with Georges about staying on for the duration of *Here Comes the Bride*, but he kept to the topic of his lordship.

"You must have noticed, Ellie, that the man couldn't take his eyes off you."

"Only because I remind him of a portrait. A foolish fixation from the sound of it, seeing the subject is Eleanor Belfrey, second wife of his cousin and predecessor Giles, and a woman who sullied the illustrious family name by making off at dead of night with the jewel collection and Giles's beloved Scottie."

"I don't think you give yourself enough credit, Ellie."

"Rubbish!" I said. "Just because I snared you by a witch's spell cast on the night of the full moon does not mean that every handsome man who crosses my path falls victim to my fatal charm."

"The fellow *is* handsome, damn him."

"I'd say reasonably good-looking."

"Tall, too."

"Now stop that," I scolded. "I don't know why you have this hang-up about being of medium height. I wouldn't want to have to crane my neck when gazing starrily into your eyes." Ben kissed me again, but I wasn't entirely sure I had convinced him. And when he didn't bring up Georges LeBois, I told him about Thumper's arrival through the window, Livonia's subsequent appearance on the scene, and the unfolding of other events. It was when I got to the encounter with Georges in the kitchen that I paused and said: "Your turn."

Ben did not answer immediately because Thumper, who had been prowling the room presumably in search of hidden recording devices installed as per the great man's instructions, climbed onto the bed and spread out between us.

"Wouldn't seem to have heard the saying about

two being company, three a crowd." My husband, who along with the children had always been keen to have a dog if Tobias could be persuaded to give way on the issue, stroked a hand over the silken black head.

"No shifting from the point," I said. "What's this about your agreeing to stay on as Georges LeBois's chef?"

"I haven't agreed to anything."

"Lower your voice." I dropped mine down a couple of notches. "This room may be bugged."

"Why on earth . . . ?"

"We're on the set of a reality show, remember?" My alarm was only half feigned. "That man you've decided to work for has lots of nasty surprises in store for the contestants." Any one of whom might walk in here at any moment thinking herself safe from prying eyes and ears.

"Again, Ellie, I haven't made a decision about Georges LeBois. I told him you'd have to be for the idea and my guess was that you wouldn't want to delay a minute in getting out of here."

"That was you last night," I reminded him.

"At first because I felt embarrassed at barging in on strangers, and then," drawing his eyebrows together as he does when annoyed, "because I didn't appreciate Lord Belfrey scooping you up in his arms after you fainted and marching you into that living room as though it was his right to do so."

"A householder assuming that the blame was his, which was the case; it was his suit of armor, along with Mrs. Foot peering menacingly through the banisters, that scared me half to death."

"I admit he doesn't seem to be a bad fellow—not after talking to him for a while, although I can't imagine how any man could decide on the course he's taking. I'd let the ancestral house rot before selecting a bride from a group of total strangers."

"Perhaps it doesn't matter to him whom he marries if his heart is elsewhere, so long as it is someone he believes he can grow to like and respect. And it's not as though his wife wouldn't be getting what she wanted in return, whether it's the title, the house, or the grounds. Or that's how it should be—a practical arrangement between two people with their eyes open."

"Including Mrs. Malloy, Ellie?"

"She is my worry," I replied over Thumper's snores. "There'll be no squashing her romantic dreams. I'll need to be around to help her to pick up the pieces if she isn't the chosen bride."

"And if she is?" Ben reached across the furry divider to hold my hand.

"I'll be happy for her."

"You're sure?"

"Well, of course I'll miss having her around at Merlin's Court and I wouldn't want to take on any sleuthing without her should the opportunity arise. The children will take her absence hard, but we'll all have to handle the adjustment. However, any of that is at least a week ahead. Meanwhile, I'd be grateful if you'd stay on and prepare meals for Georges. Maybe he'll turn into someone nice once he's back to dining in style. It's not only Mrs. Malloy, although naturally she is primary, that I'd like to keep an eye on. There's Livonia to be saved from bolting back to the awful Harold, like Whitey scurrying into that rat hole."

"Don't tell me he escaped! I left the creature caged in a bolted room."

"Obviously someone let him out. My guess is Mr. Plunket or Boris; either of those two men would do anything for Mrs. Foot. It really is sad, Ben, all three of them were homeless at some point before they ended up here. I wish I didn't find them all so spooky. Forced to a choice, I'd rather spend half an hour with Georges than five minutes with one of them, which makes me a despicably unkind person. By the way, has he promised to pay you handsomely for your services?"

"Payment wasn't mentioned."

"Good." I squeezed his hand. "I would hate to be married to a man who can be bought by trifles. But what about the children? Will your parents mind staying on with them for another week?"

"They'll be knocked silly with delight. I phoned them last night to explain the delay and will give them another call, if you're sure about this."

"It works for both of us."

"You won't be bored hovering on the sidelines in the midst of all the activity?"

"I'll hole up here with a book from the local library. But first," it was surprisingly hard to say, "I have to try to find Thumper's owner and achieve a reunion."

Sensing my mood, Ben again stroked the black satin head. "Georges did promise to list me among the credits for *Here Comes the Bride.*"

"Did you get that in writing?"

"There'll be a typed contract complete with witnessed signatures."

"Get it before you boil him an egg."

"Ellie, I think the guy's to be trusted."

"Oh, ye of too much faith!" I tapped him on the knuckles. "What about the phony name and designating himself a Monsieur?"

"All right! He's from Tottenham, a dozen or so streets away from where I grew up. So he reinvented himself!"

"Hmm!" Hadn't I suspected as much?

"That doesn't necessarily make him a complete fraud."

"No," I agreed, while thinking how awful it would be for Lord Belfrey and the contestants if *Here Comes the Bride* turned out to be a complete sham. My elastic mind painted the scenario: Georges taking the opportunity to hole up at Mucklesfeld because the law was after him for a train robbery, multiple murders, or selling secrets to the Russians in return for a land deal in Siberia. I smiled at Ben, telling him that he had lucked into a marvelous opportunity. "Such great exposure! Your name rolling down television screens all over the country. Think of the increase in book sales for you, and the numbers that will come flocking to eat at Abigail's! How wonderfully providential that the fog brought us to Mucklesfeld on the eve of *Here Comes the Bride.* Speaking of which, where is Mrs. Malloy?"

The door opened, Thumper raised a sleepy head, and in she stalked, resplendent in purple taffeta and clearly in a bit of a mood.

"Well, I must say, Mrs. H, it's good of you to show up at last, although I'd have thought you'd have come along to my room as is two doors down and helped me pick my ensemble instead of sitting canoodling."

Getting to his feet, Ben said he would go downstairs and see if the provisions had arrived from Smithers, Smithers & Smithers, smiled at me, patted Mrs. Malloy on the shoulder, and went out of the room.

"We were not canoodling," I said mildly. "We were discussing our plans for staying on at Mucklesfeld. That's right," in response to elevated painted brows, "Ben is going to be Monsieur LeBois's personal chef for the duration and I'll be your shoulder to lean on if you run into trouble with any of the other contestants."

"Well, I must say," she did a good job of not looking overly relieved, "it won't be bad having you around. Although, of course, I don't suppose as we'll see much of each other what with a busy filming schedule. And don't go expecting me to share anything personal that goes on between me and his lordship."

"Certainly not." I got off the bed. "You can keep your canoodling moments to yourself. Now let me make sure you're up to snuff." I turned her around—a tottery business given her four-inch heels. "Good, no wrinkles."

"I should think not! Smooth as a baby's bottom, my face!"

"I was talking about the frock."

"Oh! Well, of course. So you think I'll do?" She crackled with nerves, something so unlike her that I had to fight down the urge to tell her to give up on this silly business. "Is me hair all right, Mrs. H? Not too much jewelry?"

The fake ruby necklace and three diamanté brooches *were* perhaps a bit much. "Perfect! You're a credit to me and the members of the Chitterton Fells Charwomen's Association."

"That reminds me!" She stuck a hand in her skirt pocket and drew out a folded piece of paper. "I daresay you'll like to go into the village when things start rolling and you get to feeling in the way of the cameras and whatnot. Meaning there's no reason you can't take this note down to Dr.

Rowley's house; he gave me the address and it's written down. Right here," tapping with a sparkly flamingo-pink nail. "And what I want you to do, Mrs. H, is . . ."

"Dr. Rowley is here—or he was when I came upstairs."

Mrs. Malloy sighed impatiently. "This isn't for him; it's for Mrs. Spuds, as comes in to clean for him of a morning, and a very nice woman too from the way he went on about her last night. I'm hoping she can give me the names of a couple of likely ladies to come up here and help me give some of the rooms a cleaning. Although why you couldn't have offered to pitch in and help, Mrs. H, is beyond me."

"I haven't seen you since last night when I was flat out with a headache!"

"Well, there is that," she gave her skirts a yank, "although like I've often said, your timing isn't the best. But we'll let that go; what do you think of my showing Lord Belfrey I'm the wife for him by rolling up me sleeves and . . ."

"Getting some women to come in and clean? Couldn't he have come up with that one himself?"

"Not if he's down to his last bean. I'm going to pay out of me own pocket. Besides, most like he hasn't wanted to put the noses of them three scary faces out of joint. Never heard of elbow grease, any of them, from the look of the place."

"Somehow I can't see Lord Belfrey succumbing

to pressure from whomever he marries to sack them. It turns out they were all homeless for a while." I eyed her now lopsided skirts.

"So you have talked to him?"

"Not since last night."

Mrs. Malloy heaved an annoyed sigh. "Well, that's nice! After me telling you as how he wanted a word with you about me being one of the contestants! Sometimes, Mrs. H, I can't make you out. Anyone would think you was trying to put spokes in the wheels of him marrying me."

"Don't take your jitters out on me." I grabbed at her elbow as she swayed dangerously on those silly high heels. "I'm sure Ben will have given him his blessing, there's no reason it had to come from my mouth. What you need to do," a glance at my watch, "is get downstairs and join the remaining contestants, who should be arriving in ten minutes."

"What do you mean, *remaining?*" She was always good at picking up nuances.

"Two, besides yourself, are already here." I steered her toward the door. "Judy Nunn and a rather pretty woman in her early forties named Livonia Mayberry. I want you to be particularly kind to Livonia, Mrs. Malloy."

"And why's that?"

"She's the sort who'll always need someone on her side."

"Well, let that be you, Mrs. H!" Outrage shot

sparks out the back of her head. "I've got to think of meself for a change."

Talk about a nose out of joint! The door banged behind her and I turned to return Thumper's speaking look. "*Here Comes the Bride* could turn ugly," I told him sadly. "I think you should leave Mucklesfeld before a murder takes place."

7

Some five minutes later, with Mrs. Malloy's note to Mrs. Spuds in my jacket pocket and Thumper at my heels, I descended to the hall by way of the front stairs because that was the way Thumper took me and I didn't want to argue. Especially when we must soon part. I hoped the timing would prevent my being caught up in a mob of activity with Georges LeBois and his crew milling feverishly around in readiness for Lord Belfrey's formal greeting of the contestants. As it was, the hall was empty save for Judy Nunn, still wearing the same brown twill slacks and the hiking jacket with its numerous buttoned-down outer pockets. She stood, dwarfed by most of the furnishings, writing in a notebook. Looking up at my approach, she closed it after tucking the pencil inside.

"Hello, there!" she said in her brisk, friendly way. "Five minutes to go before I have to be outside for the opening scene—'The Contestants Arrive.' As per instructions from a young woman named Lucy, your friend Mrs. Malloy, Livonia, and I are to join the other three in coming up the drive as if we too are just getting here."

"Have you met Mrs. Malloy?"

"We introduced ourselves. She and Livonia went with Lucy to do a practice walk. I was just jotting down some suggestions I have for Lord Belfrey in regard to the gardens and outlying grounds. I haven't yet managed to see him." A smile flitted across her face. "It took longer than needed to find his study because Livonia and I didn't open the door with the posted order to keep out, by authority of Georges LeBois."

"Oh?"

"When I finally realized that he might have sent us on a wild goose chase and decided to risk penalty of whatever the fiendish fellow had in mind, Lord Belfrey wasn't in the study. That was after I had lost Livonia down that passageway," pointing with the notebook—a sensibly sized brown leather one.

"I know," I said, negotiating my way further toward her with Thumper as my shadow. "I'd just come from the kitchen when she came back out here."

"Upset? Not inclined to think I'd ditched her on purpose, I hope?"

"For a moment perhaps, but she decided you

were too nice to join Georges in pulling not so funny tricks."

"Good!" Judy looked relieved. "Right after we divided up, I came to a door that instead of opening into a room took me outside."

"The one we came in?"

"Don't think so, although this place is such a warren. On the bright side, who should be coming my way from the wooded area with the broken wall but that sad-faced man Boris, so I waited to ask him about the study. And after he told me which room it was, I couldn't bring myself to rush off, not when he kept standing there like he had a knife stuck in his back. I'm sorry to say," she tucked the notebook into a chest pocket and her hands into the capacious side ones, "I forgot about Livonia and had a little chat with him."

"A chat?" My mind boggled.

"A rather confused one about begonias." Again the smile. "He thought they were people from the land of Begonia. He told me he had mixed with a lot of foreigners when he worked in circuses. I wanted to ask why he had left that world, but I remembered Livonia—too late as it turned out, and now if I don't want to goof up things some more, I suppose I'd better get outside. Nice getting to know you, Ellie." Hands removed from the pockets, right arm raised in a sideways salute, she sped away—shoulders forward, short fly-away beige hair matching the jacket.

There went stiff competition for Mrs. Malloy. If ever a woman had energy to spare, it was Judy Nunn. And energy would certainly be a key virtue in bringing the house and grounds back to life. I also had the feeling that Judy was kind, something to which I sensed strongly Lord Belfrey would respond and Mr. Plunket, Mrs. Foot, and Boris would need from whoever was to become mistress of Mucklesfeld.

These thoughts were nudged aside by what she had said about Boris. A circus worker! It went together with Mrs. Foot saying he had enjoyed seeing Whitey swinging from the frying pan handle like a trapeze artist. A politely inquiring woof from Thumper brought me back into focus. He was eyeing the front door hopefully. The word *walk* floated in a balloon over his head. But of course we couldn't exit that way. I could picture all too well Georges's fury if we blundered into what would have been a successful take, if that was the right word. It also wouldn't be fair to distract the contestants. I wondered if Mrs. Malloy had overcome her case of the jitters and how Livonia was holding up. Would it turn out that Georges LeBois had determined it would add an extra dollop of drama if the six contestants discovered on arrival that they were each a link in a chain of acquaintances, if not actual friends? It would be particularly interesting to learn the identity of the woman coming after Livonia. Meanwhile, I looked down at Thumper.

"Come on, we'll look for the exit Judy found down that passageway." It seemed like one of Georges's tricks to let him think we were off on a casual walk. Perhaps I flattered myself unduly in assuming Thumper would miss me terribly. Perhaps he showed no sign of being desperate to return to the bosom of his family because he was suffering from doggie amnesia. Perhaps he had an intense interest in home decorating and hoped I could teach him a thing or two on the subject. My gaze shifted away from his. Enough of this sentimental slosh! What must be had better be done fast or I'd have to go into mourning for a year and black is not my best color.

This decided, I strode in the impressive Judy Nunn manner for all of six steps, before stopping beside the huge jardinière displaying the dead plant. Next to it was the door that Georges had posted off-limits. The study. I made to move on, but stopped . . . seized by an impulse that had nothing to do with a desire to snoop or a wish to find a book. Mucklesfeld possessed a library. No, the shameful truth is I had that sudden, unbidden urge to defy authority. My late mother, lovely mercurial creature that she was, once told me with scarcely veiled pride that sometimes when she came up behind a policeman on duty she experienced an almost irresistible impulse to tip his helmet over his face. But in my case it was personal. Georges LeBois needed stamping on good and proper, to use a familiar phrase from Mrs. Malloy. Thinking of how I'd let her down that morning, in part because Georges had delayed me in the kitchen, I reached without a quiver of remorse for the door handle.

The thrill of wickedness faded the moment I stepped into the study. I had been confident of finding it empty. Certainly the last person I expected to see standing, head bent, his back to me, in front of a desk almost the width of the room was Lord Belfrey. He should have been at the top of the drive watching the women who would soon be vying for his hand make their way toward him. Shock switched the drive to a church aisle and his lordship into Henry VIII. So silly! His lordship wasn't aiming for six wives, just one out of that number. But then neither had Henry, whatever his faults, been greedy enough to want all at once. He'd had to go through a lot to find the happiness a king deserved. The memory jingle learned at school returned to me: *Divorced, beheaded, died, divorced, beheaded, outlived.* A nervous giggle tickled its way up my throat, but mercifully subsided when Lord Belfrey turned around to face me . . . us. Thumper was seated to attention, demonstrating that he at least had some manners.

"I'm sorry, your lordship, I should have knocked. But . . . that's neither here nor there; I've no business coming in."

His expression was serious, solemn even, until

slowly warming into a smile of such subtle masculine—make that virile—charm that it was impossible not to relax a little and smile back.

"Who's your friend?" He beckoned to Thumper, who went willingly, although at a sedate pace, to be stroked. The image came of Ben's hand on the dark head and I felt myself blushing, which was so silly. What woman on the better side of eighty wouldn't experience a small fluttery thrill when looking into the dark eyes under well-shaped black brows? The left eyebrow quirked and the smile deepened as he straightened up after a final pat. "You look guilty. Did you kidnap him, Mrs. Haskell?"

"Ellie, please."

"But not short for Eleanor." The smile faded slightly.

Instantly, the rosy cloudlike feeling vanished.

"Giselle." I was glad when Thumper returned to sit beside me, warm against my leg.

"I remember." He reached behind him for a pencil. "Your resemblance to her portrait is uncanny."

"It happens," I said at my most inane, then quickly. "Mrs. Malloy told me you wanted to speak to me about her becoming one of the contestants. We both thought it very gallant of you . . . but of course the decision is hers . . . and yours. And now I'll get out of here. I was sure you were outside and . . . again; I should never have come in here. You will be wishing me at the moon when you'll be anxious to be greeting your arriving . . . guests."

"Georges doesn't want me out on the drive for another half hour. Until then I'm not a contributing factor." The smile was there—wry, self-deprecating, and unable to conceal . . . what? Minor misgivings? Or a deep-rooted sorrow? "He wants to get some shots of the women meeting for the first time, sizing each other up, before bringing me on camera. Cold-blooded, wouldn't you say, Ellie?"

"Well," looking down at Thumper for moral support, "I suppose that's the nature of a reality show."

"Have you ever watched one?" He sounded as though my answer was important to him. But did he really want to know my thoughts for their own sake, or because the opinion he desired was that of Eleanor Belfrey? How well had he known her, if at all? Could any sensible man succumb to a portrait without having seen the original?

"No, but that doesn't mean that I think there's anything innately wrong with them. It's just that I," blundering on, "prefer fictional entertainment and had parents who," unable to keep from smiling, "thought reality highly overrated."

He raised a dark inquiring eyebrow, genuine amusement again hovering around his mouth. "That must have made for an interesting childhood."

"Rather magical in its way."

"Did it leave you still believing in fairy tales?"

"Perhaps." I stood there feeling as though the conversation was taking place underwater.

"And do any of us get to write our own happy endings, or are we all the powerless pawns of fate, Ellie?"

Hadn't Carson Grant posed the same question to Wisteria Whitworth? And hadn't she wondered, before succumbing to his demanding lips, whether something sinister lurked behind his willingness to lay bare his romantic soul? Fortunately, Lord Belfrey's motives were immaterial. He had no motive for wishing to either marry or murder me. We were overnight acquaintances. I had not stumbled upon a maleficent secret that he had striven ruthlessly through the years to conceal. Neither was I the possessor of a vast fortune that, if he could get his wicked hands on, would enable him to continue a life of depravity without the vulgar restrictions imposed by a lack of cash. What rubbish I was thinking! All blame to my parents' life view! His lordship had come up with a twenty-first-century scheme to settle his financial difficulties and I was a married woman. I pictured Ben slogging in this man's archaic kitchen and swam back up to the surface at a nudge on my left by Thumper.

"You're not leaving your life up to fate, Lord Belfrey." I concentrated on the hand twiddling the pencil. "Neither do most of us. I hope *Here Comes the Bride* will be a smashing success and you will be very happy with the woman of your choice."

"Even if that woman is Mrs. Malloy?"

"Of course."

"You will miss her."

"That doesn't enter into it. I really should be going."

"Wait just a moment. I do have to get outside but"—his eyes caught mine in their dark, compelling gaze—I admit to dragging my feet. "This wasn't an easy decision to reach and I'd like you to understand how I came to it."

I nodded mutely.

"Mucklesfeld is pretty much all I have to show for my life. I've had two failed marriages and a career that was unremarkable before the firm I worked for collapsed. Saving the ancestral home may not seem the noblest of ambitions, but it could be my last chance of doing something that will put a stamp on my life. I spent very little time here before going out to America, but it always had a pull for me. Something in the blood and bone perhaps."

"I can understand that." It was true. Merlin's Court had come down to me through the family. Thumper sat looking empathetic. "But is it worth . . . ?" I gestured awkwardly.

"Selling myself on a television show?"

"I wouldn't put it that way."

"No?"

"You'll be making a bargain." I was eager to escape the study. "I can see there could be benefits to both concerned, but it just seems a rather sad arrangement to me. Luckily, six women, including Mrs. Malloy, don't see it that way. But if you find yourself uncertain, why not at least postpone the filming? You've good reason surely after what happened to Suzanne Varney."

Lord Belfrey's expression darkened, as Carson Grant's had done on so many occasions when dealing with the sorrows of Wisteria Whitworth's incarceration at Perdition Hall. "I'd met her . . . years ago on a Caribbean cruise. We spent the better part of a week together, dining, dancing. I was between marriages at the time. And she was a very attractive, likable woman."

I stared at him.

"Let me show you, Ellie." He stepped sideways, beckoning me forward. Accompanied by the faithful Thumper, I joined him at the desk. Scattered across it were a series of eight-by-ten photos displaying the faces of women. His hand went to one in the middle. "This is Suzanne."

"As you say" (and so had Tommy) "she is . . . was . . . very attractive."

"The applicants were all instructed to submit a photo of this size. They went to Georges. I told him that I wasn't interested in seeing them, that I didn't wish to be influenced by looks one way or the other. The selections were up to him, based on the personality criteria we had agreed upon. When he arrived at Mucklesfeld, he took over this room. Yesterday afternoon I came in and saw these," waving a hand over the photos, "and recognized Suzanne despite not having thought of her in years. I told Georges at once."

"Was it specified on the application form that the contestants must have no prior acquaintance with you?"

"Yes."

"Perhaps Suzanne didn't connect you with the man she had met on the cruise."

The line of his mouth was bitter. "I wasn't traveling under an assumed name."

"But you weren't Lord Belfrey at the time." Looking at her face, I decided it was etched with sorrow and felt a reluctance to believe she had broken the rules intentionally. "What did Georges say?"

"That the situation could be put to dramatic use. Either on Suzanne's arrival or further down the road."

"The other contestants would have a right to be upset."

"Especially as Georges had made his selections based on an interlocking connection between them. Her death is going to come as a shock to the ones who knew her."

I thought of Livonia and Judy. "Does it have to come out now that you and Suzanne knew each other? Even Georges must see there's no point in setting that cat among the pigeons." I looked studiedly at my watch. "And now I really must get out of here. Thumper's owners must be getting dread-fully worried about him. I'll need to find some sort of lead . . ."

"Take this," he began unknotting his tie, and to my embarrassment I felt my face flush. Ridiculous to feel that something so ordinary implied an inti-macy between us. "Why don't you stop at Witch Haven, home of my late cousin Giles's daughter Celia, and inquire there about him, if you can get the door opened to you? I haven't been allowed in and neither has she come here since the day she demanded that I hand over Eleanor Belfrey's por-trait, saying Giles had given it to her because she admired the artist, if not the subject." He handed me the tie and I took it wordlessly. "If you do get inside Witch Haven, you might get to see the por-trait and discover whether or not I am exaggerating your resemblance to Eleanor."

"Am I right in thinking you didn't know her?"

"Giles was never welcoming of family visits." His lordship turned his back on the desk and the spread-out photos. "Nevertheless, I showed up in defiance of that attitude shortly after their mar-riage. When the butler grudgingly allowed me into the hall, she was going up the stairs wearing the dress in the portrait, ankle-length and of pale filmy gauze. She must have been sitting for the artist. Halfway up she turned and looked down before going on her way. I stayed until late evening, despite the frequent glares from Giles, and from

Celia, who was twenty-three at the time. A couple of years younger than myself. Despite Giles and I being first cousins he would have been fifty or fifty-one at the time. The ages stick in my mind. He was so damnably proud of having snared so young a bride." Lord Belfrey moved a hand around his shirt collar as if fingering for his tie, looked at what was in my hand, stared for a moment in puzzlement, and then said gently: "Go on, Ellie Haskell, make your getaway with the dog."

"As did Eleanor," I replied, "only *she* didn't come back."

"Thank God for that. Don't let my dislike of Celia put you off stopping at Witch Haven. She certainly isn't a woman to answer her own door."

"Did she marry?" Just being incurably nosy.

"Not to my knowledge. I think of her as devotedly wedded to herself; but don't picture her as a recluse. Tommy claims to get on well with her. She has plenty of help in the house, including an elderly handyman named Forester she doesn't deserve, and, so I've been told, a recently acquired paid companion. God help the woman!" He gave Thumper a farewell pat before holding the study door open for us.

I had to ask, "Are you over your cold feet?"

"Whoever she is, she won't be a vulnerable girl living in fear of her life while wishing she were dead. That was the look I saw on Eleanor's face when she looked down at me from the stairs."

The study door closed behind him. Thumper looked up at me expectantly and together we crossed the hall to the passageway that Judy had said led to an outside door. I did think about going to the kitchen and telling Ben that I would be gone for a while. But he was bound to be busy. I knew that I had to try to return Thumper, and also felt compelled to make myself scarce before the house became a hotbed of activity.

Once outside, I knotted the tie around Thumper's collar, but let it dangle loose. Time enough to take hold when we got out onto the road. But how to get there? I couldn't do so by way of the drive. Even to sidle down the wooded side would be an intrusion; I didn't flatter myself I was sufficiently slim to be easily hidden by the trees. Diminutive Judy with her muted coloring might have managed this feat, although I couldn't imagine her sidling anywhere. Practical, kindly Judy—or so I saw her on early acquaintance—what would she have thought of his lordship's recounting of seeing Eleanor Belfrey on the stairs?

Thumper was trotting a little ahead of me across the weed-ridden lawn as I searched for a path through the woods that might take me out onto the road sufficiently beyond the gates for me to head toward the village without drawing attention. Most particularly, I didn't want to be seen by Lord Belfrey. How awful if he thought I was checking to make sure he had stuck with his decision and was now greeting the contestants with the requisite amount of pleasure and pageantry.

I stopped and looked in the direction of the dell, with its broken fountain and misshapen tumbles of mossy stone. A silken breeze brushed my face and rippled questing fingers through my hair—loosening strands that I did not bother to tuck back in place. The sky was a pure, pale blue between the skeined fleece of the clouds. Thumper stopped to look back at me before apparently deciding that the only way to keep his doggie figure was by racing in ever-narrowing circles and cheering himself on by a series of congratulatory barks. I found myself wondering what the garden had looked like when Eleanor Belfrey was here. Had she liked flowers, reveled in birdsong, been happy during any of her time at Mucklesfeld? I pictured her coming up from the dell wearing the dress from the portrait; I saw the soft filmy material as the color of moonlight. I saw the look on her face described by his lordship. Had she hated the idea of returning to the house, hated and feared the husband old enough to be her father? I shivered despite my light jacket. A dreadful thought socked me in the chest.

What if Eleanor had suspected Giles was planning to murder her? What if she had never left Mucklesfeld on that fateful night . . . and her body concealed along with the maligned Scottie was somewhere in the house? Or buried in one of the wooded areas . . . perhaps even the ravine where

Suzanne Varney had met her death? The present faded, taking Thumper's joyful barks with it. The dreadful scenario continued to unfurl from the wrappings of shadow woven into a shroud thirty years before. Whatever Eleanor's reasons for marrying Giles, her feelings had turned to revulsion and loathing . . . the eyes that watched her every movement, followed her even when she was briefly alone, the grasping of her shrinking flesh. And he had known with bitterness and despair that she could never be his—except in death. It all fitted. The missing jewels buried with her to give credence to her flight. The dog killed first to prevent his barking. The sightings of her ghost, the house left to rot around him as Giles completed his descent into madness. But, rational thought (something my parents had vaguely despised as too close to reality) crept back. Who knew if the legend was the true story?

I turned to follow Thumper, who had now reached the woods and was looking back at me. The cornerstone of my wild flight of fancy was what Lord Belfrey had told me. And how much were his impressions to be relied upon? He was a young man at the time, not overly fond of his much older cousin, perhaps determinedly eager to condemn the marriage. To base so much on one glimpse of Eleanor, halfway up a staircase at that, had to be implausible. Wasn't it clear that his lordship was obsessed with her memory, and that he—

rather than Giles—had been driven mad by desire, in his case for an illusion that had transferred itself to a portrait and possibly to me? I wished I could talk my thoughts over with Mrs. Malloy, but that was out of the question at this time.

I caught up with Thumper as he was nosing around some nettles on the edge of the ravine. "Be careful," I warned, "you'll come out in blisters." He gave me a tender look, took a couple of steps toward me, then turned tail to plunge into the brush. A succession of barks indicated his wish that I follow him, but I had no desire to descend a treacherous slope, especially when the opening he had used was too narrow for me to get through without gashing myself or twisting an ankle.

Some barking, then silence. I stood waiting, rubbing my arms—the breeze had picked up and the clouds had thickened, making for fewer, smaller patches of blue. But was that what had made me shiver? I felt the prickling of the skin, the cold stealth of fingers down my spine that accompanies that sense of being watched from a hidden vantage point by someone . . . or something . . . exuding menace. Eleanor's ghost? But even if that were credible, why would she have it in for me? An answer formed. A ridiculous one. Lord Belfrey might have fallen in love at first sight, but to believe that Eleanor had been struck by the same bolt of lightning, dazzled by the same stardust, swept up in the same whirlwind of wonderment, was a stretch even for me. Then, if not Eleanor, who? Something shifted, a soft settling sound . . . a foot replacing itself after slipping? Why didn't I call out, requesting the watcher identify himself? Because common sense (not all that common in my case) said there was no one at Mucklesfeld who would wish me harm. It could be a trespassing fauna hunter or, even more likely, a rabbit or squirrel.

I heard Thumper coming back, and following the sound of his greeting I came to the wide gap in the wall, responsible presumably for last evening's tragedy. I had a brief, sharp glimpse of a broad track of flattened branches and brambles before he came lolloping along with a bunch of multicolored flowers in his mouth. *Oh, my goodness!* I thought, as he sat down in front of me with the look of proffering his heart along with the bouquet. They'd be the ones Tommy placed in remembrance! An irreverent part of me wanted to laugh. Nerves, of course. It suddenly occurred to me that I could be seen by those gathered on the drive, but when I looked around what I saw was a swarm of backs, the movement, including equipment, being toward the house. Evidently the arrival scene had been completed without a hitch.

"Naughty boy!" I scolded with less heat than required, because I hated to see the sorrow fill his eyes. "Take them back this minute." I didn't expect him to do as told. The thought of descending to the place where Suzanne had met her death, seeing the tree the car had hit, was not pleasant, but it would be unkind not to return the flowers, leaving them in a mangled heap for Tommy to come across. He had been nice to me, cured my headache; and with chubby schoolboy gallantry he had saved Livonia from the clutches of the Metal Knight. I hesitated. Again that intense feeling of being covertly watched. Thumper also hesitated, before turning and to my amazement wending his way back down into the ravine, to return brief moments later absent the flowers.

"Wonderful boy," I praised while bending to knot Lord Belfrey's tie, which I had forgotten I was holding around his collar, before setting off down the drive, there being no reason now not to use it to reach the road. We had just passed through the gates when I realized he still had something in his mouth. Inserting fingers and gently prying his teeth apart, I pulled out something flat, irregularly shaped, and about two inches in size. On closer inspection this proved to be a piece of broken-off plastic. "Very nice," I told a pleased Thumper. "I'll keep it as a souvenir of you." I'd do nothing of the sort, of course, but to have tossed it aside would have been hurtful to his feelings, even if my parents hadn't brought me up to believe that littering was a deadly sin, worse than any of the others, although they could never recall what they were.

Thumper took amicably to the tie as we proceeded down the road bounded on our near side by Mucklesfeld's wall and by more woods on the other. It was a good-sized road with a crossing a short way down, but very little traffic. We came to a Norman church surrounded by an iron-fenced cemetery. It reminded me of St. Anselm's, which Ben and I attend fairly frequently (meaning if we don't oversleep or decide that a leisurely breakfast in bed would be nice). We passed nobody during the five or so minutes it took us to reach the village. Grimkirk looked to be more pleasant than its name. There was the familiar juxtaposing of half-timbered Tudor buildings, with sharply peaked roofs and narrow latticed windows, converted into boutiques and bakeries, and the modern wide-glass-fronted shops, banks, and electrical appliance showrooms. All of which make up the usual English high street. After crossing at the only traffic light in sight, I stopped a middle-aged woman in a head scarf and winter coat. A mistake. She had that blind, bustling stare of the morning shopper who is adding sausages and that nice sharp Cheddar—and mustn't forget the vinegar—to her shopping list. Understandably startled, she asked me to repeat my question.

"You don't happen to recognize this dog?"

"What dog?"

"This one," pointing down.

"No." Remembering the pork pie to have on hand in the fridge, in case the son and his wife showed up unannounced like they often did at teatime. "Why?"

"He's a stray and I'm trying to return him."

A smile appeared. "Well, isn't that kind of you! Wish I could help you, dearie. Always been fond of animals, I have, but can't have a dog or a cat because our Ted's allergic. Why don't you ask at the sweetshop, two doors along? One of the girls that work there might know something to help you."

I took her advice, and feeling I couldn't leave Thumper outside, took him in with me. The woman behind the counter, with the rows of large, enticingly filled glass jars on the shelves behind her, hadn't been a girl in a very long time. But her ornately piled and puffed white hair, stuck through here and there with sparkly topped pins, the heavy makeup, and the exceedingly tight black top made clear that she was still vigorously fighting the battle against Time.

Had there been other customers, she might not have immediately noticed Thumper, sitting like an obedience champion.

"No dogs in here." She had a rasping voice that suggested she stirred gravel into her morning black coffee for the benefits.

Again I explained the situation without success. She didn't remember seeing the dog before. Nor had she been asked to post a Missing notice by the owners of a black Lab. She suggested I inquire at the estate agents on the opposite corner, who never seemed all that busy these days. I thanked her but decided against trooping from shop to shop and bothering passersby. I would take Lord Belfrey's advice and call at Witch Haven. Hadn't I been hoping it would come to that . . . the chance to meet Giles Belfrey's daughter, Celia? And if that didn't work out successfully, I might reap results when delivering Mrs. Malloy's note to Mrs. Spuds. Working for Tommy must have given her some insights into the lives of those who had inhabited Mucklesfeld.

When I asked directions to Witch Haven, the pained expression altered, but not more pleasantly so. Interest both sly and avid flickered in the narrow strips of eyes between the gummy black mascara.

"Miss Belfrey likes her privacy, so if it's just about the dog, you'd better be ready to have the door shut in your face. If it's something more personal . . ." She let the words drift.

"Lord Belfrey suggested I go there."

"Did he then? And how do you come to know his lordship?" Usually I don't mind curiosity, especially when it's my own, but hers was accompanied by a barely suppressed sneer tinged with glee, as if she were hoarding some delicious secret.

"I'm staying at Mucklesfeld."

"One of the contestants?" She pulled a tissue out of its box and wiped it across the top of the cash register, while the real activity remained in those eyes.

"My husband and I got stranded in the fog. If you could kindly tell me how to get to Witch Haven?"

Scrunching the tissue, she tossed it into a plastic bin behind the counter. "Arrive before or after the accident?"

"After."

"How's his lordship taking it, then?"

"My husband and I just met him."

"What sort of lot are they—the contestants, the ones that made it into Mucklesfeld alive?" She shrugged. "Can't blame us locals for being interested, especially me, seeing as . . . but that's for me to know and others to find out." There it flashed again—the look of being the holder of a gleeful secret. The door jangled, and a woman came in with a couple of small children who instantly dropped down to fuss over Thumper. The mother said: "Mustn't touch strange doggies." I assured her that this one was friendly, made the necessary inquiry, got the negative result; then asked her, turning my back on the woman behind the counter and all those wonderfully filled jars of old-fashioned sweets— humbugs, gobstoppers, aniseed balls—if she could direct me to Witch Haven.

Back out on the pavement, I told Thumper that there was always a bright side. "Had the guillotine not intervened, Marie Antoinette could have ended up looking like that Terror in there. And then who'd give a hoot whether or not she had said, *Let them eat cake.*" This naturally reminded me that I hadn't eaten breakfast, leading me into the bakery, where I purchased a Chelsea bun and a Bakewell tart with no objection to Thumper from the assistant.

Paper bag in hand, I continued down the high street, munching as I went. As instructed by the mum in the sweetshop, I turned at the jewelers, proceeded down a narrow road lined with narrow gray brick houses opening directly onto the pavement, their elderly appearance cheered in some cases by glowing white steps, geranium pots in the windows, and wicker trellises around the doors. Few people were about, and none showed any undue interest in Thumper. Halfway down, I crossed over to turn left at the next corner into a tree-shaded lane that looked as though it had never seen a car, let alone a bus.

Set back in a charming garden with a weeping willow leaning toward a brook was a whitewashed, green-roofed, comfortably sized cottage-style house. It had a welcoming look that made me wish it was Witch Haven, but the instructions had been to continue on until the lane broadened into an avenue. There were only two other houses in the lane, both thatched cottages and picture-postcard charming, but I did not linger to admire. The green shade provided by the canopied branches of two rows of trees drew me in and dappled Thumper's black fur with shadow as he trotted contentedly along beside me, the tie hanging loose in my hand. What a pleasant way to spend a morning. A woman and her dog taking a walk, neither thinking particularly deep thoughts, just enjoying the moment— peaceful in silent companionship. Far too abruptly, we came to the narrow, meandering drive leading up to the faded redbrick house with its ivy and latticed windows.

Here was Witch Haven. I expected to find it dark and drear, and so it might prove on the inside, but I was enchanted by the exterior. I could sense the history in which it was steeped . . . Cromwell's Roundheads pounding on the door on a rainy winter's night, the brave resistance from the Royalist household within. Then later, a Jacobite supporter, with a clear crush on Bonnie Prince Charming, hiding out in the priest hole. And on down time to Queen Anne telling the mistress of the house while paying an informal visit that she was pleased with the new style of furniture but feared it wouldn't last.

My mind thus occupied, I reached the end of the drive, from which flowed a velvet lawn made for idyllic afternoons of croquet and tea under what looked like Longfellow's "spreading chestnut tree." Up the short wide brick steps Thumper and I went to the dark oak, iron-studded front door. It did present a daunting appearance. But if it had opened to Cromwell's men (conveniently forgetting I had created that scene), why shouldn't it do so for us? Unable to find a bell, I lifted the saucer-sized iron knocker. It fell with a thud that sent half a dozen crows flapping madly from some lofty perch, darkening the air around them.

"Perhaps she isn't home," I said, and then the door opened to reveal a tallish woman of uncertain age wearing horn-rimmed glasses and bundled into a thick cardigan above a shapeless tweed skirt. A painfully pale face, faded hair twisted into a high bun, and clumpy lace-up shoes completed the image of a woman who spent her days hurrying back and forth performing a hundred and one uninteresting tasks at the behest of the lady of the house.

In little doubt I was looking at the recently hired secretary-companion Lord Belfrey had mentioned, I gave my name and explained my errand, including the fact that his lordship had suggested I try his cousin for information.

"I'm new to the area and don't go out much." Her voice was devoid of regional accent or personality. "My employer has the groceries delivered, does her banking herself, and therefore rarely sends me into the village. I don't think I've seen him before and I think I would remember. To some people all black Labs would look alike, but I'm a dog lover—being allowed to bring my Sealyham with me was one of the reasons I decided to come to Witch Haven, and that boy there does have a particularly lovable face." Even this was said without inflection.

After a momentary hesitation, during which I expected her to close the door, she beckoned me into a handsomely wainscotted hall with a beautiful Persian carpet picking up the tones of the warmly glowing red-tiled floor and the cobalt blue of the glass lantern overhead. Unlike Mucklesfeld, the ceiling here was low, but its arched timbers along with the graceful curve of the staircase drew the eye upward. I was aware of gilt-framed portraits of bewigged gentlemen and ladies in richly hewn satin gowns, a dark oak dower chest, and a painted black-and-gold chair in the Empire style with a fringed, dark blue velvet shawl tossed upon it to artistic effect. A silk fan with a tassel would have been too much; but I wondered if it had been tried.

"I'm Nora Burton, Celia Belfrey's assistant." The woman bent her head to look with a vestige of a smile down at Thumper and I noticed both the creping of her neck and the fine white tracing of a scar above and below the corner of her left eye. Or was that an age line brought into sharper relief than the rest by the overhead light under which she was directly standing? Perhaps sensing my glance, she ceased the flow of words to Thumper . . . that he looked a nice boy, a good dog, someone had to be waiting anxiously at home . . . and raised her eyes to mine. The dutiful employee was replaced by a flesh-and-blood woman. "I hate the thought of dogs running loose, ready to get run down by the next passing car, but they do get out despite watching, especially the bigger ones, I imagine. It wouldn't be fair to think nasty thoughts about the owner."

"No, I wouldn't do that." Callous person that I was, I preferred not to think about the owner at all. "And the search isn't a chore. Actually, I'm glad to get away from Mucklesfeld for a bit."

"Is it like a madhouse, with the television show?"

It was nice of her to show a polite interest, though perhaps anything was a break in the daily drudge. I was getting a good feeling from Celia Belfrey's house, possibly because likable people might have lived in it once upon a time, but I wasn't predisposed, from what Lord Belfrey had told me, to be equally charmed by the present owner—should I be granted the opportunity to meet her. On the other hand, was it entirely fair to assume that because Nora Burton was dowdy, she was also downtrodden? Or even that his lordship's view might not be slanted by Celia's removal of Eleanor's portrait on the grounds that it belonged to her? I dragged my mind back to what Nora Burton had asked about what was currently going on at Mucklesfeld.

"Things are just getting under way, but I expect the drama will increase rapidly. If it doesn't, Georges will have a major disappointment tantrum."

213

"Lord Belfrey?"

"No, the director."

"I'm new here," she reminded me, "and haven't met his lordship. Forester, the handyman here who was with Miss Belfrey's father for years, says his lordship rarely visited at Mucklesfeld as a boy or a young man."

"Miss Burton," came an irritable, well-carrying voice from a room down the hall with its door, I now noticed, ajar, "who are you talking to out there?"

"Excuse me." The dutiful employee slipped back into place behind the horn-rimmed glasses. "I'll explain to Miss Belfrey why you came." She departed without saying she would return, but I took that to be left hanging in the air; if I were to be evicted, Cousin Celia would not dilly-dally giving the order. Several slow-ticking minutes passed. I thought about the children with yearning. Thumper availed himself of the opportunity to sit down and scratch. A paunchy periwigged gentleman on the wall kept me in his sideways leer whichever way I moved. And if the door had not suddenly reopened, I might have decided that Celia Belfrey had died from an overdose of smelling salts on being told his lordship had sent me to spy on her.

"Miss Belfrey will see you and the dog," Nora Burton informed me in the neutral tones of the impeccably trained maidservant seen on old black and white movies—invariably named Mary or Ethel and too dimwitted to reveal to the mustached, laconic inspector from Scotland Yard what she had overheard when giving the drawing-room brass doorknob a good polish. Thus ensuring she would get herself strangled, to be found in the butler's pantry in an ungainly sprawl of thick stockings, with an adenoidal gape on her face.

"Thank you." I picked up the tie lead I had dropped on entering the house and drew Thumper to my side.

"If you will kindly follow me into Miss Belfrey's sitting room."

Nora stood aside as I entered, but remained in the doorway as I crossed parquet turned golden by the sunlight entering through the latticed windows despite the raindrops spattering the glass. It was a room as lovely as the hall, with the richness of red and cobalt blue accenting perfectly other time-muted shades. The furniture was an unerring mingling of exquisite antiques and some fine contemporary pieces, including two ivory linen sofas on either side of the Adam fireplace. The woman seated on the one with its back to the windows, face turned toward the door, bore a strong resemblance to Lord Belfrey, despite the fact that she could never have been a beauty even when young. The female version of his features and black eyes conveyed a hardness impervious to rose pink silk blouse and matching cashmere cardigan draped around the shoulders. The straight, midlength hair was too black for her middle-aged skin, although I found myself doubting that it was dyed, and the slash of red that comprised her mouth suggested a woman who would stop at nothing to get her own way. She did not shift position on the sofa, let alone rise to her feet. As she watched my approach, those eyes never dipping to take in Thumper, a slow, cruel smile curved that mouth into a scythe.

"Look your fill," her voice was low and throaty.

"I'm sorry . . . ?"

"At the portrait of my stepmother above the mantel." She raised a silk-sleeved arm, which fell back to reveal a ringless hand. "It's why he sent you, isn't it?"

8

If you'll forgive my saying so," Celia Belfrey continued with obvious indifference to whether I did or not, "but you're a pale copy of her. My father's second wife, previously Eleanor Lambert-Onger, was undoubtedly a beauty."

"Yes, she was." I rounded the piecrust coffee table for a closer look and admitted to myself the truth of what she had said. I could see the resemblance to myself in the upswept light brown hair . . . the shape of the eyes and the mouth; but even had I been painted wearing that softly drifting dream of a dress evocative of the turn of the twentieth century when creamy lace and organza made women look as though they belonged always in rose gardens, I didn't have that look . . . nor could I ever achieve it . . . of infinite femininity coupled with an elusive loveliness. "Lord Belfrey did mention the portrait," I said.

"And did he tell you I marched into Mucklesfeld and snatched it away from under his furious nose?" Enjoyment seethed through that husky voice. I was a stranger intruding into her home, making me the ideal object onto which to spew her venom. It would be like talking aloud to herself, only better. The thought curled up in my mind that Celia Belfrey's reclusiveness might not be entirely self-imposed. Had she over time lost the goodwill of the locals? Had old friendships dwindled away to the obligatory Christmas card; leaving only kindly Tommy Rowley willing to spend time with her? When I didn't answer, the black eyes flashed slyly. "Of course he told you. Being a fool, Aubrey would be incredibly taken with the resemblance, such as it is, and would grasp at any opportunity to talk to you about her. The fact that Eleanor made off with not only the family jewels but Father's dog, too, wouldn't cut any ice with him. The only time he came to Mucklesfeld during the less than a year of the marriage, it was laughably apparent that after getting one look at her going up the stairs he was lost. It was also clear that he saw something sinister in her not coming down to join us for tea or dinner—but I was glad not to have to see Father watching her as though he wouldn't be able to get enough if he kept her in bed all day. He'd bought her by agreeing to pay off her father's gambling debts, but having her wasn't enough for him—he wanted her love, would have done anything including groveling on the ground to get it."

Celia Belfrey's bile would have been ugly anywhere, but in that lovely room with the onset silvery rain on the windows and Thumper looking gently perplexed it was a violation. When I still remained silent, she turned her head sharply toward Nora Burton still standing in the doorway—looking taller within that framing than I had thought in the hall. It was the bulky cardigan and shapeless skirt that shortened her up close.

"Why are you hovering like that?"

"I wondered, Miss Belfrey," Nora Burton replied evenly, "if you might wish me to bring in a pot of tea. You usually ask for one around this time."

"And you thought our visitor might like one?" The black eyes shifted back to me, intent on discomfiting, although I suspected she wanted me to stay.

"No, thank you. If you can tell me whether you know this dog, I'll be on my way."

Celia Belfrey flicked dismissing fingers in the direction of the doorway. When the door closed, the eyes went to Thumper. "I'm not sure. I don't like dogs; that Scottie of Father's once nipped me quite badly. His cousin Tommy Rowley had to come round and give me some stitches, but my reasonable demand that the creature be put down was ignored, although Father sometimes said he could throttle the wretch when it wouldn't come when called or chewed on his shoes."

"Then I'll . . ."

"Not so fast," raising an imperious hand. "I've said I'm not sure if I've seen this dog before. Sit down," it was an order, "while I think. I abhor being rushed."

Reluctantly, I seated myself on the sofa facing the one she occupied. "Forester, the old man who works for me, mentioned that the vicar's wife, Mrs. Spendlow—word has it that she's an atheist—recently got a dog from Animal Rescue. That's *them,* isn't it, out to save the planet and every life-form on it? One would have thought a man of the cloth could have found a member of some other fringe group to marry. But I do believe that dog was a poodle mix."

"Then not Thumper here." I started to rise, to be waved back into place.

"I also remember hearing that Mr. Manning from Grange Cottage had a dog, and in his case I believe it was a black Lab." She had me hooked and knew it. "He died a couple of months ago. Crossed the road in front of a car and got hit."

"Oh, the poor dear!" I fought down the urge to cover Thumper's ears. Grimkirk being a small place, the deceased might have been a relative of his.

"Hardly cut down in his prime."

"Even so . . ."

"Well into his eighties."

"Oh!"

Celia Belfrey read my look and grimaced a smile. "You thought I meant the dog. What are you—a member of your own wacky bleeding hearts group? This excessive interest in a stray!" Her insolence froze me in place, as it must have done so many others that she no longer anticipated outrage and was left fully basking in her successes as a verbal slasher. As a girl she had perhaps heard herself described too often as spirited: *You should hear her—the things Celia Belfrey says, really too marvelously funny and clever! People just fall apart when she lets them have it.* "Speaking of Mr. Manning's fatal accident brings me back to Mrs. Spendlow and the spectacle Aubrey Belfrey has chosen to make of himself with this dreadful reality show. I'm referring, of course, to last night's car crash."

"What does Mrs. Spendlow have to do with that?"

"According to Tommy Rowley, who came rushing round to bring the news early this morning, the woman killed was named Suzanne Varning—"

"Varney."

Celia Belfrey shrugged. "What does it matter, she won't be using any name from now on. My point about Mrs. Spendlow is that yesterday afternoon, Nora mentioned that a woman had come to the door saying she had managed to get herself lost and asking for directions to the vicarage. She claimed to have made arrangements to spend a few hours with Mrs. Spendlow, an old friend whom she hadn't seen in years. I told Nora I hoped she'd had sufficient sense to ask the woman's name . . . she could have shown up hoping to get into Witch Haven and have a look around. As you can see, everything I have is valuable and women living alone can be easy prey. Yes, I have Forester, but he's getting doddery. Years ago he would have grabbed that and provided some protection." She indicated a longbow that I had not previously noticed—perhaps because it melded with the ambience of the room surprisingly well—hanging above a low bookcase.

"The woman was Suzanne Varney?" I experienced a pang of guilt for having wondered if her real reason for coming a day ahead of the other contestants had been to get a head start on the competition.

"So she told Nora, although one might suppose someone going on a television show in hopes of winning a husband might be inclined to use an assumed name. But tell me, how has my cousin Aubrey

221

responded to this spanner thrown in the works?"

Clearly everything else had been a prelude to this question. Those dark eyes and red lips were eager to absorb any description I could provide of Lord Belfrey dropping his handsome face into his hands when the realization sunk in that his scheme for saving Mucklesfeld might be doomed by the loss of a contestant. Tommy Rowley must not have provided enough succulent details, either out of loyalty to his lordship or because he was a man and typically incapable of bringing the scene to life: *Nasty shock for the old boy. Understandably upset. Cup of tea the best medicine under the circumstances. Any chance of my getting one now, Celia?*

"I'm a stranger," I said tightly, "and as such, not in his confidence. Do you know what became of Mr. Manning's dog?"

"I imagine it was put down. Who wants somebody else's pet, except of course for my stepmother when taking Father's Scottie for spite." A thin-smiled pause. "How is Aubrey's so-called household staff reacting to the excitement? Did you know he found those three zombies squatting at Mucklesfeld when he moved in?"

"They are clearly devoted to him."

"Don't be pettish." She sat further back on her sofa, settling in for the beans I would inevitably spill. "It's a wonder one of them hasn't murdered him in his bed for his wristwatch. As if one couldn't tell just from looking at them, the word is they all have unsavory pasts. But enough of Wart Face and the other duo. Is the ludicrously named *Here Comes the Bride* to continue with one fewer contestant, or is some other desperate woman to be roped in as a replacement?"

"I can't say."

The black eyes narrowed. "Are they all every bit as vulgar as might be anticipated?"

"I'm not up on vulgarity. As my parents used to say—better to leave that to the experts." Getting to my feet, I felt I had finally scored a point, but Celia Belfrey was focused solely on the longbow, which would I felt sure have come from Mucklesfeld, along with every piece of furniture worth grabbing with her greedy hands.

"Why don't you suggest to my cousin Aubrey," she said with husky relish, "that if he wants to instill some excitement into what promises to be a very dull television show, he should have the contestants engage in an archery contest. In my father and grandfather's time—perhaps even further back than that—one was held every year in commemoration of the legend that William Rufus went boar-hunting in the area with one of our Norman ancestors. If it would be helpful," she smoothed a hand down the knee of her skirt, before returning her eyes to mine, "I could send Forester to provide instructions. He taught me archery as a girl. And what an opportunity for these women to learn something new!"

Oh, my goodness! I thought. The vile woman is hoping one of the contestants will get shot. That there might even be a second death! She hates Lord Belfrey because he has Mucklesfeld—which even in its ruined state represents her place as daughter of the manor.

Suddenly, the loveliness of the room ebbed into dusk. The reasonable explanation was that the sun had moved behind the clouds, but I blamed the fading colors and the emergence of a dank odor on the evil flowing out of Celia Belfrey. I got out of the room with the speed of an arrow shot from that longbow, pulling Thumper along with me. Nora Burton stood at the foot of the stairs. I had the presence of mind to remember the note from Mrs. Malloy to Mrs. Spuds, and ask how to get to Tommy Rowley's house, before making a dash out the front door and down the steps.

It was still raining in halfhearted fashion, but Thumper did not seem bothered and the walk would be a short one. From Nora Burton's description, which even mentioned the weeping willow in the garden, it had to be the cottage-style house we had passed on our way to Witch Haven. I didn't want to think about Celia Belfrey until time veiled the memory of those eyes and that voice, and I could persuade myself that I had overreacted. Instead, I concentrated on wondering about the woman behind the horn-rimmed glasses. How could she bear to stay at Witch Haven? My mind nudged toward something she had said—obviously nothing striking or I would have remembered—something that niggled afterward around the edges of my mind. Something to do with Georges LeBois and Lord Belfrey . . . I almost had it. Then it was gone.

The overspreading boughs of the avenue shed green droplets that turned iridescent on the ground, shadows brindled Thumper's black fur, and again I determinedly shifted my thoughts to wondering about Suzanne Varney's friendship with the vicar's wife. Had the authorities sought information from Mrs. Spendlow? Livonia had said she knew Suzanne only as an acquaintance, but Judy Nunn might know about family members and others she had left behind. Perhaps as sad was the thought of no one sufficiently close to mourn her passing. It was the rain—making me think of tears. I forced myself to step out more briskly as I left the trees for the narrower lane, which soon brought Tommy's house into view, along with another thought about Suzanne's visit to Mrs. Spendlow.

Had she wanted to confide in an old friend—and one likely to know his lordship—that contrary to the rules for *Here Comes the Bride*, she had a prior acquaintance with him? Or was it more likely, as I hoped, that she had not connected the name Belfrey with a man met years before . . . at least not until she had seen a photo accompanying a newspaper story about the proposed reality show? If indeed Georges LeBois would have agreed to such a photo, rather than leaving the physical appearance of the bridegroom up to conjecture. A more important question was why was I becoming fixated with Suzanne Varney's personality when her motives and decisions were immaterial, given that she had been doomed never to enter Mucklesfeld as a contestant?

Thumper looked hopefully toward the brook splashing over its stones to a tune it was making up as it went along. Its banks were low and of rock-studded grass sprinkled with wildflowers. The garden with its spacious lawns and broad flowerbeds was having its final fling before moving into October and the approach of autumn. Then it would wear copper and bronze and smell of woodsmoke and cidery windfall apples.

"Sorry." I led Thumper past the brook and up the drive that was of similar length to the one at Witch Haven. He looked up at me, his eyes instantly sympathetic. Trust him to know that I was downhearted. Why, I didn't know. I wasn't worried that Mrs. Spuds would turn out to be another nasty female avid for bad news from Mucklesfeld. Indeed, I pictured her as a kindly, motherly woman who took pleasure in *doing* for nice Dr. Rowley, who like most general practitioners worked too hard, skipped more meals than he should, and was lucky to get two full nights' sleep in a row. Didn't she always tell him it was a privilege to worry over him until the right woman came along to take on that nice responsibility?

Her image was so clear in my mind that I started when the green front door opened and there she stood, exactly to order—the snowy white hair, cozy figure, and best of all the kind face. Even so, her first words plunged a stake through my heart. "My word! Who have you got there but old Mr. Manning's Archie!"

"Archie?"

"Mr. Manning named him after the Archbishop of Canterbury." Mrs. Spuds beckoned us inside. "He said that even as a puppy there was something uplifting in those dear brown eyes."

"There is." I could not look into them. Did he sense that the moment of parting was closing in? "I'm Ellie Haskell. My husband and I are staying at Mucklesfeld for the coming week."

"Bless you, love, I know who you are from Dr. Rowley's description. What a shame you were taken poorly like that! Feeling a lot better this morning, I hope? How did you come upon Archie?"

"He came in through my bedroom window."

Mrs. Spuds didn't seem to find anything particularly strange in this. Perhaps she thought I had been sleeping on the ground floor. "You've taken to him, I can see that. What needs explaining is that Mr. Manning died some months back and his daughter took Archie to live with her and the hubby like she promised her dad."

"I heard about Mr. Manning from Celia Belfrey when I went to Witch Haven at his lordship's suggestion, but she thought that"—my voice caught—"the dog had been put down."

"That would be her, always hoping for the worst. How that acid-tongued woman can be related to Dr. Rowley or Lord Belfrey—although I don't know him as well—beats me." Mrs. Spuds shook her head. "I'm amazed you got your foot in the door, love. No wonder you're looking in need of a sitdown. If you don't mind the kitchen, I'll make you a cup of tea, and afterwards, if you like, I'll phone Mr. Manning's daughter and let her know Archie's turned up."

"Won't she be terribly worried?" I followed her through an open door with Thumper—Archie—pressing closer than usual, and sat down on the chair Mrs. Spuds pulled back from the table. It had a yellow and white checked cloth and in the middle was a bottling jar filled with leafy twigs. Altogether the kitchen, with its wide modern window above the sink, cream Aga, and old-fashioned dresser with blue and white china, looked much more cheerful than I was feeling with that soft nose nudging my knee.

"I wouldn't think she'll be in a panic, love." Mrs. Spuds set the kettle on the stove and reached for the tea caddy. "She's a nice woman is Linda Dawkins, though ready enough to say she's not an animal lover. Which isn't a crime. What would please me would be for . . . Dr. Rowley to get himself a nice puss." She opened the fridge for the milk. "Both Linda and the hubby are Dr. Rowley's patients." I nodded before bending down to unknot Lord Belfrey's tie from around . . . Archie's collar, my fingers lingering in the black velvet fur.

Having placed a cup and saucer in front of me, Mrs. Spuds patted my shoulder. "I also know Linda from playing whist at the church hall when they need someone to fill in. I'm not one of those keen card players, like she is. Both goers, her and the hubby. Never ones for a night by the telly." She fetched her own tea and joined me at the table. "Home's where I like to be when I'm not working—although you can't call it work when it comes to doing for Dr. Rowley."

"He seems very nice."

"Kindness itself. Such a shame he's never married. Shy with women like my Frank was until we got together. And like he'd have said, God rest his soul, it's a good thing we're all different. He wouldn't have liked to hear me sounding critical of Linda Dawkins. I hope you didn't take it that's what I was doing."

"Not at all." I smiled at her. "You were filling in the picture."

"Celia Belfrey's another story, although I have tried to feel sorry for her. Imagine growing up and living out your youth at Mucklesfeld! To my mind it's a Chamber of Horrors," Mrs. Spuds stirred her tea, "which I've said to Dr. Rowley when I shouldn't, him almost certain to come into the place one day, unless he goes before Lord Belfrey. Is the tea how you like it? I didn't put in much milk," she moved a small pansy-painted jug my way, "add more if you like."

"It's just right, thank you."

"Do you have a dog of your own, love?"

I shook my head, while a voice inside me cried out that Archbishop Thumper was my dog.

"Understandable Linda finds it a bind having to get back from her outings to see to Archie, or that—not being used to having an animal—she sometimes forgets to keep the garden gate shut. Like she said to me when we met in the high street, the responsibility all falls to her during the day, and when the hubby gets home at night he's entitled not to be bothered. But there, she'll stick to the promise she made her dad."

"That's something." My heart sank and my hand went down to Archbishop Thumper's head.

"A finer old gentleman you'd never wish to meet than Mr. Manning. Feeling all right, love?" Her kindly face searched mine.

"Fine. I'm interested in Mr. Manning." How could I not be in the man who had raised such a wonderful dog?

"Terrible what happened." She watched me take a swallow, as I might have done when glad to see the children start downing their milk. "Crossing the road, he was, on his way to have a chat with Mrs. Jenkins from the house opposite, and mustn't have seen the car coming, although the driver told the police he was going slow, which a couple of witnesses agreed was true. Well below the speed limit, they said. Probably Mr. Manning had his mind on his Brussels sprouts. Devoted to his sprouts, was the old gentleman, used to get worked up about them coming out in brown speckles the way a mother worries when she thinks her child may get the illness with the rash that's going around. If only he'd looked right, left, and right again like we were taught in kindergarten. The one blessing, love, was that Archie was inside at the time."

"If only" . . . those had to be among the most agonizingly futile words in the English language. If only the exterior lights had been on when Suzanne Varney drove through the gates at Mucklesfeld. If only she had parked on the drive and sounded her horn. If only the phone hadn't been out and medical help could have been fetched more quickly. Dr. Rowley had said death would have been instantaneous, but could that be certain? Might he not have wished to provide some minimal comfort to Lord Belfrey?

"The poor doctor, who'd have his job? is what I used to say to Frank." She poured us both a second cup. "He was making a house call just a few doors down the afternoon the old gentleman got run down. Someone recognized his car and fetched him to the scene. Very upset he was when I saw him next." I guessed what was coming. "And now there's been this other terrible accident. That awful fog! I don't know when I've seen one so bad in a long time. But no need to tell you that, love, when you and your hubby and friend were out driving in it like the poor young woman, just a short time before."

"It was like driving through a mattress," I said.

"I was here when Lord Belfrey came to fetch the doctor. These last few years I haven't had Frank to hurry home to, so I'm more than pleased to stay on and put his dinner in the oven. The mercy was that he'd just got back from going on a walk."

"In the fog?"

My startled exclamation roused Archbishop Thumper to place his head on my knee as if to save me from bouncing up in the air. Mrs. Spuds's periwinkle blue eyes twinkled. "Wonderful as he is, Dr. Rowley has his odd ways. Same as most men, including my Frank—for him it was going on peculiar diets, like the time all he would eat was butter beans with vinegar. For years the doctor's kept a skeleton from his medical student days in the hall wardrobe. When he comes in, I'll be asking him where it's gone because it wasn't there this morning. The fog wasn't so bad when he set off—saying he was stiff from sitting in the surgery late into the afternoon and a walk would help

232

loosen his back—but between you and me, love, it had seemed to me he'd been a little down in the dumps all week."

"Might that have had something to do with the start of filming *Here Comes the Bride*?"

"You mean that he might not have approved? I wouldn't think so, love. What goes on at Mucklesfeld has never seemed to interest him overmuch. There was a rift, you see, between his father and grandfather that led to the change of name to Rowley, and the doctor was brought up not expecting any closeness with the Belfreys. His late lordship treated him strictly as the local GP. As for Celia Belfrey, I've always thought the only reason she's accepted him halfways as a relation is he's the only person willing to spend half an hour in her company. His mother—that wasn't considered good enough to marry into the family—was the same wonderfully kind sort. A lovely home she made here," Mrs. Spuds looked around the kitchen, "and bless him, Dr. Rowley has kept things just like she had them. And now," she got to her feet, "why don't you stay resting yourself while I go into the sitting room and give Linda Dawkins a ring?" She hesitated in the doorway when Archbishop Thumper gave a low whine before putting his head down on his paws. "Just listen to him; anyone would think he's not keen to go home."

"Will she really want him back?"

"Not want, love, but there's that promise to her father, and Linda's the sort who'd worry she'd go to hell if she broke it. A shame," the blue eyes took in every inch of my face, "that he can't be with someone who'd love him as much as Mr. Manning did. And him such a young dog—not more than two, I'd say. But sadly, life's what it is, as my Frank used to say."

Mrs. Spuds disappeared and, with the kitchen door left ajar I soon heard her voice, although not what she was saying, speaking in interrupted intervals. Meanwhile, I sat with hands clenched in my lap. I must not allow Archbishop Thumper or myself to hope. For what? That Mr. Manning had contacted Mrs. Dawkins from beyond the grave to tell her he was releasing her from her promise, and that she should let the nice woman who'd found his beloved dog seek a loving home for him, if keeping him herself was out of the question. Which of course it was. Hadn't I for years told Ben and the children that bringing in another animal wouldn't be fair to Tobias, who was used to being a pampered *only* pet? That the time for a dog would be when he went to cat heaven? Besides . . . what to do with my new friend in the meantime? It would be too much of an imposition to take him back to Mucklesfeld, although I was sure Lord Belfrey would be nice about it—if only because I was the one asking the favor. No, I must bite the bullet.

When Mrs. Spuds came back into the kitchen, I turned to look up at her. "Were you able to reach Mrs. Dawkins?" My voice stayed steady even when I felt the soft furry face shift to my foot.

"Caught her just as she was about to leave for the hairdresser. Like I thought, she hadn't worked herself into a state about Archie, but said she'd be around to fetch him after her appointment if I didn't mind keeping him for another hour. Which of course I don't, love."

"Thank you."

"No trouble, is he? Now," avoiding looking directly at me, "how about you staying for a bite of lunch?" Her eyes went to the wall clock. "It's close on noon and I always get something ready before half past in case the doctor decides to come in between morning surgery and his afternoon rounds. Most often he doesn't, being pressed for time, his patients do like to keep him chatting, so I always do something that can be saved for his tea. Just before you arrived, I'd decided on making salmon and cucumber sandwiches. It's red salmon. I don't mind the pink myself, but as I used to say to Frank, you can't expect a doctor to eat pink salmon. Especially one that works as hard as my Dr. Rowley."

"That's awfully kind of you, but I should get going." Moving would necessitate dislodging Archbishop Thumper's face from my foot. While I was bracing myself, I remembered my reason for coming here. Putting my hand in my pocket, I felt the piece of plastic that had been in his mouth when coming up from the ravine after replacing the bouquet. My hand felt for his silken head. Then I drew out Mrs. Malloy's note, got to my feet, and handed it to Mrs. Spuds.

"One of the contestants asked me to give this to you." I didn't add that she was a friend of mine, so as not to put pressure on Mrs. Spuds. She unfolded and read it. When she looked up, I saw the uncertainty on her face.

"I don't know, love. Even if this lady is paying, I wouldn't feel it right to speak to any of the ladies I know about giving a hand at Mucklesfeld without first talking to Lord Belfrey. And I'm not sure I want to put myself in the middle like that. He and Dr. Rowley have begun to establish a nice relationship—working toward becoming friends after all these years of not having contact, let alone seeing each other. No, love, I think I'd best stay out of things. Would you mind telling that to the lady?"

"Of course not," I said, sensing there was something held back.

Mrs. Spuds pressed a hand to her snowy white hair. "There's the three people now working for his lordship; I gather he's fond . . . protective of them. Could be he'd worry that bringing in extra help might put their noses out of joint."

Silently I agreed with her on this, but still felt there was more going on. "What about the staff employed by Lord Giles Belfrey? Are they still in the area?"

Now we were getting to the root of the matter. "Bless you, love, there wasn't anyone for near on thirty years, excepting old Forester. He didn't go to Miss Belfrey at Witch Haven until after her father died. The rest—butler, housekeeper, and maids— were all got rid of right after Lord Giles's young wife left him. It was like he went mad with grief. Those that went to Mucklesfeld hoping to help— friends and acquaintances along with the vicar, not Mr. Spendlow but the one before—were met at the door by a disheveled, sunken-faced man they had trouble believing was the one they had known. Like you can imagine, love, the nightmare stories grew and Mucklesfeld became a place to be avoided as quickly as possible, even in daylight. Miss Belfrey stayed on for several years before, so she told Dr. Rowley, deciding that if she didn't move to Witch Haven, she'd end up as crazy as her father."

"She struck me as unpleasantly sane."

Mrs. Spuds smiled faintly. "Apart from her obsession with shoes. Apparently she has stacks and stacks still in their boxes, never worn— enough to fill an entire closet to the ceiling. But then I suppose a lot of women are nutty about shoes." She paused. "There, love, I didn't like to tell you how people around here think of Mucklesfeld—not with you staying as a guest of his lordship—but sometimes beating around the bush can make the point you're trying to avoid. And Dr. Rowley says he's never felt any evil vibrations or what have you, and if ever there's a man of sense, he's it. Like he says, it's not as though Lord Giles murdered his young wife."

"But is that the local theory?"

"That's people for you—a young wife vanishes overnight. It makes a better story than her getting fed up and bunking off."

"Did you know her?" I gave Archbishop Thumper a firmly final pat and moved toward the doorway.

"Only from seeing her at church or in the high street. I could never make out if she was stand-offish or deeply unhappy."

There was no doubt about the whine that accompanied us along with the patter of paws into the hall. My farewell to Mrs. Spuds was speedier than politeness required, but she clearly understood, saying she would close the front door as soon as I was outside to prevent an attempt to follow me.

It had stopped raining; but instead of thinking kind thoughts of Mother Nature, I took exception to the happy blue of the sky. Dear, dear Archbishop . . . no, just Thumper. That's who he would always be to me when I looked back to our hours together. Love had been ours for one brief, shimmering moment in time. It had happened: to his lordship at the moment of looking into Eleanor Belfrey's eyes as she turned to face him on the staircase at Mucklesfeld . . . to all those others down through the ages whose souls had communicated in a moment of instant recognition more clearly than the spoken word. Our bond took nothing away from what Thumper had shared with Mr. Manning. Not having witnessed the accident that took his master's life, Thumper must have continued to expect his return. This explained his making off whenever Mr. or Mrs. Dawkins left the garden gate open. Searching, forever searching, until he came through my bedroom window and the truth revealed itself: that Mr. Manning was gone, never to return except in hallowed memory, and now was the time to live again.

The poignant leaning of the weeping willow brought tears to my eyes. Stop it! I brushed them away sternly. Cease this ridiculous wallowing! Thumper is a dog. A very nice one—affectionate, sweet-natured, but unlikely to remember me except as a pleasant sniff or two if we crossed paths in a fortnight. Which wouldn't happen anyway because within the week I would be back at Merlin's Court with all who mattered most, Ben and the children and Tobias on my lap. I resolutely ignored the possible absence of Mrs. Malloy. That too—of far greater significance than a black Lab— must be borne if necessary.

I trod purposely on through the high street. When coming up the drive at Mucklesfeld, I saw Lord

Belfrey and Judy Nunn standing in front of the broken wall. She appeared particularly diminutive next to his tall figure, but it was clear from her feet-apart stance and energetic gesturing that she was in no way intimidated by him. I saw him nod as if in agreement. To walk behind them to reach one of the back doors into the house seemed inappropriate, particularly when I noticed a long-haired cameraman who on shifting position looked to be the girl named Lucy. It would have to be the front door, I decided.

This meant ringing the bell, sending a rumble of thunder down my spine if not throughout the entire interior. Fortunately, for me if not for him, Mr. Plunket must have been standing with nothing to do within inches of the door. He opened it as if expecting the black-hooded Grim Reaper complete with scythe and logbook . . . sorry, no death quips after yesterday evening. Stepping aside to allow me to creep around him, he wished me a good afternoon as if announcing that there had been an official statement from Buckingham Palace that the world was to end in twenty minutes, and all who were able should immediately vacate the planet or face a heavy fine. I parted the shadows with my hands and smiled at him through my own sorrow.

"Hello, Mr. Plunket. I see you escaped from the pantry."

"Pantry?" That could have been him or the mournful echo of my own voice.

"Or whatever cubicle you and Mrs. Foot disappeared into when Monsieur LeBois ordered you out of the kitchen this morning." I pictured a dark space where tuftless brooms and rank-smelling mops were sent to die. Oh, bother! I was doing it again!

"The artistic temperament. I'm sure he means to be nice."

I stared at Mr. Plunket and thought: Here is a man who can make allowances for the foibles of others when surely he must know that some— meaning Georges LeBois—spoke of him as Wart Face and others (including myself) harbored equally unkind thoughts. Never again, I vowed, would I notice anything except his devotion to Lord Belfrey, Mrs. Foot, and Boris.

"How did the rest of the morning go?" I asked him.

"Very exciting." No gleam of enthusiasm accompanied this response. "His nibs met with all the contestants as a group and afterwards with each in turn. Them camera people kept coming from every which way with their equipment, giving orders like they're the ones owning the place. It's a wonder his nibs isn't worn to the bone, but he made sure to pass the time of day when he saw me crawling one of the upstairs passageways calling for Whitey. It turns out he'd escaped from his cage—not his nibs, I don't mean."

"I understand."

"Poor little Whitey! Mrs. Foot and Boris has both been frantic. She broke down in tears after your husband asked for a torch to check something inside the cooker, and the one that's always wedged under a corner of the sink cupboard to keep it straight wasn't there. Must have got knocked out and rolled somewhere. Boris and me both knew what was really getting to her. Whitey's like the child she never had." Mr. Plunket wiped an eye. "But then she remembered a hole in the wall in that upper passageway and thought perhaps he'd hidden out in there. I thought I heard a squeaking, but it could've been wishful thinking."

"He'll show up." I spoke with awful certainty.

Mr. Plunket's eyes widened. "Are you one of those, Mrs. Halibut . . . ?"

"Haskell."

He nodded. "One of those with psychotic tendencies?"

It took a second for the penny to drop, at which point I saw no harm in giving him the response he wanted without lying. "I don't claim to be psychic, but I do have feelings." The air around us hummed portentously. "My husband calls me a sensitive." True. Ben said something to this effect every time I presented him with his missing watch or reading glasses.

"Then you think Whitey is all right?" Mr. Plunket's voice throbbed with hope.

"I'm certain," I closed my mind to the thought,

"that in the very near future he will make a grand reentrance. Speaking of my husband . . ."

Mr. Plunket displayed a clairvoyance of his own by finishing my sentence: ". . . he was in the kitchen less than five minutes ago serving Monsieur LeBois his lunch. Tadpoles in some savory sauce, I think it was. Perhaps, if you won't mind me saying so," he stared through me, "it's the house."

"What is?" I was struggling to think what Ben could possibly have cooked. It would serve Georges right if it really was something scooped out of an algae-covered pond with a net. Let him stick that in his bouche. Sometimes nastiness is good for the soul, especially when one's heart is aching for a black Lab.

"Sending you messages about Whitey. And who knows what else." Suddenly, a shadow overlaid the enthusiasm, succeeded by a look of dread.

"Oh, I wouldn't think there'll be anything more! One premonition a day . . . a week . . . a month is the most I, a rank amateur, can produce." I hated to leave him standing there, but my powers were sufficient for me to realize he wanted me gone, preferably from the face of the earth. So I headed for the kitchen.

Did he fear that those supposed powers would produce a meeting between myself and a visitor from beyond the grave? One who would impart information amidst much moaning and shimmering of vapors that Giles Belfrey had murdered his young wife, and then lead me to where Eleanor's remains had been concealed all these years. His concern of course would be for Lord Belfrey. Perhaps he was unaware that these days it is not considered politically correct to judge people by their relatives. And a good thing, too, considering most of us have ones that would make the devil blush. But his lordship was a stranger to each of his prospective brides, and perhaps only a woman madly in love could be expected not to wonder if there might be a family tendency to do away with wives who forgot to say please when asking to have the butter passed.

I had not expected to be thrilled at the sight of Georges LeBois. But seeing him pulled up in his wheelchair to the kitchen table countered the ache I was feeling. He had a giant-sized serviette (possibly a tea towel) tucked into the neck of his waistcoat, while he chomped down on what I hoped were not tadpoles—however wondrous the savory sauce.

"So you're back," not bothering to look up. "Find the owners of that dog you had stitched to your leg?"

"I did. What are you devouring?"

"Baby frog legs in a Champagne reduction. Care to join me in a spoonful?" He flourished a paw, indicating any of the available chairs.

"I'd rather die in the clutches of the Metal Knight." Seating myself across from him, I watched him close his eyes in ecstasy. "Apparently you are satisfied with my husband's services as temporary personal chef."

"*Ma chèr enfante*, I would marry him had you not beaten me to punch." He raised his lids to survey me sorrowfully. "And do you, naive creature that you appear to be, appreciate his gift to the world? Do you worship at his sautéing pan? Do you so much as know the difference between a flan and a crème caramel?"

I ignored this. "Where is my husband? I hope you haven't got him locked up in a cellar until he promises never to leave you."

"Gone to search his lordship's desk. He needs to check some malfunction inside the cooker and I remembered seeing a red torch in one of the drawers. As a boy I longed for a pair of bicycle clips, a paper punch, and a red torch. Those ambitions, simple as they may sound, shaped my life— drove me to succeed. I do hope our mutual friend won't be long." Georges set aside his empty plate with one last, lingering look. "I am aquiver with anticipation to know what he has planned for dessert. A white chocolate mousse Grand Marnier would do very well, although my hopes are set on an old-fashioned bread and butter pudding, with lots of raisins and a thick hot custard on top."

Either would have suited me down to the ground, but I hardened my heart against any prospect of emotional bonding with the awful man. "What of the peasants?" I asked.

He removed the napkin from his neck and dabbed his lips. "Who?"

"The contestants. Do they get to scuffle around the scraps from your table or have they been assigned kitchen time to prepare their own meals?"

"Your husband has a fault—an affinity for the common man, or in this case woman. He discussed the matter with his lordship and it has been agreed that for today at least he will also prepare their meals. All six will shortly gather in the dining room for a simple—though assuredly delectable— luncheon of soup, salad, and I believe blackberry and apple pie."

Feeling starved to death, I reached for the bread plate and lavished a slice with butter. "How did this morning's filming go?"

"Reasonably well. Lord Belfrey did all that was required, looking handsome and making a graceful welcoming speech. Among the women, Judy Nunn responds the most naturally to the camera. Livonia Mayberry isn't as stiffly timid as I thought she'd be and of course your friend Mrs. Malloy is the consummate scenehogger."

"Good for her," I responded stoutly. "Who else?"

Georges gusted a sigh. "There is a Mrs. Wanda Smiley, who unfortunately smiles too much and is altogether full of herself; an Alice Jones equally enchanted with her post-hippie self; and a Molly Duggan who doesn't have a self. I have yet to pull the takes up on-screen in the inner room off his lordship's study. You're about to say you didn't notice any such door when you went in against written instructions. Oh, fear not! No one informed against you. I know a born snooper when I see one." He smiled smugly and I started to munch. "There's a sliding panel behind the desk. Mucklesfeld boasts several such cunning devices."

"Oh, Monsieur LeBois," I pressed a hand to my throat, "pray do not fail to make use of them!"

The bird eyes twinkled nastily above the Roman nose. "Trust me to do my worst, dear lady. Do come to the inner sanctum, only when I am there, of course, and take a look at what we have before the editing."

"That's a lovely invitation, but I've been thinking I may go home and return for Ben . . . and possibly Mrs. Malloy . . . at the end of *Here Comes the Bride*. After all, there is nothing for me to do here." Before I could make a fool of myself by explaining that it would surely be easier to recover from the loss of Thumper away from Mucklesfeld, Georges pounced as if I were a baby frog leg materializing on the empty plate.

"Leave? My dear, you must do nothing of the sort. I'm sure your husband depends on you to fire his culinary genius, and if such obligations do not move you, I require your presence."

"Why?"

"To keep your friend Mrs. Malloy from disrupting the cordial relationship that seems presently to exist between the other five contestants. That woman is a cat amongst the pigeons if ever I saw one. It is clear she has taken a dislike to Judy Nunn and Livonia Mayberry and is itching to set the feathers of the other three flying."

I reached for a second slice of bread. "She's bound to feel a bit of an outsider, not being a link in your human chain."

Georges smirked. "The possibility of sparks ignited from an interconnection between the contestants has irresistible appeal. I flatter myself I have set matters up very nicely, but ideas spring eternal. And my most recent one involves you."

"Me?"

"No need to gape. You're a nice-looking young woman, but even a beauty with a capital B does not come off well with goggle eyes and a dropped chin. All I require of you is your presence at some of the sessions in which the contestants get together outside the presence of Lord Belfrey. I realized this morning when recording their stilted gibbering that an outsider was needed to nudge the conversation along and keep it from straying too far off course. I only have so much patience when it comes to weeding out the fluff."

"And how explain my role?"

"You are an interior designer, intent on exploring each of the contestants' plans to reinvigorate Mucklesfeld. Come, come, Mrs. Haskell, perceive the possibilities of extending your client base. You, along with your husband, will be listed amongst the credits." Georges eyed me narrowly. "Tell me, do you still want to leave?"

I told him I'd have to think about it, but I knew I'd cave. Leaving Mucklesfeld without watching *Here Comes the Bride* unfold would be the equivalent of abandoning the drawing room at Merlin's Court to its own devices in the middle of spring cleaning.

"Your first assignment will be afternoon tea at three today in the library." He pressed on as I remained silent. "Your husband has promised a fine spread."

Unfair! my heart cried out. I was ever a slave to cucumber sandwiches with the crusts removed, munchable scones, wafer-thin biscuits, and delectable little cakes, to say nothing of several fragrant cups of Earl Grey.

"Oh, all right, you win," I was saying when Ben walked in to inform Georges that he hadn't found the torch, while giving me a look that seemed just a little frosty.

9

I lay on my narrow bed in the room that had once been part of the servants' quarters, feeling tragically akin to a Victorian parlormaid who had allowed herself to dream of finding favor with the master, only to have him turn curt and dismissive.

"I understand you were anxious to locate the dog's owners," Ben had said, when we left the kitchen for the hall, "but couldn't you have spared a moment to let me know you were taking off and how long you were likely to be gone? I didn't much appreciate learning from Lord Belfrey that he knew more about your plans than I did." Before I could tell him he was being petty, he made an unarguable point. "How could I not worry after your being so under the weather last night?"

I apologized but reminded him I had told him before saying anything to Lord Belfrey that I intended to try to find Thumper's owners.

"So you did, but I assumed you'd wait at least until you'd had breakfast. Rushing off without so much as a slice of toast was asking for trouble, although," Ben's mouth tightened and his brows came down in a bar over eyes that flashed all green—no blue—"his lordship seemed to find your rescuing spirit absolutely enchanting."

The flat pillow did nothing to soften the memory of those words, let alone to cushion my head, but I closed my eyes against the strands of sunshine entering through the high window. If my headache returned, whose fault would that be? Not Lord Belfrey's. I had sometimes wondered how I would feel if Ben were ever jealous. There had never been any reason . . . and there wasn't now. I thought Lord Belfrey remarkably handsome; I might even go so far as to say rivetingly attractive; but that didn't mean I longed to be swept into his arms and kissed with the passion of Mr. Rochester for Jane Eyre. Really, I felt resentment stir; Ben might have put more focus on my sadness at parting from Thumper. When I had mentioned my reservations about his return to the Dawkinses, Ben had said absolutely the wrong thing. Because it was the truth.

"It says quite a lot about the couple that they are keeping their promise to her father when they aren't dog people. Something you can understand, Ellie. You've never wanted one."

"Only because bringing another animal into the house would upset Tobias."

"And that's more important than the children wanting a dog?"

There had seemed no point in saying I'd promised them one when . . . the right time came. And I now reminded myself that Ben was understandably irritable, with the cooker not working properly, along with having to contend with diva Georges's gourmand requirements and produce a luncheon for the contestants, presumably a solitary meal for Lord Belfrey, and yet another feed for the film crew. No problem at all at Abigail's or even Merlin's Court, but the kitchen at Mucklesfeld was lacking in what would have been considered rudimentary equipment two centuries back.

We had parted with Ben urging me to get some rest and promising to send something up to me on a tray.

"Just a sandwich and a cup of tea or coffee," I'd said, knowing he'd provide much better. But not baby frog legs; he'd never do that to me, even had he caught me in a state of déshabille in Lord Belfrey's bedroom.

The door creaked, and I opened my eyes hoping to see Ben abject with remorse at having been testy with me. But it was Mrs. Malloy who tottered in on her high heels to the accompaniment of a dark taffeta rustle, rouge heightened by exertion, a filled tray clasped in her ringed hands, and the sparkle of her iridescent eye shadow not showing up anywhere else on her face.

It was clear she was in a mood even before she set the tray down with a thump on the foot of the bed. The effect of the crisp salad, eggs mayonnaise, open-faced prawn sandwich, and lemon tartlet was offset by the tea slopped in the saucer and her folded arms.

"Thank you." I sat up cautiously. If my voice sounded flat, it was nothing to the compression of my lower legs. "It's quite a climb from the kitchen. I'd think suggesting installing a lift could gain contestant points. How are things going?"

"Nice of you to show some interest, Mrs. H, after bunking off all morning." She stared coldly down at me. "Where did you go, Hong Kong?"

"That was the plan, but when I arrived at the airport, I realized I didn't have my passport. And perhaps it was as well, seeing I never did take that seminar on which chopstick goes with what course of the meal." My hope that an attempt at levity would put a smile on Mrs. Malloy's purple-glossed mouth was doomed. If anything, she looked crosser than ever. Oh bother, I thought, knowing I was about to hear what she thought of the other contestants. "So?" I prompted.

"I can see I'm not going to get a fair shake with the others." She heaved a martyred sigh. "A pushy lot, all of them, especially that Judy Nunn you were so fired up about after spending five minutes with her. Why you couldn't have put the little snippet in your pocket and walked off with her when you disappeared, I don't know."

Now it wasn't only my lower extremities that felt weighted down. "She didn't strike me as pushy," I protested mildly.

"Well, you didn't see her in action when Lord Belfrey had us all together for the welcoming ceremony. She grabbed his attention right off the bat by talking about how she'd just love to get busy with a trowel and cement fixing that opening in the wall out front. Crafty creature, using how upset he was about the accident as a way of making her play for him!" A fierce tightening of Mrs. Malloy's folded arms pushed her bosom up under her chin. I held my breath waiting for a loud pop, but I doubted that even the air going out of those balloons would have deflated her wrath.

"How did his lordship bring up the accident?"

"He waited till we got into that room we was in last night."

"It would have the right ambience." I leaned forward, lifted the tray, and gingerly set it on the floor as far to the left of Mrs. M's feet as possible, although maybe a good stomp on crockery would make her feel better. "If ever a room was primed for nightmarish revelations, that one would be it. Did Lord Belfrey break the news with cameras and audio equipment present?"

"Of course not." She bridled at the suggestion. "That would've been insensitive, not that I expect that would have bothered your Judy Nunn. None of the *How sad!* And *What a terrible thing!* as came out of the others' mouths. Not so much as a shine of a tear in those little eyes of hers."

"She doesn't have particularly little eyes. Saucers wouldn't suit someone that petite."

"That's right; take her side, Mrs. H! If it wasn't unkind—something I leave to others," loaded pause, "I'd say that your fall knocked all the sense out of you." She shifted a high-heeled shoe nearer the tray, causing me to hope nastily that she would step in the prawn sandwich. Mrs. Malloy's footwear are her life, although to be fair to her she does not have a cardboard boxed tower of them on floor-to-ceiling shelves, as Mrs. Spuds suggested was the case with Celia Belfrey.

At any other time, I would have grabbed the opportunity to fill Mrs. Malloy in on my visit to

Witch Haven and describe for her not only Celia but also Nora Burton—the downtrodden paid companion straight out of a Gothic novel if ever there was one. Did she, like her fictional counterpart, harbor a thirst for revenge against an employer who never conceived that this fetcher and carrier had her own life history? I remembered the niggling feeling that something Nora had said was somehow odd. Just a tiny bit so, or it wouldn't keep eluding me.

It had always been such fun—so productive—talking things of this nature over with Mrs. Malloy. Were those stimulating moments on the way out? I realized sharply how fond I was of her—bossy, snide ways and all. Such qualities were her buttress against the world at large and me in particular. After all, didn't I have to be kept in my place to prevent my turning into the evil employer equal to any Celia Belfrey? The tiny bedroom, lacking all semblance of comfort without Thumper, shrank in upon itself, turning the window into a spy hole and making the sunlight look suspiciously sneaky.

"There has to be some reason, Mrs. H, for you not seeing straight. Any other time you'd be saying it's staring us smack in the face as how last night's car smash wasn't no accident. That like as not what happened to Suzanne Varney was murder plain and simple."

It was as well the loaded tray was off the bed or my convulsive start would have sent it flying.

"Murder!" I exhaled the word as though I'd never heard it before. Such a thought hadn't crossed my mind, even though I'm usually the first to suspect foul play, given (metaphorically speaking) the slightest whiff of burnt almonds.

"And who devised this murder?" I demanded of Mrs. Malloy, knowing full well what her answer would be.

"Judy Nunn; sticks out a mile. She knew Suzanne Varney . . ."

"So did Livonia Mayberry." I reached down for the slopped, now stone-cold cup of tea, and took a deep swallow.

"Oh, her!" Mrs. M shrugged a taffeta shoulder. "She's too mealy-mouthed to murder a goldfish without first sending for a priest to give it last rites. Besides, like she told you, Mayberry only entered *Here Comes the Bride* to stick it in her boyfriend's ear. Judy Nunn wants to be Lord Belfrey's choice so as to get her hands on Mucklesfeld's gardens. A nut job for horticulture she is, and who did she see standing in the way of her dream but Suzanne Varney?"

"Amongst four other contestants." I set the cup and saucer back on the tray. "Has she come clean with her plans for doing away with the rest of you?"

"Not need to be snarky, Mrs. H," baleful stare. "What I'm thinking is, she knew she wouldn't stand a chance against Suzanne Varney. Any woman as looks attractive dead—like Dr. Tommy told us she did—had to be she was a real smasher when breathing. Now, here's how I see things going down." Her voice became a touch more conciliatory. "Judy arranges for them to meet up somewhere close to Mucklesfeld for a bite to eat. Then, seeing as the fog was getting so bad, suggests they go the rest of the way in one car."

"She couldn't have counted on the fog."

Back to the baleful stare. "Do I look stupid?"

"Never in a million years."

"I'm not saying as she'd planned on killing Suzanne." Still huffy. "More a case of grabbing the opportunity by the horns when it came along."

"Okay." I ignored the call of the prawn sandwich.

"So, there they are creeping up the drive, Suzanne at the wheel unable to see a blinking thing, and Judy says: *Why don't I get out and guide you in?*"

"With or without malice aforethought?"

"Let's just say she was thinking of her own skin, but then she sees the break in the wall . . ."

"With her superwoman x-ray vision?"

Mrs. Malloy again tightened her arms under her chest, forcing the blood up her neck until I feared she'd turn purple to match her lipstick. "With the torch she got out of the glove compartment, like any reasonably clever Dick would do. Must've been then," her voice dropped to a low rasp, "that something wicked took hold of her, swamping every ounce of human decency drummed into her as a nipper. What was one life against the call of the Belfrey land?"

I can't say I shuddered to the villainy of this scenario. It was the torch that struck a note . . . because it was repetitive: Ben not being able to find the one Georges claimed was in a desk drawer in his lordship's study; and further back . . . to last evening, Plunket saying that if Boris had found a torch to take outside, things might have been different. It was probably a coincidence, but even so I felt that prickling of the skin . . . the chill down the spine.

"Look," I told Mrs. Malloy, "your not taking to Judy Nunn doesn't mean she killed anyone. And any such suggestions to Lord Belfrey, Georges LeBois, or the other women will do nothing but ruin your own chances of ending up with the bridal veil. I'm not saying you have to be Miss Congeniality, but at least try not to be the troublemaker everyone is hoping to see out on her ear."

"Well, I suppose it was too much to hope you'd remember all the times me instincts put me on the right track when we was handling other cases together," Mrs. Malloy addressed the ceiling. "So you go on telling yourself this is too close and personal for me to be objective. Don't you go worrying I'll be saying I told you so when I'm found breathing me last after being coshed on the noggin with a poker." Black head with its two inches of white roots held high, she made for the door.

"Oh, please!" I begged—caught however foolishly in superstitious dread. "Don't go off miffed. Stay and have half my prawn sandwich."

"Luncheon awaits," hand on the knob, she did not turn her head. "We'd have sat down half an hour ago if your friend Judy wasn't still outside with Lord Belfrey filling his head with promises of velvet lawns and herbaceous borders. And now it'll be me that's late." The snap of the door behind her indicated that this was entirely my fault. To blunt my chagrin, I ate my lunch without tasting it and lay back down. No chance of Ben appearing for a while at least. He must be fully occupied in the dining room or kitchen. As for Thumper, I recognized the hopeless folly of yearning for him to leap through the window. Courage! I told myself. At least I wasn't Wisteria Whitworth dreading the arrival of the malevolent wardress mouthing the names of the patients she had smothered in their beds after they refused their morning gruel that she'd put her whole heart into the stirring. That miserable old Mr. Codger . . . I smiled faintly at coming up with such a redundant name. Perhaps I was drifting off to sleep.

But that wasn't to be. Mrs. Malloy's disastrously silly suspicions kept pulling me back from the verge. Disastrous because she wasn't much good at concealing her feelings when her nose was out of joint. And silly because if someone had seized upon the fog to bring about Suzanne Varney's death, there was no reason to assume it was Judy Nunn. Someone living at Mucklesfeld could have easily heard the car coming, made sure the exterior lights were off, and nipped outside at the propitious moment with a torch. One now missing from its accustomed place. If killer there be, it would have to be someone who had more to fear from poor Suzanne's arrival than the mere possibility that Lord Belfrey would choose her as his bride.

I lay longing for another cup of tea, a hot one this time, accompanied by another lemon tartlet. I still had more than an hour to go before joining the contestants in the library. Thinking of what might be offered to eat at that time would only make my current pangs worse, so I went back to concocting nonsensical theories about a murder I hoped to convince Mrs. Malloy hadn't happened. Let the suspects seat themselves in a circle.

My mental gaze fell first on the trio of Mr. Plunket, Mrs. Foot, and Boris. Before finding refuge at Mucklesfeld, originally as squatters and then as employees on Lord Belfrey's return from America (when they must have expected to be given their marching papers), they had been homeless. The prospect of his lordship's marriage had to have rattled their rib cages. What if the new wife insisted they leave? What chance did any of them have to reestablish themselves? Would they be separated? That, I felt sure, was an anguish not to be borne; together they were the insiders, not the brutal reverse. But if the first contestant to show up conveniently died, his lordship might decide against continuing with *Here Comes the Bride*, and they—Mr. Plunket, Mrs. Foot, and Boris—would be safe, at least for the time being. What, I suddenly wondered, had caused them to be homeless in the first place?

My watch showed scant progress toward teatime. If I were to pretend seriously that Mrs. Malloy was right that murder had occurred, then I would have to add employer to employees in our group of suspects. Why might Lord Belfrey have decided to eliminate one contestant off the bat? Perhaps when he belatedly saw Suzanne Varney's photo laid out with the others by Georges in the study, he realized that she could ruin his chances for a marriage that would save Mucklesfeld. What could Suzanne have known to his detriment that had sealed her fate? I considered the possibility that he had behaved improperly toward her on the cruise they had shared, wincing away from more graphic wording. Illogically, my heart rebelled against the possibility that he had been anything other than a gentleman; after all, if a man would commit murder, he was likely capable of other hideous violations. But I desperately didn't want to believe anything of the kind about Lord Belfrey.

What other damning evidence might Suzanne

have had against him? A dire, but less ugly possibility sprang to mind. Perhaps she had reason to know, having met the genuine article, that he was not the real Lord Belfrey! Not that I condoned the behavior of imposters (or of highwaymen, for that matter), but there is a certain romantic allure to the face masked by black cloth or pretense. What if two Englishmen living in America, uncannily similar in appearance, chanced to meet—one telling the other he had just been informed by letter that his cousin Lord Giles Belfrey had died, making him heir to the title and ancestral estate? What if during an evening at his home in a remote rural community, this man had waxed nostalgic over the course of rather too many whiskeys and sodas on the family history, mentioning names, situations, before dramatically and conveniently collapsing? What if after failing to revive him, the other sized up the potential for starting over after two failed marriages (doomed from the start because of his fixation with Eleanor) and an abruptly ended career? What if the deceased was so newly arrived in the area that his passport and air ticket were in view on a table and his other identification in his wallet, waiting to be plucked from his jacket pocket and replaced by another set?

I might have warmed to such a scenario if it weren't connected to Suzanne Varney's murder. As it was, I nixed it firmly. Whatever might be false at Mucklesfeld, I was in no doubt that his lordship had lost his heart, completely and forever, when looking upward at Eleanor Belfrey in her portrait gown on the stairs.

Another glance at my watch convinced me I had spent long enough concocting motives for a murder that was all in Mrs. Malloy's head. I was about to get off the bed to do something about my face, hair, and clothes before heading down to the library for tea, when the door opened and in crowded Mrs. Foot.

"I've come for the tray." She beamed a gap-toothed smile, the heavy dusty gray locks matching matted clouds outside the window. Gone was the sunshine of a half hour before. Did the weather at Mucklesfeld tend to be this fickle, and were Mrs. Foot's moods equally changeable? Certainly, she was making more of an effort to be jolly than she had that morning. Had Whitey been returned safe and sound to her fond embrace? Before I could inquire, she asked winningly if I'd had a nice little nap.

"I tried, but my mind's been rather awhirl." I smiled up . . . way up at her. She would have to do a long bend to pick up the tray, which was perhaps why she made no attempt to do so. Quickly, I set it on the bed.

"Now don't you overdo," she admonished. Then I saw the hesitancy lurking in the greenish-yellow eyes. The smile, an overture at buttering me up perhaps, was gone. She's bracing to tell me something, I thought. And sat still, waiting. "You must have had a bad night, dear," a flicker of the spider leg lashes, "and for that I'm ever so sorry."

"It wasn't your fault that I fainted." That wasn't entirely true, and maybe she realized that peering through the banisters had spooked me.

"That's not what I'm getting at, dearie." She lowered her head, the ungainly hands smoothing down the sides of her faded print frock, plucking a thread here and poking at a tear there. A nervous gesture, no more. Why did it conjure an image of those hands closing about my throat . . . squeezing it dry of breath? Because I was again seeing her as the asylum wardress who had aroused palpitations in Wisteria Whitworth's unequaled bosom. "Before coming up, I confessed to Mr. Plunket and Boris what I'd done. *You didn't, Mrs. Foot!* said Mr. Plunket. *Not you, Mrs. Foot!* said Boris. It went against everything they know of my soft, loving nature to think of me pulling such tricks."

"What tricks?"

Her head stayed down, but I continued to feel those eyes. "Putting the hot-water bottle I knew leaked in your bed." She moved a foot, drawing a circling motion on the floor in a parody of a child enduring the indignity of confessing to a disappointed mummy or daddy. "The other I did when you were deep asleep, as I knew you would be after taking those tablets Dr. Rowley prescribed. He'd let me have some a few weeks ago when I

264

had a bout of lying awake nights fretting because Mr. Plunket was feeling down. I was scared he'd go back to the drinking that had finished him with his job and family years back, and him so lovely, like you'll have seen, when he's sober."

"What else did you do?"

"Came in and opened the window. Most couldn't reach up to that, but like I said to Mr. Plunket, I'm tall as a willow tree." She now cranked up her head, and seeing the fierce glint of pride spread over her features, I waited for her to add that height was something she had worked on her entire life, and that with continued sacrificial exercise she would gain another foot and a half by morning. Instead, she explained her object had been for me to awake damply chilled to the marrow.

"Why?" I felt entitled in sounding put out.

"Nothing personal, if that's a comfort." The gray locks could have been the fog framing a tombstone.

"Then . . ."

"Had to think what was best for his lordship, didn't I, dearie? Has to be him first and foremost with Mr. Plunket, Boris, and me. I'd seen the way he was taken by how close you looked like the portrait. The one of Eleanor Belfrey. Relieved, we'd been, when Miss Celia Belfrey marched in and took it away. It was like it had bewitched him, and that's not a happy way for a man to live. *Give his nibs time, Mrs. Foot,* said Mr. Plunket, *now he doesn't have her face to look at, he'll get back to himself right as rain. That's right,* said Boris, *don't you go on worrying, Mrs. Foot.* Always so thoughtful of me, those two. I got my hopes up that his lordship was over the lady when he decided on this plan to get married. But then . . . there was you . . . brought in by the fog. And it came to me that if you could be got rid of fast, before it all got stirred up again for him, there mightn't be too much harm done."

"You panicked on discovering that Monsieur LeBois had asked my husband to stay on beyond this morning."

"That's the nutshell, dearie."

"Frankly," it had to be said, "I'm surprised your primary concern isn't that if Lord Belfrey does select a bride at the end of the week, she might be the new broom sort and decide to replace you, Mr. Plunket, and Boris with her own choice of employees."

"Won't happen, dearie." The gummy smile was back full force and Mrs. Foot went so far as to rub her hands. "His lordship wouldn't stand for us being booted out. He's give us his word we're to stay as long as we wants—which is forever—and with him that's as sacred an oath as you'd get out of a bishop."

"I'm sure." And naively or not, I was. What puzzled me was why Mrs. Foot had confessed to the hot-water bottle and the open window. My mind primed to suspicion by my imaginings, I remembered Mrs. Malloy's throwing in my face our previous forays into sleuthing. I couldn't recall if she had closed the door after bringing in the tray. But if she had left it ajar, might not Mrs. Foot—having followed her up for the express purpose of having a listen to our conversation—be probing the reasons why Suzanne's death might be murder most foul?

"I do hope you're not ever so cross with me, dearie." Vast shake of the hoary locks. *Oh, Mrs. Foot,* said both Mr. Plunket and Boris. *What if the lady he thinks of as a rare rose goes telling his lordship about her bad night and he gets his dear self in a state worrying about her catching pneumonia? We can't have him upset—not anytime, but specially now when he needs to be thinking clear to make his choice of a bride.*

So much for my silly ideas. Why doubt this explanation for her coming clean? "Of course I won't say anything," I reassured her.

"That's a weight off my mind. I'll go tell Mr. Plunket and Boris. I should have thought about them along with his lordship when pulling my stunt." Giant sigh. No further mention of my feelings. "And now with all this drink your husband has brought into the house," her voice became edged with the anger she had displayed that morning at the raising of a foreign flag over the kitchen, "I'm scared out of my wits Mr. Plunket will succumb to a glass of oh-be-joyful."

"Ben acted upon Monsieur LeBois's instructions and surely" (perhaps wishful thinking) "he wouldn't have issued them without Lord Belfrey's approval."

"Pressured into it." Mrs. Foot's scowl deepened. "Not a drop of alcohol in the place from the day poor Mr. Plunket told his lordship about his battle fought and won with the bottle. An employer in a million, we've got. He'll have insisted that what's been brought into the house in the past twenty-four hours be kept under lock and key. But where there's a will, there's always a way to get to the booze. No stopping Mr. Plunket if the urge comes on too strong."

"I can understand your worrying."

Mrs. Foot knuckled a teary eye. "Just like there wasn't any stopping Boris from letting that lion loose from his trailer in the middle of some high street after there was talk of him being sent to a zoo if he kept balking at jumping through the ring of fire, the poor old puss! Such a lot of running and screaming when all he wanted to do was play. But of course no one thought to toss him a toy mouse! And Boris given the boot after being with the same circus since he was a boy. Talk about feeling betrayed!"

"Yes," I managed.

"What is this sad old world coming to?" Mrs.

Foot wiped the other eye with her sleeve. "It's a good thing those two men have me to mother them. Like Mr. Plunket said to Boris just this morning, their world would fall apart if I was took." She appeared to size up my reaction. "I'm not as strong as I look—hacking coughs every winter and a nasty boil on my neck just a few months back."

"Oh, dear!" I was really thinking of the time. If I rushed, I'd be five minutes late for afternoon tea. I explained the situation, to which she responded by picking up the tray with a wincing heave.

"Like I say to Mr. Plunket and Boris when they hover round, Ma—that's what the dears call me in private—isn't made of spun glass, but there's never any getting them to see I'm not about to break like a precious ornament . . ."

"But lovely they feel that way about you." I opened the door more fully. "Can I take the tray down for you? Going to the kitchen would give me the chance to remind Ben about the need to keep the alcohol under lock and key."

"And make it look that I've been telling tales out of school about Mr. Plunket?" The eyes flashed green-yellow fire. If a woman of her looming presence could have been said to flounce, she did so out into the hallway. The thudding footsteps continued to echo like doom on the march as I raced along to the twilit bathroom, splashed water on my face, raked a comb through my hair, decided against lipstick, let alone a change of clothes, and sped down the main staircase into the hall without bothering to wonder if Georges had set up a trip wire in the guise of adding thrills and spills to *Here Comes the Bride*. Fortunately, this must not have occurred to him—yet. However, as I paused in my headlong rush to ponder the location of the library, a ghastly apparition emerged out of the crepuscular gloom.

A startled sidestep into the sharp edge of a piece of furniture, a suppressed scream, and I recognized the white face and lanky figure of Boris. My request for directions met with a hollow-eyed stare, as if I were a zombie or the ghost of Eleanor Belfrey. Luckily, before I was forced to go it alone—opening up door after door until hitting the jackpot—another shadow cast itself alongside him and Mr. Plunket's voice asked if he could be of assistance. He sounded so much like a normal butler that I forgot my rush and took the opportunity to ask him if someone had been able to find a torch for Ben to use in trying to figure out what was wrong with the cooker.

Those blank looks of Boris had to be contagious because now Mr. Plunket had one.

"Monsieur LeBois said he'd seen one in his lordship's desk. A red one," the thickening silence had me babbling, "but there must be others, although in a house this size it must be hard to keep track of every little thing."

"Green," said Mr. Plunket.

"There's one that's—"

"Green the one in his nibs's study."

"Red, Mr. Plunket, dearie," said the voice of Mrs. Foot. "That one is red. There was a yellow torch once in the pantry, but that got broke when Whitey knocked it off the shelf."

"Color-blind," gloomed Boris. "That's what Mr. Plunket is, Mrs. Foot. Isn't that right, Mr. Plunket? Remember," his vocal cords sounded rasped to the limit, "you told us it came on you sudden, late in life, so it's not surprising you forget sometimes."

"That's right." Mr. Plunket nodded with such vigor I was afraid his head would fly off. "The result of the drink, that would be it, wouldn't it, Mrs. Foot?"

"Now don't you go blaming yourself, Mr. Plunket," came the tender response; "we've all had our vices."

"Not you, Mrs. Foot!" Staunch conviction.

"Not you, Mrs. Foot!" Sepulcher echo from Boris.

This was pointless. By now Ben had probably sent out for a torch or gone to purchase one himself. Mumbling something to this effect, I skirted the obstacle course of furniture and entered Mucklesfeld's library.

As in the drawing room, the lackluster lighting made it impossible to immediately grasp the size of the space other than that it wasn't poky.

Bookcases lined with leather volumes that appeared to have been purchased in matching height and width rose on all sides to a railed portrait gallery beneath the vaulted ceiling that had the drift of an overcast sky. I was able to make out a short stairway immediately across from the doorway, providing access to closer perusal of presumably dead (and hopefully gone) Belfreys.

The living were scattered into two groups. Georges LeBois in his wheelchair watched with pouting lips as his crew carted tripods, telescopic-looking cameras, and goodness knows what other necessary equipment first one way, then another, as if searching for the perfect campsite on which to pitch a tent. All six of the contestants were assembled on sofas and chairs arranged roughly in a circle beneath an unlighted chandelier that would have flattened an entire city if it fell. Here there was not the excess of furniture that encumbered the hall and drawing room—a billiard table blanketed in shadow at the other end of the room from the seating area, an oversized desk that enhanced the professorial atmosphere, and of course the library ladder suggesting either an urge to dust or search behind the highest tomes for a hidden safe.

Georges did not acknowledge my arrival, none of the crew gave me a glance, but before I could turn tail, Mrs. Malloy beckoned me toward the leather sofa she was seated upon with Livonia Mayberry and Judy Nunn, both of whom beamed at me. Three other women took up another even longer sofa: a buxom blonde giving vent to hearty laughter and one with an attractively untidy mass of red hair drawn up on top of her head, talking animatedly over the blonde to the mousy woman of indeterminate age. Something about flying cutlery. Hoping Mrs. Malloy had not been the source, I joined them in the hesitant manner of a schoolgirl walking into class ten minutes late, sat on a faded tapestry chair, and braced myself to embark on an explanation of why I was intruding.

"And about time, too, Mrs. H," Mrs. Malloy shot across at me, cutting into the blonde's continuing saga. "I'd about given up on you. And tea, like Christmas, is still a long time coming." She was looking fiercely overdressed in her forest green taffeta, especially compared to Judy Nunn, who had shed the hiking jacket but had not otherwise changed her attire, which, with mud stains added to the knees of her slacks, had acquired the look of gardening clothes kept on a rusty hook in the potting shed.

I started to explain to the newcomers who I was, but the buxom blonde cut me off with an impatient chuckle.

"I'm Wanda Smiley and we all understand why you're joining us, Mrs. Haskell. Monsieur LeBois gave us the explanation. Quite a long one, but then he is in the entertainment business." A look round to see how much responsive amusement this had achieved. "Though why we need an interior decorator to tell us how to brighten up Mucklesfeld, I'm sure I don't know, when all it needs is a good spring cleaning. But as he said, you do happen to be here, along with your husband and Roxie there." No bothering to look at Mrs. Malloy, therefore missing the glower. "And now where was I? Ah, yes, such a laugh you'll all get out of this one. I'd gone to buy a new bra and decided to get a good fitting, seeing I need all the support I can get, given my generous proportions." She made the mistake of pausing to look smugly down.

"I'm so glad you're staying, Ellie," Livonia leaned eagerly toward me, "and after being ready to bolt off like a rabbit, I'm glad I'm here, too." If the room had any glow at all, it came from the shine in her blue eyes. My goodness! I thought. What or who could be responsible for the stunning change? Did I need three guesses, or just two? Lord Belfrey or Dr. Tommy Rowley? Either way, she had gone in the flash of a few hours from mildly pretty to extremely so. "And, will you believe it, this lady," casting her radiance on the mousy-looking woman, "is Mrs. Knox's daughter. I never knew she had one, but here she is—Molly Duggan. You remember I told you about Mrs. Knox?"

"The next-door neighbor."

"And so horribly shocked to find out I'd entered *Here Comes the Bride*. And to think Molly is also a contestant!"

There was absolutely nothing wrong with mousy Molly's looks and nothing right with them, either, seeing she had left it all up to Mother Nature, who hadn't been forthcoming with a mascara wand, a lipstick, or, given that sad frizz, a comb.

"That's nothing to what she'll have to say when she finds out I did the same." She peeked a nervous look around the circle. "I've always been a disappointment to her. It's why she doesn't talk about me and hardly ever comes to see me at my bed-sitter. She's ashamed that I work the checkout at the supermarket she used to go to. Until now, my highest ambition was to be moved to the seafood department, but then this came along and I pictured the look on Mum's face if I got to marry a lord. But after what happened at lunch when that giant fork came at me . . ." She sat gulping.

"One in the eye for the old bat you marrying into the aristocracy, eh!" The woman with the red hair—who had by default to be Alice Jones—grabbed the chance to speak. "You should have heard how my parents both carried on when I joined a commune at age nineteen."

"Hurts to crane your neck back that far, I'm sure." Mrs. Malloy tempered this comment with a chuckle that to me was clearly imitative of the blonde Wanda Smiley, and my heart sank. Unless reined in, my friend was going get herself soundly disliked by the rest of the group, as Georges had predicted. But how to save her from herself without putting her in the corner or telling her no sweets for a week?

"Did you live off the earth at the commune, Alice?" Judy asked with her pleasant smile. "Grow all your own vegetables, peat fires, that sort of thing?"

"Did you weave your own clothes?" Livonia emerged from a dreamy-eyed reverie. "I've always thought that would be so romantic."

"Looks like she still does." I thought it, Mrs. Malloy said it.

Alice eyed her questioningly, before judiciously deciding to assume a compliment. "To be completely up-front . . ."

"Oh, do by all means set an example."

Really, I sighed, Nanny was going to have to get very cross indeed if this kept up.

Undeterred, Alice proceeded. "I haven't touched a loom in years, but as it happens I was thinking on the drive here that I could put my skills to use weaving blankets for all the bedrooms. I also hook rugs and make slipcovers—I put that down on my application and I have to assume it helped in my being chosen."

Wanda Smiley got her mouth open, but Mrs. Malloy was too quick off the mark. "You were another link in the chain, Alice, that was your selling feature . . ."

"Previously knowing which of the contestants?" I asked brightly, having caught a look from

276

Georges that said I wasn't doing much of a job controlling my charges.

"Me." The word came out in a squeak. Molly Duggan, daughter of the odious Mrs. Knox, looked and now sounded like a mouse peeking out of a hole. "Alice shops in the supermarket where I work."

"And," said the thus named, "Wanda comes in quite regularly to the health food café where I waitress."

"Not that I'm keen on tofu burgers or seaweed omelets." The oar was eagerly grabbed by the blonde, not relishing the sidelines. "But they do serve a decent cappuccino and a rather scrumptious blackberry and apple crumble—the sort Mother never used to make. As I said to the saleswoman when I went in to buy myself those new bras, I never worry about what I eat because I always put it on in the right places!"

"Same here! Shame we can't all be as lucky!" Mrs. Malloy slunk a look at Judy, who crossed her legs, clasped her knees, and remarked that she thought she heard the distant rattle of a tea cart. It was Livonia and Molly Duggan who looked uncomfortable.

"Into the changing room we went—me and the fitter—and out came her tape measure—you could tell from looking at her she'd only half a brain. But even so, I almost dropped from shock when she told me I was a size twenty-four—round the bust mind you, not my thigh! Me of all people! The Jayne Mansfield of my school! Of course she was before my time, but anyway, it turned out the silly woman had the tape measure round the wrong way . . ."

Laughter in varying degrees of amusement, save from Mrs. Malloy.

A sudden flare of camera lights nearly blinded me. In looking away, my eyes veered upward to the portrait gallery to fasten on the painted images of a sternly bewhiskered gentleman in a frock coat, a stout matron in a crinoline, and a woman in a tall white wig and the satins and lace of Versailles's glory days. Ruminating on her sour expression must have caused me to miss Georges's call for *Action*. I blinked back to the assemblage upon sensing a stiffening of posture, a drawing in of elbows and a replanting of feet.

"You were saying, Mrs. Haskell," Judy kindly cued me in.

"So exciting to be part of *Here Comes the Bride* in an observing capacity," my voice played back to me with its embarrassingly contrived enthusiasm. What on earth was I to say next? Fortunately, Mrs. Malloy intervened before Georges yelled *Cut!* or something equally cutting.

"Well, I've got to say, as lunch had its moments! And I'm not talking about the food, although it wasn't to be sneezed at—Mr. H being in top form. It was when the lid of the canteen opened all by itself and the cutlery flew up in the air that I said to meself this is a bit of all right. 'Course I see some of the others was petrified! But that's people being different." Smug-faced self-approbation. "Like I always say, after battling the world on me own, there's not much as will give me the willies. And anyway I wasn't a hundred percent convinced it was the Mucklesfeld poltergeist or what have you pulling a stunt."

"Special effects," voiced Judy sensibly.

"But how?" Molly stirred nervously.

"Some mechanical device in the cabinet to get the show started, followed by a visual recording when the cutlery apparently began whizzing around the dining room."

"Not much romance in your soul, Miss Nunn." Mrs. Malloy hunched a shoulder.

"I will always remember it as the silver dance." Livonia smiled dreamily.

"The idea that there are restless spirits at Mucklesfeld doesn't bother me," Wanda asserted. "I know blondes aren't supposed to have much in the way of brains, preferring to rely on our other charms," another of her self-congratulatory laughs, "but I'm convinced that a womanly hand on the helm will put paid to nerves."

"I rather like the idea of ghosts." Alice tucked in a tangle of reddish hair. "Places like Mucklesfeld should have them, along with a repaired roof and a thorough refurbishing."

"How do you all feel about an influx of capital used to restore the place to its former grandeur?" I dutifully inquired of the circle of faces after catching Georges's eye.

"First the gardens," responded Judy.

"I don't see why." Mrs. Malloy at her most petulant.

"Does anyone have a particular design vision for the interior or exterior?" I persisted nobly. "Elizabethan or Jacobean furniture would seem the obvious choice, but perhaps not . . ."

"I don't think a home is about a particular type of furniture," said Alice. "It should be about family, and I've been thinking," she looked round the circle, "that the nicest thing we could do for Lord Belfrey would be to invite his two cousins over for a meal, which I would be happy to cook . . ."

"It would provide an immediate incentive for sprucing up the place," I responded amicably.

"Our first joint project." Wanda was quick to display her team spirit.

"You're on to something." Judy nodded cheerfully. "Dr. Rowley seems a very pleasant man."

"Oh, yes!" Livonia continued her dream state. "Of course, like you I only met him briefly . . . just long enough for him to save me from the suit of armor and . . . but I wonder," striving to refocus, "what his lordship's female cousin is like—the one who lives at . . ."

"Witch Haven?" I smiled at her. "I went there

this morning to inquire if anyone knew," somehow I managed to keep my voice steady, "who owned the black Lab who'd shown up here. Celia Belfrey mentioned an archery contest that used to take place here on the grounds." I only threw this in because there was little else I could say about Miss Belfrey without revealing how unpleasant I had found her.

"Then that's it!" Alice exclaimed. "We'll bring back the event for our little get-together."

There was a general murmuring of enthusiastic agreement. If Mrs. Malloy looked sour, it was undoubtedly because she hadn't come up with the idea.

The library door opened with startling abruptness to reveal Mrs. Foot wheeling in a loaded tea trolley. Behind her came Mr. Plunket and Boris.

Georges bellowed: "Cut!"

The camera lights went out as if doused by buckets of water, casting the room into an unnatural darkness even for the late afternoon. Momentarily distracted by thoughts of the spread Ben would have laid on, it took a communal gasp for me to realize that something other than the prospect of cucumber sandwiches and iced fancies had created a palpable awareness of something major happening. The contestants were all looking upward. But it was not until Molly Duggan screamed that I noticed the white-wigged portrait lady poised on the uppermost step of the stairway.

She was swirled around by shadows that blurred her features but did little to hide the bloody gash around her neck. Undeterred by the negative reception, she extended a satin-shod foot. However, her descent was foiled by a squeaking scurry of white along the railing and a long-tailed leap atop the Marie Antoinette coiffure!

10

Whitey, being no simpleton as rodents go, avoided the apparition's clutches by performing an immediate vanishing act into the mist. Could it be I was the only one who had noticed him? That one shock at a time was more than the rest, including his nearest and dearest, could take in?

"Blimey! It's none other than Lady Annabel Belfrey," gasped Mr. Plunket. "The one that got her head sliced off by the guillotine when she was off on her holidays in France."

"Gone to see her auntie she had, bless her, and now she's paying us a visit." Mrs. Foot sounded thoroughly delighted.

"Who wouldn't die to make your acquaintance, Ma?" Boris's voice floated above the hubbub. The ghost having created a sufficient stir and perhaps enduring the fright of her afterlife retreated back up the stairs to disappear into a denser confluence of shadow. I could have destroyed the impact of her appearance by stating she was the woman who worked at the sweetshop in the high street, who had hinted broadly that she was hoarding a secret relating to Mucklesfeld. And all so easily achieved, with apparel similar to that in the portrait, access and egress through a hidden panel in the gallery, simulated mist, and camera lights turned off so that an adjustment in eyesight was required prior to adequate refocusing. But much as I might think Georges's contrivances—the flying cutlery at lunch and now this—foolishly theatrical and seriously distressing to Molly Duggan in particular (from the bleached look of her face), I had no right to interfere with the production of *Here Comes the Bride*.

If Georges was gloating, it was impossible to detect because he was surrounded by his crew. Mrs. Foot wheeled the trolley forward and Mr. Plunket and Boris assisted her in handing around cups of tea and setting down plates of fabulous-looking sandwiches, scones, and cakes on available surfaces. I was pleased and proud to see that Mrs. Malloy had come out of her sulks to join Livonia in comforting Molly.

"Now come on," she held a teacup to the rigid lips, "it's all over. And a poor excuse for a ghost she was—no wailing or icy chill. I'd be ashamed if it was me not to make more of an effort, but there you are; like I always say, there's some as put their best foot forward and others as do the minimum. How about one of Mr. H's nice ham rolls?"

"I think I'm going to be sick."

"Not on me, you're not."

"Just a bite, Molly," Livonia urged. "I can't believe I wasn't terrified. This morning I would have bolted for my car."

"We all knew coming here," Wanda drank her tea with pinky raised, "that adjusting to whatever Mucklesfeld offered was key. Being a romantic, though, I have to admit I'm a little disappointed that there aren't more of the usual type of reality show moments of alone time with his lordship, walks in the rose garden under the moonlight, intimate dinners for two in the gazebo."

"The gazebo is in ruins along with the gardens," Judy pointed out practically.

"Whatever the state of his property," Alice again poked at her abundant hair, and spread a hand caressingly over her flowing skirt, "Lord Belfrey is more of a dreamboat than I dared to hope for. Even his Christian name, Aubrey, it couldn't be more right! So distinguished. Not the forgettable sort like Jim or Tom."

"I think Tom is a lovely name." This from Livonia, but I stopped listening. Something had clicked into place for me . . . what it was Nora Burton had said that had afterwards niggled. When standing in the hall at Witch Haven, I mentioned that *Here Comes the Bride* was getting under way

284

at Mucklesfeld and if sufficient drama wasn't produced, Georges would have a tantrum. Her response had been to ask if I was talking about Lord Belfrey. At the time it had seemed understandable, seeing that she was new to Witch Haven, but was it? Moments later, Celia Belfrey had spoken of her cousin as Aubrey. Wasn't it likely she had done so previously? Could it be that Nora Burton had been overplaying her role of discreet paid companion? If so, why? A thrill coursed through me. Who was Nora Burton? Could it possibly be . . . ? I recalled his lordship asking me on the night of arrival if Ellie was short for Eleanor. I needed to get away and think. Georges provided the opportunity. He beckoned to me and informed me that I was free to leave.

"The next segment will be his lordship joining the contestants for a group chat, and you, my dear, would be *de trop*. Help yourself to whatever you wish from the tea trolley on your way out. No cause to mope, Mrs. Haskell, your services will be required again." He swung the wheelchair away with all the aplomb of a Roman charioteer prepared to mow down lions and Christians alike.

I prepared to make good my escape by piling a plate high with goodies but deciding against a cup of tea. That I could get in the kitchen from Ben, which would be preferable to a solitary ponder. I was within a foot of the door when a scream even louder than the one hurled from Molly Duggan rent the air. Turning, I beheld all the contestants on their feet, but it was Wanda who appeared to be doing some sort of tribal dance while still emitting that dreadful sound to a grim chorus of the word *Rat!*

"No need to carry on so!" Mrs. Foot's voice conveyed both contempt and annoyance. "You're all frightening the little precious! Isn't that right, Mr. Plunket and Boris?"

"They are at that, Mrs. Foot." Mr. Plunket nodded.

"I'll get him for you, Mrs. Foot." Boris made a move toward Wanda, who was now clutching at the bust of which she was so justifiably proud.

"It came down my neck. I'll never get past the feel of its vile fur and horrible raw tail." Gone—perhaps never to return—was the bubbly woman flush with her own charms. Clearly she had missed landing on Lady Annabel or she would have fled.

Despite Judy Nunn's efforts to calm her down, she was out the door, to be heard racing up the stairs, alternately sobbing and swearing. Alas, the library was not to be left in relative peace. Molly began weeping, and Mrs. Malloy overrode all other voices to state that her George had once asked if he could have a pet rat and she'd told him over his dead body! Meanwhile, Mrs. Foot, Mr. Plunket, and Boris had all dropped to their knees and were crawling around the floor making crooning noises. A pink nose twitched a whiskered peek out from under a chair, and before anyone else started screaming, Mrs. Foot was staggering to her feet with the little darling in her hands. Her cooing voice with accompaniment by Mr. Plunket and Boris followed me out of the library.

Let Georges restore order in there, not that Wanda didn't have my utmost sympathy. I made for the kitchen, plate in hand, and to my delighted relief Ben was there in his temporary kingdom. His face lit up at seeing me. My heart sang, but rushing into his arms might have caused the loss of my spoils, so I just stood smiling at him as I said: "Alone at last!"

"Sweetheart!" He removed the plate, set it on the table, and gathered me to him, kissing me with tender passion, before asking my forgiveness for earlier. "I was completely out of line; don't know what got into me going off on you like that."

"It's this house, darling! For the past thirty years or so it has been steeped in misery, haunted by whatever emotions—venomous anger or grief—that Sir Giles Belfrey felt, coupled with the spite of his daughter, Celia, toward his wife." I reached for a cucumber sandwich. "Do you have time now to talk about all that? I'd like to get your thoughts . . ."

Life at Mucklesfeld was a series of interruptions. Lord Belfrey came through the kitchen door, his presence as it must always do transforming the most mundane of surroundings into something grand.

"Am I intruding?" His smile extended to both of us, but his dark eyes appeared intent only upon my face. Fortunately, if Ben noticed, he gave no sign.

"Not at all," we both said together.

"I wanted to thank you, Mr. Has . . . Ben . . . for the wonderful meals you are providing, and," a hesitation, "no offense intended, to stress the necessity of making sure any alcohol is put where Mr. Plunket is unlikely to find it. He's done so well over recent months and for his sake I'd like to prevent a relapse."

"Of course," Ben responded with equal seriousness. "I found a couple of old metal bread boxes that from the dust on them hadn't been touched in years way to the back of the top pantry shelf. They're back up there, considerably heavier."

"I appreciate it." His lordship nodded. "Better safe than sorry. Mr. Plunket admitted to me that he was a violent drunk. Terrible thing, alcoholism—an illness, no doubt about that. Could be the fate of any of us. Sorry to put you to the trouble climbing stepladders."

"There was a bonus." Ben smiled. "When getting down the bread boxes, I found a torch I needed to look into the cooker."

"If it's not strong enough, there's one in my desk with a really powerful beam."

A further interruption when Mr. Plunket, Mrs. Foot, and Boris forged into the kitchen at once, all of them guiding the tea trolley, which typical of its kind wanted to go its own way. Conversation with my husband being effectively nixed, I again took up my plate, waved a hand at him in particular and the rest in general, and headed out into the hall and up the main staircase. By now I no longer felt in need of a map to reach the former servants' quarters, and I arrived at my corridor after no false turns to hear raised voices coming from a room two or three doors from mine. The one sounding most clearly to my ear was Mrs. Malloy's, and she was speaking kindly. Nanny would have to hand out gold stars.

"No one's saying you're making a giant fuss, Wanda. If anyone sympathizes it's me, seeing as how at least three of me husbands was rats. But what Livonia here and me is saying is the thing will be put back in its cage."

"And escape again! No, thank you! I'm packing up and getting out of here this minute."

"It's not Houdini!"

"No." Livonia sounded doubtful.

"Stuff the reassurances." A thump suggested Wanda had tossed a suitcase on the bed. "That Boris the zombie was in the circus, wasn't he? Teaching the . . . thing to open the cage door would be child's play to him. Ghosts, even the real kind, don't scare me, but rats! Let me tell you, we had chickens when I was a kid and they attract them by the dozen. One day my brother picked up a dead one and threw it so it landed on my shoulder.

That's something you don't get over. Ever! Where's my flaming nightdress?"

"Here," Livonia said.

"Ladies, I shouldn't be taking this out on you." Wanda sounded conciliatory. "But I'm leaving."

"I do understand. I do really. I was ready to bolt this morning, but life can change in an instant for the . . . the wonderful."

"Or go the other way," Mrs. Malloy the eternal pessimist, "but think of what you'll be giving up—the chance to marry a lord. Now, that opportunity don't come along with a bag of crisps, and when all's said and done, you're not a bad-looking woman. Perhaps too quick to think you're a laugh a minute, but in my book that's a lot better than yapping on about what kind of dirt is best for growing roses."

"When it comes to looks and the title, he's a catch, all right, but this place—rat-infested dump—you can keep! Sure, I know what was laid out on the application form about the emphasis on the practical, but a girl can dream, can't she? Anyway, I'm telling you the chance of this lord falling for any of us is zip. He might as well be married and about to celebrate his bloomin' golden anniversary from the shuttered look in his eyes. And I wasn't born with this figure to let it go to waste. If you'll take advice from someone who's been around the dance floor, don't either of you be fools and get stuck here for life!"

Another thump suggesting the suitcase hit the floor had me flitting into my room. Shameless to have eavesdropped. Worse that remorse did not set in as I applied myself to another cucumber sandwich, followed by another of egg and cress, a strawberry tart, and a mini coffee éclair. Having strategically left my door ajar, I heard the exodus down the hall—Mrs. Malloy and Livonia presumably returning to the library, hopefully not having kept Lord Belfrey waiting; Wanda to exit Mucklesfeld.

The number of contestants would again be reduced to five, but perhaps that was the intent now that *Here Comes the Bride* was under way. A process of attrition until only the strongest of the six remained and Lord Belfrey's choice was made for him. Georges and his scare tactics, although presumably he was not responsible for Whitey's intrusion on the scene. It was obvious why Lady Annabel's appearance had not taken place under the glaring gaze of the cameras. The less light the better in fooling the susceptible eye; but that the momentous event had not been recorded for the entertainment of future viewers was unthinkable, which meant hidden cameras. Devious Georges! Keeping the contestants continually off balance as to when or where they were being filmed.

Meanwhile, I pictured the reaction to Wanda's departure, Lord Belfrey sizing up the remaining contestants. My guess was that he would be drawn to Judy Nunn, a woman both energized and restful. Her passion might never extend beyond the grounds to the house, but she would have the organizational skills to put others successfully to work in areas not of her expertise. At this juncture the timid Molly Duggan would not have emotion to spare on jealousy of a particular rival, but would Alice Jones, like Mrs. Malloy, have already sized up Judy as the woman to beat to the altar?

The evening passed quickly despite my feeling confined like Bertha Mason Rochester to the attic. I'd unearthed the paperback I was halfway through from my suitcase and whiled away a couple of hours until Ben rescued me with the announcement that he and I were to dine in solitary state in what had once been designated the morning room, but was now another storage area for furniture that Sir Giles had grouped together in vague hope of finding a dealer willing to cart it away. Unfortunately, his lordship had told Ben, in recent years there hadn't been much of a market for Victorian ugly, and anything good had already been sold off. Or, I thought, plunging my fork into a delicious morsel of Lobster Thermidor, spirited away by daughter Celia. At least the overcrowding of the hall and drawing room was now explained. I pictured Sir Giles ordering the old handyman, now working for Miss Belfrey at Witch Haven (what was his name? Forester?), to heave the pieces of furniture into position for viewing, and when they didn't sell, closing his eyes to their presence and sinking ever further into the Slough of Despond.

From the window I saw Lord Belfrey crossing the overgrown lawn with Alice Jones of the billowy hair on his left and Molly Duggan sadly prim on his right. I wondered while reveling in a meringue glacé how Mrs. Malloy and Livonia were currently occupied. As it happened, I met them both in the hallway outside my bedroom after leaving Ben to prepare a late night five-course snack for Georges. I mentioned that I planned on going to church in the morning for Sunday service and asked if they had heard what time it would be.

"Nine o'clock," responded Livonia promptly, adding with flushed cheeks that she had also decided to go.

"And you can count me in, Mrs. H. Never let it be said I don't do me Christian duty come rain or shine, except of course when having a lie-in with a book or giving meself a manicure." Mrs. Malloy went on to reflect on what she would wear, bemoaning that she had only the one hat with her and it was dented from the lamp shade. "That Mrs. Foot and her pranks! Admitted to me as how she dropped it over the banisters for a laugh. A cackle's more like, the sad old crone. Still, I won't go holding a bit of silliness against her should I get to be lady of Mucklesfeld. Live and let live is the way I see it. And to send that trio packing isn't in me.

Shame I can't see that sort of compassion from the others," she heaved a pained sigh, "especially that Judy Nunn as seems to think she's the only body in the world as can get a job done right. Now, our Wanda might have been different if she hadn't left us."

Absence can be such a virtue! The three of us arranged to meet in the hall at eight thirty the next morning and I got ready for bed. It had been a long day. The ache of returning Thumper to his rightful owners came back in full force. I lay thinking of his dear furry face and form before drifting into sleep. The comfort of our few hours together stole over me, followed sharply by another memory— the sensation of being covertly watched while I stood by the ravine waiting for him to return from his foraging. Sometime later, I was vaguely aware of Ben creeping through the bedroom into his cubbyhole, and something in my muddled, half-submerged state shifted the ordinary into stealth, causing the echo of those padding footsteps to linger unpleasantly in my ears until sleep grabbed me back down into murkily disjointed dreams.

Suddenly I woke to lingering horror. In the nightmare the watcher in the woods had been Celia Belfrey, her features distorted into the ugliness of epitomized evil. Suzanne's face was a beautiful, alluring version of mine. Witless creature to have put herself in the path of such hatred, but I should have screamed out a warning. Even a silent one would have shown willing. The suffocating power-lessness of dreams was a poor excuse. My chest hurt from the pounding it had taken, and slow, concentrated breathing was required before I felt steady enough to sit up and face the day.

A glance at my watch showed five minutes to eight, and a peek into the cubbyhole revealed that Ben was already up and undoubtedly occupied in toiling for Georges while very possibly also providing breakfast for every other hungry mouth. I had to rush in order to be downstairs to meet Mrs. Malloy and Livonia in the hall at the appointed time. Both had the well-ordered look of women who make Sunday church attendance a priority instead of shaking off bad dreams. Mrs. Malloy wore the hat on which the lamp shade had landed and a black satin suit with rhinestone buttons. Livonia was in a navy linen dress with a sweetly prim white collar. Very pretty she looked, with not a crease to be seen. My eucalyptus green skirt and blouse were riddled with them, and I regretted not wearing a cardigan even though the morning was delightful warm, with only fluffy lamb-shaped clouds appliquéd on the blue gauze sky.

Not much was said on the brief walk to the church. Livonia and Mrs. Malloy appeared lost in their thoughts, while I was still struggling to get the wheels churning. Mercifully, I had not made us late. We arrived at the church with five minutes to spare. Lingering in the entryway with its bulletin board and wooden racks of pamphlets, we were greeted by flapping hand gestures from a middle-aged man with a mechanically propelled walk, a port wine complexion, and miraculously black hair.

"Welcome! Welcome! Ever so lovely to have visitors at St. Mary's in the Dell. Will you all be taking communion?" This question was asked in the manner of a maître d' suggesting it would have been the teensy-weensiest bit helpful if we'd phoned ahead for reservations.

"Would it be inconvenient?" Livonia asked, while edging toward the archway leading into the dimness of the nave. My suspicion that she had caught a glimpse of Dr. Tommy Rowley was confirmed by the sight of his eagerly turned profile from the back pew.

"Not at all," the man glanced flurriedly at his watch before flapping us forward. "Our vicar, Mr. Spendlow, who will be starting in a ticky-poo, will be delighted for you to come to the altar."

"We're not vestal virgins if that's what you're hoping." Mrs. Malloy sounded sourer than may have been intended. The temperature dropped pre-cipitously and I hastened to make clear we were the jocular sort.

"She was a nun in a former life and it wasn't for her."

"Oh, I see!" Clearly he didn't. Beckoning Livonia, who had been inching toward Dr.

Tommy's pew, into our orbit, he bustled us up the aisle close to the front. "Will this suit? Good, good! Enjoy!" He faded into the wash of pale light seeping in through the stained-glass windows as we seated ourselves, receiving nods from two women already ensconced to our right. Surreptitious glances sideways and over my shoulder revealed a respectable attendance. Admittedly St. Mary's in the Dell was tiny, but in this day and age Mr. Spendlow (judging from the clerical collar) now emerging from a side door to ascend the pulpit had reason for confidence that God could still draw a nice crowd. Livonia sat holding a hymnal close as if it were a dear, familiar hand. Mrs. Malloy whispered to me that this was nice, although a bit poky compared to St. Anselm's.

"Wonder if the ancestral Belfreys is buried under the floor."

I compressed my lips in prayerful contemplation.

"Have to be a terrible squash, bunk bed style." Her whisper rose.

Livonia's chin was tilted in hopeful stillness.

The air was a distilled blend of mildew and beeswax, with a hint of incense wafting down through the centuries. Mrs. Malloy adjusted the hat before reaching down for a kneeler, which she proceeded to tuck behind her back.

"Might as well make meself comfy."

Our two pew companions had their stares cut

short when Mr. Spendlow started his opening remarks. He was a man his early thirties with a—to me—surprising ponytail and stubble beard. Ever ready to make assumptions, I anticipated a hip approach to the service in general and the sermon in particular, but to my relief all proceeded along traditional lines. The choir sang in and out of key to the accompaniment of some invisible personage thumping away on an organ, a minimum of bobbing up and down was required, and the sermon was a frank talk, delivered in a sensible voice, on the requirement for positive action, extending beyond our nearest circle into the larger community.

"I am speaking, my dear friends," hands grasping the front of the pulpit he leaned forward in an earnest search of faces, "of those occasions when we allow ourselves to stand idly by—telling ourselves that speaking up . . . reaching out with words of compassionate concern to those we sense are in trouble . . . would be unwarranted interference. But it is my belief that it is our sins of omission that . . ."

A snore to my left from Mrs. Malloy, who had succeeded all too well in making herself comfy.

". . . that may come back to haunt us . . . with those unutterably sad words, if only. If only, I had asked what I could do to help. If only, I had uttered those words of warning . . ."

"Shush!" Mrs. Malloy uttered the word with sleepy ferocity.

I had to make matters worse by elbowing her in the ribs.

"Yapping on in church when people are trying to get a bit of peace!"

"He's supposed to talk," I whispered. "He's giving the sermon."

"That's his excuse! Give a man a soapbox and he won't get off till somebody starts throwing rotten tomatoes."

Livonia was sinking down in her seat; our pew companions had converted their stares into glares. But Mr. Spendlow, after an amused-looking pause, continued to his conclusion.

Fortunately, after the final hymn and brief benediction, the congregation surged to its feet, making it possible to be borne outside on a tidal wave of humanity without revealing more than the tops of our heads. When I was able to see beyond a few inches around me, it was to note that Livonia wasn't with us.

"Gone to make eyes at Dr. Rowley." Mrs. Malloy is never at her best when still groggy with sleep. "A right shame, I call it, her continuing to lead Lord Belfrey on when it's clear as daylight she's fallen hook, line, and sinker for another."

"The less of her, the merrier for you," I was pointing out, when suddenly finding Mr. Spendlow at our elbows. That hat of Mrs. Malloy's had to have been the giveaway.

"Thank you for not throwing rotten tomatoes at

me." He twinkled boyishly at her. The ponytail and suggestion of a beard reminded me of my cousin Freddy, and following Mrs. M.'s suitable abashed murmurings I congratulated him warmly on his sermon, adding my regrets that we wouldn't be in Grimkirk next Sunday.

"A pleasure to have had you with us today. I'm sorry your visit to the area" (discreetly put) "has been shadowed by the car accident."

"Terrible," I said.

"I dreamed about it all night long." Mrs. Malloy stood looking tragic in black, only the rhinestone buttons striking too bright a tone. "That's why I dozed off just now, instead of storing up every word you said, Vicar, as is my usual way when at church. Much prefer it to the pictures. Always have, isn't that right, Mrs. H?"

"What?" It had suddenly struck me as surprising that Mr. Spendlow hadn't referred to the accident during the service, requesting prayers for the deceased.

"I understand she—Suzanne Varney—was a friend of your wife?"

"That's right. Ingar was shattered when she heard. Ah, here she is now." The assembly of congregants had thinned, heading toward their cars or proceeding on their way on foot. Turning, I beheld a tall, Nordic-looking blonde, with the long-legged walk and vigorously healthy aura one imagines gained from camping next to fiords or skimming over frozen lakes on ice skates. There followed a few minutes of politely generalized conversation before Mr. Spendlow was corraled by the gentleman with the miraculously black hair, port wine complexion, and flapping hands.

"Dear Stanley," Mrs. Spendlow's eyes followed affectionately, "he's the head verger and utterly convinced St. Mary's would crumble to rubble without him. And he's absolutely right. My husband counts on him for so much. Oh, no! He's dropped his pocket handkerchief. Excuse me while I . . ."

"I'll take it to him. That's the trouble with men, need constant looking after. A woman's willing lot!" Mrs. Malloy teetered off in her high heels. Martyrdom on route to canonization after the rocky start to her day.

Seizing the moment, I brought up Suzanne Varney. "We'd heard she'd decided to come in a day ahead to spend time with a friend. And Celia Belfrey, whom I met when looking for the owners of a lost dog," it was still incredibly hard to mention Thumper, "told me you were that person. I'm so sorry." How to ask what they had talked about without appearing ghoulishly curious?

"Trust that woman to be in the know! For someone who rarely leaves the house, especially now she has that downtrodden-looking assistant, she's next to omniscient."

"Apparently Ms. Varney stopped at Witch Haven to ask directions to the vicarage."

"That was it, was it!" Ingar Spendlow brushed back a long lock of straight silk hair. "Sorry to sound spiteful, but Celia Belfrey is a horror! She's spread it around I'm an atheist because it's the last thing a clergyman's wife is supposed to be, although I can't see why not. She plays into assumptions that because I was born in Sweden—that hedonistic haven—and because my thing isn't organizing the annual bazaar, I have to be godless and my husband should be dispatched with a boot to the rear." She looked around and, seeing nobody close, continued: "Celia Belfrey is one dangerous woman. If I were Lord Belfrey, I'd be on the alert for her sticking a spoke in his reality bridal search. It's not in her to tolerate her father's heir—or anyone else, for that matter—living happily ever after at Mucklesfeld."

"I'm not one of the contestants," I explained.

"Poor Suzanne!" Another glance to assess the all clear. "No, I'm not suggesting that accident was rigged, that would be going too far, although I remember her as an excellent driver. We were never extremely close, but I always liked her. She was the one who wasn't religious—the idea of people praying for her soul would have offended her, which is why my husband did not refer to her or the accident during the service. But interestingly, I believe she wanted to talk to me because of my perspective as the wife of a clergyman. Aren't people contradictory? Lovably so."

"Did she want to discuss the wisdom of being a contestant on *Here Comes the Bride*? Any ethical concerns, for instance, that she might have about doing so?" Should I come straight out with my knowledge—gained from his lordship—that he and Suzanne had a prior acquaintance? I suspected that Ingar Spendlow's loathing for Celia Belfrey had goaded her into saying far more than she normally would with a complete stranger. But how far could I push without appearing too nosy? Or was that question now moot? Mr. Spendlow was heading back to us, still in the company of Stanley—purple silk handkerchief restored jauntily to his breast pocket. "Suzanne wanted to talk about her anger, how vengeful it made her feel. The hate eating away at her, made more explosive by having been kept bottled up. I asked about friends, but she said she didn't have any—only acquaintances, except for me, and we hadn't seen or corresponded with each other in years. She said if she believed in anything, it was fate bringing us together. But that was as far as she got. I received an urgnt phone call from a parishioner who needed to see me immediately . . ."

There was no time for more. Mr. Spendlow placed an arm around his wife's shoulders, clearly eager to talk about Stanley's suggestion of chair placement in the church hall for the youth concert that night. Mrs. Malloy, Livonia, and Dr. Tommy waited a short distance away, and how long could they be expected to stand admiring the parking area? I said my goodbyes to the accompaniment of a particularly coy handshake from Stanley—his parting words resounding in my ears as I rejoined my little group. Had anyone commented on my resemblance to the last Lady Belfrey? *Such a charming looking young lady she was. A sad loss for the parish and* (obvious afterthought) *her husband.* He had not added *and her stepdaughter.*

"Oh, there you are, Ellie." Livonia beamed at me with surprised delight, rather as though I had stepped out of a lifeboat after being feared lost on the *Titanic.* "Imagine, Dr. Rowley," looking shyly up into his equally radiant face, "being at the very same service! He could have been at the eleven o'clock, or he could have been at this one and we . . ."

"How are you today, Mrs. Haskell?" He executed more of a bend than a bow over his round tum. A gentlemanly formality that thrilled one of us to the core, warmed my heart, and produced a glower from Mrs. Malloy.

"I should try fainting next time I go somewhere and get to be an invalid for the rest of me life. 'Course, not everywhere's as conducive to a good old-fashioned attack of the vapors as is Mucklesfeld. Did my fellow contestant here tell you, Dr. Rowley, about the white rat jumping on the ghost's wig?"

"No! My dear," reaching for Livonia's blatantly willing hands, "what a ghastly experience for the tender female!" Was this the first time it had occurred to me that Grimkirk's local GP might share with some amongst us a predilection for the swoonier romance novel? I pictured him sitting up in bed at night, wearing striped pajamas, a tear trickling down a plump cheek as he hoped against hope that Wisteria Whitworth and Carson Grant would defy the odds against their walking down the aisle to soaring strains of *"Oh Perfect Love."*

"The truly gruesome thing," Livonia looked deep into his eyes, "was that for a moment she didn't seem aware that anything—let alone a rat— was on her head. She had this fixed, quite dreadful grin on her face!"

"Ghosts are above worldly disturbances," Mrs. Malloy retorted loftily.

"But she wasn't one, just someone pretending to be Lady Annabel Belfrey with her head stuck back on after being guillotined." Livonia clung ever more tightly to Dr. Tommy. "Even Molly Duggan realized that, or she would have fled Mucklesfeld along with Wanda Smiley. Poor Molly! She is even more timid than I am . . . or was before embarking on this mission of self-discovery." She explained who she was talking about to the entranced but also suddenly anxious-looking Tommy.

"So you're now one contestant down." It should have been clear as glass to Livonia why this worried him, but it had to be remembered her relationship with Harold had given her no reason to believe herself the sort of woman to arouse jealousy in the heart of a man. Sweet, guileless Livonia! Or was she singing exactly the right song for a duet?

"I think that worked to Georges LeBois's plan." I said. "Six, five . . . then four, three, two, until there is one."

"Meanwhile, we, the contestants, have an event in mind, as was the brainchild so to speak of Mrs. H here." Mrs. Malloy adjusted the hat to a more imposing angle. "She found out from your cousin Celia that there used to be an archery contest held every year at Mucklesfeld. So we thought we'd put one on to show we can get together as a group to bring back something from the good old days. 'Course, I'd rather set the thing up meself—too many hands in the pastry don't work to my way of thinking—but there's some already as resent me getting in late in the game, so it's go with the flow. Just family invited, so we hope you'll come, Dr. Rowley. Tomorrow, if poss, is what was decided. Afternoon would be best, but there's you and your patients . . ."

"Will you be able to come?" Livonia, no longer holding Tommy's hands but seeming woven to him by invisible cords, asked with no attempt to feign indifference.

"Delighted! No afternoon or evening surgery on Mondays."

"That's what his lordship said when we—well, Judy Nunn specifically—told him about the idea. He also said Miss Belfrey might be receptive to the idea of coming herself and agreeing to her handyman coaching the participants on use of the bows and arrows if you asked her."

"I would gladly have done so," Tommy looked both fervent and crestfallen, "but I'm afraid Celia and I had a falling-out last night. She said some things about . . . about Aubrey's marriage plans to which I took grave exception. And in the ensuing exchange of words she ordered me never to darken the doors of Witch Haven again."

It was an easy guess that Celia Belfrey had made derogatory remarks about the sort of woman who entered TV reality shows in search of a husband. Probably she was repeating what she'd said on earlier occasions without more than a token mumble of protest from Tommy—why bother upsetting the old girl to no purpose? But this last time would have been different; he could not allow her to malign the intent of even one of the contestants— not if he were to meet Livonia again pure of heart. I doubted that Celia would want a permanent breach, not out of any affection, but because Tommy had to be her main source of information regarding Lord Belfrey and what he had in store for Mucklesfeld. Meantime, the breach provided me with an opening that I felt driven to seize if I were to obey my conscience as Tommy had done.

"I'll go to Witch Haven and deliver the message about the archery contest," I said.

"You will?" Livonia eyed me with a mixture of respect and concern. "What if she's nasty to you?"

"Someone has to go, and it can't be Lord Belfrey as he's banned from the premises. I've a strong suspicion that, despite her protestations of eternal enmity, curiosity will bring Miss Celia Belfrey to your proposed event."

"Won't miss the chance to scoff from the sound of her." Mrs. Malloy nodded the hat. "I'll go with you, Mrs. H. After all," she added importantly, "it would be more of a proper invitation coming from one of the contestants, which you're not, when all's said and done."

This wasn't at all what I wanted, seeing my main intent was to have a private talk with Nora Burton. But there was no arguing her point. Fortunately, Livonia spoke up, reminding her of a prior commitment.

"Well, yes, being at the meeting with you and Alice Jones and Molly Duggan to decide what rooms we'll each focus on for setting to rights is important. And I know it was agreed on right after church, but . . ." It was clear from the pursing of her glossy purple lips that Mrs. Malloy was seriously torn.

"What about Judy Nunn?" I asked slyly.

"Her? She'll be out in the gardens, tearing out

308

tree stumps with her bare hands or rerouting the brook." Thunderous brow.

"She's incredible!" Livonia enthused. "His lordship seems very impressed."

"He does?" Tommy nudged at a stray stone with the tip of his shoe. "And may the best contestant win?"

"Absolutely." Livonia looked up at the sky.

"And who that may be is yet to be decided." From the fierceness of Mrs. Malloy's tone, I knew she'd made her decision. She'd be at that meeting not one second late. Breathing a sigh of relief, I suggested that either she or Livonia write a note to Miss Belfrey on behalf of the contestants, which I would take along to Witch Haven. Eager to be of service, however minimal, Dr. Tommy produced a pen and notepad. The missive was dictated by Mrs. Malloy and written down and neatly folded by Livonia.

I lost no time in making off for Witch Haven. It was tempting to linger in the leafy lane, enjoying its green shade and mosaic of shadows on the ground, the warm breeze suggesting a frolicsome mood to the day. Would I be speedily shown the door after saying what I had to say—if given the chance? My hand grasped the door knocker. My heart thudded along with its hammering fall. There was a line between sins of omission as addressed by Reverend Spendlow and sticking one's nose in other people's business. The door opened with startling speed, scattering beyond recoverable reach the words I'd been shoving into random order.

"Good morning," said Nora Burton; she was again lumpily dressed in a wintry-looking skirt and sagging cardigan. The thick-lensed glasses loomed large on her face, contracting her expression of polite inquiry to a lift of the mouth.

"Back like the bad penny!" Assuming admittance, I placed a foot on the threshold.

"Without the dog." She didn't budge. "Did you find the owner?"

"Yes . . ."

"Good, I'll let Miss Belfrey know."

"I have a message for her from the contestants in the reality show." I held it out and watched her pocket it in the shapeless cardigan. "But it's you I must talk to."

"Must?" She stepped backward into the hall.

"Somewhere private."

She stood rigidly still, as if finally the moment she had been anticipating since coming to Witch Haven was at hand.

Aware that the hall might have ears, I whispered the question. "You are Eleanor Belfrey?"

11

No need to explain last night's dream in which I had been powerless to scream a warning of impending danger, or to mention Reverend Spendlow's sermon. No steaming indignation, no guilty outrage from Nora Burton. She retained her calm demeanor, skipping the question as to why her true identity was any of my business to go directly to the core. "How did you guess?"

We were now in her bedroom, she seated on the edge of the bed, I in a cobalt blue velvet chair. A small white dog—a Sealyham terrier asleep in a basket before the fireplace—added the perfect cozy touch. I had always thought I would prefer a small dog. The furnishings were charming, the warm amber, cobalt blue, and rose color scheme reflective of the hall and drawing room. Given Celia Belfrey's demand for perfection, I doubted there was a room at Witch Haven that wasn't lovely.

"Several reasons. Lord Belfrey asked me if my name, Ellie, was short for Eleanor; but there are always any number of ways to abbreviate. I also learned that your last name, before your marriage, was Lambert-Onger. Shorten Eleanor into Nora, take the *bert* from Lambert and the *on* from Onger to concoct Burton, and there you are. But that didn't come to me first. The trigger was your asking if I were talking about Lord Belfrey when I mentioned Georges LeBois the other morning. Afterwards, it struck me as unlikely that Miss Belfrey had never in your hearing mentioned her cousin Aubrey by name. Not because she is fond of him. Quite the reverse. If she would vent her venom to me—a total stranger—then how could you escape being her frequent listening post?"

"What else are paid companions to spoiled, spiteful women for?" Nora's lips curved bitterly.

"Exactly. And Celia Belfrey is worse than either of those two adjectives, isn't she? Look." I leaned forward. "You haven't said it, but I will. I'm sticking my nose into your private affairs. But I'm not doing so for the fun of it. I've heard your story from the three people working at Mucklesfeld and from Lord Belfrey, and I think you're taking a huge risk in returning . . ."

"To the scene of my crime?"

"Lord Belfrey doesn't believe you took the jewels with you when you fled Mucklesfeld."

"Doesn't he?" pushing back her hair in a weary gesture. The thin white line of the scar tracing down from the corner of her eye to her cheek showed up sharply in the light coming in through the window framed in floor-length pale blue silk.

"No. You made a . . . very positive lasting impression on him the day he came to Mucklesfeld and saw you standing halfway up the stairs. When my husband and a friend and I arrived out of the fog the other night, he got the idea that I look something like you did then and still do in your portrait."

"Yes," she said, "I can see that."

"If there is any resemblance, it has to be very faint. You were beautiful. And I have a strong feeling that without those bottle glasses, the scraped-back hair, and frumpy clothes you still are."

"I don't spend much time in front of a mirror. Not because of this"—she touched a finger to the scar—"I just prefer not to narrow my focus down to me. I've spent my life since Mucklesfeld staying constantly busy in unexciting ways. A nursing career, a small flat, and for the last three years Sophie." The Sealyham twitched an ear, then reshuffled back to sleep in the basket. "I counted on being sufficiently uninteresting to have a good chance of getting away with this charade. At the start, fooling Celia was all that mattered. Once over that hurdle, I felt reasonably secure. Although sometimes I do wonder about Charlie Forester. He was always so kind, so eager to be of help to me. But," she shrugged her shoulders, bunching up the cardigan, "it was a very long time ago. I'm not sure I would have recognized him; he's over eighty now."

"If Miss Belfrey hadn't banned Lord Belfrey from this house, he would have presented a problem for you. No disguise or change in appearance would fool him. He seems to me a man of uncanny recall." That wasn't giving away more than was justified, was it?

"He . . . Aubrey made an indelible impression on me, too. For that one breathless moment, I thought I'd summoned up the man who would rescue me. It had been a quite dreadful day." She removed the spectacles and rubbed her forehead above the bridge of her nose. Without them, her face seemed stripped naked and I caught my first glimpse . . . just a suggestion, really, of the loveliness that had haunted Lord Belfrey and the loss of which had played its part in driving his cousin Giles to madness. Nora finally asked the question I would have raised earlier were the situation reversed, but she did so without rancor. "What are you really? Some sort of private detective?"

"Occasional amateur. I'm at Mucklesfeld quite by chance, as I told you. But there was something in the atmosphere right from the beginning, something apart from the accidental death of one of the contestants that drew me in, and that was your story."

"The absconding bride." Something in her misty gray eyes told me talking would be a release now the cat was out of the bag and in my lap.

"Was your husband cruel from the start of your marriage?"

"Giles never treated me badly."

"But Lord Belfrey thought . . . is still convinced you were terrified of your husband after being forced into a marriage contrived by your family."

"That's true. My father was in desperate financial straits as a result of some highly speculative investing. He was on the verge of losing everything and there was Giles offering to save the day in return for one small favor. Me. He'd been infatuated with me for several years after meeting me at Ascot on my twentieth birthday. I had no idea. He was older than both my parents by ten years. I suppose when I thought of him at all, it was as a courtesy uncle." Nora again brushed her hair back from her forehead. A weary gesture. "I was aghast when my father told me, quite unemotionally, what was expected of a dutiful daughter. I railed, of course, but unlike my brother—there were just the two of us—I had always toed the line. Saving the family home for Jeremy to inherit along with an income to support it was of far more importance than any squeamishness on my part. After all, what did I have to complain about? I would be married to a lord."

"So Giles dipped into the Belfrey coffers to replenish your family's."

"And I am supposed to have robbed them further by making off with the jewels."

"You didn't?"

"I'm not a thief."

"No, but I suppose it would have been an under-

315

standable revenge against a brutal, merciless husband. But you say he wasn't that."

Nora resettled the glasses on her perfect nose. "I hated him at first, thought him unnatural for wanting me, knowing I had no feelings for him. Our wedding night is something I try never to think back on. Not because he forced me to submit, he was I suppose pathetically gentle, and there was nothing . . . out of the way, that could be considered deviant. But every part of me recoiled from his body . . . his touch. When I couldn't block those times out of my mind, I told myself they would get better. But it didn't happen, and after a few weeks he moved out of our bedroom. At least I had my nights to myself. He said, very kindly really, that it didn't matter. That having me there, just being able to look at me, like a flower in a vase, was enough."

"That sounds distinctly creepy to me."

She stared straight ahead. "I might have grown kinder in my feelings toward him, if the days had not been so unendurable."

I sat silent in the cobalt blue velvet chair. Sophie the Sealyham slept on. From the continued stare into nothingness, I gauged Nora to be no longer with us but back at Mucklesfeld, avoiding whenever possible the husband who filled her with revulsion, leaving her with only one other source of companionship.

"I understood," Nora continued tonelessly, "that Celia would resent me. Having a stepmother a

316

couple of years her junior and knowing exactly why I had agreed to marry him would have been enraging for anyone in her position. I expected to be either ignored or the recipient of snide remarks, but she went further than that. This," pressing a finger to the scar on her face, "happened when she threw a cut-glass dish at me. It literally came at me out of the blue. Nothing apparent led up to the incident. Celia was sitting in the drawing room leafing through a magazine when she picked it up and aimed it at me. When she saw the blood dripping through my fingers, she said, 'Don't get that on the floor,' and swept out of the room. She and I both knew that I would have made a bad decision in telling Giles. I believed then—and I still do—that she would have found a way to get rid of me once and for all given half an opportunity. I began seriously to fear my days were numbered when Giles bought this house for me."

"Witch Haven? Yours?"

"In their arrangement with him—all very tidy and legal—my parents did seek to secure some protection for me in the event of his death; at which time of course I would've had to leave Mucklesfeld. I was to have a place of my own in waiting. Having paid substantially for the privilege of having a wife who couldn't bear him to touch her," Nora continued speaking without inflection, "Giles himself felt a financial pinch, so it had to be a reasonably priced house. Six months after our marriage, this one went up for sale and he bought it. To my surprise, having come to feel myself incapable of any positive emotion, I fell in love with the place despite its being in a shockingly run-down state. The only contented moments I spent after that at Mucklesfeld were occupied in planning how I would make Witch Haven my own—collecting ideas from magazines, positioning furniture choices on paper renditions of the rooms, deciding what colors I would use. Before leaving, I had an extensive scrapbook."

I looked around the bedroom—the word *stolen* coming to mind. Mrs. Foot had accused Ben of stealing her kitchen. "And you came here a short time ago to find Celia Belfrey occupying your creation?"

"Extremely close. Of course there are some things I would change, perhaps because I have changed, but surprisingly my anger against her didn't spill over to infect my feelings for the house. Perhaps it has the sort of aura that can't be tainted, however unpleasant the personality of the occupant?"

"Maybe." The empathy I had felt for this woman upon first hearing about her, in good part because of my attributed likeness to her, was increasing. I also saw houses as personalities; it was what I brought to my work as a designer. "How did Witch Haven get its name?"

For the first time I saw Nora . . . Eleanor . . .

really smile. "It may be a legend, but the story goes that back in the sixteen hundreds a young woman from this area was accused of witchcraft on the grounds that a young dairy farmer was savagely gored by his bull after she supposedly hexed him. Her version was that she'd had to fight him off on several occasions when he'd cornered her in the lane as she was passing. It was his wife who raised the village against her. On the day she was to be hanged, the squire's son came galloping up to the prison yard waving a writ for her release and plucking her from the gallows as the noose was lowered."

"Romantic! Or was he all about justice?"

"There must have been love, or at least passion, involved in his mission of mercy because he after-wards installed her in this house, with sufficient armed menservants to ensure her protection. And here she lived out her days to the grand old age of ninety-two."

"Was Celia Belfrey also captivated by the house and its history?"

"I'm not sure if she wanted it because it was mine or because it also spoke to her. She had an eye for beauty along with an almost manic acquis-itive streak."

"Almost?"

The smile against rested for a moment on Eleanor's lips before she turned her face away. "That day when I saw Aubrey looking up at me from the foot of the stairs, I had the mad idea that he was that squire's son, having ridden hell for leather to the rescue. As I said, it had been a dreadful day. Celia was in a glinty-eyed fury, as she always was on the days when I sat for my portrait, and Charlie Forester had come to tell me that Hamish the Scottie had been inexplicably injured—what appeared to be a torn muscle in one of his front legs. I knew Celia had taken out her rage on the poor little fellow. I think Giles did, too, but he was always afraid to stand up to her. He told me to go to my room and stay there. It was an order—quietly given, but I didn't attempt to argue. A bolted door . . . that was sanctuary. I think he knew that she was to be feared."

"His lordship's assessment of the situation was that you were his cousin's prisoner. This Charlie Forester, why would he leave Mucklesfeld to work for her here?"

"I think he feels it his duty to keep an eye on her, to be the watchguard against her doing something dreadful, especially against Aubrey now he's back. I don't think she considers Dr. Rowley someone to be dealt with right now. He hasn't taken Mucklesfeld from her . . . yet."

I shivered. The Sealyham lifted her tufted white head and clambered out of the basket onto the bed, to perform a circle before settling down on Eleanor's lap. But she didn't again close her eyes. Had she picked up on my unease? Or did she experience a more pervasive sense of danger? My time with Thumper had led me to believe fervently in the omniscient powers of man's—and woman's—best friend.

"It was during the hours spent in my room that day that I made up my mind to leave and take Hamish with me. I knew I couldn't go back to my parents or let them know any more than that I was safe. It was easier in those days to make an untraceable phone call. I had to disappear, and fortunately I had some friends—beatniks, was my mother's description—who were ready to help me set up a new identity. But I couldn't completely give up the old one. It would have been as if Celia had succeeded in murdering me—and melodramatic as that sounds, I know that was her plan. So I became Nora Burton." She sat stroking the Sealyham with a fine-boned hand.

"When did you learn you supposedly had taken the family jewels with you?"

"Within a few days of my escape. My friends had chosen to break with the circle in which they and I moved, but they still had sufficient access to the latest scuttlebutt. When they told me what was being said, I knew that Celia had taken the only revenge left to her. She would know that Giles would not go after the insurance money and thereby set up a criminal investigation. In his own way, I believe he did love me."

I didn't offer my view on this. There were some

things I did recognize were none of my business. "What finally brought you back?"

"Two things coincided. One of those friends who had helped me start over told me about seeing Celia's advert in *The Times* for a companion cum secretary, and that same week I read an article in another newspaper about Aubrey's reality show and the practical reasons for it. It came to me that if Celia had held on to the jewels, which according to the grapevine had never come on the market, then perhaps she had hidden them either at Mucklesfeld or more likely here at Witch Haven. In the article about Aubrey, it said he'd been married and divorced twice, and now he was being forced into what seemed likely to be a third mistake. And I, who have come to think of myself as the least romantic of people, found myself wondering if he wasn't in need of someone galloping to his rescue at the twelfth hour. Recovering those jewels should enable him to raise enough to get going on repairs and otherwise putting Mucklesfeld back together."

I liked the sound of that. "No luck so far? Not so much as the shimmer of a diamond or the glow of a ruby through a crack in the floorboards?"

She shook her head. "This house has its share of secret spaces behind the paneling and beneath hidden trap doors; not as many as Mucklesfeld, but enough to have kept me searching at night and every other spare minute I have. I'm beginning to think wherever the jewels are, it's not here. Or at Mucklesfeld. I've made a few predawn flits over there . . ."

"That explains Lord Belfrey's household staff claiming to have seen Eleanor Belfrey's ghost leaving the premises by way of an exterior door. Were you minus the disguising glasses on those occasions?"

"I believe so."

"With your hair down and a dark cloak flowing from your shoulders."

She actually laughed. "Yes, to the first, and wearing my old nurse's cape."

"They were all familiar with your portrait."

"Celia needed to be able look at it day in and day out and gloat. I was sure it would be the same with the jewels—that they had to be where she could feast her eyes and her malice upon them whenever the urge seized her. But I'm beginning to think she may have been afraid to risk their discovery, however cunning the hiding place."

"Whether they're here or not," I leaned urgently forward, "you're taking a terrible risk. If she is as crazed as she sounds and she figures out that Nora Burton is Eleanor Belfrey, she may make sure you don't escape her a second time."

"I have to keep looking . . . at least a little while longer."

"In the hope of saving Lord Belfrey from a potentially disastrous marriage? Eleanor, he would be appalled if he got wind of the risk you're taking."

"You won't tell him?"

I hesitated. "If you were doing this to reestablish your reputation and reclaim your old life, that would be one thing, but to walk into the lion's den out of a quixotic notion of female gallantry is an unnecessary sacrifice."

"What difference does my motive make?"

Unanswerable. Especially as I was pretty certain that in her situation I might well have felt compelled to pursue the same course of action. "No, I won't tell him. But forget the jewels and leave here now."

"Soon."

"Promise you'll be careful!"

Ten minutes later, walking back to Mucklesfeld, I mulled over Eleanor's assessment that Celia Belfrey's venom was so focused on the portrait that she couldn't see that the living woman was often in the same room where it was displayed. That might be so; hatred can shift and shape to its own design, blocking out what might otherwise be apparent. Celia might never guess that her enemy was looking at her with living eyes. Then again, something might at any moment bring the truth home to her. And then what? Eleanor might have exaggerated the threat the other woman had posed years ago. Most people, however nasty, will shrink from committing murder. But Celia? I remembered her cruel face and cringed. If only I had not made that promise not to tell Lord Belfrey that Eleanor had come back.

The ideal person with whom to discuss this predicament would of course have been Mrs. Malloy. An impossibility. The reason I had not wanted her to come to Witch Haven with me—knowing I was going to confront Nora Burton—was that as a contestant she could not be party to information that could well and truly disrupt the production of *Here Comes the Bride.* I would not only be dropping a turnip in her applecart but also putting her in the position of knowing something her fellow hopefuls didn't. The same would be true for Ben, who might feel under sufficient obligation to Georges LeBois to lay the facts before him. When it came down to it, I thought sadly, the only one I could have confided in with complete ease of mind was Thumper. He would have listened, assured me with his adoring gaze that he fully sympathized with my conflict, and felt no obligation to bark out the story to anyone.

In the hall at Mucklesfeld I met Lucy, the dingy blond female member of the crew with the dragon tatoos on her arms. She wasn't carrying any equipment, and said she had grabbed at a free moment to go to the loo, from which she was now returning.

"How's it going?" I asked.

She leaned against one of the larger pieces of furniture. "Hell if I know! We got the contestants' organizational meeting without too many retakes, which is something, I suppose. No idea if Georges was happy or not, he's just as snarly if he's satisfied or isn't."

"I'm not clear about the structure."

"As in?" Sticking a hand into her ragged jeans pocket, Lucy drew out a silver-wrapped stick of gum.

"The competition. I mean . . . what's the game plan?"

"Sure. I get you. As you'll know, Lord Belfrey had a formal meeting with each of the contestants yesterday—not much editing of those. Georges wanted all the throat-clearing and twitchy stares kept in. Today and for the duration the women will be assigned individual fifteen-minute interviews. Those will be well weeded, to bring each personality into the sharpest possible focus. I," she tucked the gum in her mouth and tossed away the wrapper, "will be doing the questioning off camera. Georges decided a female voice would be more effective in getting them to reveal more than intended. Keeping the viewers coming back for more means playing into the mentality of the kinds of people who used to pack up a picnic and look for a nice grassy spot to watch the beheading. The more blood and tears the merrier, then and now." Lucy stood chewing her gum. "More often than not, the most revealing stuff comes from trailing around after a subject when they think they're not doing anything worth recording—and most of the time they're right. Eventually, they stop noticing the camera and even the person holding it becomes invisible. At least that's the hope. We also aim for those candid moments between his lordship and one or other of the contestants—walking in the garden, taking a look at one of the rooms, conversing over a cup of tea."

"And he will come to his decision how?"

Lucy shrugged. "From watching the interviews and other film. That's the system as explained at the start of the first episode, but in reality," curling her tongue around the word, "it's bound to come down to the one he can best see himself stuck with for life . . . or at least as long as it takes to get a divorce."

"Was Georges pleased with the mayhem produced by Lady Annabel showing up in the gallery?"

"Who knows?"

"I thought it was a bit lame. He could at least have had her head fall off so she could tuck it under her arm and go bowling. It was only Whitey showing up that succeeded in creating a sufficient panic to drive off Wanda Smiley. How many more does he hope to scare away? I'd have thought a little attrition goes a long way."

"Right." Lucy reached into her pocket again, drew out a packet of cigarettes, turned it over a few times, and put it back. "The idea is to dangle the question as to who may be next at a point when hopefully the viewers are beginning to root for particular contestants. The next person to talk about bolting will be invited to sit down with his lordship and talk out her concerns. His obligation—even if he's already decided against her being the pick of the litter—will be to persuade her to stay."

"It sounds so ruthless."

"Has to be; that's the reality show for you," chewing energetically on the gum. "Sounds as though you've never watched even the first five minutes of one?"

"When it comes to a wedding story, I prefer fiction."

Lucy eyed me in surprise. "That's what the reality show is—life turned on its head so there's no longer anything real about it. Wanda Smiley being the one to leave is what took me by surprise. I'd have bet on either Livonia Mayberry or Molly Duggan, who seemed like two timid little birds of a feather."

"I like Livonia. And there may be more to Molly than meets the eye." Having established myself as a sanctimonious prig, I addressed another issue. "What I don't understand is why Georges wanted me in the library for his ghost scene. He spun me a line about my using my interior design background to draw out the contestants' views on refurbishing Mucklesfeld, but on reflection it seems a bit feeble."

"Don't take offense, but you are a dewy-eyed innocent, aren't you?"

Preferable perhaps to being too old to be scruffily attractive, but I had no idea as to her point. "Spell it out for me."

"Okay, but I'd have thought it was obvious. The great Georges isn't one to batten down his hopes, however remote, of a twist to the plot that'll strike real gold. Look," Lucy again explored her jeans pocket, but this time did not produce the packet of cigarettes, "the entire crew knows Lord Belfrey was knocked for six on first setting eyes on you—that you're the spitting image of some young woman in a family portrait that he's been yearning after like a soppy schoolboy for years."

"So?" The furniture seemed to be crowding in for a listen.

"You do want it printed out in big letters, don't you?" Lucy eyed me with, if there is such a thing, amiable contempt. "Could Georges write the script, honey, it would be bad luck for the contestants and for you the lovely moment when his lordship gets down on one knee and offers you his hand, his heart, and this god-awful house. Of course, you'll probably have to wait for the engagement ring until the money starts pouring in from the proceeds of the show . . ."

"But I'm married!" I was too astounded to fume.

"Georges would consider that kind of thinking bourgeois."

"I also have three children!"

A shrug, followed by more probing of the jeans pocket.

"And a cat!" Somehow I felt that if I could have added, *And a dog,* it would have clinched matters.

"Look," said Lucy with impatient kindness, "I understand the suburban mind-set. But Georges is more narrow in his thinking. He's only capable of taking the broad view when surveying a banquet table."

"That's another thing!" I leaped on the thought. "He seemed to like my husband. Or at least his cooking. Surely even he couldn't be as treacherous as you suggest."

Lucy's look informed me I was a poor, deluded nitwit. Even worse, she patted my arm before saying that if she didn't go outside and have a ciggy, she'd go into terminal withdrawal. I watched her negotiate her way through the obstacle course to the front door. Even from the rear, she had that air of negligent sophistication that makes an asset of unwashed dishwater-blond hair and torn jeans, leaving me feeling frumpish, over-washed, and utterly incapable of rushing after her to administer a sermon on the evils of smoking.

I was determined not to participate in any more of Georges's staged events. Not difficult, on the face of it. But what if Ben wanted to know why I was being obstructive? Would I dash his chance of the publicity for Abigail's, should *Here Comes the*

Bride make it to the small screen? Would he suspect Lord Belfrey of complicity and whack him over the head with a rolling pin? I yearned to discuss this with Mrs. Malloy, but that was out for the same reason I couldn't tell her that Nora Burton was Eleanor Belfrey. To put a spoke in her wheel, or for that matter any of the other contestants', would risk destroying a dream that might raise a mundane life to glorious heights. And then there was Lord Belfrey himself, who had charted his course and was entitled to sail toward the horizon without my sticking my paddleboat in the way. Oh, to have had the ever discreet Thumper as a confidant!

I decided to go into the library, mount the steps to the portrait gallery, and search out the entrance through which the sweetshop lady had emerged to play Lady Annabel's ghost. Opening the door into what was likely the handsomest room in Mucklesfeld, with its remnants of polish on the vast oak floor and wainscoting along with the blessedly limited furnishings, I thought myself alone until mounting the final step of the short, railed stairway, where I beheld Lord Belfrey seated on one of a pair of leather chairs at the far end of the parquet from Lady Annabel's portrait. He rose instantly on catching sight of me. I was struck again by how his most ordinary movement exuded gallantry. He would, I thought, look heroic putting a box of corn flakes in his shopping cart.

Damn Georges! The embarrassment that seized me was entirely his fault. Any woman who wasn't preoccupied by being tied to the stake with flames licking at her brand-new shoes would feel a quiver of response at his lordship's intent, dark-eyed gaze and that smile . . . so warmly welcoming, even when touched by a suggestion of nobly repressed sorrow.

"You've caught me," a rueful lift of the mouth and eyebrows.

"Doing what?" I stood as Lot's wife must have done when feeling herself turning into a pillar of salt.

"Skulking."

"Oh!"

"Escaping the infernal cameras, tripping over cords, blundering into seating that has just been positioned for a scene. Care to join me in my hide-away?" He extended a hand and at my nod drew back to the chairs. I took the closer, he the one he'd just occupied. "It's not the contestants I'm avoiding." His voice deepened with intensity. "They all seem very pleasant women." Was it me he wanted to convince or was he attempting to blot out an inner voice that was telling him he was making the mistake of his life? Backing out now might cause enormous hurt to the five hopeful females. Ticking Georges off would also be an issue, but not likely, I felt, to weigh with him to anywhere near the same extent.

"One contestant" (I had almost said *Another*) "down." I was glad to hear my voice sounding conversational. "Poor Wanda Smiley. She wasn't smiling as she threw her clothes into a suitcase before bunking off." Catching the drawn look on his face, I said hastily that he shouldn't upset himself about that. "They all know that the nasty surprise is a feature of the reality show to pick up the pace now and then. No one's going to tune in just to watch the contestants having races doing the washing up."

"I can't blame Georges if I've grown squeamish." His lordship stared bleakly across the railing. "He warned me, even whilst remaining vague, that he had some startling tricks up his sleeve. Perhaps but for Suzanne Varney's death I wouldn't have these qualms. Could take it all in my stride . . . believe as I did at the beginning that the outcome could benefit not only myself but another."

Sadly, I stifled the urge to protest that a loveless marriage, whatever the practical advantages, was not a cheery-sounding arrangement. Even harder to squash was the temptation to spill the beans that the woman who had held his heart captive these many years was presently installed at Witch Haven. To which I would have added the opinion that if swept into his impassioned embrace, she would not long remain impervious to his admiration. How cruel a fate should he happen upon her in the high street as a newly married man unable to offer her his hand except to unburden her of a shopping basket filled with delicacies to tempt his cousin Celia's peevish appetite! Perhaps there would be a way I could ultimately bring the two of them together, but for now I swallowed the bitter pill of honorable silence. Such thoughts pushed my plan to discover Lady Annabel's means of entering the gallery out of my mind.

"I spoke with the vicar's wife after church this morning," I said with a nicely casual touch.

"Normally I would have been there, but with all the curiosity that's bound to have arisen over what has been happening here, I opted out today." For the first time I caught a look of his cousin Tom in his lordship's boyishly apologetic gaze.

"Completely understandable." Awful to cause the beleaguered man a moment's discomfort, but I was about to put my foot in it further. "Your cousin Celia mentioned yesterday, when I went to her house to see if she might know who . . . the dog belonged to, that Mrs. Spendlow was the person Suzanne intended to visit before coming on to Mucklesfeld."

"And did they meet?" There was nothing guarded about his interest.

"Yes. They were old friends who hadn't met in years. Apparently, Suzanne had something on her mind that she had kept to herself for some time, but for some reason felt Mrs. Spendlow would be the right confidante. Unfortunately, their time together was interrupted before she got to the heart of the matter. All Mrs. Spendlow was able to say was that Suzanne was dealing with a great deal of anger."

"No idea what or who was the cause?" Now he did look and sound somewhat troubled.

I shook my head. "But if bracing herself to talk about whatever happened brought some of that anger to the surface, perhaps Suzanne wasn't at her best when handling the car at the time of the accident. On any other occasion she might have been just that bit more alert . . ." My voice wobbled to a halt and his lordship touched my hand. All very discreet, but something connected between us, a mingling of intense emotion. We were talking about a woman—still quite young—who had died.

"Poor Suzanne," he murmured deeply. "I remember her as very likable. And Judy Nunn speaks fondly of her. Livonia Mayberry also knew her, though rather less well. Perhaps they might have an idea what was on her mind."

"Not if Mrs. Spendlow is correct in her understanding that she was to be the first in whom Suzanne confided."

"Yes, I'd forgotten that point. But one must assume something quite dreadful . . ." He stopped. We had both heard someone enter the library below, not that whoever it was was noisy about it—indeed, there was something hesitant, tentative, it could even be said surreptitious about those footsteps, followed by a soft closing of the door. Lord Belfrey rose to his feet—his courtesy as instinctive doubtless as the curiosity that caused me to follow suit. There was no telling how visible we would have been, obscured by the gallery railing and shadows collecting in the corners, but the person who had come in did not look up. After a quick, jerking glance around the library proper, she tiptoed, head down, to stand in a bare expanse of wood floor with only the billiard table, which did not take up undue space. An island of serenity compared to the suffocatingly overcrowded drawing room and hall.

She placed a smallish rectangular object on the floor (impossible to see what it was without leaning dangerously far over the railing). Then she drew some item—or items—from the pocket of a full peasant-style skirt before bending down to remove her shoes in the same stealthy fashion that had accompanied her entrance. It did not occur to me to wonder why Lord Belfrey had not called down to her, let alone descended the stairway. He and I had become the intruders in the vignette. Setting the shoes under the billiard table, she sat down, picked up what she had taken from her pocket—slippers of some kind—placed them on her feet, and proceeded to lace them above her ankles. Before getting back up, she touched the rectangular object, and music—glorious, if at a subdued sound level, Tchaikovsky—poured into every particle of the rather musty air that was Mucklesfeld even at its best.

I felt the pressure of his lordship's shoulder, heard the catch of startled amazement in his breath, but neither of us murmured a word. Nor did it occur to me to wonder what Georges would have made of our standing glued together like the ornamental bride and groom on top of a cake. Molly Duggan—for it was she who, incredibly and improbably, raised her arms above her head, fingers touching to form a Gothic arch—started to dance on her points. Those hadn't been slippers but block-toed, satin ballet shoes. My hands gripped the railing when she teetered. She was going to fall splat on the floor in an ungainly heap of dumpy, frumpy forty-year-old woman. Unbearable to watch. We all have our dreams, ridiculously unrealistic though they may be. But no! She steadied, spread her arms, arched her back, and extended one leg behind her in the pure straight line of the arabesque. Out the corner of my eye I saw that Lord Belfrey also had a fast hold on the railing. Then he ceased to exist.

The music was from *Swan Lake* or, as my mother, who had been a ballet dancer, would have called it, *Le Lac des Cygnes*.

Gone also were the peasant skirt and black top. Molly was Odette in a white tutu with a cap of snowy feathers on her head as she leaped, twirled, and fluttered, light as down, achingly tragic . . .

The early wobble must have been caused by a moment of distraction, perhaps as her eyes went to the door in fear of someone coming in and discovering her secret. For I had no doubt that this Molly existed in absolute secrecy, quite apart from the woman who worked in a supermarket and was probably most generally known pityingly as the meddling Mrs. Knox's daughter. Suddenly, with a shift in tempo, she was Odile in black tutu and feathers, her movements no longer dreamy and sad but sharply edged, evilly bewitching, the pirouettes faster, the leaps even higher, so that it was hard to believe she could be airborne without being held up by strings. Again the music changed. No longer Tchaikovsky, but a composer I didn't recognize. This piece was not white or black, but the misty gray of cobwebs, and that is what Molly became—a filmy drift upon the air, fragile beyond belief. I held my breath in the fear that she would brush against the billiard table and disappear. Then, abruptly, it was over. The music faded away to nothing and did not resume. Molly removed the ballet shoes, replaced them with her ordinary ones, picked up the player, and after a final furtive glace around her as if fearing that the walls had tongues as well as ears, tiptoed from the room.

"Incredible!" I said into the silence that descended.

"I'll be damned!" said Lord Belfrey. After which we started down the stairs to hover speechless in

338

the space where the magic had occurred. After a couple of minutes, I looked at him, he looked at me, we both nodded and went out into the hall. Understandably, Molly had not lingered there clutching the evidence of her secret life—unless she was hiding behind one of the larger pieces of furniture, which would make no sense, especially as who knew what recording devices peered and listened out of holes that only the likes of Whitey would find charming. It spoke to Molly's desperate need to dance that she had taken so great a risk in the library. But for her surreptitious entry and exit, I might have wondered if she had entertained the possibility that his lordship might be a hidden audience to be enchanted into choosing her for his bride. No, her fearful uncertainty had seemed genuine. By now I felt sure Molly was back in her room, back pressed to the door, trembling at the enormity of her daring, yet glowing at the memory of the music that had given her wings.

I could see the lake in the moonlight as I stared rapturously into his lordship's dark, unfathomably thoughtful eyes.

"It was the same for me, Ellie."

"And yet the most incredibly beautiful moment was when she became the cobweb fairy. Oh, someone," unaware of doing so I placed a hand on his arm, "has to write a ballet just for her and call it that—*Cobweb and . . . Candlelight*. She was both, wasn't she . . . shadow and radiance!"

"Yes." His mouth curved gently.

"I suppose the reason I care so much," I continued haltingly, "is that my mother was a ballet dancer. She died when I was seventeen."

"Such a vulnerable age."

"I still miss her." Words I hadn't spoken in a very long time. A shaky laugh. "Not an ounce of her talent came my way."

"You have other gifts." There was no missing the tenderness in his voice, but he was a kind man.

"Something must be done about Molly. Oh, I don't mean," sensing his reaction, "that I think you ought to choose her as your bride, only that she can't be left to dance in hiding. It's such a waste."

He nodded. "How blind we are much of the time to who people really are. She seemed so ordinary, but she isn't . . . in fact, quite the opposite. You are absolutely right, Ellie, something so lovely should not be kept hidden."

"Yes," I whispered, enraptured by the thought of Molly curtsying amidst a shower of flowers as the curtain came down behind her.

"Pardon me for interrupting." The suavely pleasant voice belonged to my husband. In the act of turning, I saw the hand I recognized as possibly . . . just possibly . . . my own resting on Lord Belfrey's arm. It weighed a ton as I lifted it; a crane would have been useful, but there wasn't even one in that foolishly jam-packed hall. Silly! Of course I was uncomfortable for nothing. Ben couldn't possibly think his lordship and I had been looking just a little bit too cozy. Or could he? That tightening of the jaw, the brilliant flash of his blue-green eyes that accentuated the dark line of his brows did give me pause; as had been the case with Wisteria Whitworth when Carson Grant came upon her gazing limpidly into the eyes of the highly eligible justice of the peace shortly after her release from Perdition Hall. She had merely responded to his avowals of sympathy, yet she sensed with palpitating bosom and trembling lashes that Carson had misconstrued. A triumphant joy had seared her soul, before melancholy seized her. Looking into Ben's now-closed face, I missed out on the joy and had to settle for melancholy for the heart-ticking moments it took for common sense to return.

"Hello, darling!" Wide smile. "Lord Belfrey and I have been sharing a magical moment." Sensing from the lack of responsive glow that as clarifications went this was opaque at best, I entreated his lordship: "Is it all right to tell him?"

"Of course, but perhaps it should go no further at present."

"I'm afraid I haven't time just now to share whatever makes the two of you look so pleased with yourselves." Ben twitched a smile that didn't fully reach his lips, let alone his eyes. "Georges sent me looking for you, Lord Belfrey. He wants you in the dining room in ten minutes for luncheon with the contestants."

"I'll be there."

"And, Ellie, Georges has requested that you join the ladies for the sweet. Regrettably, as I understand it, his lordship won't be present for that course, but chocolate is always a great compensation, isn't it?"

Somehow it didn't seem to be quite the right time to say that I didn't wish to fall in with any other of Georges's schemes and be drawn into explaining the reason. Suddenly both men were gone and I was alone with the creaking of floorboards. Or was it the sneering whispers of ghosts? At least, I thought, as I trailed up the staircase, they wouldn't start guffawing. Even a hollow laugh would be too merry a sound at this Mucklesfeldian moment in time.

12

Applying lipstick to quivering lips is beyond my limited makeup capabilities. After staring bleakly in the spotted mirror above the bathroom basin, I tossed aside the tube and dragged myself downstairs. I was sure I could put matters right with Ben, given ten minutes alone with him—not possible when he was in the final rush of preparing lunch, but hopefully very soon thereafter? The tense scene with him and Lord Belfrey had lowered my spirits, so that my banked-down missing of the children bubbled to the surface. It was not only their dear faces that I saw through a mist of tears . . . but Thumper's also. And while I was sure that Tam, Abbey, and Rose were happy in the care of Gran and Grumpy, I had doubts that Thumper had been joyfully reunited with the Dawkinses. Rushing to open the dining-room door, I had trouble sticking a smile on my face. And really, why bother, when I would instantly have to switch to scowling at Georges?

There he was in his wheelchair, but so screened by crew and equipment that my glare was swallowed up in the tension that fogged the air. Lord Belfrey was seated at the head of the rectangular table with Mrs. Malloy to his immediate right, while Molly Duggan occupied the privileged position to the left. Alice Jones sat next to Mrs. Malloy. Livonia Mayberry had the chair next to Molly. Judy Nunn was at the foot of the table. What was to be made of that distinction?

His lordship rose to his feet at my arrival. This courtesy was accompanied by a general turning of heads and some scattered smiles, including a crack in Mrs. Malloy's cement face. Impossible to believe Ben had not provided a superb meal, but she had the look of a woman whose insides had turned to stone, requiring serious drilling if ever to be put right. A growl from Georges might or might not have been a greeting. When it came to the crew, I was patently of no more interest than a crack in the timbered ceiling.

I had not previously been inside the dining room, and though like the library not excessively burdened with furniture, it had all the hallmarks of Mucklesfeld gloom. The dark oak paneling would not appear to have been polished in a hundred years. Curtain-sized cobwebs were the only window treatments for two narrow panels of grimy glass. The sideboard was hideously carved with mythical creatures that looked ready to come to life with a vengeance at the sound of a dropped fork. The massive rusty iron light fixture above the table—unlit, as were the several lamps scattered around the room—might have seen former service when the need arose to string up a clumsy footman. As for the dark oil paintings dotting the walls, even the most menacing family portraits, instilling the urge to put oneself up for immediate adoption, would have been preferable to those gory battle scenes and lamentable shipwrecks.

His lordship stepped aside to offer me his chair, then addressed a few gracefully kind words to the contestants and myself and left the room. Georges barked something, the crew murmured back. Only Alice Jones roused herself from staring at the frayed tablecloth to flick a glance their way. Feeling very much the intruder in the wake of such lackluster greetings, I consoled myself that I no longer felt blinded by the camera lights. Either I was adapting to their glare or had permanently lost the ability to blink. I waited for Mrs. Malloy to voice her delight that I had spared time from my unoccupied day to join them. Oh, how I relished the memory of her barbed affection before her foolish urge to marry into the nobility had put a dent the size of the Grand Canyon in our relationship. As the silence mounted, I yearned to whisk off on a magic carpet to the United States or any other outback of civilization that had never cottoned on to the notion of titles. What had I walked in on this time?

Mrs. Malloy failing to take pity on one less fortunate, I was grateful when Livonia suddenly and sweetly came to life. "Look," she said, in her gentle voice, "it's a strain for everyone trying to make the best possible impression on Lord Belfrey." I doubted she included herself in this statement, but there was no doubting her sincerity. "Lunch has been so lovely—the food, I mean." She smiled at me. "Why don't we all make an effort to relax with each other and enjoy the pudding when it comes? Doesn't that sound a good idea?"

"I always say sweet," countered Mrs. Malloy, who did nothing of the sort. In any other company she would have been holding forth that a jam roly-poly was a pud, as was anyone of them fancy meringue things Mr. H was so fond of making. And don't let the Queen herself say different.

"Really?" Molly, looking neither a swan nor a cobweb fairy but ordinary to the point of frumpishness, sounded uncertain yet eager to open herself to a different view of the world. "I always think of a toffee when someone mentions sweets. I've always loved toffees, but I can't eat them now I wear dentures. Mummy will continue to say false teeth, which sounds so much worse. More . . . more dribbly, if you get what I mean."

"Oh, I do," exclaimed Livonia. "Can't mothers be awful? Not Dr. Rowley's, I don't mean her," delightful blush, "she sounds as though she was absolutely lovely. Perhaps the reason he hasn't married is that he hasn't found a woman to equal her. Of course, anyone the least bit nice would never try to compete with her late mother-in-law."

"I'm not the least competitive," Alice Jones of the abundant hair and home-woven clothes broke in. "That's why I find the situation we are all in—other, that is, than Mrs. Haskell—so stressful. I know I should have anticipated being uncomfortable, but thinking about something isn't the same as being thrust in at the deep end."

"No, it isn't," agreed Livonia, "and I think your teeth are absolutely lovely."

"Mine?" Alice looked delighted.

"Oh, yes, but I meant . . . also meant Molly's."

I heard myself say that everyone present had lovely teeth. How stupid could I sound? A diversion would have been welcome. Alas, the huge and rusty light fixture, so reminiscent of a medieval torture apparatus, did not begin swaying ominously overhead. Nor did the cutlery choose to leap out of a sideboard drawer and go skimming like unguided missiles through the air, as had reportedly happened at yesterday's lunch. It seemed that, like Homer, Georges sometimes nodded.

"I know I haven't been very chatty," Judy spoke from the foot of the table, "but I've been thinking about the grounds."

Mrs. Malloy folded her arms purposefully under her bosom and curled a damson lip. "You would be!" Honestly! Georges (I couldn't bring myself to look his way) had to be lapping this up like double cream. The woman needed to be shoved under the table and her hand trodden on if she attempted to crawl out.

"How can you not be thrilled, Judy, by the repairs you've already made to the broken wall?" I rushed to say. "I understand you all got together this morning to plan what each of you will do to improve Mucklesfeld while you are here."

"We did." Alice Jones fingered the frayed edge of the tablecloth. "I said I would go through the linen cupboards. Plunket," like a true mistress of Mucklesfeld Manor she forewent the *Mr.,* "tells me there are ten of them, although Mrs. Foot said there were not more than seven."

Mrs. Malloy stared at nothing, unless hopefully

into her conscience. Livonia looked at her hands, but whether because she wasn't deeply engaged by improvements at Mucklesfeld or was thinking of Tommy Rowley could only be a mind reader's guess.

Alice tucked up a bundle of hair that had escaped from a large tortoiseshell comb. "However many cupboards there may really be, I hope to locate a sewing machine and repair as much of the linen as I can. It doesn't match up to Judy and the wall, I know." There was none of Mrs. Malloy's rancor in her voice and Judy responded appreciatively.

"Kind of you to say, but we all do what we can. I can't sew a stitch."

"Same here," said Molly. "Working in a super-market isn't my life's dream," no faltering or conscious look here, "but like I said this morning, I started out stocking shelves." That must have thrilled Mother Knox. "Boring, unless you learn to take pride, and it taught me a thing about being quick to get organized. So I think I can help organize the furniture, at least to make better paths through it."

"I could help you with that," I offered, realizing with surprise that for several minutes now I had been unaware of Georges, crew, and moon-sized stare of the camera.

Livonia turned to me. "Oh, Ellie, you are kind. I said if it would help I'd make up inventories of what's in each room. Being a bank teller isn't the most exciting job in the world either, but you have to be quick and make sure you're correct to the penny. The only difference is I'll be adding up tables and chairs." She beamed at me. "Could you also give us some ideas of what is and what isn't valuable so I can make note of that, too?"

"I'll tell you what I think."

"That is nice." Molly looked directly at me for the first time. There was nothing in her gaze beyond gratitude, nothing to suggest that she connected me in any way with the library.

"This is all well and good," proclaimed Mrs. Malloy with a toss of her black head with its two inches of white roots and a heightening of rouge, "but what the place needs more than anything is a start on a good clean. From the looks of it, that'll be left to Muggins here."

Before offers of assistance in this nearly impossible endeavor could pour in, Mrs. Foot entered the dining room wheeling a trolley with one of Ben's delectable chocolate orange gateaux ornamented with Chantilly cream, candied almonds, and marigold petals. Knowing it to be laced with Grand Marnier, my tongue melted at the sight. Behind her came Mr. Plunket, bearing a tarnished silver coffeepot. Creeping in last came Boris. A cheery raspberry pink short-sleeved shirt emphasized quite horribly his zombie appearance. That he carried a knife, admittedly a cake one, served to heighten the impression that he had been given his orders and would perform them in glassy-eyed fashion.

Mindful, one presumed, of the need to display aplomb worthy of the mistress of Mucklesfeld even when faced with having their throats cut, not one of the contestants squealed. Indeed, a smiling Judy complimented him on the shirt.

"Taken from a dead man."

"Oh!" Livonia committed the solecism of turning pale.

Seizing the moment for additional points, Mrs. Malloy said in her best high falutin' voice: "How frightfully nice of some . . . body," capping off this *bon mot* with a posh-sounding chuckle.

Mrs. Foot placed the gateau on the very edge of the table, either unaware of the risk or daring it to attempt a flying leap so she could flatten it with a hand that outmatched it in size. "The word's *corpse*."

"So it is! So it is! Trust you, Mrs. Foot, to know the medical terminology." Mr. Plunket chuckled appreciatively. "Comes from all her years as a ward maid," he confided to the gathering, which at that moment decreased considerably with the clanging exit of Georges and the crew. "But to explain clearer, Boris didn't himself take that there shirt of his off the bod . . . corpse. He got it from an undertaker acquaintance of ours. Amazed you'd be," Mr. Plunket was now wending his way around the table with the coffeepot, missing more cups than he hit but not appearing to notice the sloshy saucers, "proper amazed at how many people don't want the clothes back that their loved ones is brought in wearing. Isn't that right, Mrs. Foot?"

"True as you, Mr. Plunket, and Boris is standing there looking so handsome. And not just clothes, neither. Tell the ladies, Boris."

"Glass eyeballs and false teeth, too. Always got customers waiting for them has our friend." The zombie voice would have produced a chill regardless of subject. As it was, Molly pressed a hand to her mouth. She had been correct in saying that the word *dentures* had a far less dribbly sound than *false teeth*.

"Nothing wrong with economizing is what I say." Mrs. Foot took the knife from Boris and began hacking up the gateau, sprinkled liberally with gray hairs.

Mrs. Malloy drew on her better nature to pass Molly the first piece.

"The waste that's going on out there in the kitchen makes my stomach turn." The wiping of the blade on her grubby apron caused my insides to perform the same feat. "All that chocolate when a tablespoon of cocoa would have done just as well."

What hadn't been wasted on Mr. Plunket, I feared, was the Grand Marnier. I got a strong whiff of orange as he again paused at my side to tilt the empty coffeepot over my cup before weaving on to do the same for the others. But he managed to inform us steadily that the one exception to Mrs. Foot's rules of economy was when it came to her tea making.

"Always a good strong cup."

Sadly, his fondness for other beverages must have destroyed his taste buds. I exchanged glances with Mrs. Malloy and experienced a spurt of pleasure when her expression mirrored my thought. There would again be times when we thought as one.

"No one brews up better than Ma," droned Boris.

"Now then," Mrs. Foot stopped licking the knife blade (mercifully having finished passing round the portions) to give him and Mr. Plunket her broad, gap-toothed smile, "that's enough about me, you two. Go to the stake for me, you would!"

"Isn't that wonderful?" said Judy warmly.

"Oh, yes! Lovely!" Livonia laid down her dessert fork after raising it halfway to her lips.

"Nothing like true friends," chimed in Alice.

"When they're not being awkward." Mrs. Malloy sailed a look over my head.

Molly ventured a closed-mouth smile.

"There was something I was meant to tell you ladies." Mr. Plunket stood scratching at his face, when he didn't miss it by a yard. "Now, what was it, Mrs. Foot? Do you remember, Boris? Never mind," lowering a wobbly hand, "I've got it. His nibs asked me to tell you his cousin Miss Celia Belfrey will append . . . attend the archery contest.

She sent word round just a few mim . . . minutes ago by Charlie Forester, who said he'll be haffy . . . happy to . . ."

"Provide instruction? How very kind of him!" Poor Mr. Plunket, I had to rescue him before he stumbled over his tongue and fell flat on the floor. Presumably the same thought caused Mrs. Foot to grasp him by the elbow and airlift him out of the dining room with Boris lurching behind.

"He's been at the booze!" Alice said, on the possibility, I supposed, that no one else had noticed.

"Ben will have done his best to keep it away from him." I hoped I didn't sound defensive. "But he'd have to turn his back sometimes. He may not have seen Mr. Plunket come into the kitchen . . ."

"No one could blame your husband." Livonia's blue eyes brimmed with sympathy. Was she swept up in a new understanding of the burning need to protect one's beloved against even a hint of unjust criticism?

"Never knows who's there or who isn't, does Mr. H, when he's in cookery heaven." Mrs. Malloy sounded so much like her old self that I found myself relaxing on her account as well as Ben's.

"Mr. Plunket seemed all right when he first came in," said Molly, seemingly restored after the false teeth business.

"I don't know a lot about drink, but Harold told me—he was always telling me things—that alcohol takes effect less slowly in people with severe post nasal drip. But," she added cheerfully, "I'm beginning to think he wasn't nearly as clever as he thought, except when it came to door and window handles, which was his job."

Nobody asked who Harold was or the nature of his career in handles, either because Livonia had already explained him to the other contestants or because he sounded such a dreadful bore. Judy demonstrated a knack of knowing when to change the subject by bringing up the archery contest.

"I'd forgotten it's set for tomorrow. I do hope Lord Belfrey is pleased his cousin seems willing to bury the hatchet at least for an afternoon. I don't like to think we've put him in a difficult position."

"If anyone's up a tree, it's me." Alice speared a piece of gateau but didn't attempt a bite. "I've never held a bow, let alone shot an arrow in my life. I know what will happen. My hair will fall down all over my face," a poke at the recalcitrant tresses, "and I'll shoot myself in the foot, or worse yet someone else in the eye."

"Remember," pointed out Judy, "this nice-sounding man Charlie Forester will be there to show those of us new to the sport what to do."

"That's right." Molly, who had been looking twitchy, smoothed out.

"And Tommy . . . Dr. Rowley is coming," said Livonia to her coffee cup.

"With an ambulance?" Alice, whom I was beginning to like, slumped theatrically back in her chair.

"Naturally some of you will be glad of the lessons." Mrs. Malloy smoothed a hand down her majestic bosom and assumed a look of unconvincing modesty. "As for meself, I don't claim to be an expert in the sport, but I do believe I've acquired sufficient knowledge to do Mrs. H, here, proud."

I yearned to wipe the smug look off her face; instead, I forced myself to sound admiring. "How exactly have you come by this knowledge of archery?"

"And you asking me that, Mrs. H! As if you didn't read that book by Doris McCrackle same as I did."

"Perdition Hall?"

" 'Course not! *The Landcroft Legacy* is what I'm talking about. Remember how when Semolina Gibbons was coming back across the moor—after visiting old Mrs. Weathervane, who wouldn't tell what she knew about the body in the bog on account of her varicose veins putting her in a mood—someone shot an arrow at her . . ."

"Who?" Livonia was so intent, her elbow went into her cup.

"Unfortunately," Mrs. Malloy was brought to the brink of a smile by the recollection, "Semolina couldn't see who had tried to kill her, because of the mist that she didn't want to admit to herself was really a fog, seeing as she'd promised the rector who had taken her into his household when he came upon her as a waif selling matches one dark and dismal night in a mean little street . . ."

"Oh, I love match girls!" Livonia's eyes remained riveted on Mrs. Malloy's face, even as she wiped off her elbow with her table napkin.

"So do I!" Molly was looking equally entranced.

"Certainly enterprising," said Judy, after absently (it must be assumed) swallowing a forkful of gateau.

"The rector, as was named Reverend Goodhope—you'll remember that, Mrs. H— couldn't bring himself to buy any of Semolina's matches because he disapproved of their use for lighting up pipes and cigars . . . cigarettes too, although I don't remember him mentioning them. It's a very politically correct book. All Doris McCrackle's books are politically correct."

"How did he light his fires?" Alice asked reasonably enough.

"With a flint box," Mrs. Malloy said. "He was a very flinty gentleman, but kind in his way to Semolina. The reason he had made her promise never to go out in a fog was that his sister had left the house in a temper—no custard with the jam sponge was the trouble, I think—got caught in a pea souper, and never returned. Although," Mrs. Malloy's voice took on a sepulchral overtone, "her ghost was said be glimpsed in the avenue between the rectory and Landcroft Lodge. And there had been a number of other deaths before her; Doris

McCrackle can't never be accused of being stingy when it comes to the number of bodies."

"Corpses," Alice corrected naughtily.

Mrs. Malloy waved a dismissive hand. "Semolina briefly suspected the dean's butler, but he had led a blameless life, unless you'd call giving innocent young girls tours of the Deanery pantries, with particular emphasis on the bottled fruit, wicked."

"Oh, I do love Deaneries," exclaimed Livonia. "They're so Trollope!"

"Splendid author," said Judy, "although perhaps rather too focused on the indoors. A little more about herbaceous borders and potting soil would . . ."

"Interestingly," Mrs. Malloy placed unnecessary emphasis on the word, "all the deceased women had spoken fluent Flemish. As did Semolina's mother that was Belgian before the consumption took her."

"I never have time to read anything but shelving manuals," Molly said from the edge of her seat.

Mrs. Malloy rewarded her with a magnanimous nod. " 'Course the villain didn't always stick to the same weapon. Variety gave him his thrill, the nasty bugger! He'd been bullied as a boy, you see, by being called a stick-in-the-mud. But he did like bows and arrows best."

"Surely not the rector!" Alice gamely took part. "His own sister added to the laundry list!"

"That's what we was supposed to suspect, either him or Sir Lucimus Landcroft as had dared to love Semolina despite his twitchy left eye and nasty allergy to red vegetables. It was his new undergardener as had the bad speech impediment—only that turned out to be put on because he was really Inspector Smith from Scotland Yard as solved the crime. There'd been a second attack on Semolina, you see, and the inspector explained, without a hint of a stammer, that even an experienced archer can miss if he tenses up and releases the arrow too soon."

Mrs. Malloy drew up straighter, expanding her majestic bosom. Only the orb and scepter were lacking. "It is the memory of Inspector Smith's detailed explanation—at least eight pages, of what an archer should and shouldn't do—as makes me confident that, all modesty aside, I won't show meself up in tomorrow's competition."

Modesty was several miles down the road.

"But must it be won? Why can't we all go out and enjoy ourselves?" Judy looked down the table.

"Because, like it or not," retorted a tight-mouthed Mrs. Malloy, "everyone for themselves is the nature of a competition!"

And I had thought for a brief, flickering glimmer that she was coming back into her own! Full of herself, long-winded, but able to capture the interest of most of her listeners. Now, as sure as she had a hundred pairs of shoes, she was going to blow any gained goodwill. Then again—hope reared its foolish head—maybe not.

"It was a lovely story." Molly's look of beholding some distant vision suggested she might have missed Mrs. Malloy's biting comment. "I can picture it made into a breathtaking ballet; the murder parts set to Beethoven's Fifth, and the scenes at the Deanery to Handel, with interspersions of Wagner, Chopin, and Liszt."

"Not Wagner, if you don't mind my saying so, Molly," demurred Livonia with utmost seriousness. "Not because of his music, but I don't think he was a very nice man. I picture him as much more like Harold than Tommy . . . Rowley, for . . . just one vague example."

"I don't like the bally, in fact," Mrs. Malloy added a self-congratulatory chuckle, "I think it's bally awful."

Nobody could have missed that one. Before Molly's face had finished crumbling, and before Alice could get her mouth more than a third open, Judy said, with an obvious attempt at keeping a grip on her temper, that it was always a matter of each to his or—this case her—own opinion.

"So, what's your idea of enjoying yourself, Miss Candidate for Sainthood?" Mrs. Malloy's defiant attempt at a laugh came out as a snort, quite unfitting a future mistress of Mucklesfeld. "Would it be thinking you've already won Lord Belfrey's heart with your looks and charm? A shame you're not tall enough to look in a mirror once in ten years!"

The ensuing silence was the loudest I had ever heard. A pinched-faced Judy made no reply, but the gleam of tears in her eyes spoke paragraphs. No one else said peep, fearing perhaps, as I did, that to say anything would only make matters worse. If I could have produced a clap of thunder to startle Mrs. Malloy back to sense—demonstrated by a crawling, sniveling apology—I would have done so. As it was, I would have to wait until I got her alone. Or so I thought for the second and a half before a deafening crash of what sounded like vast wooden cymbals blasted us all back in our chairs, followed by an immediate plunge into darkness. A higher power at work? But just how much higher? Even in my shattered, trembling state, I couldn't help thinking that Georges had been remarkably quiescent during this gathering. Had he just made up for such restraint with a bang?

Judy's voice pierced the blackness. "That sounded to me like exterior shutters being clapped shut outside. There weren't any at these windows when I was walking around that side of the house this morning, but it wouldn't have taken any time even for one person to install them."

" 'Course not." The meek voice sounded vaguely like Mrs. Malloy's. Too little too late, I feared, to put her instantly back in anyone's good books, but at least she wasn't (as yet) ratcheting up the tension. "It could have been done right before lunch; no one was likely to go outdoors when waiting for the gong to bong, so to speak."

"There aren't any shutters at any of the windows." This sounded like Livonia. "It isn't the house for them, is it? I mean, it's not a villa in the South of France or that type of place."

"I'll feel my way over to the door and try for a light switch." That was Alice. As with Judy's, her voice was instantly recognizable. A scraping back of chairs, followed by some blundering into one another (the dark truly was impenetrable), and then Alice again. "I've found it." Minuscule pause. "Nothing! The power's off, at least in here."

"That Georges!" Judy sounded back to her bracing self. "No one can accuse him of not doing things in style. Have you tried the door handle?"

"Won't turn."

"Could I try?" Livonia offered. "One thing I got out of my relationship with Harold were a few, supposedly top secret company tricks on how to wiggle a lock. If someone would pass me a knife . . . Oh, thanks, whoever you are! A butter one, that's perfect!"

Hope flamed . . . flickered . . . ebbed and died.

"Sorry. It has to be bolted on the outside. Harold didn't have any solutions to that one."

"Good try, Livonia," said Judy. Echoes of agreement rose and fell.

"Well," Mrs. Malloy said (perhaps a little less

puffily than usual), "like Wisteria Whitworth exclaimed when the padded cell door closed on her . . ."

"Who?" several voices inquired.

"Another of Doris McCrackle's heroines," I supplied. "On that occasion she told herself there was no reason to panic and absolutely no use in screaming because no one would hear her. We'll be heard, but no one will come because they'll be under orders not to interfere. Even my husband will feel compelled to stuff his fingers in his ears. Luckily, unlike Wisteria, we aren't dealing with reality—except in the silly sense of the word. This is a game. Another of Georges's wacky challenges to see if the five of you can display steel under pressure. Meaning there has to be a way out of here. You just have to find it."

"But you'll help, won't you, Ellie?" said Livonia steadily. "Perhaps your being here is Georges's way of giving us a bonus card. You have a professional understanding of houses."

"If anyone can find a secret exit, it'll be Mrs. H here." Even though my anger at Mrs. Malloy for bringing that gleam of tears into Judy's eyes did not evaporate, I couldn't help being touched by the pride in her voice. "Couldn't put in a book all she knows about old places. Wouldn't brag about it herself, she wouldn't—modest to a fault, always was and always will be."

This was laying it on too thick. Aware that

362

attempting to sound self-deprecating would come off as self-satisfied, I kept silent.

"Glad for the silver lining," said Alice. "Of course it's too much to hope that Georges has supplied us with a torch."

"Even if they aren't remarkably scarce at Mucklesfeld, he wouldn't make it that easy."

"And to be fair to him, Ellie," Judy's voice came from close beside me, "it's not to be expected that he would make things easier. A shame I'm not one wearing my hiking jacket; there's a penlight in one of the pockets."

A general murmur of resigned disappointment.

Molly spoke up. "I don't know anything about secret passages and that sort of thing, but it doesn't seem likely we'd find an opening on the window wall."

"I don't know all that much either," I said in the direction of her voice. "Despite Mrs. Malloy's praise, I'm not an expert on houses the age of Mucklesfeld." Answering snort. "Most of what I've gleaned—rightly or wrongly—comes from reading books of the sort written by Doris McCrackle. And in those fictional accounts the hidden opening is often found, after a great deal of tapping of the wainscoting, on one side or other of the fireplace."

"There's a lot of paneling," said Molly, "but I didn't notice a fireplace."

"Well, I don't suppose you would have done,"

came Mrs. Malloy's determinedly mellow rejoinder, "but it's there on the back wall at the top of the table, closed off with a piece of metal sheeting." Something I, the authority, hadn't noticed.

Although not good in the dark (Ben might disagree), I managed to fumble my way without excessive bumping into furniture—hard-edged—or the other women—softer-edged—to the wall in question. A sharp yelp preceded Molly's warning to be cautious of the metal fireplace covering. With considerable overlapping of hands, we proceeded to frisk the wainscoting. To be frank, I wasn't entirely convinced we would locate a means of escape from the dining room other than the ones bolted against us. But just when I was thinking that past inhabitants of Mucklesfeld must have been a very dull, unimaginative lot, who hadn't deserved the treat of being scared out of their wits by being forced to hide from the Roundheads or harbor a popish priest, someone bumped into me, causing my knee to jerk forward.

"Is whoever that was all right?" inquired Judy from somewhere to my right.

"Blissful," I said, staring into an opening the size of a cupboard door, which though shadowy revealed the start of a passageway, suggesting that somewhere ahead was a window or even an exit. "Don't anyone trample on me as we escape Georges's clutches!"

Exuberant exclamations, cheers, and laughter exploded as I stepped forward. There was, however, nothing of a stampede in the surge behind me. The light neither brightened nor waned as we made our crocodile march down the narrow, timbered face fifteen or so feet before finding ourselves at the top of a stone stairway.

It was Judy who noticed the candlestick and box of matches. "A clue that we're meant to go down," she said, and to my relief Mrs. Malloy did not inform her that this was too obvious to bother mentioning.

"Oh, I do love clues," said Molly from my immediate rear. "I'm actually enjoying this adventure."

Judy lit the candle, put the matches in a hip pocket, and we began the downward procession.

"It is rather fun, isn't it?" I could hear the smile in Livonia's voice as we continued down, girded on both sides by walls that looked as though they had been around before Hadrian got busy doing his showing off. "Or maybe it's just the relief of being out of the dining room, which I didn't much like even before we got locked in."

"New curtains could make a difference in there and everywhere else." Alice also sounded chipper.

I thought of Witch Haven's restful charm that could withstand Celia Belfrey's personality. Cross as I might be with Mrs. Malloy, I couldn't bear the thought of her living out her days at Mucklesfeld.

Whatever was needed to restore both the structure and the spirit of the house could not be provided by even the most happily married couple, let alone two people brought together out of practicality or ambition. What the place needed was to be crammed as full of life as the hall and drawing room were currently full of furniture.

Having reached the bottom, we found ourselves in an empty cellar small enough to show itself reasonably clearly in the candlelight. No wine racks, filled or empty, no sprouting sacks of potatoes. The only thing to say for it was that it appeared dry—no lichen or mold on the walls. Indeed, the air smelled reasonably fresh. The faces of the other women seemed more clearly defined, more fleshed out than they had done in the dining room before the lights went out. I put that down to a reaction from the plunge into darkness, but then I felt the energy flowing from each of the contestants, with the exception of Mrs. Malloy, who suddenly looked all her sixty-some years.

Alice stood bundling her hair back up. "Georges and his crew have to be filming us through spy holes, otherwise where would be the fun for the viewing audience? May we all agree we're showing the jokester that any one of us could deal with a crisis as Lady Belfrey?"

"Ellie found the way out of the dining room and she isn't in the running," Livonia reminded her.

Take that, Georges! You and your twisted hope

of an uncontrollable passion arising between Lord Belfrey and a wedded woman!

"It's not a bad cellar as such places go, but I'd love to get back out into the gardens." Judy smiled ruefully. "Should we start prying apart the walls and floor?"

"Please don't anyone think I'm pushing myself forward," said Livonia at her most tentative, "but it seems to me that even without the candle we wouldn't be in pitch dark, so there has to be a faint amount of light creeping in somehow, doesn't there?"

"What if," suggested Molly, who looked and sounded breezily confident, "those spy holes Alice mentioned are cracks between the stones in the wall? The ventilation they provide could explain why the cellar is dry." Taking the candle from Judy, she paced left, then right—eyes shifting from walls to ceiling. "Maybe the cracks—even the widest of them—aren't easy to see because they're filmed over with cobwebs of the same gray as the stone. Except, of course, for the one being used to spy on us; that would likely be high up, even in the ceiling."

"Knowing Georges, he would prefer looking down on us," I said. "Also, he won't want to be caught on the spot when we do manage to break out of here."

"Okay, but even if there are cracks big enough to get our fingers into," Mrs. Malloy stood a shade wobbly on her high heels and looking as though she'd have dearly liked to sit down and melt into the flagged floor, "how do they help us? Even if we could get a grip, stone's not what you could call lightweight." She and I share a gift for pointing out the obvious. "Unless," she reenergized sufficiently to purse her lips and raise a black painted-on eyebrow, "a section of wall has been replaced with something made up to look just like the rest. You know, Mrs. H, one of them faux finishes you're always going on about, now everyone's wanting the insides of their semidetached to look like a Tuscan villa these days."

"Work done in this case courtesy of Georges's minions." I nodded. "That secret panel in the dining room must have been mentioned to Georges as one of Mucklesfeld's manifold charms, and he went from there. I remember now his mentioning to me, in his usual conceited way, earlier in the week, before the crew came on board, he ordered some stage work done."

"What's the betting we're closing in on what he was boasting about?" Alice gave a comradely hug to Judy, who said that if she were Georges she would have camouflaged the removable section of wall with a thicker layer of cobwebs.

"Shall we start scouting?" Livonia turned to Molly, at which point we heard the faintest sound of organ music, so thready it was almost like someone humming, which reminded me of the dean's butler in *The Landcroft Legacy*. I remembered how the evil-sounding tune had drifted into Semolina's ears when she was lost in the moorland fog. The onset of music from an unseen source can be one of the scariest sounds in the world, even . . . I reminded myself, even when knowing, almost a hundred percent, that it was being filtered into the cellar on the instructions of Georges, if he wasn't rapaciously twiddling knobs himself.

We all looked at each other, before gathering closer together.

"It's all right," said Molly without a quaver. "All part of the fun."

"I'm getting meself worked up to chuckle me head off!" said Mrs. Malloy.

"Perverted sense of fun," amended Alice rather jerkily. "I've . . . never cared much for that tune. It's so bouncily jolly . . . it's creepy."

What tune? The music swelled to fill the cellar, making it impossible for any one of us not to recognize "Here Comes the Bride." Silly not to have instantly known from the organ. The tempo picked up to skipping speed, then slowed . . . deepened . . . scraped the bottom of a misery a dirge could not have found. I could picture it—St. Mary's in the Dell so welcoming when I was there that morning, the veiled bride being dragged, clutching and moaning, toward the now sacrificial altar.

"I told you it's a horrible tune." Most of Alice's voluminous hair had tumbled down and she made no move to pile it back up.

"Any music can be twisted around." Molly moved up close to her.

"Georges is a pain in the neck," said Judy in her mild voice, "but seeing he must want us to get out of here sometime today, I wouldn't be surprised if he gave us a hint, by having the music come in loudest near the removable stone, if there is such a piece."

" 'Course the trouble is," I could hear the effort Mrs. Malloy made not to sound irritably contradictory, "this isn't no great big space. So the music's bloomin' loud everywhere."

At that moment the music gentled down to the point of sleepiness . . . or death. There followed a rush over to various walls, a pressing of ears to stone, a narrowed riveting of the eyes. Within moments, Livonia, the formerly timid and repressed, let out a whoop of joy.

"I've found it—the section of wall that shifts! The tune was piping directly into my ear. Oh, these cobwebs on my hands! But it doesn't matter . . . the gap's big enough for me to get a good grip. Some of you come and help me. I don't want to be knocked backward, even if it is only Styrofoam coming down on me."

I wasn't among the first to rush forward. To be honest, I was glued to the floor, stunned that what had been posed as a farfetched theory appeared to be on the money. Mrs. Malloy wasn't speedy, either. In her case the problem seemed be aching feet, although I pretended not to notice because even though she had behaved so badly to Judy at lunch, she was my pal and, as she often says, if you don't have your pride and an egg in the fridge, what do you have?

As she and I discovered on making up the rear, the fake portion of wall came out in easily controllable portions, leaving us facing a door-sized opening, beyond which according to Alice—the first to go through—was a passageway. Ubiquitous at Mucklesfeld. This turned out to be similar in size and length to the one leading from the dining room's secret exit, though less shadowy, due to a good-sized window above a door to our right. Of recording devices or human activity there was no sign, suggesting that immediately before the wall came down there had been rapid flight. But there was no budging the door when Judy tried the handle.

"It has to open to the outdoors," I said, "or there would be no sense to the passage, just as there has to be a way up to our left. Did anyone notice when the music stopped? Or were we all too focused on the wall?"

With hardly another word said, we headed in hope of the staircase which, unless it had been blocked up for the pure enjoyment of doing so by Belfreys past or Georges present, had to be there. It was, and even Mrs. Malloy was renewed sufficiently that she ceased to hobble. Indeed, as we mounted the steps—wooden ones this time, which somehow seemed encouraging—her high heels tapped out a beat that I suddenly realized made an accompaniment to a renewal of organ music. That same oh so merrily macabre tune I would never again hear without thinking of death and decay, which was what we came upon as we headed around a turn of the stairs. In the corner of the dusk-filled landing, in a sitting sprawl, was a hideously grinning skeleton, gowned as for a debutante's ball in diaphanous chiffon.

"Well," exclaimed Mrs. Malloy over the now insanely pounding "Here Comes the Bride," "don't anyone tell me that isn't Eleanor Belfrey—murdered by the husband just like I said. Wonder what closet Georges found her in?"

13

It was the gown that chilled me to the core. Something about the cruelly draped neckline convinced me that here was the lovely ivory creation Eleanor had worn when posing for the portrait. I knew it was impossible that the hideously grinning skull and dangle of bones were her remnants, unless Nora Burton had lied to me and the physical resemblance to the vanished bride had been a lucky (for her) happenstance.

The spirit of adventure that had sustained us to

this point evaporated. Not a word was spoken as we edged past the appalling object and hurried en masse up the next flight of stairs. But numbed though I was, I remembered Mrs. Spuds mentioning that Dr. Rowley's skeleton from his student days was missing from the cupboard in his study.

Had it been nabbed or given willingly? More likely the latter. If Georges had mentioned to Tommy his need for one as part of the activities planned to help choose the right bride for Lord Belfrey, who could blame a fond cousin for stepping into the breach? The more sinister question was, who had suggested and perhaps offered up Eleanor's gown? And why? Why take the risk of grievously wounding Lord Belfrey, knowing that he cherished her memory? Or was that exactly the point? Was someone seeking to provoke his lordship into putting a stop to the filming? If that was the hope, it would fall flat if none of the contestants babbled a description of the skeleton's ensemble, which from the current vibes I was getting seemed likely.

On reaching the final steps, we were faced with a piece of paneling, which after a limited amount of poking and pushing by Judy slid sideways to reveal the library gallery. So this was how Lady Annabel had gained admittance, shielded from blatant sight by the sudden dimming of the lights. The place above and below was unoccupied. No audience to greet the return of the wanderers, no disembodied applause, not even a door ajar to provide mirthful or sympathetic peeking. Judy said she was more than ready to go outside and continue working, while the others, including Mrs. Malloy, seemed eager to scatter without further comment. I was ready for a word with the evil mastermind. I'm sorry to say that the thought I gave to Ben was a passing one. Events had pushed from my mind his witnessing the starry-eyed moment I'd shared with his lordship. Had I remembered, it would have seemed too silly to need bringing up. And really, after all, I shouldn't have to explain myself. If anyone was at fault, it was Ben for being irritated. As a faithful wife I didn't deserve suspicion.

I was the last to leave the library, and beheld Georges wheeling down the hall from the direction of Lord Belfrey's study.

"You, sir, are a fiend," I informed him glacially.

"Spare me your compliments," he replied with gleeful contempt. "What part of this afternoon's festivities delighted you most, Ellie Haskell? Was it not generous of me not to leave you out of the entertainment?"

"Not if your hope was for me to faint dead away, as I did the other evening, and have to be deposited on a sofa, causing Lord Belfrey's chivalrous heart to stir at the sight." Or, I wondered, had someone else hoped for that outcome, not necessarily with myself but one of the other contestants? Pushing this niggling thought aside, I continued.

"Understand, Monsieur LeBois, that I'm on to your idea of setting me as a cat among the pigeons, and if you keep it up, I'll lock myself in my poke-hole bedroom and not come out till it's time to leave Mucklesfeld."

"Speaking of holes . . ."

"Let's not."

"Then the music?"

"The only thing I'm willing to spend time talking to you about is . . ."

"Madame Skeleton? The pièce de résistance, would you not agree, my dear Ellie?" His eyes burned above the beaky nose, the fleshy face quivered with sly pleasure. "Was it not sporting of Tommy Rowley to loan it to me?"

"Did he," I asked with a sinking recollection of Livonia's sweetly gentle face when talking about the doctor, "also give you the dress that pathetic bag of bones was wearing? And if so, did he tell you to whom it belonged?"

"Of its provenance I am ignorant," Georges said with supreme indifference; then a dawning alertness passed over his bloodhound features, suggesting he was telling the truth. "From your manner, dear child, I now hazard the guess that the onetime wearer was Eleanor Belfrey. I was told— by whom I will not divulge, so much do I adore hoarding secrets—that its well-preserved condition was due to its having been carefully stored."

"In a drawer or chest in Lord Giles Belfrey's

bedroom," I said more to myself than to Georges, the one room perhaps that his daughter, Celia, had been prevented from entering, since it was locked and the key placed in his pocket on leaving. But what if—another possibility came hard on the heels of the first—Celia had taken the gown to Witch Haven, to gloat over as she did the portrait, and it was she who had given it to Georges?

"If you don't want Lord Belfrey to tell you *Here Comes the Bride* is done with before it's finished, you'd better make sure whoever provided that gown understands the necessity of keeping his or her mouth shut. The sense I get from the contestants is they're a decent bunch, uninclined to chatter beyond themselves about such a mockery of death." With this parting thrust, I left him to make my way up to my room, where I found Ben asleep on the bed. A few minutes later, he stirred and elbowed himself up to stare bleary-eyed at me. Bending forward, I kissed the top of his dark head.

"Hello, darling, back from prowling the rabbit warrens," I said, plopping down at his feet. "How's Georges been treating you?"

"Haven't seen him. I wasn't worried about your surviving his fun and games—you thrive on that sort of thing, although why he included you in his theatrical folly I've no idea—but how did the other contestants hold up?"

"Gamely. We ended up in a cellar, but it didn't take us long to discover the way out."

"Mrs. Malloy still reveling in the hope of becoming the next Lady Belfrey?"

"I'm not so sure," I smoothed a hand over the bedspread, "but I certainly haven't said anything to discourage her."

"That would be unsporting, sweetheart." Was there a hint of sarcasm in his voice? "Not just a lord, but a king among men. You don't, I gather, hold the nature of these challenges against him?"

"How can anyone? The women must all have had some idea of what they were getting into. If there weren't anything to be endured, it wouldn't be the kind of show anyone would watch on television. And if Georges is inclined to go overboard at times, that's on him."

"Shouldn't his lordship insist on knowing exactly what is going on?" Ben swung his legs off the side of the bed and stood looking down at me with that appraising look that he normally reserves for the children when suspecting they aren't facing up to facts.

"Oh, I know what's getting to you," I said crossly. "You've got this bee in your bonnet that Lord Belfrey has a thing for me, and like any fool of a woman I'm incapable of not being ridiculously flattered. Well, it is good to know that he likes me—he's nice and any bright spot is welcome at Mucklesfeld—but what he and I were talking about outside the library was Molly

Duggan's dancing. Ballet. She'd crept in, turned on Tchaikovsky, and morphed into a swan. Oh, I know," interpreting his blank expression, "that no one would guess from looking at her. That's swans for you—exquisitely graceful on water, and disappointingly waddly on land. Not that Molly waddles, but she is ordinary, even frumpy, just like the poor little ugly duckling."

"Are you saying," Ben sounded both surprised and interested, "that she's good at all that leaping, twirling on tiptoe stuff?"

"I don't know enough to tell if she's an Anna Pavlova or a Margot Fonteyn, but she certainly blew me and Lord Belfrey away. I'd gone into the library to look for the entrance onto the gallery used by Lady Annabel, and he was there . . ." I got no further because Mrs. Malloy came in and gave Ben a look that suggested he make himself scarce. She plunked herself down on the bed, forcing me to shift to the edge.

"They're few and far between, but thank God some men can take a hint," she observed morosely after Ben had shot out the door. "And don't you go spoiling this little visit, Mrs. H, by harping on about me going off on Judy Nunn."

"I've no intention of doing any such thing," I said. "The fact that your feet were aching afterwards was a clear sign of remorse, considering you've so often told me you've been wearing high heels since you were two. Obviously you've got it in for her because you're convinced she's going to be Lord Belfrey's choice . . ."

"That's not it," a sigh ruffled the bedclothes, "although I don't think I'm the only one as thinks she'll be picked."

"Then why? She seems such a nice woman."

"That's it in a nutshell, I suppose, Mrs. H. She's one of them sort as never has to bother about what she's wearing, or if she has her eyebrows on or off, because nobody else cares neither; she's just Judy as seems to suit everybody down to the ground. Makes me feel kind of inferior, and that don't happen often on account of me having been three times chairwoman of the Chitterton Fells Charwomen's Association. 'Course I'm not saying she does it on purpose, but right from the first I got me back up."

"Get over it," I retorted the more firmly because, despite my liking for Judy, I empathized. "I've been in that boat at one time or another and it goes nowhere. Besides, if his lordship gets wind that you're picking on her, you're likely to dish your chances."

A pause, causing me to wonder if she had nodded off to sleep.

"That's another thing bothering me, Mrs. H. At first you could say I was in a dream, picturing meself Lady Belfrey, but like I got to thinking in church this morning, call it a sacred revelation if you like, what's lovely in books don't have quite the same thrill in the day to day. A husband's a husband whatever way you slice him—wanting to know where his socks are when they're right there on his feet, or stuck in bed with lumbago, banging on the table if you don't fly up the stairs the moment he wants helping to the loo! And then," a hesitation suggesting we were getting to the crux of the matter, "it's not like Lord Belfrey will worship the ground I tread on like Carson Grant did with Wisteria Whitworth. To be picked because I'm good at flapping round with a feather duster won't have me floating on air, however handsome he is. And anyway," disgruntled stare, "what woman needs a man as would have you wanting to pick up the nearest knife and give yourself a face-lift when he comes sashaying into the bedroom in his silk pajamas?"

"You underrate your mature charms," I was saying when the door opened and in came Livonia, clearly eager to talk about the afternoon's events although displaying an awkwardness in Mrs. Malloy's presence.

"Sorry to interrupt, but I wanted to ask you, Ellie, what you thought of this afternoon's escapade? Wasn't the skeleton awful? So . . . so disrespectful to the poor creature. I wonder where Georges got it?"

"I wouldn't put it past him if it was his own mother." Mrs. Malloy got off the bed; as she often says—usually when it's time for the washing up—she knows when she's not wanted, "Or his father, for that matter. Looked like a man in drag to me; my third husband had that same silly grin when I'd catch him in one of me best frocks. And them teeth! Women always do a better job brushing!"

I was glad of her interruption. Certainly I wasn't going to tell Livonia who I believed to be the source of poor Nellie or Ned. But something in my look must have given me away, because the moment Mrs. Malloy went out the door, Livonia sank down on the bed to stare up at me in wide blue-eyed distress.

"Oh, not Tommy—Dr. Rowley, I should say— surely he wouldn't allow Georges to make such a cruel mockery of . . ."

"Calm down." I sat beside her. "If it was his skeleton, I'm sure he never dreamed she'd be put in that dress, which is what made it all vicious."

"But he seems so very sensitive. So noble . . . in the sweetest way. When I was telling him on the walk back from church this morning about Daddy's final days at Shady Oaks, he said he had worked there for a couple of weeks one summer filling in for a colleague, giving up his own holiday to do so. Isn't that an amazing coincidence? He wanted to know what I thought of the care provided and . . . well, he was just so kind."

"Which is why you shouldn't be bothering your head about that skeleton. By the way, did you ever talk to Suzanne about her father's treatment at Shady Oaks?"

"I expect so. When we met there, our dads were our only connection. But I don't remember anything specific. That day in London she said she'd taken her dad's death hard and changed the subject. She was the type uninclined to give much of herself away."

"That's what Mrs. Spendlow, the vicar's wife, said, although if they hadn't been interrupted she's sure Suzanne was going to open the floodgates to her." I explained the relationship. "Did you get the feeling that inside Suzanne might be a very angry person?"

"No, controlled is how I saw her. Judy, who knew her better—although not close friends—described her as intensely private. She knew nothing about Shady Oaks when I brought it up, or of any personal relationships, with men I mean, only that Suzanne had been briefly married. But she did say she believes Suzanne signed on for *Here Comes the Bride* to try to escape some haunting sorrow."

I doubted Judy had used that exact phrase, but I got the point. Fond as I had grown of Livonia, I was relieved when she went. Lying back down on the bed, my mind shifted, lighting on scraps of remembered this and that, until it became a whirl of conjecture. I suspected that Suzanne Varney's arrival at Mucklesfeld had placed someone in a most awful dither. But murder? I still tried to tell myself that that was carrying things into the realm of a Doris McCrackle novel.

That evening Ben brought a meal up on a tray, which we shared companionably without saying very much. He did mention that no one had eaten the gateau at lunch, and hoped that was because the meal had been interrupted. Not wishing to put any blame on Mrs. Foot, I assured him that was the case and told him I'd love him to make another; it had looked so delicious, I would dream of it for days if not given the opportunity to sample three or four slices. Telling me I looked tired, he asked if I would be offended if he slept in the bedroom Wanda Smiley had been set to occupy before her abrupt departure. Knowing how claustrophobic he must find the cubbyhole, I said he should enjoy a good night's rest, returned his kiss, and after he had left with the tray, thought about reading. Instead, I did more thinking, before turning off the light and going out like one myself.

I awoke the next morning to find some comfort in the offing. Nothing—meaning Georges—was going to persuade me to participate in that afternoon's archery contest. A half hour later, I informed Mrs. Malloy of this decision on meeting her in the hall. I was wearing my outdoor jacket— the weather having looked sufficiently dull to suggest the possibility of rain—and was going out for a prowl around the village.

"Well, don't make a week of it, Mrs. H!" She eyed me through lashes given a furry application of mascara, which brought into lurid play the neon eye shadow, brick red rouge, and purple lipstick. Whatever her despondency of last evening, she had her war paint on today. "You owe it to me to be there to watch, and don't go denying it. Who got me reading them silly romance novels? And who's going to cheer me on to a bull's-eye if you don't? Won't be Mr. H, he'll be inside busy preparing a spread for those as feels like a little something to celebrate the winner. Which I'm not saying will be me, seeing as the Bible says boasters will taste the bitter ashes of despair and wallow in the welter that is the land of Woebegone."

Although I can't claim to be a biblical scholar, this sounded more like Doris McCrackle to me, but I did promise to return to witness the event.

"However, don't expect me to stay if you're wearing a Robin Hood hat and calling people Friar Tuck, Maid Marion, and Little John."

"No need to make jokes, Mrs. H!"

I reminded her that I'm always nastiest at dawn, which to me includes nine in the morning, asked her to tell Ben I would be gone with luck for the entire morning, and set off for Grimkirk. After not much wandering down the high street, I came upon a café with an overtly ye olde worlde exterior that suggested more than prepackaged sandwiches and instant coffee. Over very satisfactory bacon, sausage, fried tomatoes, and cups of tea that helped ease the memory Mrs. Foot's tepidly nasty brew, I again allowed my thoughts to wander down dark alleys. The only sanguinity I could arrive at was that if Mrs. Malloy and I were alone in our suspicions that Suzanne Varney's death had been engineered, no immediate danger appeared to loom. I pictured myself marching into the police station and pouring out my concerns to the man or woman at the desk and the winking side glance directed at a cohort.

I killed—such an unfortunate word under the circumstances—the next half hour wandering in and out of shops, avoiding the sweetshop on principle. On the brink of buying a couple of finger puppets for Abbey and Rose at the Jack and Jill's, I reached into my jacket pocket for my purse and felt the piece of plastic I had taken from Thumper when he returned from his excursion into the ravine. The memory was so achingly poignant that I left the puppets on the counter and set off in the direction of Tommy Rowley's house. What harm would there be in asking Mrs. Spuds if she knew how Thumper had settled back with the Dawkinses? Besides, a longer walk would revive the appetite presently sated by the kind of breakfast I ate at home only on weekends. I planned to stop for lunch before my return to Mucklesfeld and a possible attempt at ensnarement by Georges. Turning onto the long drive off the leafy lane, I wondered if Monsieur Malevolent had hoped that yesterday's challenge would cause one or both of the more timid contestants to follow Wanda Smiley's example and flee Mucklesfeld. I doubted he could have guessed that the lure of a dance floor for Molly, and Livonia's burgeoning feelings for Tommy, had enabled them to withstand all he had dragged out of his sleeve thus far.

I found Tommy prowling around the flowerbeds at the front of the house and explained that although very pleased to see him, it was Mrs. Spuds I had come to see, telling him why.

"She's gone down to the butcher's, always does on a Monday. Talked about lamb chops for dinner, very nicely she does them, too, makes the mint sauce herself, famous for it. But you should see her this afternoon, if that helps; she's planning on going with me to watch the archery contest. Imagine one being held again at Mucklesfeld after all these years; of course there's no telling if Giles would have been pleased or not. There was no reading him at all during the last twenty years." Finally drawing a much-needed breath, he stood staring at me in awkward schoolboy fashion. That he was aware he'd been babbling, I doubted. Some strong emotion had him by the throat, forcing a series of gulps as he now looked pleadingly at me.

"Miss Mayberry . . . Livonia . . . how is she? Last night in bed, I remembered the skeleton I loaned Georges LeBois. I'm afraid I didn't think much about it at the time, not then being acquainted with any of the contestants. It seemed a harmless enough prank, since I'm given to understand that a show like *Here Comes the Bride* must have some scary moments; it's why I never watch that sort of program. But this seemed mild after someone told me they'd watched one where the contestants had to eat slugs and . . ."

"That would have been a straight survival show; this one is a mix of romance, if you can call it that, and life's nitty-gritty." I studied the weeping willow. "Livonia did seem a little upset at the thought of your lending the skeleton, but I don't think she will hold it against you if you want to be her . . . friend."

"A friend! Dear Mrs. Haskell, my feelings for her go so much deeper! But would one so lovely . . ." he went on in this vein at such length that I couldn't not help wondering how much of his reading was confined to medical journals, but he was a dear man—or I was prepared to assume he was, so I listened, made sympathetic noises, was tempted to pat him on the head and tell him he was a good boy, and tried not to look relieved when he wound down. I didn't mention lunch for fear he would invite me in and offer me a Marmite sandwich while continuing to wax rhapsodic about Livonia. I could have told him about every quivering breath she took, but a perennial schoolboy had to grow up sometime and do his own finding out.

Remembering his providing the tablets that had cured my headache, I wished him well before bidding him a firmly motherly goodbye.

The weather had now turned sufficiently chill to make me glad of my jacket, and thinking that another decent cup of tea would be welcome, I returned to the same café. Shepherd's pie sounded good and just right for a Monday that had seen said meal served up in many an English household when what was left of Sunday's joint wasn't sufficient to be served cold.

The place was crowded, and I was joined at the table for two by a woman in a pink wooly hat and beige raincoat who proceeded to surround her legs and mine with shopping bags that should have needed six arms to carry them. She very kindly told me the haddock would have been a better choice, and then seemed to feel she owed me her life history, which I would have reveled in at any other time. The son-in-law with the ring through his eyebrow who'd never worked a day since the first kiddy was born, and them all three of them such sweet little things, though it was a shame Emma—just four as of last Wednesday—every now and then showed signs of a temper that had to come from her other granny who'd had trouble with all of her neighbors going back years, but of course it did no good saying anything . . .

The waitress, rushed off her feet, was a little slow bringing out our meals, so to show her I hadn't been in any rush, I ordered the treacle tart and coffee, heard about Mrs. Pink Wooly Hat's other daughter—the one who'd never given a moment's worry, except that she did keep changing jobs, and although it couldn't be said she was living above her means . . . Sneaking a look at my watch, I discovered it was a quarter to two, fifteen minutes before the archery contest was due to start. And start on time I knew it would. One of those unpleasant rules of life is that nothing starts late when you hope it will. Also the contestants would be galvanized to punctuality either in the hope of gaining points for themselves or because of a growing team spirit.

I hoped my hasty departure did not offend my table companion, but it was as I expected on reaching the end of Mucklesfeld's drive and rounding the rear of the house. Mr. Plunket and Boris were adding a final couple of lawn chairs to a row some yards in front of the ravine. Even now, two chairs were occupied by Mrs. Spendlow and the woman I had sat next to in church. I nodded and smiled but did not go over to them. The contestants were grouped together on the lawn above the terrace near the fountain and a motley assortment of worse for wear statues. Perhaps not all of the contestants; I couldn't see Judy, although being diminutive she could have been invisible inside the huddle. Georges and the crew were positioned close to the house wall. A sturdy, middle-height elderly man in a jacket and cap moved between the two groups, occasionally extending a hand, palm up, as if testing the wind. There didn't seem to be much of one, but Charlie Forester—for that's who he had to be—had in his manner of moving and the tilt of his head the look of an expert on all things nature. I could see the bows and arrows on a table alongside Georges's wheelchair and the round target on a tree to the forefront of one of several small, unpruned groves.

Mrs. Foot came out the door by which Judy, Livonia, and I had entered the house on arrival. I heard her asking Georges if he would like a nice cup of tea, only to be rudely ignored. At which moment I heard Mr. Plunket's voice raised in what sounded like a greeting, and turned to see Celia Belfrey seat herself in queenly fashion, and to my amazement Nora Burton—alias I knew who—take the chair next to her. Before I could finish gaping, Tommy Rowley joined the audience with Mrs. Spuds, who waved at me in friendly fashion.

But this was not the moment for pondering. Lord Belfrey made his appearance, went up to the group of contestants, and was heard offering words of encouragement and warnings to take care. Echoes of which were then instilled in a crusty, confident voice by Charlie Forester.

"Safety first, for your own good as well as others. Never—repeat, never—turn if someone calls your name or there are any other interruptions. That's the way serious accidents happen." He rumbled informatively on longbows and recurve bows. "The thirty-five-pound bows cause more damage than the twenty-five, which will be used this afternoon, along with target arrows—wooden ones with wooden fletches."

"It all sounds rather intimidating," I heard Alice say, but with an edge of laughter. "Do we get a good practice in first?" Charlie assured her that they'd all have the basics down pat before firing their first arrows.

Livonia and Molly stood in what to me looked like nervous conversation, while Mrs. Malloy, having actually replaced her high heels with lace-up shoes she must have borrowed, pivoted this way and that, pulling an imaginary bow, eyes narrowed in deepest concentration. Lord Belfrey retreated to stand alongside Georges. What, I wondered, would be his reaction upon approaching his cousin Celia? Would something deep in his being cry out in recognition upon beholding her hired companion? My thoughts had been so occupied with this question I had forgotten the absent Judy, but in turning my head to see if I could detect anything from Nora Burton's posture, I saw Judy emerge in the familiar hiking jacket from the ravine at a fast pace. Head down as if to carve out more speed, she did not look up until nearing her fellow contestants still hearkening with various signs of interest—Mrs. Malloy's the least—to the words of Charlie Forester.

"So sorry to keep you all waiting," Judy said with remorseful embarrassment. "Afraid I lost track of time down there hunting for a few final pieces of stone to finish the wall. Have to go inside and wash my hands, but will speed on back."

Mrs. Foot, who had the entry door open prior to going back inside—perhaps to make herself one of those cups of tea that no one else seemed to appreciate—held it for Judy and they went in together. At that point, I became increasingly absorbed by what was going on immediately in front of me. If the entire audience and crew had got up and left, I wouldn't have noticed.

Charlie continued his flow of instructions while the bows were handed out by a blank-faced Boris, hindered rather than helped by Mrs. Foot, when she returned from the house. Provided with their sporting weaponry, the women—still absent Judy—wandered around in circles, occasionally pausing to bump into each other.

"Line up your stance and look directly at target when preparing to shoot," instructed Charlie, moving, bravely in my opinion, among them. There was quite a bit of turning when being spoken to, despite having been told this was taboo, and much dropping of arrows.

"If you don't listen, I'll never make shooters out of you. Anchor index finger to corner of the mouth. That's not your finger, it's your wrist," he informed Mrs. Malloy, who bared her teeth in a smile. "Keep shooting arm straight," he told Alice. And then to Molly: "Make sure nock is firmly on string."

What was a nock? I wondered.

"Elbow high," he said to Livonia.

How very confusing it all was! Which elbow; hadn't he just said to keep the shooting arm straight?

"Don't release, still practicing!" For the first time he raised his voice when looking at Mrs. Malloy, who indeed appeared poised to let fly.

Judy came out of the house. Lord Belfrey crossed the lawn toward the audience, halting midway for what seemed like a full minute before moving slowly on. A joyous barking rent the air and . . . could it be? Yes! It was! Thumper came flying into view, colliding with his lordship and several others—the audience having grown since I last looked. What was to have been a family affair had turned into a village outing. Knowing it was me he had come to see, bless his dear faithful heart, I hurried to greet him before he could further disrupt the archers. I was kneeling on pebbly ground, holding his wonderful furry warmth close, when there was a scream to my rear followed by a torrent of exclamations.

Heart in my mouth, I released Thumper, ordering him to stay, and raced back to the source of whatever had happened. Georges, for once looking anxious, was wheeling himself at speed in the same direction, the crew hurrying along with him, while Lord Belfrey and Tommy Rowley came up behind me. On the ground, encircled by the other contestants, lay Judy. Charlie was kneeling beside her. For a long—excruciatingly long—moment I was sure she was dead. There was an arrow protruding from her chest that had to be close to her heart. Tommy brushed urgently by me, but before he could take medical action, Judy opened her eyes and against instructions from all sides sat up, looking dazed but sounding quite coherent when responding to the babble of questioning coming from all sides.

"I'm fine," she kept repeating.

"But how's that possible?" Livonia stood twisting her hands. "You've got an arrow . . ."

"So I have." Judy looked down and—without a blink—pulled it out. "It must have gone in the notebook in my jacket pocket." She managed a shaky laugh. "How lucky I am, although," she added ruefully, "I think I may have sprained an ankle when I went down."

Here was something for Tommy, at Lord Belfrey's anxious urging, to examine. While doing so, he admonished Judy in a very grown-up doctor voice for removing the arrow herself. He talked about tetanus shots, and for all the grimness of the situation I sensed his awareness of the glowing looks bestowed on him by Livonia. But the troubling question hung heavy in the air: How had Judy come to be shot? No one asked until Tommy rose to his feet, saying the only injury appeared to be the ankle, which was already beginning to swell.

"What happened, Charlie?" Lord Belfrey placed a hand on Forester's shoulder.

The keen eyes in the leathery face returned his look man-to-man. "I was talking to this lady here," nodding at Molly. "They'd all been told not to shoot till I gave word for the first to move in front of the target. Sometimes it happens that someone gets a little too pumped up and releases without thinking." He didn't direct his gaze toward Mrs. Malloy, but I saw Livonia, Alice, and Molly steal glances at her. She was gripping her bow . . . but arrow she held not.

"It wasn't me!" I could tell from the defiant anger in her voice that she was frightened. "I'd dropped me arrow and was bending looking for it when something whizzed past me. It's a wonder it didn't take me ear off! I can tell," darting looks this way and that, "as how my word won't be good enough for some." And why would it be? I thought sadly. Her spite toward Judy—particularly at lunch yesterday, must be fresh in the minds of the other contestants, even if word of it had not spread further to Lord Belfrey and the rapacious Georges.

"It was my own fault entirely," Judy said, looking pitifully defenseless on the ground over a wince of pain from shifting her ankle. "I blundered toward the others without paying the least attention to what was going on. My mind was elsewhere, so please don't anyone make something big out of what happened."

No one had anything helpful to add.

That was the problem; there had been a great deal of preoccupation at the crucial moment. A lack of reliable witnesses, and a continuing suspicion I feared directed at Mrs. Malloy. For the shooter, that muddying of the waters was a gift if the object had been to kill Judy, which I perhaps stupidly, was fiercely sure was the case. If Mrs. Malloy had been hit in the first attempt, another arrow would have been speedily drawn. As it was, expertise or at least a natural hand-eye coordination, coupled with daring desperation, would have achieved the objective, but for the life-saving notebook.

Coming up to me, Ben squeezed my hand. "I'll offer to help get Judy into the house," he said.

"And I'll go and get a glass of water for her. With all the furor, maybe no one has thought to do so." As I headed off, I felt the comfort of Thumper keeping pace beside me. "Sorry to have ignored you," I told him, "but being the perceptive fellow you are, you'll have noticed we had a crisis." Time later to consider his necessary return to the Dawkinses. Pushing open the entry door, I was grateful for some time to think, but that opportunity was doomed. Halfway down the passageway that would take us through the hall to the kitchen, I heard the familiar hateful scurrying, glimpsed a flash of white, felt Thumper bristle, then all was shrill squeaking, raucous yelping, and flying fur.

"Thumper, stop!" My voice may have reached the tip of his tail as he rounded the corner, but he so outdistanced me that there was not a flicker of black to be seen when I reached the hall. I could, however, hear him with increasingly deafening clarity as I neared the kitchen. That he was capable in this mood of feverish pursuit of standing on his hind legs and turning the doorknob seemed all too probable. The scene I entered upon was mayhem, with hostile overtones coming forcibly from Mrs. Foot, who stood clasping Whitey to her apron chest, while Thumper raced in circles around her like an Oliver Twist sent berserk after being denied a reasonable request for more. Mr. Plunket, weaving like a tree in the wind, stood close by, Boris beside him, wearing the bright pink shirt of yesterday, his right hand—I noted numbly— clamped around his left arm.

"Just look at the sweet darling trembling like a leaf in my arms," Mrs. Foot bellowed at me. "That dog of yours should be put down—going after Whitey like he was vermin! I'd kill him with my bare hands if it wouldn't mean dropping my precious!"

It didn't occur to me to say that Thumper wasn't my dog. Nor was I compelled to order him to quiet down. Having successfully treed what would have been a very small snack, he looked to me for approval before lying down, nose on front paws, in sighing contentment.

"I came in for a glass of water for Judy, who's been hurt," I said as calmly as I could manage.

"That girl Lucy's already been in for one. We know all about the hoopla, don't we, Mr. Plunket and Boris? No, don't you go bothering answering, poor dears. Just look at the two of them." She rounded on me again. "Poor Mr. Plunket was so upset with everything gone wrong for his nibs, just when his lady cousin decides to visit again, he needed a restorative tipple. It was that husband of yours leaving bottles in an old bread bin where anyone with a stepladder to climb to the top pantry would think to look that started him back on after years of laying off the stuff. Who can wonder at a little lapse the way this week's gone! My kitchen being taken over! That Monsieur LeBois rolling around the place like he's king on wheels, never so much as lifting his bottom when I hand him one of my nice cups of tea. Oh, I know his kind—can't budge a muscle for themselves unless it suits them. Ask me and I'll tell you he doesn't need that chair any more than I need wings. But for him, none of you lot would be here stirring up trouble. And Mr. Plunket and I've got Boris standing there with his arm tore up by that dog leaping at him when Whitey ran up his leg."

"Missed that." Grinning foolishly, Mr. Plunket continued to sway as if in a quickening breeze. "Always did love his uncle Boris, but not more than you, Mrs. Foot. Nobody in the whole wide world," spreading his arms, "is loved more than you, Mrs. Foot."

"There, there, Mr. Plunket! But it's our Boris that matters most right now. Look at him," this to me, "standing there white as a sheet"—as this was normal for Boris, I hadn't panicked on looking at him—"and him waiting so patient for a proper bandage!"

I thought snappishly that she was right about that. A dead man couldn't have looked more patient. "I'm sorry," I said . . . suddenly meaning it. There was something heartrendingly sad about Boris's empty-eyed stare and his rigor mortis stance. I remembered Judy's kind way with him and suddenly felt close to tears. So much so that when Mrs. Foot worked herself back to a roar—letting me know that if I didn't get that dog out of the house right now she'd ring the police—I replied meekly that I was sure Mrs. Spuds or Dr. Rowley would agree to return him to his owners.

Whitey bade us a triumphant squeak of good riddance as we left the kitchen, but I didn't leave the house. Instead, I went into Lord Belfrey's study—currently the dominion of Georges. I had been seized by the urge to take another look at Suzanne Varney's photo. Foolish, I know, but I thought that if I could look into her face I might get a clearer sense of who she was . . . that she might even tell me something. The photos of the contestants were no longer spread over the table. I knew it was wrong, but the impulse to revisit her image was so strong that I crossed to the desk and opened the top right-hand drawer first. Inside were some notepads, pencils, and a torch . . . a dull red torch. I picked it up, turned it over in my hands, and saw the uneven crack in the plastic and the small jagged gap where a piece had broken off. My hand found its way into my jacket pocket and drew out what I had taken from Thumper's mouth on his return from the ravine.

He sat, looking up at me with sympathetic curiosity as I sank down in the desk chair and fitted the broken-off plastic back into the torch. Suddenly it was as though Suzanne were in the room with me, striving to tell me what she must have intended to tell Mrs. Spendlow. I felt her anger and grief pour into me. If only . . . if only fate had not brought her to Mucklesfeld. But it had, and all I could do was unmask her killer.

I now strongly suspected who had lured her down into the ravine with the torch. If I was right as to the who, the why stared me in the face. But if I were wrong, even a subtle change in attitude toward the person in question might be enough to give the tip that the game was up. Also, I risked besmirching the good name of someone who might never be able to convincingly prove innocence of both crimes—the murder of Suzanne and the attempt on Judy's life.

After repocketing the piece of plastic, I returned

the torch to the drawer and was on my way out into the hall when, as so often seemed to happen, I nearly collided with Lord Belfrey. He did not ask what I had been doing in his study. It was apparent that he was as preoccupied as I.

"How's Judy?" I asked.

"Doing well, apart from the ankle. Your husband and I carried her into the drawing room, where Tommy is administering the required care. What a plucky woman she is. I admire her tremendously, more so I have to admit than the other contestants, fine and likable as they are." He hesitated and I detected a change in him, a lightening of the heart and a barely restrained joy.

"I saw her, Ellie; something drew me across the lawn. Of course I had to greet those who had come to watch, in particular, Celia—whatever my feelings toward her—but there was a summons more powerful than required politeness. Before I could fully make out her form and features, my heart knew, recognized her despite all the years gone past . . . those," he smiled, "those ridiculous glasses."

"Nora Burton," I said, "once and always the Eleanor you saw standing on those stairs," looking toward them, "when you came to Mucklesfeld for the day."

"You knew?"

"The likeness to her portrait was there, despite the attempt at disguise."

"There was no time to say more than ask her to meet me at noon tomorrow at the end of the lane leading from Witch Haven. Ellie, I'm consumed with remorse about the contestants, but whatever happens, I realize now, my mercenary plan makes a mockery of marriage. I had increasingly come to know I couldn't go through with it—mainly because of you. Your resemblance to Eleanor was the reminder I needed that love is worth the wait, even if it takes an eternity."

"So it is," I said. "I was lucky meeting Ben when I did. And you still have a long life ahead of you."

"I'll always be grateful you turned up out of the fog that night."

"Thank you. Will you do something for me?"

"Gladly. What is it?

"Put down your foot as master of Mucklesfeld and insist that tonight Judy sleep in one of the beds in my suite. She is going to need some looking after and must not on any account be left alone."

14

One other thing," I said, on receiving Lord Belfrey's agreement to my request, "suggest to Eleanor that she take a good look at every pair of your cousin Celia's shoes. I understand she has a closet full of them, most still in their boxes. Perhaps Eleanor's already done so, but if not, I think that's where she may find what she's been looking for over the past few months. Shoes make good hiding places because a lot of people are squeamish about handling those that aren't theirs. Oh, and would you kindly," looking sadly down at Thumper, "ask Dr. Rowley if he'd be willing to return my friend here to his owners?"

"Of course. As for . . ."

"Eleanor will explain. I'm going upstairs now. Perhaps another of your ties for a lead . . ."

Once in my room I endeavored by stripping down both beds to work off the jumble of troublesome emotions the day had brought. Fortunately Alice popped her head round the door a short time later to say that she'd heard from Molly, who'd heard it from Livonia, that Judy would be rooming with me that night, and did I need a change of sheets? I was relieved that Judy had agreed to my plan, and also grateful that I wouldn't have to further enrage Mrs. Foot by asking her to supply fresh linens. Alice obligingly fetched them for me, apologized that she hadn't yet mended the pillowcases, and got busy helping me remake the beds. I explained that both needed doing because Judy might balk at taking the one I'd been sleeping in.

"Awful what happened to her," Alice plumped up the final pillow, "but imagine getting shot in the chest with an arrow and not at the very least ending up in the hospital. When you think it could have been the morgue, all I can say is whoever shot that arrow should be counting their lucky stars along with Judy."

"Yes," I said, straightening the cubbyhole bedspread.

"I don't want to think it was your friend Roxie Malloy . . ."

"Then please don't."

"Of course you can't bear to think it, but there's no getting round it that she's had her knife into Judy from the beginning. I doubt you'll get Livonia and Molly to admit what they're thinking but . . ."

"Alice, you've been awfully good about helping with the beds. I do appreciate it, but . . ."

"You'd like me out of here." She paused in the doorway, bundling back up the forever falling hair. "Look, you're the only one who really knows Roxie, so who's most likely to be right? Why not get some shut-eye before Judy is brought up? I'm going to lie down myself and think about not becoming the next Belfrey bride. According to Molly, who heard it from Livonia, who heard it from Dr. Rowley, the Master of Mucklesfeld seems likely to make his pick the old-fashioned way."

When the door closed behind her it hit me that I was holed up, skulking from Mrs. Malloy, who needed me more than at any time in our relationship. Three words into talking to her, she would have known for sure I was acting solo on a hunch.

Something I would never have done, but for her being suspected by some of deliberately shooting Judy. Until I was proved right or wrong, it seemed kinder in the long run to keep my own counsel. And the same seemed true when it came to considering my obligation to warn Judy. I did not allow myself to focus on the entirely likely possibility that the killer would not obligingly step forward as I both hoped and feared. One thing of which I was confident was that Mrs. Malloy would not pay me a visit once Judy was with me. In fact, knowing what the situation was to be, as she had surely learned by now, would explain why she had not yet marched in upon me. Astute though she is, wounded feelings mount rapidly to unreasoning huffiness with Mrs. Malloy, which interestingly was one of the things that touched me most about her.

The person who came in next was Livonia, looking radiantly pretty, despite her opening words being an expression of regret over Judy's ordeal, followed by the information she knew would hurt, despite my need to know.

"I went with Tommy," the name curved lovingly on her lips, "to take dear Thumper back to his owners. Mrs. Spuds gave us directions—she seems such a lovely person, those kind blue eyes and beautiful white hair. Oh, Ellie, I do wish you could keep that dear dog. He so obviously believes he belongs with you. Tommy had tears in his eyes when we talked about it. He's wonderfully sensitive. And terribly upset about the skeleton. But how could he have known how Georges would dress it up? Or that . . . that I would be one of those to see it?"

"I knew you shouldn't be cross with him."

"Oh, dear, dear, Ellie!" She perched on the bed in the main room. "He's so caring of my feelings. I've never been this happy in my life. Don't you think he's the dearest man and such a clever doctor? Wasn't it amazing how quickly he diagnosed Judy's sprained ankle?"

"He is perfect." Her joy was so contagious, all else fled my mind for the moment. "Perfect for you. And you and Mrs. Spuds will be the best of friends, and you'll get a couple of cats you and Tommy will both dote on and have friends, including Lord Belfrey, over for Sunday lunch and everyone will say the Rowleys are what Grimkirk should be all about."

"His lordship confided in Tommy—isn't it wonderful to think of them growing close?—that he isn't going on with *Here Comes the Bride*. Not only did that free Tommy so he could speak honorably of his longing to marry me, he also thinks that something has happened to transform his cousin into a blissfully happy man. I know it has to be very disappointing for the other contestants, but I can't help believing that even for them it is all for the best. To marry without love . . ." She sat staring dreamily into space.

"Let's hope something splendid happens to each of them," I was saying, when edging in sideways came her beloved and mine carrying Judy between them in a linked armlift. She looked quite chirpy in her seated position, but I noted the shadows under her eyes and the twitch of the mouth that suggested she was battling pain. As I had expected, she insisted on taking the bed in the cubbyhole, saying she would be cozily cocooned in there. To have tried to persuade her otherwise would have delayed getting her into bed, which Livonia and I accomplished as soon as the men left. Ben had smiled at me in a way that at that moment felt more enveloping than an embrace, before saying he would send a meal up in half an hour, although Judy might be asleep by then as a result of the tablets Tommy had given her.

"I wouldn't worry if she's not awake to eat; what she needs most is rest. What happened must have been a severe shock to her system," whispered Livonia, sounding very much a doctor's wife when we returned to the bigger space after spreading the bedclothes gently over Judy and folding back a triangle to leave the injured foot uncovered.

"Thanks for the help and the shared confidences," I said.

"Oh, I do hope you'll stay in touch." The hug she gave me had a warmth I would never have expected from the frozen creature she had been on first meeting. "I want so much to go on being friends."

"So do I, Livonia; already you feel like a close pal."

She blinked tearily. "Promise to fetch me if you need help of any kind with Judy, getting her to bathroom or just someone else to talk to her? Remember, I'm just a few steps away. And do try to get some rest yourself, I know you have to be worried about Mrs. Malloy. She has to be feeling under a cloud because of," lowering her voice, "not liking Judy, but I believe she was telling the truth about not being the one who shot that arrow, deliberately or otherwise. She's your friend and that's enough for me."

"Out," I said, edging her toward the door. "You're so dear you'll have me bawling if you stay a moment longer. Go to Tommy and fall into his arms, you deservedly lucky girl."

"I only wish that Molly, with that awful Mrs. Knox as a mother, can end up as happy. Mummy could be controlling in that plaintive way of hers, but if I'd had a talent for ballet and it had been my grand passion as is the case with Molly, I think she would have been proud enough to have encouraged me instead of saying that a lump of a girl would be booed offstage. Oh, I do hope someone can wave a magic wand for her, and for Judy and Alice, who also have their very special gifts. Okay, Ellie! I'm leaving before you toss me out."

Of course the moment she was gone, I selfishly wished her back; a peek into the cubbyhole showed Judy to be asleep, breathing evenly and otherwise revealing no sign of restlessness. It was still early—only six fifteen—and the evening stretched endlessly ahead. Ben would come whether or not he was the one to bring up the meal. Mrs. Foot, Mr. Plunket, and Boris might insist on doing that, but in either case he would not linger talking because of risking disturbing Judy.

Half an hour later, Tommy put in a return appearance to check on the patient. He nodded in a satisfied way and left a couple of tablets with me that he said I should give to her at ten if she woke up, but not to disturb her if she slept on. I was struck by his new aplomb, but the boyish beam was very much in evidence when telling me he was taking Livonia back to his home for dinner.

"Mrs. Spuds is preparing something special and will stay to observe the proprieties," he added earnestly. "As Livonia may have told you, she was not treated with greatest respect by a man named Harold, and I intend to proceed gently with her."

Not too gently, I hoped. On his departure I put the tablets in a little dish on the chair and picked up the book that still had me on chapter one. It was by an author who was new to me and I hadn't found it particularly gripping, but it might take off in the next fifty or so pages. I was on the bed, having read no more than three pages, when Ben came through the door empty-handed.

"Judy sleeping?" he asked in a hushed voice, with an eye to the cubbyhole.

I nodded up at him.

"Sweetheart," he continued to whisper, "when I said I'd bring up the tray for you and Judy, Mrs. Foot looked close to tears."

Being a woman capable of compassion, I refrained from saying that must have been a gruesome sight.

"She went on about having snapped at you earlier."

"That," I too kept my voice way down, "is an understatement; but she was under stress. Thumper chased Whitey up Boris's trousers, and from the sound of it he's going to need thrice weekly sessions with a psychiatrist."

"Boris?"

"Whitey." Poor Thumper . . .

"My poor Ellie," he bent and kissed my cheek, "was it a terrible wrench parting with him?"

"Yes, but I have to accept that he isn't mine. Speaking of low spirits, is Georges in the dumps now that Lord Belfrey has decided not to continue with *Here Comes the Bride*? Or hadn't you heard about that?"

Ben whispered that he had, and from what was being floated around, it sounded as though congratulations might be in order anyway. Was that an assessing glance he was giving me?

"That leaves me heartbroken." For a moment I

forgot to whisper. "I've always relished having a man enjoy looking at me because I remind him of the woman he loves. Oh, all right! I admit to being flattered. He's handsome and if a woman doesn't have some ego, she's dead. But would I want to put him in a shopping bag and take him home? The answer is no. He doesn't make me laugh or want to throw things at him. And I doubt he can boil an egg. Now go before you wake Judy."

"I've had terrible pangs of jealousy." He stroked my hair.

"Well, think of some way to make it up to me—some wonderful present, although I can't for the moment think of anything I desperately want."

"Can't you?" Ben said on his way out the door.

I picked up my book and had read another page and a half during what length of time I did not know—my mind having wandered so far afield that I hadn't checked my watch—when my next visitor, the least welcome by far, arrived. Mrs. Foot with a loaded tray.

"Let me help you with that—it looks heavy," I said, jumping up.

"Mr. Plunket came down with a headache." She allowed me to take the tray from her and watched me place it on the bed. "It's taking up the drink after being off it so long, but I'll get him sorted once Mucklesfeld is back to itself again."

"I'm sure. Judy's sleeping."

"Is she now?" No attempt at lowering her voice.

411

"Best thing for her, I'm sure she'll be fine in the morning. After all, in the scheme of things, what's a sprained ankle? If she'd watched where she fell, it shouldn't have happened. When I picture dear Boris swinging from one trapeze to another and never a stubbed toe, bless him, my heart melts."

One thing to be said for Mrs. Foot, I always felt dainty as a buttercup in her presence. "How is Boris?"

"Gone to bed like I said he must. A right shock he got, being attacked by that dog."

"Did he have Dr. Rowley take a look at his arm?"

"What, go making a fuss? That's not my Boris! Never a thought for his self when there's others to be worried about. It's Whitey he's thinking on, wondering if the dear wee fellow will ever be quite right in the head again after the fright he took."

"How's Mr. Plunket?"

"Been crying his eyes out from going back on the bottle; got him tucked in with a hot-water bottle."

Preferably one that didn't leak.

"Anyway," Mrs. Foot finally got to it, "I'm sorry I flared at you like I did this afternoon and me usually so sunny. I realized soon as you went off in a huff that it really wasn't your fault. The dog isn't yours; though you can't say you haven't encouraged him to hang around. I hope you'll eat your meal in the spirit it was brought up in and drink the tea I put in a thermos to keep warm, though as Mr.

Plunket and Boris always say, one of my cups tastes just as good cold, even better often as not. Milk and sugar's already in. And there's orange juice in a glass for the invalid if she has to take more of those tablets Dr. Rowley will have left for her."

"Thank you, Mrs. Foot," I said meekly, "and no hard feelings on either side, I hope."

A noticeable thawing. "That's nice of you to say. I'm sure I wish you and the lady sleeping in there," eyes shifting toward the cubbyhole, "nothing but the best. And now I'm off—back down to my boys, the dear loves! And once I see they're well settled, I sit down for a nice cuddle with Whitey. Nothing better than a mum's love for putting things right if it can be done."

Upon her none too soon departure, I sized up the tray. Ben had very sensibly sent up a meal intended to be served cold—containers of fruit, a leafy salad, asparagus vinaigrette, slivered ham, eggs mayonnaise, and crusty bread. Enough for two; there was a second plate, should Judy wake and wish to eat. Best of all, he had made another chocolate orange gateau. The Chantilly cream had been spread instead of piped into rosettes, but I wasn't inclined to be the least picky.

Needless to say, I wasn't about to drink Mrs. Foot's tea. Neither did I think the orange juice the wisest accompaniment to the pills should Judy wake and need them. Heaven only knew what was floating in it. So before starting my meal, I tiptoed

413

rapidly down to the bathroom, emptied out both thermos and glass, and having replaced the former with water, returned as fast as I could to my room. My attempt at silence was mainly due to a concern that Mrs. Malloy—a sliver of light had shown under her door—would come out to see if the patter of feet were mine.

Once safely reinstalled, I checked on Judy, found her still sleeping with apparent soundness, and settled down to my meal. Determined on keeping up my strength for what the night might bring, I ate heartily—enjoying every morsel, especially of the two slices of gateau I didn't feel it wrong to take as my share, since there was still one good-sized piece left for Judy. Covering the plate I had arranged for her with a napkin, I placed it on the chair with the empty thermos and glass, made sure the little dish with the pills was securely positioned, and then put the tray with its remaining contents outside the door. Ben, I was sure, would return for it and assume I preferred him not to come in because of Judy.

My face stretched into a yawn as I unwrapped the one treat I'd bought myself in Yorkshire. How long ago the visit to Tom and Betty's now seemed as I lifted the heavy . . . oh so heavy . . . bronze candlestick and trolled back to the bed to place it under the pillow . . . which seemed to shift shape in the most peculiar way. Indeed. How long ago and far away everything seemed. Slapping my face with flopping hands, I came back to myself sufficiently to decide I was giving way to panic. A sound from Judy roused my ministering instincts. I found her half awake and clearly in pain from the ankle. Staggering to the chair which served as a chest, I sloshed water from the thermos into the glass, picked up the tablets, and managed to accomplish my Florence Nightingale turn without falling on top of her. I think she thanked me, she would have, must have done—that was Judy, although who Judy was or why she was in Ben's bed became less clear by the second. The next I knew . . . and that groggily . . . was that I was on my bed and after that . . . swirling darkness, drawing me down, down into nothingness.

Afterwards, I was to reflect wryly on how I'd felt rather smug when getting rid of the beverages, but they hadn't contained the crushed sleeping pills. For all Mrs. Foot's pride in her lovely cup of tea, she must have doubted my proper appreciation, so she had doctored the Chantilly cream instead. Something I should have suspected by the lack of rosettes, which had required flattening out in the process. If Judy had eaten a slice, all the better. Mrs. Foot had used the tablets that Dr. Rowley had prescribed for her when she'd told him she was having trouble sleeping and that she'd held on to in case of need. Life always offered the unexpected and it was best to be prepared.

She admitted all this to the police, in the early hours of the next morning, along with a great deal more—that she had smothered Suzanne Varney's father, Mr. Codger, as well as several other of the difficult patients during her days as a ward maid at Shady Oaks. It was Livonia's mentioning that Tommy had helped out there during his summer holidays that jolted my memory of where Mrs. Foot had worked. But unfortunately not until I was sitting in Lord Belfrey's study that afternoon had I pictured her nosing around in there shortly before the contestants were due to arrive and coming across Suzanne's photo.

"A proper start of surprise, it gave me," she told the police in wounded fashion. As they recorded in her statement.

Suzanne had had concerns about Mrs. Foot for some time, and on her father's death, insisted to the administrator that she be investigated.

"Such a fuss about one old man . . . well, yes, there were others, helped on the way to a better place. Not that there was any proof, I'd been that careful, but I wasn't going to stay around to be looked at funny every time I came into one of the wards with my lovely trolley. It seemed best just not to show up again. So, out of a job and forced to live in the streets it was, but always the silver lining, it was there I met dear Mr. Plunket and sweet Boris. And now here we were landed on our feet, happy as larks at Mucklesfeld, and now she

416

was coming . . . bound to go telling stories to his nibs so that he'd decide—lovely though he is— that the three of us would have to go."

So much I had guessed. The use of the torch to lure Suzanne down into the ravine, the concern that it had been dropped and lost in the fog, Mr. Plunket's early search for it the next morning, Boris's similar attempts to find it—yes, it turned out to be he who had been watching from a strategic vantage point among the trees when I stood debating whether to follow Thumper down on his scramble. And then Judy coming up from the ravine this afternoon and going almost immediately into the house to hand over the torch she had found. Its having been discovered in the ravine wasn't likely to seriously interest the police. But it wasn't the police that mattered; it was the sad thought that his nibs might wonder who had removed the torch from his drawer and put two and two together. If life was to continue happily, Judy must be disposed of before she could talk, and the chances seemed good that she wouldn't bring the matter up during the archery contest. That oh so convenient contest! She hadn't died, yet even then all was not lost. The injured ankle was bound to put so trivial a find out of her mind for the immediate future. And Mrs. Foot set great store by Dr. Rowley's sleeping tablets.

And now there I was, drugged to the gills, the

candlestick a wasted attempt at protection under my pillow, my chivalrous whim not to confide my suspicions until proved true precluding rescue by Mrs. Malloy, who would have so thrilled to the opportunity. Later, Ben would tell me in no uncertain terms that if I ever attempted such heroics again, he would never make me another chocolate orange gateau—which didn't have quite the impact it would once have done. I had been a well-meaning fool, undeserving of the passionate devotion that brought Thumper to the rescue, leaping through the window onto the bed, barking to raise the dead . . . or in my case the stupored. But, unlike Whitey, who so needed his little cuddles, he lingered not a moment beyond the one it took to pry myself up. Away he raced into the cubbyhole. To my horror in following him, I saw Judy's bed was empty. Nor had Thumper dallied there; he was out on the rooftop growling menacingly.

I had not taken Mrs. Foot for the killer, and I had been right in thinking that one of the two who loved her beyond her deserts had taken care of matters for her. It was Boris who stood like death personified holding Judy in his arms. The empty eyes stared through me before he laid her down with a gentleness she had seen in him and remarked upon, and took the graceful leap of a trapeze artist to his death.

Epilogue

I hope I'm a woman as learns from trial and tribulation," said Mrs. Malloy from the backseat as we left the gates of Mucklesfeld behind us. "'Course there's no overlooking quite yet your leaving me in the dark about what you was up to. Could be you thought I needed being taught a lesson, what with me not being overly nice to Judy Nunn, that I have come to see as a good egg, and a brave one at that, though she didn't remember any of the night, which is a blessing. Although it could be said she missed out on one of the most exciting moments in her life, and for most of us they don't come along often."

"I'd think you'd be glad of some peace and quiet after all that's happened," said Ben, looking remarkably handsome behind the steering wheel. Thumper had not, as it turned out, been the only hero of the hour. Lord Belfrey had mentioned to Ben his belief that I wanted Judy in my room in case something happened to her. He believed I feared she might take a turn for the worse, but Ben construed it differently, explained my concern might be from a different cause, and the two of them in manly accord had kept watch outside my door throughout the evening, neither of course making anything of Mrs. Foot's arrival with the tray. What neither they nor I had anticipated was that Boris would come up by way of the fire escape, and then creep through both rooms to lock my door. Thumper's frantic barking had alerted the men of trouble, but also drowned out their subsequent pounding on the door. So they had broken down the door and entered upon the scene to lift Judy from the roof edge and carry her back to bed.

"Mr. Plunket is the one I now feel most sorry for," I said. "His worried knowledge was what turned him back to drink. But I'm sure Lord Belfrey and Dr. Rowley will come up with a solution as to where he should go, if the police let him off lightly, which won't be the case with Mrs. Foot after her unremorseful confession."

"Glad of some peace and quiet!" Mrs. Malloy had fastened on Ben's words. "There won't much of that waiting at Merlin's Court, what with the children and Tobias and everything that will need putting to rights, after your parents leave—no offense, Mr. H, but your mother will keep putting out doilies no matter where I hide them."

"Speaking of hiding places," I turned my head, "it was your treasured collection of shoes that gave me the idea where Celia Belfrey might have hidden the family jewels that Eleanor was thought to have stolen. And then there was your talking at lunch about the clue that revealed the identity of the murderer in *The Landcroft Legacy*—the contusion left on the arm of an archer releasing too soon.

On a right handed person, the abrasion would be on the left arm between wrist and elbow, remember? Boris had his right hand around his left arm when I went into the kitchen to get a glass of water for Judy. Mrs. Foot made a big thing about Thumper having scratched him—nerves making her overly eager, I suppose, to have an explanation ready in case Charlie Forester should suggest checking people's arms."

"Did I do anything else?"

"Yes. Giving me a living person to fight for in addition to Suzanne."

A sniff, followed by, "I still say you should have told me it was Boris."

"But I wasn't sure, right up to the end. I had this dreadful fear that it might have been Tommy Rowley. Mrs. Spuds said he went out for a walk in spite of the fog, and he might have gone down with the bouquet into the ravine to look for the torch. When I found out that he too had worked at Shady Oaks, I couldn't write him off entirely, and there was Livonia so in love with him."

"Well, I suppose I can see . . ."

"There was always the possibility that Lord Belfrey had done away with Suzanne because of something that happened when they met on that cruise. Or it could have been Celia . . . she could have followed Suzanne after she stopped at Witch Haven for directions to the rectory. To ruin any plan of Lord Belfrey's would cause her delight, and then there was Nora . . . Eleanor, who could be expected to hate the family. Oh! One last detail. It was Lucy who found Eleanor's gown in a trunk in Giles's room and thought it perfect for the skeleton. No sinister motive there."

"At least some of those we've met would seem to have a good chance of happiness."

"Yes, but there are Judy and Alice and Molly!"

"Don't you worry," answered Mrs. Malloy with her old confidence. "Things will work out perfect for them, along with everyone else. Celia Belfrey will do a bunk, Lord and Lady will go to live at Witch Haven, but they'll keep Mucklesfeld as a refuge for the homeless old and young. Sad the way some can't manage to put roofs over their children's heads. Molly will stay on to teach dancing; Alice handwork; and Judy will turn part of the grounds into a paying proposition as a market garden. She'll have plenty of help. And because it will all be a great big success, Georges LeBois will make a documentary about it that will help pour in money for a staff of health professionals under the direction of Dr. Belfrey. Livonia will help out as much as poss, but she'll have two cats and a new son named Thomas after his dad and . . ."

I didn't interrupt. Fiction makes such a wonderful change from reality. Or—maybe not. Amazingly, everything turned out much as she predicted, except that Livonia also had a little girl named Eleanor . . . Ellie, for short. Alice married the detective involved in the case, who proved to be a great help with the sometimes troubled youth. And Molly gained fame from choreographing a ballet titled *The Cobweb Fairy*, but refused to give up teaching her Mucklesfeld pupils.

But all that was for the future, and I was entirely in the present. I had fallen in love during that week, passionately, irrevocably in love. When I confided this to Ben, he had not shown the smallest jealousy. It was he who managed it all . . . the talk with Tommy and Livonia, who talked to Mrs. Spuds, who talked to Mrs. Spendlow, who talked to her husband . . . who better than the rector to lift the burden of guilt over an ill-made promise from Mrs. Dawkins's shoulders?

She was waiting at the gate with Thumper when we pulled up outside the house. He had on a new collar and a bright red lead.

"Just look at his lordship," said Mrs. Malloy, sticking her head out the car window. "Now don't go thinking you'll be keeping him all to yourself, Mrs. H. I'll be the one fixing up his dinner a treat and making sure he gets enough walkies. Like I've always said, who needs a man when you can have a dog?"

To my knowledge she'd never said anything of the sort. But perhaps neither reality nor fiction can ever be quite sufficient on its own . . . and life at its richest must be a perfect blending of the two.

Center Point Publishing

600 Brooks Road ● PO Box 1
Thorndike ME 04986-0001 USA

(207) 568-3717

US & Canada:
1 800 929-9108
www.centerpointlargeprint.com